Saga Six Pack 2

The Poetic Edda

The Nibelungenlied

The Saga of Thorstein

Fridthjof the Bold

King Harald's Saga

Ingolf's Saga

Saga Six Pack 2

The Poetic Edda Volume I by Anonymous. Edited by Damian Stevenson

The Nibelungenlied by Anonymous. Translated by George Henry Needler. First published in 1904.

The Saga of Thorstein and *Fridthjof the Bold* by Rasmus Bjorn Anderson. First published in *Viking Tales of the North: The sagas of Thorstein, Viking's son, and Fridthjof the Bold* in 1901.

King Harald's Saga and *Ingolf's Saga* by Jennie Hall. First published in *Viking Tales* by Jennie Hall in 1902.

All rights reserved. This book or any portion thereof may not be reproduced or used in any manner whatsoever without the express written permission of the publisher except for the use of brief quotations in a book review.

Printed in the United States of America. First printing, 2015. Enhanced Media Publishing.

ISBN-10: 1514708531
ISBN-13: 978-1514708538

CONTENTS

The Poetic Edda 1

The Nibelungenlied 66

The Saga of Thorstein 275

Fridthjof the Bold 318

King Harald's Saga 342

Ingolf's Saga 369

Saga Glossary 384

THE POETIC EDDA

VOLUME I: LAY OF THE GODS

BY

ANONYMOUS

VOLUSPO

The Wise-Woman's Prophecy

1. Silence I ask from the holy races,
From Heimdall's sons, both high and low;
Thou wilt, Valfather, that well I relate
Old tales I remember of men long ago.

2. I remember still the giants of old,
Who gave me bread back in the day;
Nine worlds I recall, the nine in the tree
With mighty roots beneath the mold.

3. Of old was the age when Ymir lived;
Sea nor cool waves nor sand there were;
Earth had not been, nor heaven above,
But a yawning gap, and grass nowhere.

4. Before Bur's sons raised up heaven's vault,
They who the noble mid-earth shaped.
The sun shone from the south over the structure's rocks:
Then was the earth begrown with herbage green.

5. The sun from the south,
The moon's companion,
Her right hand cast about the heavenly horses.
The sun knew not where she a dwelling had.

6. Then sought the gods their assembly-seats,
The holy ones, and council held;
Names then gave they to noon and twilight,
Morning they named, and mid-day, afternoon,
Night and evening, the years to number.

7. The mighty gods met on Ida's plain,
Shrines and temples they timbered high;
Forges they set, and they smithied ore,
Tongs they wrought, and tools they fashioned.

8. In their dwellings at peace they played at tables,
Of gold no lack did the gods then know,
Till thither came up giant-maids three,
Huge of might, out of Jotunheim.

9. Then sought the gods their assembly-seats,
The exhalted ones, and council held,
To decide who should create the race of dwarfs
From the sea giant's blood and bones.

10. There was Motsognir the mightiest made
Of all the dwarfs, and Durin next;
Many a likeness of men they forged,
The dwarfs on earth, as Durin related.

11. Nyi and Nithi, Northri and Suthri,
Austri and Vestri, Althjof, Dvalin,
Nar and Nain, Niping, Dain,
Bifur, Bofur, Bombur, Nori,
An and Onar, Ai, Mjothvitnir.

12. Vigg and Gandalf Vindalf, Thrain,
Thekk and Thorin, Thror, Vit and Lit,
Nyr and Nyrath, now have I told --
Regin and Rathsvith -- the list aright.

13. Fili, Kili, Fundin, Nali,
Heptifili, Hannar, Sviur,
Frar, Hornbori, Fraeg and Loni,
Aurvang, Jari, Eikinskjaldi.

14. The race of the dwarfs in Dvalin's throng
Down to Lofar the list must I tell;
The rocks they left, and through wet lands
They sought a home in the fields of sand.

15. There were Draupnir and Dolgthrasir,
Hor, Haugspori, Hlevang, Gloin,
Dori, Ori, Duf, Andvari,
Skirfir, Virfir, Skafith, Ai.

16. Alf and Yngvi, Eikinskjaldi,

Fjalar and Frosti, Fith and Ginnar;
So for all time shall the tale be known,
The list of all the forbears of Lofar.

17. Then from the throng did three come forth,
From the home of the gods, the mighty and gracious;
Two without fate on the land they found,
Ask and Embla, empty of might.

18. Soul they had not, sense they had not,
Heat nor motion, nor goodly hue;
Soul gave Othin, sense gave Honir,
Heat gave Lothur and goodly hue.

19. There lives a towering ash named Yggdrasil,
With water white is the great tree wet;
Thence come the dews that fall in the dales,
Green by Urth's well does it ever grow.

20. Thence come the maidens,
Much knowing, three from the hall,
Which under that tree stands; Urd hight the one,
The second Verdandi,—on a tablet they graved—Skuld the third.
Laws they established, life allotted to the sons of men.

21. The war I recall, the first in the world,
When the gods with spears had smitten Gollveig,
And in the hall of Hor had burned her,
Three times burned, and three times born,
Oft and again, yet ever she lives.

22. Heith they named her who sought their home,
The wide-seeing witch, in magic wise;
Minds she bewitched that were moved by her magic,
To evil women a joy she was.

23. On the host his spear did Othin hurl,
Then in the world did war first come;
The wall that girdled the gods was broken,
And the field by the warlike Wanes was trodden.

24. Then sought the gods their assembly-seats,
The holy ones, and council held,

Whether the gods should tribute give,
Or to all alike should worship belong.

25. Then sought the gods their assembly-seats,
The holy ones, and council held,
To find who with venom the air had filled,
Or had given Oth's bride to the giants' brood.

26. In swelling rage then rose up Thor,
Seldom he sits when he such things hears,
And the oaths were broken, the words and bonds,
The mighty pledges between them made.

27. I know of the horn of Heimdall, hidden
Under the high-reaching holy tree;
On it there pours from Valfather's pledge
A mighty stream: would you know yet more?

28. Alone I sat when the Old One sought me,
The terror of gods, and gazed in mine eyes:
"What hast thou to ask? why comest thou hither?
Othin, I know where thine eye is hidden."

29. I know where Othin's eye is hidden,
Deep in the wide-famed well of Mimir;
Mead from the pledge of Othin each morn
Does Mimir drink: would you know yet more?

30. Necklaces had I and rings from Heerfather,
Wise was my speech and my magic wisdom …
…Widely I saw over all the worlds.

31. On all sides saw I Valkyries assemble,
Ready to ride to the ranks of the gods;
Skuld bore the shield, and Skogul rode next,
Guth, Hild, Gondul, and Geirskogul.
Of Herjan's maidens the list have ye heard,
Valkyries ready to ride o'er the earth.

32. I saw for Baldr, the bleeding god,
The son of Othin, his destiny set:
Famous and fair in the lofty fields,
Full grown in strength the mistletoe stood.

33. From the branch which seemed so slender and fair
Came a harmful shaft that Hoth should hurl;
But the brother of Baldr was born ere long,
And one night old fought Othin's son.

34. His hands he washed not, his hair he combed not,
Till he bore to the bale-blaze Baldr's foe.
But in Fensalir did Frigg weep sore
For Valhall's need: would you know yet more?

35. One did I see in the wet woods bound,
A lover of ill, and to Loki like;
By his side does Sigyn sit, nor is glad
To see her mate: would you know yet more?

36. From the east there pours through poisoned vales
With swords and daggers the river Slith…

37. Northward a hall in Nithavellir
Of gold there rose for Sindri's race;
And in Okolnir another stood,
Where the giant Brimir his beer-hall had.

38. A hall I saw, far from the sun,
On Nastrond it stands, and the doors face north,
Venom drops through the smoke-vent down,
For around the walls do serpents wind.

39. Then the Vala knew the fatal bonds
Were twisting, most rigid,
Bonds from entrails made.

40. The giantess old in Ironwood sat,
In the east, and bore the brood of Fenrir;
Among these one in monster's guise
Was soon to steal the sun from the sky.

41. There feeds he full on the flesh of the dead,
And the home of the gods he reddens with gore;
Dark grows the sun, and in summer soon
Come mighty storms: would you know yet more?

42. On a hill there sat, and smote on his harp,
Eggther the joyous, the giants' warder;
Above him the cock in the bird-wood crowed,
Fair and red did Fjalar stand.

43. Then to the gods crowed Gollinkambi,
He wakes the heroes in Othin's hall;
And beneath the earth does another crow,
The rust-red bird at the bars of Hel.

44. Further forward I see,
Much can I say of Ragnarök and the gods' conflict.

45. Brothers shall fight, and slay each other;
Cousins shall kinship violate. The earth resounds, the giantesses flee;
No man will another spare.

46. Hard is it in the world,
Great whoredom, an axe age, a sword age,
Shields shall be cloven, a wind age, a wolf age, ere the world sinks.

47. Yggdrasil shakes, and shiver on high
The ancient limbs, and the giant is loose;
To the head of Mim does Othin give heed,
But the kinsman of Surt shall slay him soon.

48. How fare the gods? How fare the elves?
All Jotunheim groans, the gods are at council;
Loud roar the dwarfs by the doors of stone,
The masters of the rocks: would you know yet more?

49. Now Garm howls loud before Gnipahellir,
The fetters will burst, and the wolf run free
Much do I know, and more can see
Of the fate of the gods, the mighty in fight.

50. From the east comes Hrym with shield held high;
In giant-wrath does the serpent writhe;
O'er the waves he twists, and the tawny eagle
Gnaws corpses screaming; Naglfar is loose.

51. O'er the sea from the north there sails a ship
With the people of Hel, at the helm stands Loki;

After the wolf do wild men follow,
And with them the brother of Byleist goes.

52. How is it with the Æsir?
How with the Alfar? All Jötunheim resounds; the Æsir are in council.
The dwarfs groan before their stony doors, the sages of the rocky walls.
Understand ye yet, or what?

53. Then arises Hlin's second grief,
When Odin goes with the wolf to fight,
And the bright slayer of Beli with Surt.
Then will Frigg's beloved fall.

54. Then comes Sigfather's mighty son,
Vithar, to fight with the foaming wolf;
In the giant's son does he thrust his sword
Full to the heart: his father is avenged.

55. Hither there comes the son of Hlothyn,
The bright snake gapes to heaven above;
Against the serpent goes Othin's son.

56. In anger smites the warder of earth,
Forth from their homes must all men flee;
Nine paces fares the son of Fjorgyn,
And, slain by the serpent, fearless he sinks.

57. The sun turns black, earth sinks in the sea,
The hot stars down from heaven are whirled;
Fierce grows the steam and the life-feeding flame,
Till fire leaps high about heaven itself.

58. Now Garm howls loud before Gnipahellir,
The fetters will burst, and the wolf run free;
Much do I know, and more can see
Of the fate of the gods, the mighty in fight.

59. Now do I see the earth anew
Rise all green from the waves again;
The cataracts fall, and the eagle flies,
And fish he catches beneath the cliffs.

60. The gods in Ithavoll meet together,

Of the terrible girdler of earth they talk,
And the mighty past they call to mind,
And the ancient runes of the Ruler of Gods.

61. In wondrous beauty once again
Shall the golden tables stand mid the grass,
Which the gods had owned in the days of old…

62. Then fields unsowed bear ripened fruit,
All ills grow better, and Baldr comes back;
Baldr and Hoth dwell in Hropt's battle-hall,
And the mighty gods: would you know yet more?

63. Then Honir wins the prophetic wand ….
And the sons of the brothers of Tveggi abide
In Vindheim now: would you know yet more?

64. More fair than the sun, a hall I see,
Roofed with gold, on Gimle it stands;
There shall the righteous rulers dwell,
And happiness ever there shall they have.

65. There comes on high, all power to hold,
A mighty lord, all lands he rules…

66. From below the dragon dark comes forth,
Nithhogg flying from Nithafjoll;
The bodies of men on his wings he bears,
The serpent bright: but now must I sink.

VAFTHRUTHNISMOL

The Ballad of Vafthruthnir

Othin spake:

1. "Counsel me, Frigg, for I long to fare,
And Vafthruthnir fain would find;
fit wisdom old with the giant wise
Myself would I seek to match."

Frigg spake:

2. "Heerfather here at home would I keep,
Where the gods together dwell;
Amid all the giants an equal in might
To Vafthruthnir know I none."

Othin spake:

3. "Much have I fared, much have I found.
Much have I got from the gods;
And fain would I know how Vafthruthnir now
Lives in his lofty hall."

Frigg spake:

4. "Safe mayst thou go, safe come again,
And safe be the way thou wendest!
Father of men, let thy mind be keen
When speech with the giant thou seekest."

5. The wisdom then of the giant wise
Forth did he fare to try;
He found the hall of the father of Im,
And in forthwith went Ygg.

Othin spake:

6. "Vafthruthnir, hail! to thy hall am I come,

For thyself I fain would see;
And first would I ask if wise thou art,
Or, giant, all wisdom hast won."

Vafthruthnir spake:

7. "Who is the man that speaks to me,
Here in my lofty hall?
Forth from our dwelling thou never shalt fare,
Unless wiser than I thou art."

Othin spake:

8. "Gagnrath they call me, and thirsty I come
From a journey hard to thy hall;
Welcome I look for, for long have I fared,
And gentle greeting, giant."

Vafthruthnir spake:

9. "Why standest thou there on the floor whilst thou speakest?
A seat shalt thou have in my hall;
hen soon shall we know whose knowledge is more,
The guest's or the sage's gray."

Othin spake:

10. "If a poor man reaches the home of the rich,
Let him wisely speak or be still;
For to him who speaks with the hard of heart
Will chattering ever work ill."

Vafthruthnir spake:

11. "Speak forth now, Gagnrath, if there from the floor
Thou wouldst thy wisdom make known:
What name has the steed that each morn anew
The day for mankind doth draw?"

Othin spake:

12. "Skinfaxi is he, the steed who for men
The glittering day doth draw;

The best of horses to heroes he seems,
And brightly his mane doth burn."

Vafthruthnir spake:

13. "Speak forth now, Gagnrath, if there from the floor
Thou wouldst thy wisdom make known:
What name has the steed that from East anew
Brings night for the noble gods?"

Othin spake:

14. "Hrimfaxi name they the steed that anew
Brings night for the noble gods;
Each morning foam from his bit there falls,
And thence come the dews in the dales."

Vafthruthnir spake:

15. "Speak forth now, Gagnrath, if there from the floor
Thou wouldst thy wisdom make known:
What name has the river that 'twixt the realms
Of the gods and the giants goes?"

Othin spoke:

16. "Ifing is the river that 'twixt the realms
Of the gods and the giants goes;
For all time ever open it flows,
No ice on the river there is."
Vafthruthnir spake:

17. "Speak forth now, Gagnrath, if there from the floor
Thou wouldst thy wisdom make known:
What name has the field where in fight shall meet
Surt and the gracious gods?"

Othin spake:

18. "Vigrith is the field where in fight shall meet
Surt and the gracious gods;
A hundred miles each way does it measure.
And so are its boundaries set."

Vafthruthnir spake:

19. "Wise art thou, guest! To my bench shalt thou go,
In our seats let us speak together;
Here in the hall our heads, O guest,
Shall we wager our wisdom upon."

Othin spake:

20. "First answer me well, if thy wisdom avails,
And thou knowest it, Vafthruthnir, now:
In earliest time whence came the earth,
Or the sky, thou giant sage?"

Vafthruthnir spake:

21. "Out of Ymir's flesh was fashioned the earth,
And the mountains were made of his bones;
The sky from the frost-cold giant's skull,
And the ocean out of his blood."

Othin spake:

22. "Next answer me well, if thy wisdom avails,
And thou knowest it, Vafthruthnir, now:
Whence came the moon, o'er the world of men
That fares, and the flaming sun?"
Vafthruthnir spake:

23. "Mundilferi is he who begat the moon,
And fathered the flaming sun;
The round of heaven each day they run,
To tell the time for men."

Othin spake:

24. "Third answer me well, if wise thou art called,
If thou knowest it, Vafthruthnir, now:
Whence came the day, o'er mankind that fares,
Or night with the narrowing moon?"

25. "The father of day is Delling called,

And the night was begotten by Nor;
Full moon and old by the gods were fashioned,
To tell the time for men."
Othin spake:

26. "Fourth answer me well, if wise thou art called,
If thou knowest it, Vafthruthnir, now:
Whence did winter come, or the summer warm,
First with the gracious gods?"

Vafthruthnir spake:

27. "Vindsval he was who was winter's father,
And Svosuth summer begat…

Othin spake:

28. "Fifth answer me well, if wise thou art called,
If thou knowest it, Vafthruthnir, now:
What giant first was fashioned of old,
And the eldest of Ymir's kin?"

Vafthruthnir spake:

29. "Winters unmeasured ere earth was made
Was the birth of Bergelmir;
Thruthgelmir's son was the giant strong,
And Aurgelmir's grandson of old."

Othin spake:

30. "Sixth answer me well, if wise thou art called,
If thou knowest it, Vafthruthnir, now:
Whence did Aurgelmir come with the giants' kin,
Long since, thou giant sage?"

Vafthruthnir spake:

31. "Down from Elivagar did venom drop,
And waxed till a giant it was;
And thence arose our giants' race,
And thus so fierce are we found."

Othin spake:

32. "Seventh answer me well, if wise thou art called,
If thou knowest it, Vafthruthnir, now:
How begat he children, the giant grim,
Who never a giantess knew?"

Vafthruthnir spake:

33. "They say 'neath the arms of the giant of ice
Grew man-child and maid together;
And foot with foot did the wise one fashion
A son that six heads bore."

Othin spake:

34. "Eighth answer me well, if wise thou art called,
If thou knowest it, Vafthruthnir, now:
What farthest back dost thou bear in mind?
For wide is thy wisdom, giant!"

35. "Winters unmeasured ere earth was made
Was the birth of Bergelmir;
This first knew I well, when the giant wise
In a boat of old was borne."

Othin spake:

36. "Ninth answer me well, if wise thou art called
If thou knowest it, Vafthruthnir, now:
Whence comes the wind that fares o'er the waves
Yet never itself is seen?"

Vafthruthnir spake:

37. "In an eagle's guise at the end of heaven
Hraesvelg sits, they say;
And from his wings does the wind come forth
To move o'er the world of men."

Othin spake:

38. "Tenth answer me now, if thou knowest all

The fate that is fixed for the gods:
Whence came up Njorth to the kin of the gods,
(Rich in temples and shrines he rules,)
Though of gods he was never begot?"

Vafthruthnir spake:

39. "In the home of the Wanes | did the wise ones create him,
And gave him as pledge to the gods;
At the fall of the world | shall he fare once more
Home to the Wanes so wise."

Othin spake:

40. "Eleventh answer me well,
What men ... in … home
Each day to fight go forth?"

Vafthruthnir spake:

41. "The heroes all in Othin's hall
Each day to fight go forth;
They fell each other, and fare from the fight
All healed full soon to sit."

Othin spake:

42. "Twelfth answer me now how all thou knowest
Of the fate that is fixed for the gods;
Of the runes of the gods and the giants' race
The truth indeed dost thou tell,
(And wide is thy wisdom, giant!)"

Vafthruthnir spake:

43. "Of the runes of the gods and the giants' race
The truth indeed can I tell,
(For to every world have I won;)
To nine worlds came I, to Niflhel beneath,
The home where dead men dwell."

Othin spake:

44. "Much have I fared, much have I found,
Much have I got of the gods:
What shall live of mankind when at last there comes
The mighty winter to men?"

Vafthruthnir spake:

45. "In Hoddmimir's wood shall hide themselves
Lif and Lifthrasir then;
The morning dews for meat shall they have,
Such food shall men then find."

Othin spake:

46. "Much have I fared, much have I found,
Much have I got of the gods:
Whence comes the sun to the smooth sky back,
When Fenrir has snatched it forth?"

Vafthruthnir spake:

47. "A daughter bright Alfrothul bears
Ere Fenrir snatches her forth;
Her mother's paths shall the maiden tread
When the gods to death have gone."

Othin spake:

48. "Much have I fared, much have I found,
Much have I got of the gods:
What maidens are they, so wise of mind.
That forth o'er the sea shall fare?"

Vafthruthnir spake:

49. "O'er Mogthrasir's hill shall the maidens pass,
And three are their throngs that come;
They all shall protect the dwellers on earth,
Though they come of the giants' kin."

Othin spake:

50. "Much have I fared, much have I found,

Much have I got of the gods:
Who then shall rule the realm of the gods,
When the fires of Surt have sunk?"

Vafthruthnir spake:

51. "In the gods' home Vithar and Vali shall dwell,
When the fires of Surt have sunk;
Mothi and Magni shall Mjollnir have
When Vingnir falls in fight."

Othin spake:

52. "Much have I fared, much have I found,
Much have I got of the gods:
What shall bring the doom of death to Othin,
When the gods to destruction go?"

Vafthruthnir spake:

53. "The wolf shall fell the father of men,
And this shall Vithar avenge;
The terrible jaws shall he tear apart,
And so the wolf shall he slay."

Othin spake:

54. "Much have I fared, much have I found,
Much have I got from the gods:
What spake Othin himself in the ears of his son,
Ere in the bale-fire he burned?"

Vafthruthnir spake:

55. "No man can tell what in olden time
Thou spak'st in the ears of thy son;
With fated mouth the fall of the gods
And mine olden tales have I told;
With Othin in knowledge now have I striven,
And ever the wiser thou art."

LOKASENNA

Loki's Wrangling

Loki spoke:

1. "Speak now, Eldir, for not one step
Farther shalt thou fare;
What ale-talk here do they have within,
The sons of the glorious gods?"

Eldir spake:
2. "Of their weapons they talk, and their might in war,
The sons of the glorious gods;
From the gods and elves who are gathered here
No friend in words shalt thou find."

Loki spake:
3. "In shall I go into Aegir's hall,
For the feast I fain would see;
Bale and hatred I bring to the gods,
And their mead with venom I mix."

Eldir spake:
4. "If in thou goest to Aegir's hall,
And fain the feast wouldst see,
And with slander and spite wouldst sprinkle the gods,
Think well lest they wipe it on thee."

Loki spake:
5. "Bethink thee, Eldir, if thou and I
Shall strive with spiteful speech;
Richer I grow in ready words
If thou speakest too much to me."

Then Loki went into the hall, but when they who were there saw who had entered, they were all silent.

Loki spake:

6. "Thirsty I come into this thine hall,
I, Lopt, from a journey long,
To ask of the gods that one should give
Fair mead for a drink to me.

7. "Why sit ye silent, swollen with pride,
Ye gods, and no answer give?
At your feast a place and a seat prepare me,
Or bid me forth to fare."

Bragi spake:
8. "A place and a seat will the gods prepare
No more in their midst for thee;
For the gods know well what men they wish
To find at their mighty feasts."

Loki spake:
9. "Remember, Othin, in olden days
That we both our blood have mixed;
Then didst thou promise no ale to pour,
Unless it were brought for us both."

Othin spake:
10. "Stand forth then, Vithar, and let the wolf's father
Find a seat at our feast;
Lest evil should Loki speak aloud
Here within Aegir's hall."

Then Vithar arose and poured drink for Loki; but before he drank he spoke to the gods:

11. "Hail to you, gods! ye goddesses, hail!
Hail to the holy throng!
Save for the god who yonder sits,
Bragi there on the bench."

Bragi spake:
12. "A horse and a sword from my hoard will I give,
And a ring gives Bragi to boot,
That hatred thou makst not among the gods;
So rouse not the great ones to wrath."

Loki spake:
13. "In horses and rings thou shalt never be rich,

Bragi, but both shalt thou lack;
Of the gods and elves here together met
Least brave in battle art thou,
(And shyest thou art of the shot.)"

Bragi spake:
14. "Now were I without as I am within,
And here in Aegir's hall,
Thine head would I bear in mine hands away,
And pay thee the price of thy lies."

Loki spake:
15. "In thy seat art thou bold, not so are thy deeds,
Bragi, adorner of benches!
Go out and fight if angered thou feelest,
No hero such forethought has."

Ithun spake:
16. "Well, prithee, Bragi, his kinship weigh,
Since chosen as wish-son he was;
And speak not to Loki such words of spite
Here within Aegir's hall."

Loki spake:
17. "Be silent, Ithun! thou art, I say,
Of women most lustful in love,
Since thou thy washed-bright | arms didst wind
About thy brother's slayer."

Ithun spake:
18. "To Loki I speak not with spiteful words
Here within Aegir's hall;
And Bragi I calm, who is hot with beer,
For I wish not that fierce they should fight."

Gefjun spake:
19. "Why, ye gods twain, with bitter tongues
Raise hate among us here?
Loki is famed for his mockery foul,
And the dwellers in heaven he hates."

Loki spake:
20. "Be silent, Gefjun! for now shall I say

Who led thee to evil life;
The boy so fair gave a necklace bright,
And about him thy leg was laid."

Othin spake:
21. "Mad art thou, Loki, and little of wit,
The wrath of Gefjun to rouse;
For the fate that is set for all she sees,
Even as I, methinks."

Loki spake:
22. "Be silent, Othin! not justly thou settest
The fate of the fight among men;
Oft gavst thou to him who deserved not the gift,
To the baser, the battle's prize."

Othin spake:
23. "Though I gave to him who deserved not the gift,
To the baser, the battle's prize;
Winters eight wast thou under the earth,
Milking the cows as a maid,
(Ay, and babes didst thou bear;
Unmanly thy soul must seem.)"

Loki spake:
24. "They say that with spells | in Samsey once
Like witches with charms didst thou work;
And in witch's guise among men didst thou go;
Unmanly thy soul must seem."

Frigg spake:
25. "Of the deeds ye two of old have done
Ye should make no speech among men;
Whate'er ye have done in days gone by,
Old tales should ne'er be told."

Loki spake:
26. "Be silent, Frigg! thou art Fjorgyn's wife,
But ever lustful in love;
For Vili and Ve, thou wife of Vithrir,
Both in thy bosom have lain."

Frigg spake:

27. "If a son like Baldr were by me now,
Here within Aegir's hall,
From the sons of the gods thou shouldst go not forth
Till thy fierceness in fight were tried."

Loki spake:
28. "Thou wilt then, Frigg, that further I tell
Of the ill that now I know;
Mine is the blame that Baldr no more
Thou seest ride home to the hall."

Freyja spake:
29. "Mad art thou, Loki, that known thou makest
The wrong and shame thou hast wrought;
The fate of all does Frigg know well,
Though herself she says it not."

Loki spake:
30. "Be silent, Freyja! for fully I know thee,
Sinless thou art not thyself;
Of the gods and elves who are gathered here,
Each one as thy lover has lain."

Freyja spake:
31. "False is thy tongue, and soon shalt thou find
That it sings thee an evil song;
The gods are wroth, and the goddesses all,
And in grief shalt thou homeward go."

Loki spake:
32. "Be silent, Freyja! thou foulest witch,
And steeped full sore in sin;
In the arms of thy brother the bright gods caught thee
When Freyja her wind set free."

Njorth spake:
33. "Small ill does it work though a woman may have
A lord or a lover or both;
But a wonder it is that this womanish god
Comes hither, though babes he has borne."

Loki spake:

34. "Be silent, Njorth; thou wast eastward sent,
To the gods as a hostage given;
And the daughters of Hymir their privy had
When use did they make of thy mouth."

Njorth spake:
35. "Great was my gain, though long was I gone,
To the gods as a hostage given;
The son did I have whom no man hates,
And foremost of gods is found."

Loki spake:
36. "Give heed now, Njorth, nor boast too high,
No longer I hold it hid;
With thy sister hadst thou so fair a son,
Thus hadst thou no worse a hope."

Tyr spake:
37. "Of the heroes brave is Freyr the best
Here in the home of the gods;
He harms not maids nor the wives of men,
And the bound from their fetters he frees."

Loki spake:
38. "Be silent, Tyr! for between two men
Friendship thou ne'er couldst fashion;
Fain would I tell how Fenrir once
Thy right hand rent from thee."

Tyr spake:
39. "My hand do I lack, but Hrothvitnir thou,
And the loss brings longing to both;
Ill fares the wolf who shall ever await
In fetters the fall of the gods."

Loki spake:
40. "Be silent, Tyr! for a son with me
Thy wife once chanced to win;
Not a penny, methinks, wast thou paid for the wrong,
Nor wast righted an inch, poor wretch."

Freyr spake:
Till the gods to destruction go;

Thou too shalt soon, if thy tongue is not stilled,
Be fettered, thou forger of ill."

Loki spake:
42. "The daughter of Gymir with gold didst thou buy,
And sold thy sword to boot;
But when Muspell's sons through Myrkwood ride,
Thou shalt weaponless wait, poor wretch."

Byggvir spake:
43. "Had I birth so famous as Ingunar-Freyr,
And sat in so lofty a seat,
I would crush to marrow this croaker of ill,
And beat all his body to bits."

Loki spake:
44. "What little creature goes crawling there,
Snuffling and snapping about?
At Freyr's ears ever wilt thou be found,
Or muttering hard at the mill."

Byggvir spake:
45. "Byggvir my name, and nimble am I,
As gods and men do grant;
And here am I proud that the children of Hropt
Together all drink ale."

Loki spake:
46. "Be silent, Byggvir! thou never couldst set
Their shares of the meat for men;
Hid in straw on the floor, they found thee not
When heroes were fain to fight."

Heimdall spake:
47. "Drunk art thou, Loki, and mad are thy deeds,
Why, Loki, leavst thou this not?
For drink beyond measure will lead all men
No thought of their tongues to take."

Loki spake:
48. "Be silent, Heimdall! in days long since
Was an evil fate for thee fixed;
With back held stiff must thou ever stand,

As warder of heaven to watch."

Skathi spake:
49. "Light art thou, Loki, but longer thou mayst not
In freedom flourish thy tail;
On the rocks the gods bind thee with bowels torn
Forth from thy frost-cold son."

Loki spake:
50. "Though on rocks the gods bind me with bowels torn
Forth from my frost-cold son,
I was first and last at the deadly fight
There where Thjazi we caught."

Skathi spake:
51. "Wert thou first and last at the deadly fight
There where Thjazi was caught,
From my dwellings and fields shall ever come forth
A counsel cold for thee."

Loki spake:
52. "More lightly thou spakest with Laufey's son,
When thou badst me come to thy bed;
Such things must be known if now we two
Shall seek our sins to tell."

Then Sif came forward and poured mead for Loki in a crystal cup, and said:
53. "Hail too thee, Loki, and take thou here
The crystal cup of old mead;
For me at least, alone of the gods,
Blameless thou knowest to be."

He took the horn, and drank therefrom:
54. "Alone thou wert if truly thou wouldst
All men so shyly shun;
But one do I know full well, methinks,
Who had thee from Hlorrithi's arms,
(Loki the crafty in lies.)"

Beyla spake:
55. "The mountains shake, and surely I think
From his home comes Hlorrithi now;
He will silence the man who is slandering here

Together both gods and men."

Loki spake:
56. "Be silent, Beyla! thou art Byggvir's wife,
And deep art thou steeped in sin;
A greater shame to the gods came ne'er,
Befouled thou art with thy filth."

Then came Thor forth, and spake:
57. "Unmanly one, cease, or the mighty hammer,
Mjollnir, shall close thy mouth;
Thy shoulder-cliff shall I cleave from thy neck,
And so shall thy life be lost."

Loki spake:
58. "Lo, in has come the son of Earth:
Why threaten so loudly, Thor?
Less fierce thou shalt go to fight with the wolf
When he swallows Sigfather up."

Thor spake:
59. "Unmanly one, cease, or the mighty hammer,
Mjollnir, shall close thy mouth;
I shall hurl thee up and out in the East,
Where men shall see thee no more."

Loki spake:
60. "That thou hast fared on the East-road forth
To men shouldst thou say no more;
In the thumb of a glove didst thou hide, thou great one,
And there forgot thou wast Thor."

Thor spake:
61. "Unmanly one, cease, or the mighty hammer,
Mjollnir, shall close thy mouth;
My right hand shall smite thee with Hrungnir's slayer,
Till all thy bones are broken."

Loki spake:
62. "Along time still do I think to live,
Though thou threatenest thus with thy hammer;
Rough seemed the straps of Skrymir's wallet,
When thy meat thou mightest not get,

(And faint from hunger didst feel.)"

Thor spake:
63. "Unmanly one, cease, or the mighty hammer,
Mjollnir, shall close thy mouth;
The slayer of Hrungnir shall send thee to hell,
And down to the gate of death."

Loki spake:
64. "'I have said to the gods and the sons of the god,
The things that whetted my thoughts;
But before thee alone do I now go forth,
For thou fightest well, I ween.

65. "Ale hast thou brewed, but, Aegir, now
Such feasts shalt thou make no more;
O'er all that thou hast which is here within
Shall play the flickering flames,
(And thy back shall be burnt with fire.)"

THRYMSKVITHA

The Lay of Thrym

1. Wild was Vingthor when he awoke,
And when his mighty hammer he missed;
He shook his beard, his hair was bristling,
As the son of Jorth about him sought.

2. Hear now the speech that first he spake:
"Harken, Loki, and heed my words,
Nowhere on earth is it known to man,
Nor in heaven above: our hammer is stolen."

3. To the dwelling fair of Freyja went they,
Hear now the speech that first he spake:
"Wilt thou, Freyja, thy feather-dress lend me,
That so my hammer I may seek?"

Freyja spake:

4. "Thine should it be though of silver bright,
And I would give it though 'twere of gold."
Then Loki flew, and the feather-dress whirred,
Till he left behind him the home of the gods,
And reached at last the realm of the giants.

5. Thrym sat on a mound, the giants' master,
Leashes of gold he laid for his dogs,
And stroked and smoothed the manes of his steeds.

Thrym spake:
6. "How fare the gods, how fare the elves?
Why comst thou alone to the giants' land?"

Loki spake:
"Ill fare the gods, ill fare the elves!
Hast thou hidden Hlorrithi's hammer?"

Thrym spake:
7. "I have hidden Hlorrithi's hammer,
Eight miles down deep in the earth;
And back again shall no man bring it
If Freyja I win not to be my wife."

8. Then Loki flew, and the feather-dress whirred,
Till he left behind him the home of the giants,
And reached at last the realm of the gods.
There in the courtyard Thor he met:
Hear now the speech that first he spake:

9. "Hast thou found tidings as well as trouble?
Thy news in the air shalt thou utter now;
Oft doth the sitter his story forget,
And lies he speaks who lays himself down."

Loki spake:
10. "Trouble I have, and tidings as well:
Thrym, king of the giants, keeps thy hammer,
And back again shall no man bring it
If Freyja he wins not to be his wife."

11. Freyja the fair then went they to find
Hear now the speech that first he spake:

"Bind on, Freyja, the bridal veil,
For we two must haste to the giants' home."

12. Wrathful was Freyja, and fiercely she snorted,
And the dwelling great of the gods was shaken,
And burst was the mighty Brisings' necklace:
"Most lustful indeed should I look to all
If I journeyed with thee to the giants' home."

13. Then were the gods together met,
And the goddesses came and council held,
And the far-famed ones a plan would find,
How they might Hlorrithi's hammer win.

14. Then Heimdall spake, whitest of the gods,
Like the Wanes he knew the future well:
"Bind we on Thor the bridal veil,
Let him bear the mighty Brisings' necklace;

15. "Keys around him let there rattle,
And down to his knees hang woman's dress;
With gems full broad upon his breast,
And a pretty cap to crown his head."

16. Then Thor the mighty his answer made:
"Me would the gods unmanly call
If I let bind the bridal veil."

17. Then Loki spake, the son of Laufey:
"Be silent, Thor, and speak not thus;
Else will the giants in Asgarth dwell
If thy hammer is brought not home to thee."

8. Then bound they on Thor the bridal veil,
And next the mighty Brisings' necklace.

19. Keys around him let they rattle,
And down to his knees hung woman's dress;
With gems full broad upon his breast,
And a pretty cap to crown his head.

20. Then Loki spake, the son of Laufey:
"As thy maid-servant thither I go with thee;

We two shall haste to the giants' home."

21. Then home the goats to the hall were driven,
They wrenched at the halters, swift were they to run;
The mountains burst, earth burned with fire,
And Othin's son sought Jotunheim.

22. Then loud spake Thrym, the giants' leader:
"Bestir ye, giants, put straw on the benches;
Now Freyja they bring to be my bride,
The daughter of Njorth out of Noatun.

23. "Gold-horned cattle go to my stables,
Jet-black oxen, the giant's joy;
Many my gems, and many my jewels,
Freyja alone did I lack, methinks."

24. Early it was to evening come,
And forth was borne the beer for the giants;
Thor alone ate an ox, and eight salmon,
All the dainties as well that were set for the women;
And drank Sif's mate three tuns of mead.

25. Then loud spake Thrym, the giants' leader:
"Who ever saw bride more keenly bite?
I ne'er saw bride with a broader bite,
Nor a maiden who drank more mead than this!"

26. Hard by there sat the serving-maid wise,
So well she answered the giant's words:
"From food has Freyja eight nights fasted,
So hot was her longing for Jotunheim."

27. Thrym looked 'neath the veil, for he longed to kiss,
But back he leaped the length of the hall:
"Why are so fearful the eyes of Freyja?
Fire, methinks, from her eyes burns forth."

28. Hard by there sat the serving-maid wise,
So well she answered the giant's words:
"No sleep has Freyja for eight nights found,
So hot was her longing for Jotunheim."

29. Soon came the giant's luckless sister,
Who feared not to ask the bridal fee:
"From thy hands the rings of red gold take,
If thou wouldst win my willing love,
(My willing love and welcome glad.)"

30: Then loud spake Thrym, the giants' leader:
"Bring in the hammer to hallow the bride;
On the maiden's knees let Mjollnir lie,
That us both the band of Vor may bless."

31. The heart in the breast of Hlorrithi laughed
When the hard-souled one his hammer beheld;
First Thrym, the king of the giants, he killed,
Then all the folk of the giants he felled.

32. The giant's sister old he slew,
She who had begged the bridal fee;
A stroke she got in the shilling's stead,
And for many rings the might of the hammer.

33. And so his hammer got Othin's son.

ALVISSMOL

The Ballad of Alvis

Alvis spake:
1. "Now shall the bride my benches adorn,
And homeward haste forthwith;
Eager for wedlock to all shall I seem,
Nor at home shall they rob me of rest."

Thor spake:
2. "What, pray, art thou? Why so pale round the nose?
By the dead hast thou lain of late?
To a giant like dost thou look, methinks;
Thou wast not born for the bride."

Alvis spake:

3. "Alvis am I, and under the earth
My home 'neath the rocks I have;
With the wagon-guider a word do I seek,
Let the gods their bond not break."

Thor spake:
4. "Break it shall I, for over the bride
Her father has foremost right;
At home was I not when the promise thou hadst,
And I give her alone of the gods."

Alvis spake:
5. "What hero claims such right to hold
O'er the bride that shines so bright?
Not many will know thee, thou wandering man!
Who was bought with rings to bear thee?"

Thor spake:
6. "Vingthor, the wanderer wide, am I,
And I am Sithgrani's son;
Against my will shalt thou get the maid,
And win the marriage word."

Alvis spake:
7. "Thy good-will now shall I quickly get,
And win the marriage word;
I long to have, and I would not lack,
This snow-white maid for mine."

Thor spake:
8. "The love of the maid I may not keep thee
From winning, thou guest so wise,
If of every world thou canst tell me all
That now I wish to know.

9. "Answer me, Alvis! thou knowest all,
Dwarf, of the doom of men:
What call they the earth, that lies before all,
In each and every world?"

Alvis spake:
10. " 'Earth' to men, 'Field' to the gods it is,
'The Ways' is it called by the Wanes;

'Ever Green' by the giants, 'The Grower' by elves,
'The Moist' by the holy ones high."

Thor spake:
11. "Answer me, Alvis! thou knowest all,
Dwarf, of the doom of men:
What call they the heaven, beheld of the high one,
In each and every world?"

Alvis spake:
12. " 'Heaven' men call it, 'The Height' the gods,
The Wanes 'The Weaver of Winds';
Giants 'The Up-World,' elves 'The Fair-Roof,'
The dwarfs 'The Dripping Hall.'"

Thor spake:
13. "Answer me, Alvis! thou knowest all,
Dwarf, of the doom of men:
What call they the moon, that men behold,
In each and every world?"

Alvis spake:
14. "'Moon' with men, 'Flame' the gods among,
'The Wheel' in the house of hell;
'The Goer' the giants, 'The Gleamer' the dwarfs,
The elves 'The Teller of Time.'"

Thor spake:
15. "Answer me, Alvis! thou knowest all,
Dwarf, of the doom of men:
What call they the sun, that all men see,
In each and every world?"

Alvis spake:
16. "Men call it 'Sun,' gods 'Orb of the Sun,'
'The Deceiver of Dvalin' the dwarfs;
The giants 'The Ever-Bright,' elves 'Fair Wheel,'
'All-Glowing' the sons of the gods."

Thor spake:
17. "Answer me, Alvis! thou knowest all,
Dwarf, of the doom of men:
What call they the clouds, that keep the rains,

In each and every world?"

Alvis spake:
18. "'Clouds' men name them, 'Rain-Hope' gods call them,
The Wanes call them 'Kites of the Wind';
'Water-Hope' giants, 'Weather-Might' elves,
'The Helmet of Secrets' in hell."

Thor spake:
19. "Answer me, Alvis! thou knowest all,
Dwarf, of the doom of men:
What call they the wind, that widest fares,
In each and every world?"

Alvis spake:
20. "'Wind' do men call it, the gods 'The Waverer,'
'The Neigher' the holy ones high;
'The Wailer' the giants, 'Roaring Wender' the elves,
In hell 'The Blustering Blast.'

Thor spake:
21. "Answer me, Alvis! thou knowest all
Dwarf, of the doom of men:
What call they the calm, that quiet lies,
In each and every world?"

Alvis spake:
22. " 'Calm' men call it, 'The Quiet' the gods,
The Wanes 'The Hush of the Winds';
'The Sultry' the giants, elves 'Day's Stillness,'
The dwarfs 'The Shelter of Day.'

Thor spake:
23. "Answer me, Alvis! thou knowest all,
Dwarf, of the doom of men:
What call they the sea, whereon men sail,
In each and every world?"

Alvis spake:
24. " 'Sea' men call it, gods 'The Smooth-Lying,'
'The Wave' is it called by the Wanes;
'Eel-Home' the giants, | 'Drink-Stuff' the elves,
For the dwarfs its name is 'The Deep.'

Thor spake:
25. "Answer me, Alvis! thou knowest all,
Dwarf, of the doom of men:
What call they the fire, that flames for men,
In each of all the worlds?"

Alvis spake:
26. " 'Fire' men call it, and 'Flame' the gods,
By the Wanes is it 'Wildfire' called;
'The Biter' by giants, 'The Burner' by dwarfs,
'The Swift' in the house of hell."

Thor spake:
27. "Answer me, Alvis! thou knowest all,
Dwarf, of the doom of men:
What call they the wood, that grows for mankind,
In each and every world?"

Alvis spake:
28. "Men call it 'The Wood, gods 'The Mane of the Field,'
'Seaweed of Hills' in hell;
'Flame-Food' the giants, 'Fair-Limbed' the elves,
'The Wand' is it called by the Wanes."

Thor spake:
29. "Answer me, Alvis! thou knowest all,
Dwarf, of the doom of men:
What call they the night, the daughter of Nor,
In each and every world?"

Alvis spake:
30. "'Night' men call it, 'Darkness' gods name it,
'The Hood' the holy ones high;
The giants 'The Lightless,' the elves 'Sleep's joy"
The dwarfs 'The Weaver of Dreams.'"

Thor spake:
31. "Answer me, Alvis! thou knowest all,
Dwarf, of the doom of men:
What call they the seed, that is sown by men,
In each and every world?"

Alvis spake:
32. "Men call it 'Grain,' and 'Corn' the gods,
'Growth' in the world of the Wanes;
'The Eaten' by giants, 'Drink-Stuff' by elves,
In hell 'The Slender Stem.'

Thor spake:
33. "Answer me, Alvis! thou knowest all,
Dwarf, of the doom of men:
What call they the ale, that is quaffed of men,
In each and every world?"

Alvis spake:
34. "'Ale' among men, 'Beer' the gods among,
In the world of the Wanes 'The Foaming';
'Bright Draught' with giants, 'Mead' with dwellers in hell,
'The Feast-Draught' with Suttung's sons."

Thor spake:
"In a single breast I never have seen
More wealth of wisdom old;
But with treacherous wiles must I now betray thee:
The day has caught thee, dwarf!
(Now the sun shines here in the hall.)"

BALDRS DRAUMAR

Baldr's Dreams

1. Once were the gods together met,
And the goddesses came and council held,
And the far-famed ones the truth would find,
Why baleful dreams to Baldr had come.

2. Then Othin rose, the enchanter old,
And the saddle he laid on Sleipnir's back;
Thence rode he down to Niflhel deep,
And the hound he met that came from hell.

3. Bloody he was on his breast before,

At the father of magic he howled from afar;
Forward rode Othin, the earth resounded
Till the house so high of Hel he reached.

4. Then Othin rode to the eastern door,
There, he knew well, was the wise-woman's grave;
Magic he spoke and mighty charms,
Till spell-bound she rose, and in death she spoke:

5. "What is the man, to me unknown,
That has made me travel the troublous road?
I was snowed on with snow, and smitten with rain,
And drenched with dew; long was I dead."

Othin spake:
6. "Vegtam my name, I am Valtam's son;
Speak thou of hell, for of heaven I know:
For whom are the benches bright with rings,
And the platforms gay bedecked with gold?"

The Wise-Woman spake:
7. "Here for Baldr the mead is brewed,
The shining drink, and a shield lies o'er it;
But their hope is gone from the mighty gods.
Unwilling I spake, and now would be still."

Othin spake:
8. "Wise-woman, cease not! I seek from thee
All to know that I fain would ask:
Who shall the bane of Baldr become,
And steal the life from Othin's son?"

The Wise-Woman spake:
9. "Hoth thither bears the far-famed branch,
He shall the bane of Baldr become,
And steal the life from Othin's son.
Unwilling I spake, and now would be still."

Othin spake:
10. "Wise-woman, cease not! I seek from thee
All to know that I fain would ask:
Who shall vengeance win for the evil work,
Or bring to the flames the slayer of Baldr?"

The Wise-Woman spake:
11. "Rind bears Vali in Vestrsalir,
And one night old fights Othin's son;
His hands he shall wash not, his hair he shall comb not,
Till the slayer of Baldr he brings to the flames.
Unwilling I spake, and now would be still."

Othin spake:
12. "Wise-woman, cease not! I seek from thee
All to know that I fain would ask:
What maidens are they who then shall weep,
And toss to the sky the yards of the sails?"

The Wise-Woman spake:
13. "Vegtam thou art not, as erstwhile I thought;
Othin thou art, the enchanter old."

Othin spake:
"No wise-woman art thou, nor wisdom hast;
Of giants three the mother art thou."

The Wise-Woman spake:
14. "Home ride, Othin, be ever proud;
For no one of men shall seek me more
Till Loki wanders loose from his bonds,
And to the last strife the destroyers come."

RIGSTHULA

The Song of Rig

1. Men say there went by ways so green
Of old the god, the aged and wise,
Mighty and strong did Rig go striding.

2. Forward he went on the midmost way,
He came to a dwelling, a door on its posts;
In did he fare, on the floor was a fire,

Two hoary ones by the hearth there sat,
Ai and Edda, in olden dress.

3. Rig knew well wise words to speak,
Soon in the midst of the room he sat,
And on either side the others were.

4. A loaf of bread did Edda bring,
Heavy and thick and swollen with husks;
Forth on the table she set the fare,
And broth for the meal in a bowl there was.
(Calf's flesh boiled was the best of the dainties.)

5. Rig knew well wise words to speak,
Thence did he rise, made ready to sleep;
Soon in the bed himself did he lay,
And on either side the others were.

6. Thus was he there for three nights long,
Then forward he went on the midmost way,
And so nine months were soon passed by.

7. A son bore Edda, with water they sprinkled him,
With a cloth his hair so black they covered;
Thraell they named him….

8. The skin was wrinkled and rough on his hands,
Knotted his knuckles…
Thick his fingers, and ugly his face,
Twisted his back, and big his heels.

9. He began to grow, and to gain in strength,
Soon of his might good use he made;
With bast he bound, and burdens carried,
Home bore faggots the whole day long.

10. One came to their home, crooked her legs,
Stained were her feet, and sunburned her arms,
Flat was her nose; her name was Thir.

11. Soon in the midst of the room she sat,
By her side there sat the son of the house;
They whispered both, and the bed made ready,

Thraell and Thir, till the day was through.

12. Children they had, they lived and were happy,
Fjosnir and Klur they were called, methinks,
Hreim and Kleggi, Kefsir, Fulnir,
Drumb, Digraldi, Drott and Leggjaldi,
Lut and Hosvir; the house they cared for,
Ground they dunged, and swine they guarded,
Goats they tended, and turf they dug.

13. Daughters had they, Drumba and Kumba,
Okkvinkalfa, Arinnefla,
Ysja and Ambott, Eikintjasna,
Totrughypja and Tronubeina;
And thence has risen the race of thralls.

14. Forward went Rig, his road was straight,
To a hall he came, and a door there hung;
In did he fare, on the floor was a fire:
Afi and Amma owned the house.

15. There sat the twain, and worked at their tasks:
The man hewed wood for the weaver's beam;
His beard was trimmed, o'er his brow a curl,
His clothes fitted close; in the corner a chest.

16. The woman sat and the distaff wielded,
At the weaving with arms outstretched she worked;
On her head was a band, on her breast a smock;
On her shoulders a kerchief with clasps there was.

17. Rig knew well wise words to speak,
Soon in the midst of the room he sat,
And on either side the others were.

18. Then took Amma....
The vessels full with the fare she set,
Calf's flesh boiled was the best of the dainties.

19. Rig knew well wise words to speak,
He rose from the board, made ready to sleep;
Soon in the bed himself did he lay,
And on either side the others were.

20. Thus was he there for three nights long,
Then forward he went on the midmost way,
And so nine months were soon passed by.

21. A son bore Amma, with water they sprinkled him,
Karl they named him; in a cloth she wrapped him,
He was ruddy of face, and flashing his eyes.

22. He began to grow, and to gain in strength,
Oxen he ruled, and plows made ready,
Houses he built, and barns he fashioned,
Carts he made, and the plow he managed.

23. Home did they bring the bride for Karl,
In goatskins clad, and keys she bore;
Snor was her name, 'neath the veil she sat;
A home they made ready, and rings exchanged,
The bed they decked, and a dwelling made.

24. Sons they had, they lived and were happy:
Hal and Dreng, Holth, Thegn and Smith,
Breith and Bondi, Bundinskeggi,
Bui and Boddi, Brattskegg and Segg.

25. Daughters they had, and their names are here:
Snot, Bruth, Svanni, Svarri, Sprakki,
Fljoth, Sprund and Vif, Feima, Ristil:
And thence has risen the yeomen's race.

26. Thence went Rig, his road was straight,
A hall he saw, the doors faced south;
The portal stood wide, on the posts was a ring,
Then in he fared; the floor was strewn.

27. Within two gazed in each other's eyes,
Fathir and Mothir, and played with their fingers;
There sat the house-lord, wound strings for the bow,
Shafts he fashioned, and bows he shaped.

28. The lady sat, at her arms she looked,
She smoothed the cloth, and fitted the sleeves;
Gay was her cap, on her breast were clasps,

Broad was her train, of blue was her gown,
Her brows were bright, her breast was shining,
Whiter her neck than new-fallen snow.

29. Rig knew well wise words to speak,
Soon in the midst of the room he sat,
And on either side the others were.

30. Then Mothir brought a broidered cloth,
Of linen bright, and the board she covered;
And then she took the loaves so thin,
And laid them, white from the wheat, on the cloth.

31. Then forth she brought the vessels full,
With silver covered, and set before them,
Meat all browned, and well-cooked birds;
In the pitcher was wine, of plate were the cups,
So drank they and talked till the day was gone.

32. Rig knew well wise words to speak,
Soon did he rise, made ready to sleep;
So in the bed himself did he lay,
And on either side the others were.

33. Thus was he there for three nights long,
Then forward he went on the midmost way,
And so nine months were soon passed by.

34. A son had Mothir, in silk they wrapped him,
With water they sprinkled him, Jarl he was;
Blond was his hair, and bright his cheeks,
Grim as a snake's were his glowing eyes.

35. To grow in the house did Jarl begin,
Shields he brandished, and bow-strings wound,
Bows he shot, and shafts he fashioned,
Arrows he loosened, and lances wielded,
Horses he rode, and hounds unleashed,
Swords he handled, and sounds he swam.

36. Straight from the grove came striding Rig,
Rig came striding, and runes he taught him;
By his name he called him, as son he claimed him,

And bade him hold his heritage wide,
His heritage wide, the ancient homes.

37. Forward he rode through the forest dark,
O'er the frosty crags, till a hall he found.

38. His spear he shook, his shield he brandished,
His horse he spurred, with his sword he hewed;
Wars he raised, and reddened the field,
Warriors slew he, and land he won.

39. Eighteen halls ere long did he hold,
Wealth did he get, and gave to all,
Stones and jewels and slim-flanked steeds,
Rings he offered, and arm-rings shared.

40. His messengers went by the ways so wet,
And came to the hall where Hersir dwelt;
His daughter was fair and slender-fingered,
Erna the wise the maiden was.

41. Her hand they sought, and home they brought her,
Wedded to Jarl the veil she wore;
Together they dwelt, their joy was great,
Children they had, and happy they lived.

42. Bur was the eldest, and Barn the next,
Joth and Athal, Arfi, Mog,
Nith and Svein, soon they began-
Sun and Nithjung -- to play and swim;
Kund was one, and the youngest Kon.

43. Soon grew up the sons of Jarl,
Beasts they tamed, and bucklers rounded,
Shafts they fashioned, and spears they shook.

44. But Kon the Young learned runes to use,
Runes everlasting, the runes of life;
Soon could he well the warriors shield,
Dull the swordblade, and still the seas.

45. Bird-chatter learned he, flames could he lessen.,
Minds could quiet, and sorrows calm;

The might and strength of twice four men.

46. With Rig-Jarl soon the runes he shared,
More crafty he was, and greater his wisdom;
The right he sought, and soon he won it,
Rig to be called, and runes to know.

47. Young Kon rode forth through forest and grove,
Shafts let loose, and birds he lured;
There spake a crow on a bough that sat:
"Why lurest thou, Kon, the birds to come?

48. " 'Twere better forth on thy steed to fare,
... and the host to slay.

49. "The halls of Dan and Danp are noble,
Greater their wealth than thou hast gained;
Good are they at guiding the keel,
Trying of weapons, and giving of wounds.

HYNDLULJOTH

The Poem of Hyndla

Freyja spake:

1. "Maiden, awake! wake thee, my friend,
My sister Hyndla, in thy hollow cave!
Already comes darkness, and ride must we
To Valhall to seek the sacred hall.

2. "The favor of Heerfather seek we to find,
To his followers gold he gladly gives;
To Hermoth gave he helm and mail-coat,
And to Sigmund he gave a sword as gift.

3. "Triumph to some, and treasure to others,
To many wisdom and skill in words,
Fair winds to the sailor, to the singer his art,
And a manly heart to many a hero.

4. "Thor shall I honor, and this shall I ask,
That his favor true mayst thou ever find;
Though little the brides of the giants he loves.

5. "From the stall now one of thy wolves lead forth,
And along with my boar shalt thou let him run;
For slow my boar goes on the road of the gods,
And I would not weary my worthy steed."

Hyndla spake:

6. "Falsely thou askest me, Freyja, to go,
For so in the glance of thine eyes I see;
On the way of the slain | thy lover goes with thee.
Ottar the young, the son of Instein."

Freyja spake:

7. "Wild dreams, methinks, are thine when thou sayest
My lover is with me on the way of the slain;
There shines the boar with bristles of gold,
Hildisvini, he who was made
By Dain and Nabbi, the cunning dwarfs.

8. "Now let us down from our saddles leap,
And talk of the race of the heroes twain;
The men who were born of the gods above,

9. "A wager have made in the foreign metal
Ottar the young and Angantyr;
We must guard, for the hero young to have,
His father's wealth, the fruits of his race.

10. "For me a shrine of stones he made,--
And now to glass the rock has grown;--
Oft with the blood of beasts was it red;
In the goddesses ever did Ottar trust.

11. "Tell to me now the ancient names,
And the races of all that were born of old:
Who are of the Skjoldungs, who of the Skilfings,
Who of the Othlings, who of the Ylfings,

Who are the free-born, who are the high-born,
The noblest of men that in Mithgarth dwell?"

Hyndla spake:

12. "Thou art, Ottar, the son of Instein,
And Instein the son of Alf the Old,
Alf of Ulf, Ulf of Saefari,
And Saefari's father was Svan the Red.

13. "Thy mother, bright with bracelets fair,
Hight, methinks, the priestess Hledis;
Frothi her father, and Friaut her mother;--
Her race of the mightiest men must seem.

14. "Of old the noblest of all was Ali,
Before him Halfdan, foremost of Skjoldungs;
Famed were the battles the hero fought,
To the corners of heaven his deeds were carried.

15. "Strengthened by Eymund, the strongest of men,
Sigtrygg he slew with the ice-cold sword;
His bride was Almveig, the best of women,
And eighteen boys did Almveig bear him.

16. "Hence come the Skjoldungs, hence the Skilfings,
Hence the Othlings, hence the Ynglings,
Hence come the free-born, hence the high-born,
The noblest of men that in Mithgarth dwell:
And all are thy kinsmen, Ottar, thou fool!

17. "Hildigun then her mother hight,
The daughter of Svava and Saekonung;
And all are thy kinsmen, Ottar, thou fool!
It is much to know, wilt thou hear yet more?

18. "The mate of Dag was a mother of heroes,
Thora, who bore him the bravest of fighters,
Frathmar and Gyrth and the Frekis twain,
Am and Jofurmar, Alf the Old;
It is much to know, wilt thou hear yet more?

19. "Her husband was Ketil, the heir of Klypp,

He was of thy mother the mother's-father;
Before the days of Kari was Frothi,
And horn of Hild was Hoalf then.

20. "Next was Nanna, daughter of Nokkvi,
Thy father's kinsman her son became;
Old is the line, and longer still,
And all are thy kinsmen, Ottar, thou fool!

21. "Isolf and Osolf, the sons of Olmoth,
Whose wife was Skurhild, the daughter of Skekkil,
Count them among the heroes mighty,
And all are thy kinsmen, Ottar, thou fool!

22. "Gunnar the Bulwark, Grim the Hardy,
Thorir the Iron-shield, Ulf the Gaper,
Brodd and Horvir both did I know;
In the household they were of Hrolf the Old.

23. "Hervarth, Hjorvarth, Hrani, Angantyr,
Bui and Brami, Barri and Reifnir,
Tind and Tyrfing, the Haddings twain,
And all are thy kinsmen, Ottar, thou fool!
24. "Eastward in Bolm were born of old
The sons of Arngrim and Eyfura;
With berserk-tumult and baleful deed
Like fire o'er land and sea they fared,
And all are thy kinsmen, Ottar, thou fool!

25. "The sons of Jormunrek all of yore
To the gods in death were as offerings given;
He was kinsman of Sigurth, hear well what I say,
The foe of hosts, and Fafnir's slayer.

26., "From Volsung's seed was the hero sprung,
And Hjordis was born of Hrauthung's race,
And Eylimi from the Othlings came,
And all are thy kinsmen, Ottar, thou fool!

27. "Gunnar and Hogni, the heirs of Gjuki,
And Guthrun as well, who their sister was;
But Gotthorm was not of Gjuki's race,
Although the brother of both he was:

And all are thy kinsmen, Ottar, thou fool!

28. "Of Hvethna's sons was Haki the best,
And Hjorvarth the father of Hvethna was...

29. "Harald Battle-tooth of Auth was born,
Hrorek the Ring-giver her husband was;
Auth the Deep-minded was Ivar's daughter,
But Rathbarth the father of Randver was:
And all are thy kinsmen, Ottar, thou fool!"

Fragment of "The Short Voluspo"

30. Eleven in number the gods were known,
When Baldr o'er the hill of death was bowed;
And this to avenge was Vali swift,
When his brother's slayer soon he slew.

31. The father of Baldr was the heir of Bur,

32. Freyr's wife was Gerth, the daughter of Gymir,
Of the giants' brood, and Aurbotha bore her;
To these as well was Thjazi kin,
The dark-loving giant; his daughter was Skathi.

33. Much have I told thee, and further will tell;
There is much that I know; wilt thou hear yet more?

34. Heith and Hrossthjof, the children of Hrimnir.

35. The sybils arose from Vitholf's race,
From Vilmeith all the seers are,
And the workers of charms are Svarthofthi's children,
And from Ymir sprang the giants all.

36. Much have I told thee, and further will tell;
There is much that I know; wilt thou hear yet more?

37. One there was born in the bygone days,
Of the race of the gods, and great was his might;
Nine giant women, at the world's edge,
Once bore the man so mighty in arms.

38. Gjolp there bore him, Greip there bore him,
Eistla bore him, and Eyrgjafa,
Ulfrun bore him, and Angeyja,
Imth and Atla, and Jarnsaxa.

39. Strong was he made with the strength of earth,
With the ice-cold sea, and the blood of swine.

40. One there was born, the best of all,
And strong was he made with the strength of earth;
The proudest is called the kinsman of men
Of the rulers all throughout the world.

41. Much have I told thee, and further will tell;
There is much that I know; wilt thou hear yet more?

42. The wolf did Loki with Angrbotha win,
And Sleipnir bore he to Svathilfari;
The worst of marvels seemed the one
That sprang from the brother of Byleist then.

43. A heart ate Loki, in the embers it lay,
And half-cooked found he the woman's heart;
With child from the woman Lopt soon was,
And thence among men came the monsters all.

44. The sea, storm-driven, seeks heaven itself,
O'er the earth it flows, the air grows sterile;
Then follow the snows and the furious winds,
For the gods are doomed, and the end is death.

45. Then comes another, a greater than all,
Though never I dare his name to speak;
Few are they now that farther can see
Than the moment when Othin shall meet the wolf.

Freyja spake:

46. "To my boar now bring the memory-beer,
So that all thy words, that well thou hast spoken,
The third morn hence he may hold in mind,
When their races Ottar and Angantyr tell."

Hyndla spake:

47. "Hence shalt thou fare, for fain would I sleep,
From me thou gettest few favors good;
My noble one, out in the night thou leapest
As. Heithrun goes the goats among.

48. "To Oth didst thou run, who loved thee ever,
And many under thy apron have crawled;
My noble one, out in the night thou leapest,
As Heithrun goes the goats among."

Freyja spake:

49. "Around the giantess flames shall I raise,
So that forth unburned thou mayst not fare."

Hyndla spake:

50. "Flames I see burning, the earth is on fire,
And each for his life the price must lose;
Bring then to Ottar the draught of beer,
Of venom full for an evil fate."

Freyja spake:

51. "Thine evil words shall work no ill,
Though, giantess, bitter thy baleful threats;
A drink full fair shall Ottar find,
If of all the gods the favor I get."

SVIPDAGSMOL

The Ballad of Svipdag

I. GROUGALDR

GROA'S SPELL

Svipdag spake:

1. "Wake thee, Groa! wake, mother good!
At the doors of the dead I call thee;
Thy son, bethink thee, thou badst to seek
Thy help at the hill of death."

Groa spake:

2. "What evil vexes mine only son,
What baleful fate hast thou found,
That thou callest thy mother, who lies in the mould,
And the world of the living has left?"

Svipdag spake:

3. "The woman false whom my father embraced
Has brought me a baleful game;
For she bade me go forth where none may fare,
And Mengloth the maid to seek."

Groa spake:

4. "Long is the way, long must thou wander,
But long is love as well;
Thou mayst find, perchance, what thou fain wouldst have,
If the fates their favor will give."

Svipdag spake:

5. "Charms full good then chant to me, mother,
And seek thy son to guard;
For death do I fear on the way I shall fare,
And in years am I young, methinks."

Groa spake:

6. "Then first I will chant thee the charm oft-tried,
That Rani taught to Rind;
From the shoulder whate'er mislikes thee shake,
For helper thyself shalt thou have.

7. "Then next I will chant thee, if needs thou must travel,
And wander a purposeless way:
The bolts of Urth shall on every side

Be thy guards on the road thou goest.

8. "Then third I will chant thee, if threatening streams
The danger of death shall bring:
Yet to Hel shall turn both Horn and Ruth,
And before thee the waters shall fail.

9. "Then fourth I will chant thee, if come thy foes
On the gallows-way against thee:
Into thine hands shall their hearts be given,
And peace shall the warriors wish.

10. "Then fifth I will chant thee, if fetters perchance
Shall bind thy bending limbs:
O'er thy thighs do I chant a loosening-charm,
And the lock is burst from the limbs,
And the fetters fall from the feet.

11. "Then sixth I will chant thee, if storms on the sea
Have might unknown to man:
Yet never shall wind or wave do harm,
And calm is the course of thy boat.

12. "Then seventh I chant thee, if frost shall seek
To kill thee on lofty crags:
The fatal cold shall not grip thy flesh,
And whole thy body shall be.

13. "Then eighth will I chant thee, if ever by night
Thou shalt wander on murky ways:
Yet never the curse of a Christian woman
From the dead shall do thee harm.

14. "Then ninth will I chant thee, if needs thou must strive
With a warlike giant in words:
Thy heart good store of wit shall have,
And thy mouth of words full wise.

15. "Now fare on the way where danger waits,
Let evils not lessen thy love!
I have stood at the door of the earth-fixed stones,
The while I chanted thee charms.

16. "Bear hence, my son, what thy mother hath said,
And let it live in thy breast;
Thine ever shall be the best of fortune,
So long as my words shall last."

II. FJOLMINNSMOL

THE LAY OF FJOLSVITH

17. Before the house he beheld one coming
To the home of the giants high.

Svipdag spake:

"What giant is here, in front of the house,
And around him fires are flaming?"

Fjolsvith spake:

18. "What seekest thou here? for what is thy search?
What, friendless one, fain wouldst thou know?
By the ways so wet must thou wander hence,
For, weakling, no home hast thou here."

Svipdag spake:

19. "What giant is here, in front of the house,
To the wayfarer welcome denying?"

Fjolsvith spake:

"Greeting full fair thou never shalt find,
So hence shalt thou get thee home.

20. "Fjolsvith am I, and wise am I found,
But miserly am I with meat;
Thou never shalt enter within the house,--
Go forth like a wolf on thy way!"

Svipdag spake:

21. "Few from the joy of their eyes will go forth,

When the sight of their loves they seek;
Full bright are the gates of the golden hall,
And a home shall I here enjoy."

Fjolsvith spake:

22. "Tell me now, fellow, what father thou hast,
And the kindred of whom thou camst."

Svipdag spake:

"Vindkald am I, and Varkald's son,
And Fjolkald his father was.

23. "Now answer me, Fjolsvith, the question I ask,
For now the truth would I know:
Who is it that holds and has for his own
The rule of the hall so rich?"

Fjolsvith spake:

24. "Mengloth is she, her mother bore her
To the son of Svafrthorin;
She is it that holds and has for her own
The rule of the hall so rich."

Svipdag spake:

25. "Now answer me, Fjolsvith, the question I ask,
For now the truth would I know:
What call they the gate? for among the gods
Ne'er saw man so grim a sight."
Fjolsvith spake:

26. "Thrymgjol they call it; 'twas made by the three,
The sons of Solblindi;
And fast as a fetter the farer it holds,
Whoever shall lift the latch."

Svipdag spake:

27. "Now answer me, Fjolsvith, the question I ask,
For now the truth would I know:

What call they the house? for no man beheld
'Mongst the gods so grim a sight."

Fjolsvith spake:

28. "Gastropnir is it, of old I made it
From the limbs of Leirbrimir;
I braced it so strongly that fast it shall stand
So long as the world shall last."

Svipdag spake:

29. "Now answer me, Fjolsvith, the question I ask,
For now the truth would I know:
What call they the tree that casts abroad
Its limbs o'er every land?"

Fjolsvith spake:

30. "Mimameith its name, and no man knows
What root beneath it runs;
And few can guess what shall fell the tree,
For fire nor iron shall fell it."

Svipdag spake:

31. "Now answer me, Fjolsvith, the question I ask,
For now the truth would I know:
What grows from the seed of the tree so great,
That fire nor iron shall fell?"

Fjolsvith spake:

32. "Women, sick with child, shall seek
Its fruit to the flames to bear;
Then out shall come what within was hid,
And so is it mighty with men."

Svipdag spake:

33. "Now answer me, Fjolsvith, the question I ask,
For now the truth would I know:
What cock is he on the highest bough,
That glitters all with gold?"

Fjolsvith spake:

34. "Vithofnir his name, and now he shines
Like lightning on Mimameith's limbs;
And great is the trouble with which he grieves
Both Surt and Sinmora."

Svipdag spake:

35. "Now answer me, Fjolsvith, the question I ask,
For now the truth would I know:
What call they the hounds, that before the house
So fierce and angry are?"

Fjolsvith spake:

36. "Gif call they one, and Geri the other,
If now the truth thou wouldst know;
Great they are, and their might will grow,
Till the gods to death are doomed."

Svipdag spake:

37. "Now answer me, Fjolsvith, the question I ask,
For now the truth would I know:
May no man hope the house to enter,
While the hungry hounds are sleeping?"

Fjolsvith spake:

38. "Together they sleep not, for so was it fixed
When the guard to them was given;
One sleeps by night, the next by day,
So no man may enter ever."

Svipdag spake:

39. "Now answer me, Fjolsvith, the question I ask,
For now the truth would I know:
Is there no meat that men may give them,
And leap within while they eat?"
Fjolsvith spake:

40. "Two wing-joints there be in Vithofnir's body,
If now the truth thou wouldst know;
That alone is the meat that men may give them,
And leap within while they eat."

Svipdag spake:

41. "Now answer me, Fjolsvith, the question I ask,
For now the truth would I know:
What weapon can send Vithofnir to seek
The house of Hel below?"

Fjolsvith spake:

42. "Laevatein is there, that Lopt with runes
Once made by the doors of death;
In Laegjarn's chest by Sinmora lies it,
And nine locks fasten it firm."

Svipdag spake:

43. "Now answer me, Fjolsvith, the question I ask,
For now the truth would I know:
May a man come thence, who thither goes,
And tries the sword to take?"

Fjolsvith spake:

44. "Thence may he come who thither goes,
And tries the sword to take,
If with him he carries what few can win,
To give to the goddess of gold."

Svipdag spake:

45. "Now answer me, Fjolsvith, the question I ask,
For now the truth would I know:
What treasure is there that men may take
To rejoice the giantess pale?"

Fjolsvith spake:

46. "The sickle bright in thy wallet bear,
Mid Vithofnir's feathers found;
To Sinmora give it, and then shall she grant
That the weapon by thee be won."

Svipdag spake:

47. "Now answer me, Fjolsvith, the question I ask,
For now the truth would I know:
What call they the hall, encompassed here
With flickering magic flames?"

Fjolsvith spake:

48. "Lyr is it called, and long it shall
On the tip of a spear-point tremble;
Of the noble house mankind has heard,
But more has it never known."

Svipdag spake:

49. "Now answer me, Fjolsvith, the question I ask,
For now the truth would I know:
What one of the gods has made so great
The hall I behold within?"

Fjolsvith spake:

50. "Uni and Iri, Bari and Jari,
Var and Vegdrasil,
Dori and Ori, Delling, and there
Was Loki, the fear of the folk."

Svipdag spake:

51. "Now answer me, Fjolsvith, the question I ask,
For now the truth would I know:
What call they the mountain on which the maid
Is lying so lovely to see?"

Fjolsvith spake:

52. "Lyfjaberg is it, and long shall it be

A joy to the sick and the sore;
For well shall grow each woman who climbs it,
Though sick full long she has lain."

Svipdag spake:

53. "Now answer me, Fjolsvith, the question I ask,
For now the truth would I know:
What maidens are they that at Mengloth's knees
Are sitting so gladly together?"
Fjolsvith spake:

54. "Hlif is one named, Hlifthrasa another,
Thjothvara call they the third;
Bjort and Bleik, Blith and Frith,
Eir and Aurbotha."

Svipdag spake:

55. "Now answer me, Fjolsvith, the question I ask,
For now the truth would I know:
Aid bring they to all who offerings give,
If need be found therefor?"

Fjolsvith spake:

56. "Soon aid they all who offerings give
On the holy altars high;
And if danger they see for the sons of men,
Then each from ill do they guard."

Svipdag spake:

57. "Now answer me, Fjolsvith, the question I ask,
For now the truth would I know:
Lives there the man who in Mengloth's arms
So fair may seek to sleep?"

Fjolsvith spake:

58. "No man there is who in Mengloth's arms
So fair may seek to sleep,
Save Svipdag alone, for the sun-bright maid

Is destined his bride to be."

Svipdag spake:

59. "Fling back the gates! make the gateway wide!
Here mayst thou Svipdag see!
Hence get thee to find if gladness soon
Mengloth to me will give."

Fjolsvith spake:

60. "Hearken, Mengloth, a man is come;
Go thou the guest to see!
The hounds are fawning, the house bursts open,
Svipdag, methinks, is there."

Mengloth spake:

61. "On the gallows high shall hungry ravens
Soon thine eyes pluck out,
If thou liest in saying that here at last
The hero is come to my hall.

62. "Whence camest thou hither? how camest thou here?
What name do thy kinsmen call thee?
Thy race and thy name as a sign must I know,
That thy bride I am destined to be."

Svipdag spake:

63. "Svipdag am I, and Solbjart's son;
Thence came I by wind-cold ways;
With the words of Urth shall no man war,
Though unearned her gifts be given."

Mengloth spake:

64. "Welcome thou art, for long have I waited;
The welcoming kiss shalt thou win!
For two who love is the longed-for meeting
The greatest gladness of all.

65. "Long have I sat on Lyfjaberg here,
Awaiting thee day by day;

And now I have what I ever hoped,
For here thou art come to my hall.

66. "Alike we yearned; I longed for thee,
And thou for my love hast longed;
But now henceforth together we know
Our lives to the end we shall live."

THE NIBELUNGENLIED

By

Anonymous

TRANSLATED BY GEORGE HENRY NEEDLER

FIRST ADVENTURE

Kriemhild's Dream

To us in olden story are wonders many told
Of heroes rich in glory, of trials manifold:
Of joy and festive greeting, of weeping and of woe,
Of keenest warriors meeting, shall ye now many a wonder know.
There once grew up in Burgundy a maid of noble birth,
Nor might there be a fairer than she in all the earth:
Kriemhild hight the maiden, and grew a dame full fair,
Through whom high thanes a many to lose their lives soon doomèd were.
'Twould well become the highest to love the winsome maid,
Keen knights did long to win her, and none but homage paid.
Beauty without measure, that in sooth had she,
And virtues wherewith many ladies else adorned might be.
Three noble lords did guard her, great as well in might,
Gunther and Gernot, each one a worthy knight,
And Giselher their brother, a hero young and rare.
The lady was their sister and lived beneath the princes' care.
These lords were free in giving, and born of high degree;
Undaunted was the valor of all the chosen three.
It was the land of Burgundy o'er which they did command,
And mighty deeds of wonder they wrought anon in Etzel's land.

At Worms amid their warriors they dwelt, the Rhine beside,
And in their lands did serve them knights of mickle pride,
Who till their days were ended maintained them high in state.
They later sadly perished beneath two noble women's hate.
A high and royal lady, Ute their mother hight,
Their father's name was Dankrat, a man of mickle might.
To them his wealth bequeathed he when that his life was done,
For while he yet was youthful had he in sooth great honor won.
In truth were these three rulers, as I before did say,
Great and high in power, and homage true had they
Eke of knights the boldest and best that e'er were known,
Keen men all and valiant, as they in battle oft had shown.
There was of Tronje Hagen, and of that princely line
His brother valiant Dankwart; and eke of Metz Ortwein;
Then further the two margraves, Gere and Eckewart;
Of Alzei was Volker, a doughty man of dauntless heart.
Rumold the High Steward, a chosen man was he,
Sindold and Hunold they tended carefully
Each his lofty office in their three masters' state,
And many a knight beside them that I the tale may ne'er relate.
Dankwart he was Marshal; his nephew, then, Ortwein
Upon the monarch waited when that he did dine;

Sindold was Cup-bearer, a stately thane was he,
And Chamberlain was Hunold, masters all in courtesy.
Of the kings' high honor and their far-reaching might,
Of their full lofty majesty and how each gallant knight
Found his chiefest pleasure in the life of chivalry,
In sooth by mortal never might it full related be.
Amid this life so noble did dream the fair Kriemhild
How that she reared a falcon, in beauty strong and wild,
That by two eagles perished; the cruel sight to see
Did fill her heart with sorrow as great as in this world might be.
The dream then to her mother Queen Ute she told,
But she could not the vision than thus more clear unfold:
"The falcon that thou rearedst, doth mean a noble spouse:
God guard him well from evil or thou thy hero soon must lose."
"Of spouse, O darling mother, what dost thou tell to me?
Without a knight to woo me, so will I ever be,
Unto my latest hour I'll live a simple maid,
That I through lover's wooing ne'er be brought to direst need."
"Forswear it not so rashly," her mother then replied.
"On earth if thou wilt ever cast all care aside,
'Tis love alone will do it; thou shalt be man's delight,
If God but kindly grant thee to wed a right good valiant knight."
"Now urge the case, dear mother," quoth she, "not further here.
Fate of many another dame hath shown full clear
How joy at last doth sorrow lead oft-times in its train.
That I no ruth may borrow, from both alike I'll far remain."
Long time, too, did Kriemhild her heart from love hold free,
And many a day the maiden lived right happily,
Ere good knight saw she any whom she would wish to woo.
In honor yet she wedded anon a worthy knight and true.
He was that same falcon she saw the dream within
Unfolded by her mother. Upon her nearest kin,
That they did slay him later, how wreaked she vengeance wild!
Through death of this one hero died many another mother's child.

SECOND ADVENTURE

Siegfried

There grew likewise in Netherland a prince of noble kind,
Siegmund hight his father, his mother Siegelind—
Within a lordly castle well known the country o'er,
By the Rhine far downward: Xanten was the name it bore.
Siegfried they did call him, this bold knight and good;
Many a realm he tested, for brave was he of mood.
He rode to prove his prowess in many a land around:

Heigh-ho! what thanes of mettle anon in Burgundy he found!
In the springtime of his vigor, when he was young and bold,
Could tales of mickle wonder of Siegfried be told,
How he grew up in honor, and how fair he was to see:
Anon he won the favor of many a debonair lady.
As for a prince was fitting, they fostered him with care:
Yet how the knightly virtues to him native were!
'Twas soon the chiefest glory of his father's land,
That he in fullest measure endowed with princely worth did stand.
He soon was grown in stature that he at court did ride.
The people saw him gladly, lady and maid beside
Did wish that his own liking might lead him ever there.
That they did lean unto him the knight was soon right well aware.
In youth they let him never without safe escort ride;
Soon bade Siegmund and Siegelind apparel rich provide;
Men ripe in wisdom taught him, who knew whence honor came.
Thus many lands and people he won by his wide-honored name.
Now was he of such stature that he could weapons bear:
Of what thereto he needed had he an ample share.
Then to think of loving fair maids did he begin,
And well might they be honored for wooer Siegfried bold to win.
Then bade his father Siegmund make known to one and all
That he with his good kinsmen would hold high festival.
And soon were tidings carried to all the neighboring kings;
To friends at home and strangers steeds gave he and rich furnishin
Wherever they found any who knight was fit to be
By reason of his kindred, all such were courteously
Unto the land invited to join the festal throng,
When with the prince so youthful on them the knightly sword was hung.
Of this high time of revelry might I great wonders tell.
Siegmund and Siegelind great honor won full well,
Such store of goodly presents they dealt with generous hand,
That knights were seen full many from far come pricking to their land.
Four hundred lusty squires were there to be clad
In knight's full garb with Siegfried. Full many a beauteous maid
At work did never tire, for dear they did him hold,
And many a stone full precious those ladies laid within the gold,
That they upon the doublets embroidered cunningly
Of those soon to be knighted: 't was thus it had to be,
Seats bade the host for many a warrior bold make right
Against the high midsummer, when Siegfried won the name of knight.
Then went unto the minster full many a noble knight
And gallant squires beside them. The elder there with right
Did wait upon the younger, as once for them was done.
They were all light-hearted, in hope of pleasure every one.
God to praise and honor they sang the mass' song;
There, too, were crowds of people, a great and surging throng,

When after knightly custom knighthood received they then,
In such a stately pageant as scarce might ever be again.
They hastened where they found them saddled many a steed;
In the court of Siegmund's castle they tilted with such speed
That far the din resounded through castle and through hall,
As in the play with clamor did join the fiery riders all.
Well-tried old knights and youthful met there in frequent clash,
There was sound of shattered lances that through the air did crash,
And along before the castle were splinters seen to fly
From hands of knights a many: each with other there did vie.
The king he bade give over: they led the chargers out:
There was seen all shattered many a boss well-wrought,
And many a stone full costly lay there upon the sward
From erstwhile shining shield-bands, now broken in the jousting hard.
The guests all went thereafter where seats for them were reared;
They by the choicest viands from weariness were cheered,
And wine, of all the rarest, that then in plenty flowed.
Upon both friends and strangers were fitting honors rich bestowed.
In such merry manner all day did last the feast.
Many a wandering minstrel knew not any rest,
But sang to win the presents dealt out with bounteous hand;
And with their praise was honored far and wide King Siegmund's land.
The monarch then did order Siegfried his youthful son
In fee give lands and castles, as he erstwhile had done.
To all his sword-companions he gave with such full hand,
That joyed they o'er the journey they now had made unto that land.
The festival yet lasted until the seventh day.
Siegelind after old custom in plenty gave away
—For so her son she honored— rich gifts of shining gold:
In sooth deserved she richly that all should him in honor hold.
Never a wandering minstrel was unprovided found:
Horses there and raiment so free were dealt around,
As if to live they had not beyond it one day more.
I ween a monarch's household ne'er bestowed such gifts before.
Thus closed the merry feasting in this right worthy way,
And 't was well known thereafter how those good knights did say
That they the youthful hero for king would gladly have;
But this nowise he wished for, Siegfried the stately knight and brave.
While that they both were living, Siegmund and Siegelind,
No crown their son desired, —thereto he had no mind.
Yet would he fain be master o'er all the hostile might
That in the lands around him opposed the keen and fiery knight.

THIRD ADVENTURE

How Siegfried came to Worms

Seldom in sooth, if ever, the hero's heart was sad.
He heard them tell the story, how that a winsome maid
There lived afar in Burgundy, surpassing fair to see:
Great joy she brought him later, but eke she brought him misery.
Of her exceeding beauty the fame spread far and near,
And of the thing, moreover, were knights oft-times aware
How the maid's high spirit no mortal could command:
The thing lured many a stranger from far unto King Gunther's land.
Although to win her favor were many wooers bent,
In her own heart would never Kriemhild thereto consent
That any one amongst them for lover she would have:
Still to her was he a stranger to whom anon her troth she gave.
To true love turned his fancy the son of Siegelind.
'Gainst his, all others' wooing was like an idle wind:
Full well did he merit a lady fair to woo,
And soon the noble Kriemhild to Siegfried bold was wedded true.
By friends he oft was counselled, and many a faithful man,
Since to think of wooing in earnest he began,
That he a wife should find him of fitting high degree.
Then spoke the noble Siegfried: "In sooth fair Kriemhild shall it be,
"The noble royal maiden in Burgundy that dwells,
For sake of all her beauty. Of her the story tells,
Ne'er monarch was so mighty that, if for spouse he sighed,
'Twere not for him befitting to take the princess for his bride."
Unto King Siegmund also the thing was soon made known.
His people talked about it, whereby to him was shown
The Prince's fixéd purpose. It grieved him sorely, too,
That his son intent was the full stately maid to woo.
Siegelind asked and learned it, the noble monarch's wife.
For her loved son she sorrowed lest he should lose his life,
For well she knew the humor of Gunther and his men.
Then gan they from the wooing strive to turn the noble thane.
Then said the doughty Siegfried: "O father dear to me,
Without the love of woman would I ever be,
Could I not woo in freedom where'er my heart is set.
Whate'er be said by any, I'll keep the selfsame purpose yet."
"Since thou wilt not give over," the king in answer said,
"Am I of this thy purpose inwardly full glad,
And straightway to fulfil it I'll help as best I can,
Yet in King Gunther's service is many a haughty-minded man.
"And were there yet none other than Hagen, warrior-knight,
He with such haughty bearing is wont to show his might,
That I do fear right sorely that sad our end may be,
If we set out with purpose to win the stately maid for thee."
"Shall we by that be hindered?" outspake Siegfried then;

"Whate'er in friendly fashion I cannot obtain
I'll yet in other manner take that, with sword in hand.
I trow from them I'll further wrest both their vassals and their land."
"I grieve to hear thy purpose," said Siegmund the king;
"If any one this story unto the Rhine should bring,
Then durst thou never after within that land be seen.
Gunther and Gernot, —well known to me they long have been.
"By force, however mighty, no man can win the maid,"
Spake King Siegmund further, "to me hath oft been said.
But if with knightly escort thither thou wilt ride,
Good friends—an have we any— shall soon be summoned to thy side."
"No wish," then answered Siegfried, "it ever was of mine,
That warrior knights should follow with me unto the Rhine
As if arrayed for battle: 'twould make my heart full sad,
To force in hostile manner to yield to me the stately maid.
"By my own hand—thus only— trust I to win my bride;
With none but twelve in company to Gunther's land I'll ride.
In this, O royal father, thy present help I pray."
Gray and white fur raiment had his companions for the way.
Siegelind his mother then heard the story too,
And grieved she was on hearing what her dear son would do,
For she did fear to lose him at hands of Gunther's men.
Thereat with heart full heavy began to weep the noble queen.
Then came forth Sir Siegfried where the queen he sought,
And to his weeping mother thus gently spake his thought:
"No tear of grief thou shouldest ever shed for me,
For I care not a tittle for all the warriors that be.
"So help me on my journey to the land of Burgundy,
And furnish such apparel for all my knights and me,
As warriors of our station might well with honor wear.
Then I in turn right truly to thee my gratitude will swear."
"Since thou wilt not give over," Siegelind then replied,
"My only son, I'll help thee as fits thee forth to ride,
With the best apparel that riders ever wore,
Thee and thy companions: ye shall of all have goodly store."
Then bowed the youthful Siegfried the royal dame before,
And said: "Upon the journey will I take no more,
But twelve good knights only: for these rich dress provide,
For I would know full gladly how 't doth with Kriemhild betide."
Then sat at work fair women by night and eke by day,
And rest indeed but little from busy toil had they,
Until they had made ready the dress Siegfried should wear.
Firm bent upon the journey, no other counsel would he hear.
His father bade a costly garb for him prepare,
That leaving Siegmund's country he the same might wear.
For all their glittering breastplates were soon prepared beside,
And helmets firmly welded, and shining shields long and wide.

Then fast the day grew nearer when they should thence depart.
Men and likewise women went sorrowing in heart,
If that they should ever see more their native land.
With full equipment laden the sumpter horses there did stand.
Their steeds were stately, furnished with trappings rich with gold;
It were a task all bootless to seek for knights more bold
Than were the gallant Siegfried and his chosen band.
He longed to take departure straightway for Burgundian land.
Leave granted they with sadness, both the king and queen,
The which to turn to gladness sought the warrior keen,
And spake then: "Weep ye shall not at all for sake of me,
Forever free from doubtings about my safety may ye be."
Stern warriors stood there sorrowing, —in tears was many a maid.
I ween their hearts erred nothing, as sad forebodings said
That 'mongst their friends so many thereby were doomed to die.
Good cause had they to sorrow at last o'er all their misery.
Upon the seventh morning to Worms upon the strand
Did come the keen knights riding. Bright shone many a band
Of gold from their apparel and rich equipment then;
And gently went their chargers with Siegfried and his chosen men.
New-made shields they carried that were both strong and wide
And brightly shone their helmets as thus to court did ride
Siegfried the keen warrior into King Gunther's land.
Of knights before was never beheld so richly clad a band.
The points of their long scabbards reached down unto the spur,
And spear full sharply pointed bore each chosen warrior.
The one that Siegfried carried in breadth was two good span,
And grimly cut its edges when driven by the fearless man.
Reins with gold all gleaming held they in the hand,
The saddle-bands were silken. So came they to the land.
On every side the people to gape at them began,
And also out to meet them the men that served King Gunther ran.
Gallant men high-hearted, knight and squire too,
Hastened to receive them, for such respect was due,
And bade the guests be welcome unto their master's land.
They took from them their chargers, and shields as well from out the hand.
Then would they eke the chargers lead forth unto their rest;
But straight the doughty Siegfried to them these words addressed:
"Yet shall ye let our chargers stand the while near by;
Soon take we hence our journey; thereon resolved full well am I.
"If that be known to any, let him not delay,
Where I your royal master now shall find, to say,—
Gunther, king so mighty o'er the land of Burgundy."
Then told him one amongst them to whom was known where that might be:
"If that the king thou seekest, right soon may he be found.
Within that wide hall yonder with his good knights around
But now I saw him sitting. Thither do thou repair,

And thou may'st find around him   many a stately warrior there."
Now also to the monarch   were the tidings told,
That within his castle   were knights arrived full bold,
All clad in shining armor   and apparelled gorgeously;
But not a man did know them   within the land of Burgundy.
Thereat the king did wonder   whence were come to him
These knights adventure seeking   in dress so bright and trim,
And shields adorned so richly   that new and mighty were.
That none the thing could tell him   did grieve him sorely to hear.
Outspake a knight then straightway,   Ortwein by name was he,
Strong and keen as any   well was he known to be:
"Since we of them know nothing,   bid some one quickly go
And fetch my uncle Hagen: to him thou shalt the strangers show.

"To him are known far kingdoms   and every foreign land,
And if he know these strangers   we soon shall understand."
The king then sent to fetch him: with his train of men
Unto the king's high presence   in stately gear went he then.
What were the king's good pleasure,   asked Hagen grim in war.
"In the court within my castle   are warriors from afar,
And no one here doth know them: if them thou e'er didst see
In any land far distant,   now shalt thou, Hagen, tell to me."

"That will I do, 'tis certain."— To a window then he went,
And on the unknown strangers   his keen eye he bent.
Well pleased him their equipment   and the rich dress they wore,
Yet ne'er had he beheld them   in land of Burgundy before.
He said that whencesoever   these knights come to the Rhine,
They bear a royal message,   or are of princely line.
"Their steeds are so bedizened,   and their apparel rare:
No matter whence they journey,   high-hearted men in truth they are."

Further then spake Hagen: "As far as goes my ken,
Though I the noble Siegfried   yet have never seen,
Yet will I say meseemeth,   howe'er the thing may be,
This knight who seeks adventure,   and yonder stands so proud, is he.

"'Tis some new thing he bringeth   hither to our land.
The valiant Nibelungen   fell by the hero's hand,
Schilbung and Nibelung,   from royal sire sprung;
Deeds he wrought most wondrous   anon when his strong arm he swung.

"As once alone the hero   rode without company,
Found he before a mountain   —as hath been told to me—
With the hoard of Nibelung   full many stalwart men;
To him had they been strangers   until he chanced to find them then.

"The hoard of King Nibelung   entire did they bear
Forth from a mountain hollow.   And now the wonder hear,
How that they would share it,   these two Nibelung men.
This saw the fearless Siegfried,   and filled he was with wonder then.

"He came so near unto them   that he the knights espied,
And they in turn him also.   One amongst them said:

'Here comes the doughty Siegfried, hero of Netherland.'
Since 'mongst the Nibelungen strange wonders wrought his mighty hand.
"Right well did they receive him, Schilbung and Nibelung,
And straight they both together, these noble princes young,
Bade him mete out the treasure, the full valorous man,
And so long time besought him that he at last the task began.
"As we have heard in story, he saw of gems such store
That they might not be laden on wagons full five score;
More still of gold all shining from Nibelungenland.
'Twas all to be divided between them by keen Siegfried's hand.
"Then gave they him for hire King Nibelung's sword.
And sooth to say, that service brought them but small reward,
That for them there performed Siegfried of dauntless mood.
His task he could not finish; thereat they raged as were they wood.
"They had there of their followers twelve warriors keen,
And strong they were as giants: what booted giants e'en?
Them slew straightway in anger Siegfried's mighty hand,
And warriors seven hundred he felled in Nibelungenland
"With the sword full trusty, Balmung that hight.
Full many a youthful warrior from terror at the sight
Of that deadly weapon swung by his mighty hand
Did render up his castle and pledge him fealty in the land.
"Thereto the kings so mighty, them slew he both as well.
But into gravest danger through Alberich he fell,
Who thought for his slain masters vengeance to wreak straightway,
Until the mighty Siegfried his wrath with strong arm did stay.
"Nor could prevail against him the Dwarf, howe'er he tried.
E'en as two wild lions they coursed the mountainside,
Where he the sightless mantle from Alberich soon won.
Then Siegfried, knight undaunted, held the treasure for his own.
"Who then dared join the struggle, all slain around they lay.
Then he bade the treasure to draw and bear away
Thither whence 'twas taken by the Nibelungen men.
Alberich for his valor was then appointed Chamberlain.
"An oath he had to swear him, he'd serve him as his slave;
To do all kinds of service his willing pledge he gave"—
Thus spake of Tronje Hagen— "That has the hero done;
Might as great before him was never in a warrior known.
"Still know I more about him, that has to me been told.
A dragon, wormlike monster, slew once the hero bold.
Then in its blood he bathed him, since when his skin hath been
So horn-hard, ne'er a weapon can pierce it, as hath oft been seen.
"Let us the brave knight-errant receive so courteously
That we in nought shall merit his hate, for strong is he.
He is so keen of spirit he must be treated fair:
He has by his own valor done many a deed of prowess rare."
The monarch spake in wonder: "In sooth thou tellest right.

Now see how proudly yonder he stands prepared for fight,
He and his thanes together, the hero wondrous keen!
To greet him we'll go thither, and let our fair intent be seen."
"That canst thou," out spake Hagen, "well in honor do.
He is of noble kindred, a high king's son thereto.
'Tis seen in all his bearing; meseems in truth, God wot,
The tale is worth the hearing that this bold knight has hither brought."
Then spake the mighty monarch: "Be he right welcome here.
Keen is he and noble, of fame known far and near.
So shall he be fair treated in the land of Burgundy."
Down then went King Gunther, and Siegfried with his men found he.
The king and his knights with him received so well the guest,
That the hearty greeting did their good will attest.
Thereat in turn the stranger in reverence bowed low,
That in their welcome to him they did such courtesy bestow.
"To me it is a wonder," straightway spake the host,
"From whence, O noble Siegfried, come to our land thou dost,
Or what here thou seekest at Worms upon the Rhine."
Him the stranger answered: "Put thou away all doubts of thine.
"I oft have heard the tiding within my sire's domain,
How at thy court resided —and know this would I fain—
Knights, of all the keenest, —'tis often told me so—
That e'er a monarch boasted: now come I hither this to know.
"Thyself have I heard also high praised for knightly worth;
'Tis said a nobler monarch ne'er lived in all the earth.
Thus speak of thee the people in all the lands around.
Nor will I e'er give over until in this the truth I've found.
"I too am warrior noble and born to wear a crown;
So would I right gladly that thou of me shouldst own
That I of right am master o'er people and o'er land.
Of this shall now my honor and eke my head as pledges stand.
"And art thou then so valiant as hath to me been told,
I reck not, will he nill he thy best warrior bold,
I'll wrest from thee in combat whatever thou may'st have;
Thy lands and all thy castles shall naught from change of masters save."
The king was seized with wonder and all his men beside,
To see the manner haughty in which the knight replied
That he was fully minded to take from him his land.
It chafed his thanes to hear it, who soon in raging mood did stand.
"How could it be my fortune," Gunther the king outspoke,
"What my sire long ruled over in honor for his folk,
Now to lose so basely through any vaunter's might?
In sooth 'twere nobly showing that we too merit name of knight!"
"Nowise will I give over," was the keen reply.
"If peace through thine own valor thy land cannot enjoy,
To me shall all be subject: if heritage of mine
Through thy arm's might thou winnest, f right shall all hence-forth be thine.

"Thy land and all that mine is, at stake shall equal lie.
Whiche'er of us be victor when now our strength we try,
To him shall all be subject, the folk and eke the land."
But Hagen spake against it, and Gernot too was quick at hand.
"Such purpose have we never," Gernot then said,
"For lands to combat ever, that any warrior dead
Should lie in bloody battle. We've mighty lands and strong;
Of right they call us master, and better they to none belong."
There stood full grim and moody Gernot's friends around,
And there as well amongst them was Ortwein to be found.
He spake: "This mild peace-making doth grieve me sore at heart,
For by the doughty Siegfried attacked all undeserved thou art.
"If thou and thy two brothers yourselves to help had naught,
And if a mighty army he too had hither brought,
I trow I'd soon be able to make this man so keen
His manner now so haughty of need replace by meeker mien."
Thereat did rage full sorely the hero of Netherland:
"Never shall be measured 'gainst me in fight thy hand.
I am a mighty monarch, thou a king's serving-knight;
Of such as thou a dozen dare not withstand me in the fight."
For swords then called in anger of Metz Sir Ortwein:
Son of Hagen's sister he was, of Tronje's line.
That Hagen so long was silent did grieve the king to see.
Gernot made peace between them: a gallant knight and keen was he.
Spake he thus to Ortwein: "Curb now thy wrathful tongue,
For here the noble Siegfried hath done us no such wrong;
We yet can end the quarrel in peace,—such is my rede—
And live with him in friendship; that were for us a worthier deed."
Then spake the mighty Hagen: "Sad things do I forebode
For all thy train of warriors, that this knight ever rode
Unto the Rhine thus arméd. 'Twere best he stayed at home;
For from my masters never to him such wrong as this had come."
But outspake Siegfried proudly, whose heart was ne'er dismayed:
"An't please thee not, Sir Hagen, what I now have said,
This arm shall give example whereby thou plain shall see
How stern anon its power here in Burgundy will be."
"Yet that myself will hinder," said then Gernot.
All his men forbade he henceforth to say aught
With such unbridled spirit to stir the stranger's ire.
Then Siegfried eke was mindful of one most stately maid and fair.
"Such strife would ill befit us," Gernot spake again;
"For though should die in battle a host of valiant men
'Twould bring us little honor and ye could profit none."
Thereto gave Siegfried answer, good King Siegmund's noble son:
"Wherefore bides thus grim Hagen, and Ortwein tardy is
To begin the combat with all those friends of his,
Of whom he hath so many here in Burgundy?"

Answer him they durst not, for such was Gernot's stern decree.
"Thou shalt to us be welcome," outspake young Giselher,
"And all thy brave companions that hither with thee fare.
Full gladly we'll attend thee, I and all friends of mine."
For the guests then bade they pour out in store of Gunther's wine.
Then spake the stately monarch: "But ask thou courteously,
And all that we call ours stands at thy service free;
So with thee our fortune we'll share in ill and good."
Thereat the noble Siegfried a little milder was of mood.
Then carefully was tended all their knightly gear,
And housed in goodly manner in sooth the strangers were,
All that followed Siegfried; they found a welcome rest.
In Burgundy full gladly anon was seen the noble guest.
They showed him mickle honor thereafter many a day,
And more by times a thousand than I to you could say.
His might respect did merit, ye may full well know that.
Scarce a man e'er saw him who bore him longer any hate.
And when they held their pastime, the kings with many a man,
Then was he ever foremost; whatever they began,
None there that was his equal, —so mickle was his might—
If they the stone were putting, or hurling shaft with rival knight.
As is the knightly custom, before the ladies fair
To games they turned for pastime, these knights of mettle rare;
Then ever saw they gladly the hero of Netherland.
But he had fixed his fancy to win one fairest maiden's hand.
In all that they were doing he'd take a ready part.
A winsome loving maiden he bore within his heart;
Him only loved that lady, whose face he ne'er had seen,
But she full oft in secret of him spake fairest words, I ween.
And when before the castle they sped in tournament,
The good knights and squires, oft-times the maiden went
And gazed adown from casement, Kriemhild the princess rare.
Pastime there was none other for her that could with this compare.
And knew he she was gazing whom in his heart he bore,
He joy enough had found him in jousting evermore.
And might he only see her, —that can I well believe—
On earth through sight none other his eyes could such delight receive.
Whene'er with his companions to castle court he went,
E'en as do now the people whene'er on pleasure bent,
There stood 'fore all so graceful Siegelind's noble son,
For whom in love did languish the hearts of ladies many a one.
Eke thought he full often: "How shall it ever be,
That I the noble maiden with my own eyes may see,
Whom I do love so dearly and have for many a day?
To me is she a stranger, which sorely grieves my heart to say."
Whene'er the kings so mighty rode o'er their broad domain,
Then of valiant warriors they took a stately train.

With them abroad rode Siegfried, which grieved those ladies sore:
—He too for one fair maiden at heart a mickle burden bore.
Thus with his hosts he lingered —'tis every tittle true—
In King Gunther's country a year completely through,
And never once the meanwhile the lovely maid did see,
Through whom such joy thereafter for him, and eke such grief should be.

FOURTH ADVENTURE

How Siegfried fought with the Saxons

Now come wondrous tidings to King Gunther's land,
By messengers brought hither from far upon command
Of knights unknown who harbored against him secret hate.
When there was heard the story, at heart in sooth the grief was great.
Of these I now will tell you: There was King Luedeger
From out the land of Saxons, a mighty warrior,
And eke from land of Denmark Luedegast the king:
Whene'er they rode to battle went they with mighty following.
Come were now their messengers to the land of Burgundy,
Sent forth by these foemen in proud hostility.
Then asked they of the strangers what tidings they did bring:
And when they heard it, straightway led them to court before the king.
Then spake to them King Gunther: "A welcome, on my word.
Who 'tis that send you hither, that have I not yet heard:
Now shall ye let me know it," spake the monarch keen.
Then dreaded they full sorely to see King Gunther's angry mien.
"Wilt them, O king, permit us the tidings straight to tell
That we now have brought thee, no whit will we conceal,
But name thee both our masters who us have hither sent:
Luedegast and Luedeger, —to waste thy land is their intent.
"Their hate hast thou incurréd, and thou shalt know in sooth
That high enraged against thee are the monarchs both.
Their hosts they will lead hither to Worms upon the Rhine;
They're helped by thanes full many— of this put off all doubts of thine.
"Within weeks a dozen their march will they begin;
And if thy friends be valiant, let that full quick be seen,
To help thee keep in safety thy castles and thy land:
Full many a shield and helmet shall here be cleft by warrior's hand.
"Or wilt thou with them parley, so let it quick be known,
Before their hosts so mighty of warlike men come down
To Worms upon Rhine river sad havoc here to make,
Whereby must death most certain many a gallant knight o'ertake."
"Bide ye now the meanwhile," the king did answer kind,
"Till I take better counsel; then shall ye know my mind.
Have I yet warriors faithful, from these I'll naught conceal,

But to my friends I'll straightway these warlike tidings strange reveal."
The lordly Gunther wondered thereat and troubled sore,
As he the message pondered in heart and brooded o'er.
He sent to fetch grim Hagen and others of his men,
And bade likewise in hurry to court bring hither Gernot then.
Thus at his word his trusted advisers straight attend.
He spake: "Our land to harry foes all unknown will send
Of men a mighty army; a grievous wrong is this.
Small cause have we e'er given that they should wish us aught amiss."
"Our swords ward such things from us,"   Gernot then said;
"Since but the fated dieth, so let all such lie dead.
Wherefore I'll e'er remember what honor asks of me:
Whoe'er hath hate against us shall ever here right welcome be."
Then spake the doughty Hagen: "Methinks 'twould scarce be good;
Luedegast and Luedeger are men of wrathful mood.
Help can we never summon, the days are now so few."
So spake the keen old warrior, "'Twere well Siegfried the tidings knew."
The messengers in the borough were harbored well the while,
And though their sight was hateful, in hospitable style
As his own guests to tend them   King Gunther gave command,
Till 'mongst his friends he learnéd who by him in his need would stand.
The king was filled with sorrow and his heart was sad.
Then saw his mournful visage a knight to help full glad,
Who could not well imagine what 'twas that grieved him so.
Then begged he of King Gunther the tale of this his grief to know.
"To me it is great wonder," said Siegfried to the king,
"How thou of late hast changéd to silent sorrowing
The joyous ways that ever with us thy wont have been."
Then unto him gave answer   Gunther the full stately thane:
"'Tis not to every person I can the burden say
That ever now in secret upon my heart doth weigh:
To well-tried friends and steady   are told our inmost woes."
—Siegfried at first was pallid, but soon his blood like fire up-rose.
He spake unto the monarch: "To thee I've naught denied.
All ills that now do threaten I'll help to turn aside.
And if but friends thou seekest, of them the first I'll be,
And trow I well with honor till death to serve thee faithfully."
"God speed thee well, Sir Siegfried, for this thy purpose fair:
And though such help in earnest thy arm should render ne'er,
Yet do I joy at hearing thou art so true to me.
And live I yet a season, right heartily repaid 'twill be.
"Know will I also let thee wherefore I sorrowing stand.
Through messengers from my foemen have tidings reached my land
That they with hosts of warriors will ride my country o'er;
Such thing to us did never thanes of any land before."
"Small cause is that for grieving," said then Siegfried;
"But calm thy troubled spirit and hearken to my rede:

Let me for thee acquire honor and vantage too,
And bid thou now assemble for service eke thy warriors true.
"And had thy mighty enemies to help them now at hand
Good thanes full thirty thousand, against them all I'd stand,
Had I but one good thousand: put all thy trust in me."
Then answered him King Gunther: "Thy help shall full requited be."
"Then bid for me to summon a thousand of thy men,
Since I now have with me of all my knightly train
None but twelve knights only; then will I guard thy land.
For thee shall service faithful be done alway by Siegfried's hand.
"Herein shall help us Hagen and eke Ortwein,
Dankwart and Sindold, those trusted knights of thine;
And with us too shall journey Volker, the valiant man;
The banner he shall carry: bestow it better ne'er I can.
"Back to their native country the messengers may go;
They'll see us there right quickly, let them full surely know,
So that all our castles peace undisturbed shall have."
Then bade the king to summon his friends with all their warriors brave.
To court returned the heralds King Luedeger had sent,
And on their journey homeward full joyfully they went.
King Gunther gave them presents that costly were and good,
And granted them safe convoy; whereat they were of merry mood.
"Tell ye my foes," spake Gunther, "when to your land ye come,
Than making journeys hither they better were at home;
But if they still be eager to make such visit here,
Unless my friends forsake me, cold in sooth shall be their cheer."
Then for the messengers rich presents forth they bore,
Whereof in sooth to give them Gunther had goodly store:
And they durst not refuse them whom Luedeger had sent.
Leave then they took immediate, and homeward joyfully they went.
When to their native Denmark the messengers returned,
And the king Luedegast the answer too had learned,
They at the Rhine had sent him, —when that to him was told,
His wrath was all unbounded to have reply in words so bold.
'Twas said their warriors numbered many a man full keen:
"There likewise among them with Gunther have we seen
Of Netherland a hero, the same that Siegfried hight."
King Luedegast was grievéd, when he their words had heard aright.
When throughout all Denmark the tidings quick spread o'er,
Then in hot haste they summoned helpers all the more,
So that King Luedegast, 'twixt friends from far and near,
Had knights full twenty thousand all furnished well with shield and spear.
Then too his men did summon of Saxony Luedeger,
Till they good forty thousand, and more, had gathered there,
With whom to make the journey 'gainst the land of Burgundy.
—At home likewise the meanwhile King Gunther had sent forth decree
Mighty men to summon of his own and brothers twain,

Who against the foemen would join the armed train.
In haste they made them ready, for right good cause they had.
Amongst them must thereafter full many a noble thane lie dead.
To march they quick made ready. And when they thence would fare,
The banner to the valiant Volker was given to bear,
As they began the journey from Worms across the Rhine;
Strong of arm grim Hagen was chosen leader of the line.
With them there rode Sindold and eke the keen Hunold
Who oft at hands of Gunther had won rewards of gold;
Dankwart, Hagen's brother, and Ortwein beside,
Who all could well with honor in train of noble warriors ride.
"King Gunther," spake then Siegfried, "stay thou here at home;
Since now thy knights so gallant with me will gladly come,
Rest thou here with fair ladies, and be of merry mood:
I trow we'll keep in safety thy land and honor as we should.
"And well will I see to it that they at home remain,
Who fain would ride against thee to Worms upon the Rhine.
Against them straight we'll journey into their land so far
That they'll be meeker minded who now such haughty vaunters are."
Then from the Rhine through Hesse the hosts of knights rode on
Toward the land of Saxons, where battle was anon.
With fire and sword they harried and laid the country waste,
So that both the monarchs full well the woes of war did taste.
When came they to the border the train-men onward pressed.
With thought of battle-order Siegfried the thanes addressed:
"Who now shall guard our followers from danger in the rear?"
In sooth like this the Saxons in battle worsted never were.
Then said they: "On the journey the men shall guarded be
By the valiant Dankwart, —a warrior swift is he;
So shall we lose the fewer by men of Luedeger.
Let him and Ortwein with him be chosen now to guard the rear."
Spake then the valiant Siegfried: "Myself will now ride on,
And against our enemies will keep watch in the van,
Till I aright discover where they perchance may be."
The son of fair Queen Siegelind did arm him then immediately.
The folk he left to Hagen when ready to depart,
And as well to Gernot, a man of dauntless heart.
Into the land of Saxons alone he rode away,
And by his hand was severed many a helmet's band that day.
He found a mighty army that lay athwart the plain,
Small part of which outnumbered all those in his own train:
Full forty thousand were they or more good men of might.
The hero high in spirit saw right joyfully the sight.
Then had eke a warrior from out the enemy
To guard the van gone forward, all arméd cap-a-pie.
Him saw the noble Siegfried, and he the valiant man;
Each one straight the other to view with angry mien began.

Who he was I'll tell you that rode his men before,
—A shield of gold all shining upon his arm he bore—
In sooth it was King Luedegast who there the van did guard.
Straightway the noble Siegfried full eagerly against him spurred.
Now singled out for combat him, too, had Luedegast.
Then full upon each other they spurred their chargers fast,
As on their shields they lowered their lances firm and tight,
Whereat the lordly monarch soon found himself in sorry plight.
After the shock their chargers bore the knights so fast
Onward past each other as flew they on the blast.
Then turned they deftly backward obedient to the rein,
As with their swords contested the grim and doughty fighters twain.
When Siegfried struck in anger far off was heard the blow,
And flew from off the helmet, as if 'twere all aglow,
The fiery sparks all crackling beneath his hand around.
Each warrior in the other a foeman worth his mettle found.
Full many a stroke with vigor dealt eke King Luedegast,
And on each other's buckler the blows fell thick and fast.
Then thirty men discovered their master's sorry plight:
But ere they came to help him had doughty Siegfried won the fight.

With three mighty gashes which he had dealt the king
Through his shining breastplate made fast with many a ring.
The sword with sharpest edges from wounds brought forth the blood,
Whereat King Luedegast apace fell into gloomy mood.
To spare his life he begged him, his land he pledged the knight,
And told him straight moreover, that Luedegast he hight.
Then came his knights to help him, they who there had seen
How that upon the vanguard fierce fight betwixt the twain had been.
After duel ended, did thirty yet withstand
Of knights that him attended; but there the hero's hand
Kept safe his noble captive with blows of wondrous might.
And soon wrought greater ruin Siegfried the full gallant knight.
Beneath his arm of valor the thirty soon lay dead.
But one the knight left living, who thence full quickly sped
To tell abroad the story how he the others slew;
In sooth the blood-red helmet spake all the hapless tidings true.
Then had the men of Denmark   for all their grief good cause,
When it was told them truly their king a captive was.
They told it to King Luedeger, when he to rage began
In anger all unbounded: for him had grievous harm been done.
The noble King Luedegast was led a prisoner then
By hand of mighty Siegfried back to King Gunther's men,
And placed in hands of Hagen: and when they did hear
That 'twas the king of Denmark they not a little joyful were.
He bade the men of Burgundy then bind the banners on.
"Now forward!" Siegfried shouted, "here shall yet more be done,

An I but live to see it; ere this day's sun depart,
Shall mourn in land of Saxons full many a goodly matron's heart.
"Ye warriors from Rhineland, to follow me take heed,
And I unto the army of Luedeger will lead.
Ere we again turn backward to the land of Burgundy
Helms many hewn asunder by hand of good knights there shall be."
To horse then hastened Gernot and with him mighty men.
Volker keen in battle took up the banner then;
He was a doughty Fiddler and rode the host before.
There, too, every follower a stately suit of armor wore.
More than a thousand warriors they there had not a man,
Saving twelve knights-errant. To rise the dust began
In clouds along the highway as they rode across the fields,
And gleaming in the sunlight were seen the brightly shining shields.
Meanwhile eke was nearing of Saxons a great throng,
Each a broadsword bearing that mickle was and long,
With blade that cut full sorely when swung in strong right hand.
'Gainst strangers were they ready to guard their castles and their land.
The leaders forth to battle led the warriors then.
Come was also Siegfried with his twelve chosen men,
Whom he with him hither had brought from Netherland.
That day in storm of battle was blood-bespattered many a hand.
Sindold and Hunold and Gernot as well,
Beneath their hands in battle full many a hero fell,
Ere that their deeds of valor were known throughout the host.
Through them must many a stately matron weep for warrior lost.
Volker and Hagen and Ortwein in the fight
Lustily extinguished full many a helmet's light
With blood from wounds down flowing,— keen fighters every one.
And there by Dankwart also was many a mickle wonder done.
The knights of Denmark tested how they could weapons wield.
Clashing there together heard ye many a shield
And 'neath sharp swords resounding, swung by many an arm.
The Saxons keen in combat wrought 'mid their foes a grievous harm.
When the men of Burgundy pressed forward to the fight,
Gaping wounds full many hewed they there with might.
Then flowing down o'er saddle in streams was seen the blood,
So fought for sake of honor these valiant riders keen and good.
Loudly were heard ringing, wielded by hero's hand,
The sharply-cutting weapons, where they of Netherland
Their master followed after into the thickest throng:
Wherever Siegfried led them rode too those valiant knights along.
Of warriors from Rhine river could follow not a one.
There could be seen by any a stream of blood flow down
O'er brightly gleaming helmet 'neath Siegfried's mighty hand,
Until King Luedeger before him with his men did stand.
Three times hither and thither had he the host cut through

From one end to the other. Now come was Hagen too
Who helped him well in battle to vent his warlike mood.
That day beneath his valor must die full many a rider good.
When the doughty Luedeger Siegfried there found,
As he swung high in anger his arm for blows around
And with his good sword Balmung knights so many slew,
Thereat was the keen warrior filled with grief and anger too.
Then mickle was the thronging and loud the broadswords clashed,
As all their valiant followers 'gainst one another dashed.
Then struggled all the fiercer both sides the fight to win;
The hosts joined with each other: 'twas frightful there to hear the din.
To the monarch of the Saxons it had been told before,
His brother was a captive, which grieved his heart right sore.
He knew not that had done it fair Siegelind's son,
For rumor said 'twas Gernot. Full well he learned the truth anon.
King Luedeger struck so mighty when fierce his anger rose,
That Siegfried's steed beneath him staggered from the blows,
But forthwith did recover; then straight his rider keen
Let all his furious mettle in slaughter of his foes be seen.
There helped him well grim Hagen, and Gernot in the fray,
Dankwart and Volker; dead many a knight there lay.
Sindold and Hunold and Ortwein, doughty thane,
By them in that fierce struggle was many a valiant warrior slain.
Unparted in storm of battle the gallant leaders were,
Around them over helmet flew there many a spear
Through shield all brightly shining, from hand of mighty thane:
And on the glancing armor was seen full many a blood-red stain.
Amid the hurly-burly down fell many a man
To ground from off his charger. Straight 'gainst each other ran
Siegfried the keen rider and eke King Luedeger.
Then flew from lance the splinters and hurled was many a pointed spear.
'Neath Siegfried's hand so mighty from shield flew off the band.
And soon to win the victory thought he of Netherland
Over the valiant Saxons, of whom were wonders seen.
Heigh-ho! in shining mail-rings many a breach made Dankwart keen!
Upon the shining buckler that guarded Siegfried's breast
Soon espied King Luedeger a painted crown for crest;
By this same token knew he it was the doughty man,
And to his friends he straightway amid the battle loud began:
"Give o'er from fighting further, good warriors every one!
Amongst our foes now see I Siegmund's noble son,
Of netherland the doughty knight on victory bent.
Him has the evil Devil to scourge the Saxons hither sent."
Then bade he all the banners amid the storm let down.
Peace he quickly sued for: 'Twas granted him anon,
But he must now a hostage be ta'en to Gunther's land.
This fate had forced upon him the fear of Siegfried's mighty hand.

They thus by common counsel left off all further fight.
Hacked full many a helmet and shields that late were bright
From hands down laid they weary; as many as there might be,
With stains they all were bloody 'neath hands of the men of Burgundy.
Each whom he would took captive, now they had won the fight.
Gernot, the noble hero, and Hagen, doughty knight,
Bade bear forth the wounded. Back led they with them then
Unto the land of Burgundy five hundred stalwart fighting-men.
The knights, of victory cheated, their native Denmark sought,
Nor had that day the Saxons with such high valor fought,
That one could praise them for it, which caused the warriors pain.
Then wept their friends full sorely at home for those in battle slain.
For the Rhine then laden they let their armor be.
Siegfried, the knight so doughty, had won the victory
With his few chosen followers; that he had nobly done,
Could not but free acknowledge King Gunther's warriors every one.
To Worms sent Gernot riding now a messenger,
And of the joyous tiding soon friends at home were ware,
How that it well had prospered with him and all his men.
Fought that day with valor for honor had those warriors keen.
The messenger sped forward and told the tidings o'er.
Then joyfully they shouted who boded ill before,
To hear the welcome story that now to them was told.
From ladies fair and noble came eager questions manifold,
Who all the fair fortune of King Gunther's men would know.
One messenger they ordered unto Kriemhild to go.
But that was done in secret: she durst let no one see,
For he was 'mongst those warriors whom she did love so faithfully.
When to her own apartments was come the messenger
Joyfully addressed him Kriemhild the maiden fair:
"But tell me now glad tidings, and gold I'll give to thee,
And if thou tell'st not falsely, good friend thou'lt ever find in me.
"How has my good brother Gernot in battle sped,
And how my other kinsmen? Lies any of them dead?
Who wrought most deeds of valor? —That shall thou let me know."
Then spake the messenger truly: "No knight but did high valor show.
"But in the dire turmoil rode rider none so well,
O Princess fair and noble, since I must truly tell,
As the stranger knight full noble who comes from Netherland;
There deeds of mickle wonder were wrought by doughty Siegfried's hand.
"Whate'er have all the warriors in battle dared to do,
Dankwart and Hagen and the other knights so true,
Howe'er they fought for honor, 'twas naught but idle play
Beside what there wrought Siegfried, King Siegmund's son, amid the fray.
"Beneath their hands in battle full many a hero fell,
Yet all the deeds of wonder no man could ever tell,
Wrought by the hand of Siegfried, when rode he 'gainst the foe:

And weep aloud must women for friends by his strong arm laid low.
"There, too, the knight she loved full many a maid must lose.
Were heard come down on helmet so loud his mighty blows,
That they from gaping gashes brought forth the flowing blood.
In all that maketh noble he is a valiant knight and good.
"Many a deed of daring of Metz Sir Ortwein wrought:
For all was evil faring whom he with broadsword caught,
Doomed to die that instant, or wounded sore to fall.
And there thy valiant brother did greater havoc work than all
"That e'er in storm of battle was done by warrior bold.
Of all those chosen warriors let eke the truth be told:
The proud Burgundian heroes have made it now right plain,
That they can free from insult their country's honor well maintain.
"Beneath their hands was often full many a saddle bare,
When o'er the field resounding their bright swords cut the air.
The warriors from Rhine river did here such victory win
That for their foes 'twere better if they such meeting ne'er had seen.
"Keen the knights of Tronje 'fore all their valor showed,
When with their stalwart followers against their foes they rode;
Slain by the hand of Hagen must knights so many be,
'Twill long be in the telling here in the land of Burgundy.
"Sindold and Hunold, Gernot's men each one,
And the valiant Rumold have all so nobly done,
King Luedeger will ever have right good cause to rue
That he against thy kindred at Rhine dared aught of harm to do.
"And deeds of all most wondrous e'er done by warrior keen
In earliest time or latest, by mortal ever seen,
Wrought there in lusty manner Siegfried with doughty hand.
Rich hostages he bringeth with him unto Gunther's land.
"By his own strength subdued them the hero unsurpassed
And brought down dire ruin upon King Luedegast,
Eke on the King of Saxons his brother Luedeger.
Now hearken to the story I tell thee, noble Princess fair.
"Them both hath taken captive Siegfried's doughty hand.
Hostages were so many ne'er brought into this land
As to the Rhine come hither through his great bravery."
Than these could never tidings unto her heart more welcome be.
"With captives home they're hieing, five hundred men or mo',
And of the wounded dying Lady shalt thou know,
Full eighty blood-stained barrows unto Burgundian land,
Most part hewn down in battle beneath keen Siegfried's doughty hand.
"Who message sent defiant unto the Rhine so late
Must now as Gunther's prisoners here abide their fate.
Bringing such noble captives the victors glad return."
Then glowed with joy the princess when she the tidings glad did learn.
Her cheeks so full of beauty with joy were rosy-red,
That passed he had uninjured through all the dangers dread,

The knight she loved so dearly, Siegfried with doughty arm.
Good cause she had for joying o'er all her friends escaped from harm.
Then spake the beauteous maiden: "Glad news thou hast told me,
Wherefor now rich apparel thy goodly meed shall be,
And to thee shall be given ten marks of gold as well."
'Tis thus a thing right pleasant to ladies high such news to tell.
The presents rich they gave him, gold and apparel rare.
Then hastened to the casement full many a maiden fair,
And on the street looked downward: hither riding did they see
Many a knight high-hearted into the land of Burgundy.
There came who 'scaped uninjured, and wounded borne along,
All glad to hear the greetings of friends, a joyful throng.
To meet his friends the monarch rode out in mickle glee:
In joying now was ended   all his full great anxiety.
Then did he well his warriors and eke the strangers greet;
And for a king so mighty 'twere nothing else but meet
That he should thank right kindly the gallant men each one,
Who had in storm of battle the victory so bravely won.
Then of his friends King Gunther   bade tidings tell straightway,
Of all his men how many were fallen in the fray.
Lost had he none other than warriors three score:
Then wept they for the heroes, as since they did for many more.
Shields full many brought they all hewn by valiant hand,
And many a shattered helmet into King Gunther's hand.
The riders then dismounted from their steeds before the hall,
And a right hearty welcome from friends rejoicing had they all.
Then did they for the warriors lodging meet prepare,
And for his guests the monarch bade full well have care.
He bade them take the wounded and tend them carefully,
And toward his enemies also his gentle bearing might ye see.
To Luedeger then spake he: "Right welcome art thou here.
Through fault of thine now have I lost many friends full dear,
For which, have I good fortune, thou shall right well atone.
God rich reward my liegemen, such faithfulness to me they've shown."
"Well may'st thou thank them, truly," spake then Luedeger;
"Hostages so noble won a monarch ne'er.
For chivalrous protection rich goods we offer thee,
That thou now right gracious to us thy enemies shalt be."
"I'll grant you both your freedom," spake the king again;
"But that my enemies surely here by me remain,
Therefor I'll have good pledges they ne'er shall quit my land,
Save at my royal pleasure." Thereto gave Luedeger the hand.
Sweet rest then found the weary their tired limbs to aid,
And gently soon on couches the wounded knights were laid;
Mead and wine right ruddy they poured out plenteously:
Than they and all their followers merrier men there none might be.
Their shields all hacked in battle   secure were laid away;

And not a few of saddles   stained with blood that day,
Lest women weep to see them, hid they too from sight.
Full many a keen rider home came aweary from the fight.
The host in gentlest manner did his guests attend:
The land around with stranger was crowded, and with friend.
They bade the sorely wounded nurse with especial care:
Whereby the knights high-hearted 'neath all their wounds knew not despair.
Who there had skill in healing received reward untold,
Silver all unweighéd and thereto ruddy gold
For making whole the heroes after the battle sore.
To all his friends the monarch gave presents rich in goodly store.
Who there again was minded to take his homeward way
They bade, as one a friend doth, yet a while to stay.
The king did then take counsel how to reward each one,
For they his will in battle like liegemen true had nobly done.
Then outspake royal Gernot: "Now let them homeward go;
After six weeks are over, —thus our friends shall know—
To hold high feast they're bidden hither to come again;
Many a knight now lying sore wounded will be healed ere then.
Of Netherland the hero would also then take leave.
When of this King Gunther did tidings first receive,
The knight besought he kindly not yet his leave to take:
To this he'd ne'er consented an it were not for Kriemhild's sake.
A prince he was too noble to take the common pay;
He had right well deserved it that the king alway
And all his warriors held him in honor, for they had seen
What by his arm in battle bravely had accomplished been.
He stayed there yet a little for the maiden's sake alone,
Whom he would see so gladly. And all fell out full soon
As he at heart had wished it: well known to him was she.
Home to his father's country joyously anon rode he.
The king bade at all seasons keep up the tournament,
And many a youthful rider forth to the lists there went.
The while were seats made ready by Worms upon the strand
For all who soon were coming unto the Burgundian land.
In the meantime also, ere back the knights returned,
Had Kriemhild, noble lady, the tidings likewise learned,
The king would hold high feasting with all his gallant men.
There was a mickle hurry, and busy were fair maidens then
With dresses and with wimples   that they there should wear.
Ute, queen so stately, the story too did hear,
How to them were coming proud knights of highest worth.
Then from enfolding covers were store of dresses rich brought forth.
Such love she bore her children she bade rich dress prepare,
Wherewith adorned were ladies and many a maiden fair,
And not a few young riders in the land of Burgundy.
For strangers many bade she rich garments eke should measured be.

FIFTH ADVENTURE

How Siegfried first saw Kriemhild

Unto the Rhine now daily the knights were seen to ride,
Who there would be full gladly to share the festive tide.
To all that thither journeyed to the king to show them true,
In plenty them were given steeds and rich apparel too.
And soon were seats made ready for every noble guest,
As we have heard the story, for highest and for best,
Two and thirty princes at the festival.
Then vied with one another to deck themselves the ladies all.
Never was seen idle the young Prince Giselher:
The guests and all their followers received full kindly were
By him and eke by Gernot and their men every one.
The noble thanes they greeted as ever 'tis in honor done.
With gold bright gleaming saddles unto the land they brought,
Good store of rich apparel and shields all richly wrought
Unto the Rhine they carried to that high festival.
And joyous days were coming for the woúnded warriors all.
They who yet on couches lay wounded grievously
For joy had soon forgotten how bitter death would be:
The sick and all the ailing no need of pity had.
Anent the days of feasting were they o'er the tidings glad,
How they should make them merry there where all were so.
Delight beyond all measure, of joys an overflow,
Had in sooth the people seen on every hand:
Then rose a mickle joyance over all King Gunther's land.
Full many a warrior valiant one morn at Whitsuntide
All gorgeously apparelled was thither seen to ride,
Five thousand men or over, where the feast should be;
And vied in every quarter knight with knight in revelry.
Thereof the host was mindful, for he well did understand
How at heart right warmly the hero of Netherland
Loved alone his sister, though her he ne'er had seen,
Who praised for wondrous beauty before all maidens else had been.
Then spake the thane so noble of Metz Sir Ortwein:
"Wilt thou full be honored by every guest of thine,
Then do them all the pleasure the winsome maids to see,
That are held so high in honor here in the land of Burgundy.
"What were a man's chief pleasure, his very joy of life,
An 't were not a lovely maiden or a stately wife?
Then let the maid thy sister before thy guests appear."
—Brave thanes did there full many at heart rejoice the rede to hear.
"Thy words I'll gladly follow," then the monarch said,
And all the knights who heard him ere thereat right glad.
Then told was Queen Ute and eke her daughter fair,

That they with maids in waiting unto the court should soon repair.
Then in well-stored wardrobes rich attire they sought,
And forth from folding covers their glittering dresses brought,
Armbands and silken girdles of which they many had.
And zealous to adorn her was then full many a winsome maid.
Full many a youthful squire upon that day did try,
By decking of his person, to win fair lady's eye;
For the which great good fortune he'd take no monarch's crown:
They longed to see those maidens, whom they before had never known.
For her especial service the king did order then
To wait upon his sister a hundred of his men,
As well upon his mother: they carried sword in hand.
That was the court attendance there in the Burgundian land.
Ute, queen so stately, then came forth with her:
And with the queen in waiting ladies fair there were,
A hundred or over, in festal robes arrayed.
Eke went there with Kriemhild full many a fair and winsome maid.
Forth from their own apartments they all were seen to go:
There was a mickle pressing of good knights to and fro,
Who hoped to win the pleasure, if such a thing might be,
The noble maiden Kriemhild, delight of every eye, to see.
Now came she fair and lovely, as the ruddy sun of morn
From misty clouds emerging. Straight he who long had borne
Her in his heart and loved her, from all his gloom was freed,
As so stately there before him he saw the fair and lovely maid.
Her rich apparel glittered with many a precious stone,
And with a ruddy beauty her cheeks like roses shone.
Though you should wish to do so, you could not say, I ween,
That e'er a fairer lady in all the world before was seen.
As in a sky all starlit the moon shines out so bright,
And through the cloudlets peering pours down her gentle light,
E'en so was Kriemhild's beauty among her ladies fair:
The hearts of gallant heroes were gladder when they saw her there.
The richly clad attendants moved stately on before,
And the valiant thanes high-hearted stood patiently no more,
But pressed right eager forward to see the lovely maid:
In noble Siegfried's bosom alternate joy and anguish swayed.
He thought with heart despairing, "How could it ever be,
That I should win thy favor? There hoped I foolishly.
But had I e'er to shun thee, then were I rather dead."
And oft, to think upon it, the color from his visage fled.
he noble son of Siegmund did there so stately stand
As if his form were pictured by good old master's hand
Upon a piece of parchment. All who saw, confessed
That he of all good heroes was the stateliest and the best.
The fair Kriemhild's attendants gave order to make way
On all sides for the ladies, and willing thanes obey.

To see their noble bearing did every warrior cheer;
Full many a stately lady of gentle manner born was there.
Then outspake of Burgundy Gernot the valiant knight:
"To him who thus has helped thee so bravely in the fight,
Gunther, royal brother, shalt thou like favor show,
A thane before all others; he's worthy of it well, I trow.

"Let then the doughty Siegfried unto my sister go
To have the maiden's greetings, —'twill be our profit so.
She that ne'er greeted hero shall greet him courteously,
That thus the stately warrior for aye our faithful friend may be."
The king's knights hastened gladly upon his high command
And told these joyous tidings to the prince of Netherland.

"It is the king's good pleasure that thou to court shalt go,
To have his sister's greetings; to honor thee 'tis ordered so."
Then was the thane full valiant thereat soon filled with joy.
Yea, bore he in his bosom delight without alloy
At thought that he should straightway Ute's fair daughter see.
Siegfried anon she greeted in courteous manner lovingly.

As she saw the knight high-hearted there before her stand,
Blushed red and spake the maiden, the fairest of the land:
"A welcome, brave Sir Siegfried, thou noble knight and good."
As soon as he had heard it, the hearty greeting cheered his mood.
Before her low he bended; him by the hand took she,
And by her onward wended the knight full willingly.

They cast upon each other fond glances many a one,
The knight and eke the maiden; furtively it all was done.
Whether he pressed friendly that hand as white as snow
From the love he bore her, that I do not know;
Yet believe I cannot that this was left undone,
For straightway showed the maiden that he her heart had fully won.

In the sunny summer season and in the month of May
Had his heart seen never before so glad a day,
Nor one so fully joyous, as when he walked beside
That maiden rich in beauty whom fain he'd choose to be his bride.
Then thought many a warrior: "Were it likewise granted me
To walk beside the maiden, just as now I see,

Or to lie beside her, how gladly were that done!"
But ne'er a knight more fully had gracious lady's favor won.
From all the lands far distant were guests distinguished there,
But fixed each eye was only upon this single pair.
By royal leave did Kriemhild kiss then the stately knight:
In all the world he never before had known so rare delight.

Then full of strange forebodings, of Denmark spake the king:
"This full loving greeting to many woe will bring,
—My heart in secret warns me— through Siegfried's doughty hand.
God give that he may never again be seen within my land."
On all sides then 'twas ordered 'fore Kriemhild and her train

Of women make free passage. Full many a valiant thane
With her unto the minster in courtly way went on.
But from her side was parted the full stately knight anon.
Then went she to the minster, and with her many a maid.
In such rich apparel Kriemhild was arrayed,
That hearty wishes many there were made in vain:
Her comely form delighted the eye of many a noble thane.
Scarce could tarry Siegfried till mass was sung the while.
And surely did Dame Fortune upon him kindly smile,
To him she was so gracious whom in his heart he bore.
Eke did he the maiden, as she full well deserved, adore.
As after mass then Kriemhild came to the minster door,
The knight his homage offered, as he had done before.
Then began to thank him the full beauteous maid,
That he her royal brothers did 'gainst their foes so nobly aid.
"God speed thee, Sir Siegfried," spake the maiden fair,
"For thou hast well deservéd that all these warriors are,
As it hath now been told me, right grateful unto thee."
Then gan he cast his glances on the Lady Kriemhild lovingly.
"True will I ever serve them," —so spake the noble thane—
"And my head shall never be laid to rest again,
Till I, if life remaineth, have their good favor won.
In sooth, my Lady Kriemhild, for thy fair grace it all is done."
Ne'er a day passed over for a twelve of happy days,
But saw they there beside him the maiden all did praise,
As she before her kinsmen to court would daily go:
It pleased the thane full highly that they did him such honor show.
Delight and great rejoicing, a mighty jubilee,
Before King Gunther's castle daily might ye see,
Without and eke within it, 'mongst keen men many a one.
By Ortwein and by Hagen great deeds and wondrous there were done.
Whate'er was done by any, in all they ready were
To join in way right lusty, both the warriors rare:
Whereby 'mongst all the strangers they won an honored name,
And through their deeds so wondrous of Gunther's land spread far the fame.
Who erstwhile lay sore wounded now were whole again,
And fain would share the pastime, with all the king's good men;
With shields join in the combat, and try the shaft so long.
Wherein did join them many of the merry-making throng.
To all who joined the feasting the host in plenty bade
Supply the choicest viands: so guarded well he had
'Gainst whate'er reproaches could rise from spite or spleen.
Unto his guests right friendly to go the monarch now was seen.
He spake: "Ye thanes high-hearted, ere now ye part from me,
Accept of these my presents; for I would willingly
Repay your noble service. Despise ye not, I pray,
What now I will share with you: 'tis offered in right grateful way."

Straightway they of Denmark thus to the king replied:
"Ere now upon our journey home again we ride,
We long for lasting friendship. Thereof we knights have need,
For many a well-loved kinsman at hands of thy good thanes lies dead."
Luedegast was recovered from all his wounds so sore,
And eke the lord of Saxons from fight was whole once more.
Some amongst their warriors left they dead behind.
Then went forth King Gunther where he Siegfried might find.
Unto the thane then spake he: "Thy counsel give, I pray.
The foes whom we hold captive fain would leave straightway,
And long for lasting friendship with all my men and me.
Now tell me, good Sir Siegfried, what here seemeth good to thee.
"What the lords bid as ransom, shall now to thee be told
Whate'er five hundred horses might bear of ruddy gold,
They'd give to me right gladly, would I but let them free."
Then spake the noble Siegfried: "That were to do right foolishly.
"Thou shalt let them freely journey hence again;
And that they both hereafter shall evermore refrain
From leading hostile army against thee and thy land,
Therefor in pledge of friendship let each now give to thee the hand."
"Thy rede I'll gladly follow." Straightway forth they went.
To those who offered ransom the answer then was sent,
Their gold no one desired which they would give before.
The warriors battle-weary dear friends did yearn to see once more.
Full many a shield all laden with treasure forth they bore:
He dealt it round unmeasured to friends in goodly store;
Each one had marks five hundred and some had more, I ween.
Therein King Gunther followed the rede of Gernot, knight full keen.
Then was a great leave-taking, as they departed thence.
The warriors all 'fore Kriemhild appeared in reverence,
And eke there where her mother Queen Ute sat near by.
Gallant thanes were never dismissed as these so graciously.
Bare were the lodging-places, when away the strangers rode.
Yet in right lordly manner there at home abode
The king with friends around him, full noble men who were.
And them now saw they daily at court before Kriemhild appear.
Eke would the gallant hero Siegfried thence depart,
The thing to gain despairing whereon was set his heart.
The king was told the tidings how that he would away.
Giselher his brother did win the knight with them to stay.
"Whither, O noble Siegfried, wilt thou now from us ride?
Do as I earnest pray thee, and with these thanes abide,
As guest here with King Gunther, and live right merrily.
Here dwell fair ladies many: them will he gladly let thee see."
Then spake the doughty Siegfried: "Our steeds leave yet at rest,
The while from this my purpose to part will I desist.
Our shields once more take from us. Though gladly home I would,

Naught 'gainst the fond entreaties of Giselher avail me could."
So stayed the knight full gallant   for sake of friendship there.
In sooth in ne'er another country anywhere
Had he so gladly lingered: I wish it was that he,
Now whensoe'er he wished it,   Kriemhild the maiden fair could see.
'Twas her surpassing beauty that made the knight to stay.
With many a merry pastime they whiled the time away;
But love for her oppressed him, oft-times grievously.
Whereby anon the hero   a mournful death was doomed to die.

SIXTH ADVENTURE

How Gunther fared to Isenland to Brunhild

Tidings unknown to any from over Rhine now come,
How winsome maids a many far yonder had their home.
Whereof the royal Gunther bethought him one to win,
And o'er the thought the monarch of full joyous mood was seen.
There was a queenly maiden seated over sea,
Like her nowhere another was ever known to be.
She was in beauty matchless, full mickle was her might;
Her love the prize of contest, she hurled the shaft with valiant knight.
The stone she threw far distant, wide sprang thereafter too.
Who turned to her his fancy with intent to woo,
Three times perforce must vanquish the lady of high degree;
Failed he in but one trial, forfeited his head had he.
This same the lusty princess times untold had done.
When to a warrior gallant beside the Rhine 'twas known,
He thought to take unto him the noble maid for wife:
Thereby must heroes many since that moment lose their life.
Then spake of Rhine the master: "I'll down unto the sea
Unto Brunhild journey, fare as 'twill with me.
For her unmeasured beauty I'll gladly risk my life,
Ready eke to lose it, if she may not be my wife."
"I counsel thee against it," spake then Siegfried.
"So terrible in contest the queen is indeed,
Who for her love is suitor his zeal must dearly pay.
So shalt thou from the journey truly be content to stay."
"So will I give thee counsel," outspake Hagen there,
"That thou beg of Siegfried with thee to bear
The perils that await thee: that is now my rede,
To him is known so fully what with Brunhild will be thy need."
He spake: "And wilt thou help me, noble Siegfried,
To win the lovely maiden? Do what now I plead;
And if in all her beauty she be my wedded wife,
To meet thy fullest wishes honor will I pledge and life."

Thereto answered Siegfried, the royal Siegmund's son:
"Giv'st thou me thy sister, so shall thy will be done,
—Kriemhild the noble princess, in beauty all before.
For toils that I encounter none other meed I ask thee more."
"That pledge I," spake then Gunther, "Siegfried, in thy hand.
And comes the lovely Brunhild thither to this land,
Thereunto thee my sister for wife I'll truly give,
That with the lovely maiden thou may'st ever joyful live."
Oaths the knight full noble upon the compact swore,
Whereby to them came troubles and dangers all the more,
Ere they the royal lady brought unto the Rhine.
Still should the warriors valiant in sorest need and sorrow pine.
With him carried Siegfried that same mantle then,
The which with mickle trouble had won the hero keen
From a dwarf in struggle, Alberich by name.
They dressed them for the journey, the valiant thanes of lofty fame.
And when the doughty Siegfried the sightless mantle wore,
Had he within it of strength as good a store
As other men a dozen in himself alone.
The full stately princess anon by cunning art he won.
Eke had that same mantle such wondrous properties
That any man whatever might work whate'er he please
When once he had it on him, yet none could see or tell.
'Twas so that he won Brunhild; whereby him evil since befell.
"Ere we begin our journey, Siegfried, tell to me,
That we with fullest honor come unto the sea,
Shall we lead warriors with us down to Brunhild's land?
Thanes a thirty thousand straightway shall be called to hand."
"Men bring we ne'er so many," answered Siegfried then.
"So terrible in custom ever is the queen,
That all would death encounter from her angry mood.
I'll give thee better counsel, thane in valor keen and good.
"Like as knights-errant journey down the Rhine shall we.
Those now will I name thee who with us shall be;
But four in all the company seaward shall we fare:
Thus shall we woo the lady, what fortune later be our share.
"Myself one of the company, a second thou shalt be,
Hagen be the third one —so fare we happily;
The fourth let it be Dankwart, warrior full keen.
Never thousand others dare in fight withstand us then."
"The tale I would know gladly," the king then further said,
"Ere we have parted thither —of that were I full glad—
What should we of apparel, that would befit us well,
Wear in Brunhild's presence: that shalt thou now to Gunther tell."
"Weeds the very finest that ever might be found
They wear in every season in Brunhild's land:
So shall we rich apparel before the lady wear,

That we have not dishonor where men the tale hereafter hear."
Then spake he to the other: "Myself will go unto
My own loving mother, if I from her may sue
That her fair tendant maidens help that we be arrayed
As we may go in honor before the high majestic maid."
Then spake of Tronje Hagen with noble courtliness:
"Why wilt thou of thy mother beg such services?
Only let thy sister hear our mind and mood:
So shall for this our journey her good service be bestowed."
Then sent he to his sister that he her would see,
And with him also Siegfried. Ere that such might be,
Herself had there the fair one in rich apparel clad.
Sooth to tell, the visit but little did displease the maid.
Then also were her women decked as for them was meet.
The princes both were coming: she rose from off her seat,
As doth a high-born lady when that she did perceive,
And went the guest full noble and eke her brother to receive.
"Welcome be my brother and his companion too.
I'd know the story gladly," spake the maiden so,
"What ye now are seeking that ye are come to me:
I pray you straightway tell me how 't with you valiants twain may be."
Then spake the royal Gunther: "Lady, thou shall hear:
Spite of lofty spirits have we yet a care.
To woo a maid we travel afar to lands unknown;
We should against the journey have rich apparel for our own."
"Seat thee now, dear brother," spake the princess fair;
"Let me hear the story, who the ladies are
That ye will seek as suitors in stranger princes' land."
Both good knights the lady took in greeting by the hand.
With the twain then went she where she herself had sat,
To couches rich and costly, in sooth believe ye that,
Wrought in design full cunning of gold embroidery.
And with these fair ladies did pass the time right pleasantly.
Many tender glances and looks full many a one
Fondly knight and lady each other cast upon.
Within his heart he bore her, she was as his own life.
Anon the fairest Kriemhild was the doughty Siegfried's wife.
Then spake the mighty monarch: "Full loving sister mine,
This may we ne'er accomplish without help of thine.
Unto Brunhild's country as suitor now we fare:
'Tis fitting that 'fore ladies we do rich apparel wear."
Then spake the royal maiden: "Brother dear to me,
In whatsoever manner my help may given be,
Of that I well assure you, ready thereto am I.
To Kriemhild 'twere a sorrow if any should the same deny.
"Of me, O noble brother, thou shalt not ask in vain:
Command in courteous manner and I will serve thee fain.

Whatever be thy pleasure, for that I'll lend my aid
And willingly I'll do it," spake the fair and winsome maid.
"It is our wish, dear sister, apparel good to wear;
That shall now directing the royal hand prepare;
And let thy maids see to it that all is done aright,
For we from this same journey turn not aside for word of wight."
Spake thereupon the maiden: "Now mark ye what I say:
Myself have silks in plenty; now send us rich supply
Of stones borne on bucklers, so vesture we'll prepare."
To do it royal Gunther and Siegfried both right ready were.
"And who are your companions," further questioned she,
"Who with you apparelled now for court shall be?"
"I it is and Siegfried, and of my men are two,
Dankwart and Hagen, who with us to court shall go.
"Now rightly what we tell thee, mark, O sister dear:
'Tis that we four companions for four days may wear
Thrice daily change of raiment so wrought with skilful hand
That we without dishonor may take our leave of Brunhild's land."
After fair leave-taking the knights departed so.
Then of her attendants thirty maids to go
Forth from her apartments Kriemhild the princess bade,
Of those that greatest cunning in such skilful working had.
ks that were of Araby white as the snow in sheen,
And from the land of Zazamank like unto grass so green,
With stones of price they broidered; that made apparel rare.
Herself she cut them, Kriemhild the royal maiden debonair.
Fur linings fashioned fairly from dwellers in the sea
Beheld by people rarely, the best that e'er might be,
With silken stuffs they covered for the knights to wear.
Now shall ye of the shining weeds full many a wonder hear.
From land of far Morocco and eke from Libya
Of silks the very finest that ever mortal saw
With any monarch's kindred, they had a goodly store.
Well showed the Lady Kriemhild that unto them good will she bore.
Since they unto the journey had wished that so it be,
Skins of costly ermine used they lavishly,
Whereon were silken pieces black as coal inlaid.
To-day were any nobles in robes so fashioned well arrayed.
From the gold of Araby many a stone there shone.
The women long were busy before the work was done;
But all the robes were finished ere seven weeks did pass,
When also trusty armor for the warriors ready was.
When they at length were ready adown the Rhine to fare,
A ship lay waiting for them strong built with mickle care,
Which should bear them safely far down unto the sea.
The maidens rich in beauty plied their work laboriously.
Then 'twas told the warriors for them was ready there

The finely wrought apparel that they were to wear;
Just as they had wished it, so it had been made;
After that the heroes there by the Rhine no longer stayed.
To the knights departing went soon a messenger:
Would they come in person to view their new attire,
If it had been fitted short and long aright.
'Twas found of proper measure, and thanked those ladies fair each knight.
And all who there beheld them they must needs confess
That in the world they never had gazed on fairer dress:
At court to wear th' apparel did therefore please them well.
Of warriors better furnished never could a mortal tell.
Thanks oft-times repeated were there not forgot.
Leave of parting from them the noble knights then sought:
Like thanes of noble bearing they went in courteous wise.
Then dim and wet with weeping grew thereat two shining eyes.
She spake: "O dearest brother, still here thou mightest stay,
And woo another woman— that were the better way—
Where so sore endangered stood not thus thy life.
Here nearer canst thou find thee equally a high-born wife."
I ween their hearts did tell them what later came to pass.
They wept there all together, whatever spoken was.
The gold upon their bosoms was sullied 'neath the tears
That from their eyes in plenty fell adown amid their fears.
She spake: "O noble Siegfried, to thee commended be
Upon thy truth and goodness the brother dear to me,
That he come unscathed home from Brunhild's land."
That plighted the full valiant knight in Lady Kriemhild's hand.
The mighty thane gave answer: "If I my life retain,
Then shall thy cares, good Lady, all have been in vain.
All safe I'll bring him hither again unto the Rhine,
Be that to thee full sicker." To him did the fair maid incline.
Their shields of golden color were borne unto the strand,
And all their trusty armor was ready brought to hand.
They bade their horses bring them: they would at last depart.
—Thereat did fairest women weep with sad foreboding heart.
Down from lofty casement looked many a winsome maid,
As ship and sail together by stirring breeze were swayed.
Upon the Rhine they found them, the warriors full of pride.
Then outspake King Gunther: "Who now is here the ship to guide?"
"That will I," spake Siegfried; "I can upon the flood
Lead you on in safety, that know ye, heroes good;
For all the water highways are known right well to me."
With joy they then departed from the land of Burgundy.
A mighty pole then grasped he, Siegfried the doughty man,
And the ship from shore forth to shove began.
Gunther the fearless also himself took oar in hand.
The knights thus brave and worthy took departure from the land.

They carried rich provisions, thereto the best of wine
That might in any quarter be found about the Rhine.
Their chargers stood in comfort and rested by the way:
The ship it moved so lightly that naught of injury had they.

Stretched before the breezes were the great sail-ropes tight,
And twenty miles they journeyed ere did come the night,
By fair breezes favored down toward the sea.
Their toil repaid thereafter the dauntless knights full grievously.

Upon the twelfth morning, as we in story hear,
Had they by the breezes thence been carried far,
Unto Castle Isenstein and Brunhild's country:
That to Siegfried only was known of all the company.

As soon as saw King Gunther so many towers rise
And eke the boundless marches stretch before his eyes,
He spake: "Tell me, friend Siegfried, is it known to thee
Whose they are, the castles and the majestic broad country?"

Thereto gave answer Siegfried: "That well to me is known:
Brunhild for their mistress do land and people own
And Isenstein's firm towers, as ye have heard me say.
Ladies fair a many shall ye here behold to-day.

"And I will give you counsel: be it well understood
That all your words must tally —so methinks 'twere good.
If ere to-day is over our presence she command,
Must we leave pride behind us, as before Brunhild we stand.

"When we the lovely lady 'mid her retainers see,
Then shall ye, good companions, in all your speech agree
That Gunther is my master and I his serving-man:
'Tis thus that all he hopeth shall we in the end attain."

To do as he had bidden consented straight each one,
And spite of proudest spirit they left it not undone.
All that he wished they promised, and good it proved to be
When anon King Gunther the fair Brunhild came to see.

"Not all to meet thy wishes do I such service swear,
But most 'tis for thy sister, Kriemhild the maiden fair;
Just as my soul unto me she is my very life,
And fain would I deserve it that she in truth become my wife."

SEVENTH ADVENTURE

How Gunther won Brunhild

The while they thus did parley their ship did forward glide
So near unto the castle that soon the king espied
Aloft within the casements many a maiden fair to see.
That all to him were strangers thought King Gunther mournfully.

He asked then of Siegfried, who bare him company:

"Know'st thou aught of the maidens, who the same may be,
Gazing yonder downward upon us on the tide?
Howe'er is named their master, minded are they high in pride."
Then spake the valiant Siegfried: "Now thither shalt thou spy
Unseen among the ladies, then not to me deny
Which, wert thou free in choosing, thou'dst take to be thy queen."
"That will I do," then answered Gunther the valiant knight and keen.
"I see there one among them by yonder casement stand,
Clad in snow-white raiment: 'tis she my eyes demand,
So buxom she in stature, so fair she is to see.
An I were free in choosing, she it is my wife must be."
"Full well now in choosing thine eyes have guided thee:
It is the stately Brunhild the maiden fair to see,
That doth now unto her thy heart and soul compel."
All the maiden's bearing pleased the royal Gunther well.
But soon the queen commanded from casement all to go
Of those her beauteous maidens: they should not stand there so
To be gazed at by the strangers. They must obey her word.
What were the ladies doing, of that moreover have we heard.
Unto the noble strangers their beauty they would show,
A thing which lovely women are ever wont to do.
Unto the narrow casements came they crowding on,
When they spied the strangers: that they might also see, 'twas done.
But four the strangers numbered, who came unto that land.
Siegfried the doughty the king's steed led in hand:
They saw it from the casements, many a lovely maid,
And saw the willing service unto royal Gunther paid.
Then held he by the bridle for him his gallant steed,
A good and fair-formed charger, strong and of noble breed,
Until the royal Gunther into the saddle sprung.
Thus did serve him Siegfried: a service all forgot ere long.
Then his own steed he also led forth upon the shore.
Such menial service had he full seldom done before,
That he should hold the stirrup for monarch whomsoe'er.
Down gazing from the casements beheld it ladies high and fair.
At every point according, the heroes well bedight
—Their dress and eke their chargers of color snowy white—
Were like unto each other, and well-wrought shield each one
Of the good knights bore with him, that brightly glimmered in the sun.
Jewelled well was saddle and narrow martingale
As they rode so stately in front of Brunhild's Hall,
And thereon bells were hanging of red gold shining bright.
So came they to that country, as fitting was for men of might,
With spears all newly polished, with swords, well-made that were
And by the stately heroes hung down unto the spur:
Such bore the valiant riders of broad and cutting blade.
The noble show did witness Brunhild the full stately maid.

With him came then Dankwart and Hagen, doughty thane.
The story further telleth how that the heroes twain
Of color black as raven rich attire wore,
And each a broad and mighty shield of rich adornment bore.
Rich stones from India's country every eye could see,
Impending on their tunics, sparkle full brilliantly.
Their vessel by the river they left without a guard,
As thus the valiant heroes rode undaunted castleward.
Six and fourscore towers without they saw rise tall,
Three spacious palaces and moulded well a hall
All wrought of precious marble green as blade of grass,
Wherein the royal Brunhild with company of fair ladies was.
The castle doors unbolted were flung open wide
As out toward them the men of Brunhild hied
And received the strangers into their Lady's land.
Their steeds they bade take over, and also shield from out the hand.
Then spake a man-in-waiting: "Give o'er the sword each thane,
And eke the shining armor."— "Good friend, thou ask'st in vain,"
Spake of Tronje Hagen; "the same we'd rather wear."
Then gan straightway Siegfried the country's custom to declare.
"'Tis wont within this castle, —of that be now aware—
That never any stranger weapons here shall bear.
Now let them hence be carried: well dost thou as I say."
In this did full unwilling Hagen, Gunther's man, obey.
They bade the strangers welcome with drink and fitting rest.
Soon might you see on all sides full many knights the best
In princely weeds apparelled to their reception go:
Yet did they mickle gazing who would the keen new-comers know.
Then unto Lady Brunhild the tidings strange were brought
How that unknown warriors now her land had sought,
In stately apparel come sailing o'er the sea.
The maiden fair and stately gave question how the same might be.
"Now shall ye straight inform me," spake she presently,
"Who so unfamiliar these warrior knights may be,
That within my castle thus so lordly stand,
And for whose sake the heroes have hither journeyed to my land."
Then spake to her a servant: "Lady, I well can say
Of them I've ne'er seen any before this present day:
Be it not that one among them is like unto Siegfried.
Him give a goodly welcome: so is to thee my loyal rede.
"The next of the companions he is a worthy knight:
If that were in his power he well were king of might
O'er wide domains of princes, the which might reach his hand.
Now see him by the others so right majestically stand.
"The third of the companions, that he's a man of spleen,
—Withal of fair-formed body, know thou, stately Queen,—
Do tell his rapid glances that dart so free from him.

He is in all his thinking a man, I ween, of mood full grim.
"The youngest one among them he is a worthy knight:
As modest as a maiden, I see the thane of might
Goodly in his bearing standing so fair to see,
We all might fear if any affront to him should offered be.
"How blithe soe'er his manner, how fair soe'er is he,
Well could he cause of sorrow to stately woman be,
If he gan show his anger. In him may well be seen
He is in knightly virtues a thane of valor bold and keen."
Then spake the queen in answer: "Bring now my robes to hand.
And is the mighty Siegfried come unto this land,
For love of me brought thither, he pays it with his life.
I fear him not so sorely that I e'er become his wife."
So was fair Brunhild straightway well arrayed.
Then went with her thither full many a beauteous maid,
A hundred good or over, bedight right merrily.
The full beauteous maidens would those stranger warriors see.
And with them went the warriors there of Isenland,
The knights attending Brunhild, who bore sword in hand,
Five hundred men or over. Scarce heart the strangers kept
As those knights brave and seemly down from out the saddle leapt.
When the royal lady Siegfried espied,
Now mote ye willing listen what there the maiden said.
"Welcome be thou, Siegfried, hither unto this land.
What meaneth this thy journey, gladly might I understand."
"Full mickle do I thank thee, my Lady, high Brunhild,
That thou art pleased to greet me, noble Princess mild,
Before this knight so noble, who stands before me here:
For he is my master, whom first to honor fitting were.
"Born is he of Rhineland: what need I say more?
For thee 'tis highest favor that we do hither fare.
Thee will he gladly marry, an bring that whatsoe'er.
Betimes shalt thou bethink thee: my master will thee never spare.
"For his name is Gunther and he a mighty king.
If he thy love hath won him, more wants he not a thing.
In sooth the king so noble hath bade me hither fare:
And gladly had I left it, might I to thwart his wishes dare."
She spake: "Is he thy master and thou his vassal art,
Some games to him I offer, and dare he there take part,
And comes he forth the victor, so am I then his wife:
And be it I that conquer, then shall ye forfeit each his life."
Then spake of Tronje Hagen: "Lady, let us see
Thy games so fraught with peril. Before should yield to thee
Gunther my master, that well were something rare.
He trows he yet is able to win a maid so passing fair."
"Then shall ye try stone-putting and follow up the cast,
And the spear hurl with me. Do ye naught here in haste.

For well may ye pay forfeit with honor eke and life:
Bethink ye thus full calmly," spake she whom Gunther would for wife.
Siegfried the valiant stepped unto the king,
And bade him speak out freely his thoughts upon this thing
Unto the queen so wayward, he might have fearless heart.
"For to well protect thee from her do I know an art."
Then spake the royal Gunther: "Now offer, stately Queen,
What play soe'er thou mayest. And harder had it been,
Yet would I all have ventured for all thy beauty's sake.
My head I'll willing forfeit or thyself my wife I'll make."
When therefore the Queen Brunhild heard how the matter stood
The play she begged to hasten, as indeed she should.
She bade her servants fetch her therefor apparel trim,
A mail-coat ruddy golden and shield well wrought from boss to rim.
A battle-tunic silken the maid upon her drew,
That in ne'er a contest weapon piercéd through,
Of skins from land of Libya, and structure rare and fine;
And brilliant bands embroidered might you see upon it shine.
Meanwhile were the strangers jibed with many a threat;
Dankwart and Hagen, their hearts began to beat.
How here the king should prosper were they of doubtful mood,
Thinking, "This our journey shall bring us wanderers naught of good."
Ie did also Siegfried the thane beyond compare,
Before 'twas marked by any, unto the ship repair,
Where he found his sightless mantle that did hidden lie,
And slipped into 't full deftly: so was he veiled from every eye.
Thither back he hied him and found great company
About the queen who ordered what the high play should be.
There went he all in secret; so cunningly 'twas done,
Of all around were standing perceived him never any one.
The ring it was appointed wherein the play should be
'Fore many a keen warrior who the same should see.
More than seven hundred were seen their weapons bear,
That whoso were the victor they might sure the same declare.
Thither was come Brunhild; all arméd she did stand
Like as she were to combat for many a royal land;
Upon her silken tunic were gold bars many a one,
And glowing 'mid the armor her flesh of winsome color shone.
Then followed her attendants and with them thither brought
At once a shield full stately, of pure red gold 'twas wrought,
With steel-hard bands for facings, full mickle 'twas and broad,
Wherewith in the contest would guard herself the lovely maid.
To hold the shield securely a well-wrought band there was,
Whereon lay precious jewels green as blade of grass.
Full many a ray their lustre shot round against the gold.
He were a man full valiant whom this high dame should worthy hold.
The shield was 'neath the boss-point, as to us is said,

Good three spans in thickness, which should bear the maid.
Of steel 'twas wrought so richly and had of gold such share,
That chamberlain and fellows three the same scarce could bear.
When the doughty Hagen the shield saw thither brought,
Spake the knight of Tronje, and savage was his thought:
"Where art thou now, King Gunther? Shall we thus lose our life!
Whom here thou seekst for lover, she is the very Devil's wife."
List more of her apparel; she had a goodly store.
Of silk of Azagang a tunic made she wore,
All bedight full richly; amid its color shone
Forth from the queen it covered, full many a sparkling precious stone.
Then brought they for the lady, large and heavy there,
As she was wont to hurl it, a sharply-pointed spear;
Strong and massive was it, huge and broad as well,
And at both its edges it cut with devastation fell.
To know the spear was heavy list ye wonders more:
Three spears of common measure 'twould make, and something o'er.
Of Brunhild's attendants three scarce the same could bear.
The heart of noble Gunther thereat began to fill with fear.
Within his soul he thought him: "What pickle am I in?
Of hell the very Devil, how might he save his skin?
Might I at home in Burgundy safe and living be,
Should she for many a season from proffered love of mine be free."
Then spake Hagen's brother the valiant Dankwart:
"In truth this royal journey doth sorely grieve my heart.
We passed for good knights one time: what caitiff's death, if we
Here in far-off country a woman's game are doomed to be!
"It rueth me full sorely that I came to this land.
And had my brother Hagen his good sword in hand,
And had I mine to help him, a bit more gently then,
A little tame of spirit, might show themselves all Brunhild's men.
"And know it of a certain to lord it thus they'd cease;
E'en though oaths a thousand I'd sworn to keep the peace,
Before that I'd see perish my dear lord shamefully,
Amid the souls departed this fair maid herself should be."
"Well should we unhampered quit at last this land,"
Spake his brother Hagen, "did we in armor stand,
Such as we need for battle, and bore we broadswords good:
'Twould be a little softened, this doughty lady's haughty mood."
Well heard the noble maiden what the warriors spoke.
Back athwart her shoulder she sent a smiling look:
"Now thinks he him so valiant, so let them arméd stand;
Their full keen-edged broadswords give the warriors each in hand."
When they their swords received, as the maiden said,
The full valiant Dankwart with joy his face grew red.
"Now play they what them pleaseth," cried the warrior brave;
"Gunther is yet a freeman, since now in hand good swords we have."

The royal Brunhild's prowess with terror was it shown.
Into the ring they bore her in sooth a ponderous stone,
Great and all unwieldy, huge it was and round:
And scarce good knights a dozen together raised it from the ground.
To put this was her custom after trial with the spear.
Thereat the men of Burgundy began to quake with fear.
"Alack! Alack!" quoth Hagen, "what seeks the king for bride?
Beneath in hell 'twere better the Devil had her by his side!"
On her white arms the flowing sleeves she backward flung,
Then with grasp of power the shield in hand she swung,
And spear poised high above her. So did the contest start.
Gunther and Siegfried saw Brunhild's ire with falling heart.
And were it not that Siegfried a ready help did bring,
Surely then had perished beneath her hand the king.
There went he unperceived and the king's hand did touch.
Gunther at his cunning artifice was troubled much.
"What is that hath touched me?" thought the monarch keen.
Then gazed he all around him: none was there to be seen.
A voice spake: "Siegfried is it, a friend that holds thee dear.
Before this royal maiden shall thy heart be free from fear.
"Thy shield in hand now give me and leave it me to bear,
And do thou rightly mark thee what thou now shalt hear.
Now make thyself the motions, —the power leave to me."
When he did know him rightly, the monarch's heart was filled with glee.
"Now secret keep my cunning, let none e'er know the same:
Then shall the royal maiden here find but little game
Of glory to win from thee, as most to her is dear.
Behold now how the lady stands before thee void of fear."
The spear the stately maiden with might and main did wield,
And huge and broad she hurled it upon the new-made shield,
That on his arm did carry the son of Siegelind;
From the steel the sparks flew hissing as if were blowing fierce the wind.
The mighty spear sharp-pointed full through the shield did crash,
That ye from off the mail-rings might see the lightning flash.
Beneath its force they stumbled, did both those men of might;
But for the sightless mantle they both were killed there outright.
From mouth of the full doughty Siegfried burst the blood.
Full soon he yet recovered; then seized the warrior good
The spear that from her strong arm thus his shield had rent,
And back with force as came it the hand of doughty Siegfried sent.
He thought: "To pierce the maiden were but small glory earned,"
And so the spear's sharp edges backward pointing turned;
Against her mail-clad body he made the shaft to bound,
And with such might he sent it full loud her armor did resound.
The sparks as if in stormwind from mail-rings flew around.
So mightily did hurl it the son of Siegmund
That she with all her power could not the shaft withstand.

In sooth it ne'er was speeded so swiftly by King Gunther's hand.
But to her feet full sudden had sprung Brunhild fair.
"A shot, O noble Gunther, befitting hero rare."
She weened himself had done it, and all unaided he,
Nor wot she one far mightier was thither come so secretly.
Then did she go full sudden, wrathful was her mood,
A stone full high she heaved the noble maiden good,
And the same far from her with might and main she swung:
Her armor's mail-rings jingled as she herself thereafter sprung.
The stone, when it had fallen, lay fathoms twelve from there,
And yet did spring beyond it herself the maiden fair.
Then where the stone was lying thither Siegfried went:
Gunther feigned to move it, but by another arm 'twas sent.
A valiant man was Siegfried full powerful and tall.
The stone then cast he farther, and farther sprang withal.
From those his arts so cunning had he of strength such store
That as he leaped he likewise the weight of royal Gunther bore.
And when the leap was ended and fallen was the stone,
Then saw they ne'er another but Gunther alone.
Brunhild the fair maiden, red grew she in wrath:
Siegfried yet had warded from royal Gunther surest death.
Unto her attendants she spake in loud command,
When she saw 'cross the circle the king unvanquished stand.
"Come hither quick, my kinsmen, and ye that wait on me;
Henceforth unto Gunther shall all be pledged faithfully."
Then laid the knights full valiant their swords from out the hand;
At feet 'fore mighty Gunther from Burgundian land
Offered himself in service full many a valiant knight.
They weened that he had conquered in trial by his proper might.
He gave her loving greeting, right courteous was he.
Then by the hand she took him, the maiden praiseworthy,
In pledge that all around him was his to have and hold.
Whereat rejoiced Hagen the warrior valorous and bold.
Into the spacious palace with her thence to go
Bade she the noble monarch. When they had done so,
Then still greater honors unto the knight were shown.
Dankwart and Hagen, right willingly they saw it done.
Siegfried the valiant, by no means was he slow,
His sightless mantle did he away in safety stow.
Then went he again thither where many a lady sat.
He spake unto the monarch— full cunningly was done all that:
"Why bidest thus, my master? Wilt not the play begin,
To which so oft hath challenged thee the noble queen?
Let us soon have example what may the trial be."
As knew he naught about it, did the knight thus cunningly.
Then spake the queen unto him: "How hath this ever been,
That of the play, Sir Siegfried, nothing thou hast seen,

Wherein hath been the victor Gunther with mighty hand?"
Thereto gave answer Hagen a grim knight of Burgundian land.
Spake he: "There dost thou, Lady, think ill without a cause:
By the ship down yonder the noble Siegfried was,
The while the lord of Rhineland in play did vanquish thee:
Thus knows he nothing of it," spake Gunther's warrior courteously.
"A joy to me these tidings," the doughty Siegfried spoke,
"That so thy haughty spirit is brought beneath the yoke,
And that yet one there liveth master to be of thine.
Now shalt thou, noble maiden, us follow thither to the Rhine."
Then spake the maiden shapely: "It may not yet be so.
All my men and kindred first the same must know.
In sooth not all so lightly can I quit my home.
First must I bid my trusty warriors that they hither come."
Then bade she messengers quickly forth to ride,
And summoned in her kindred and men from every side.
Without delay she prayed them to come to Isenstein,
And bade them all be given fit apparel rare and fine.
Then might ye see daily 'twixt morn and eventide
Unto Brunhild's castle many a knight to ride.
"God wot, God wot," quoth Hagen, "we do an evil thing,
To tarry here while Brunhild doth thus her men together bring.
"If now into this country their good men they've brought
—What thing the queen intendeth thereof know we naught:
Belike her wrath ariseth, and we are men forlorn—
Then to be our ruin were the noble maiden born."
Then spake the doughty Siegfried: "That matter leave to me.
Whereof thou now art fearful, I'll never let it be.
Ready help I'll bring thee hither unto this land,
Knights of whom thou wotst not till now I'll bring, a chosen band.
"Of me shalt thou ask not: from hence will I fare.
May God of thy good honor meanwhile have a care.
I come again right quickly with a thousand men for thee,
The very best of warriors hitherto are known to me."
"Then tarry not unduly," thus the monarch said.
"Glad we are full fairly of this thy timely aid."
He spake: "Till I come to thee full short shall be my stay.
That thou thyself hast sent me shalt thou unto Brunhild say."

EIGHTH ADVENTURE

How Siegfried fared to his Knights, the Nibelungen

Thence went then Siegfried out through the castle door
In his sightless mantle to a boat upon the shore.
As Siegmund's son doth board it him no mortal sees;

And quickly off he steers it as were it wafted by the breeze.
No one saw the boatman, yet rapid was the flight
Of the boat forth speeding driven by Siegfried's might.
They weened that did speed it a swiftly blowing wind:
No, 'twas Siegfried sped it, the son of fairest Siegelind.
In that one day-time and the following night
Came he to a country by dint of mickle might,
Long miles a hundred distant, and something more than this:
The Nibelungen were its people where the mighty hoard was his.
Alone did fare the hero unto an island vast
Whereon the boat full quickly the gallant knight made fast.
Of a castle then bethought him high upon a hill,
And there a lodging sought him, as wayworn men are wont to still.
Then came he to the portals that locked before him stood.
They guarded well their honor as people ever should.
At the door he gan a-knocking, for all unknown was he.
But full well 'twas guarded, and within it he did see
A giant who the castle did guard with watchful eye,
And near him did at all times his good weapons lie.
Quoth he: "Who now that knocketh at the door in such strange wise?"
Without the valiant Siegfried did cunningly his voice disguise.
He spake: "A bold knight-errant am I; unlock the gate.
Else will I from without here disturbance rare create
For all who'd fain lie quiet and their rest would take."
Wrathful grew the Porter as in this wise Siegfried spake.
Now did the giant valorous his good armor don,
And placed on head his helmet; then the full doughty man
His shield up-snatched quickly and gate wide open swung.
How sore was he enraged as himself upon Siegfried he flung!
'How dared he thus awaken brave knights within the hall?'
The blows in rapid showers from his hand did fall.
Thereat the noble stranger began himself to shield.
For so a club of iron the Porter's mighty arm did wield,
That splinters flew from buckler, and Siegfried stood aghast
From fear that this same hour was doomed to be his last,
So mightily the Porter's blows about him fell.
To find such faithful warder did please his master Siegfried well.
So fiercely did they struggle that castle far within
And hall where slept the Nibelungen echoed back the din.
But Siegfried pressed the Porter and soon he had him bound.
In all the land of Nibelungen the story soon was bruited round.
When the grim sound of fighting afar the place had filled,
Alberich did hear it, a Dwarf full brave and wild.
He donned his armor deftly, and running thither found
This so noble stranger where he the doughty Porter bound.
Alberich was full wrathy, thereto a man of power.
Coat of mail and helmet he on his body wore,

And in his hand a heavy scourge of gold he swung.
Where was fighting Siegfried, thither in mickle haste he sprung.
Seven knobs thick and heavy on the club's end were seen,
Wherewith the shield that guarded the knight that was so keen
He battered with such vigor that pieces from it brake.
Lest he his life should forfeit the noble stranger gan to quake.
The shield that all was battered from his hand he flung;
And into sheath, too, thrust he his sword so good and long.
For his trusty chamberlain he did not wish to slay,
And in such case he could not grant his anger fullest sway.
With but his hands so mighty at Alberich he ran.
By the beard then seized he the gray and aged man,
And in such manner pulled it that he full loud did roar.
The youthful hero's conduct Alberich did trouble sore.
Loud cried the valiant steward: "Have mercy now on me.
And might I other's vassal than one good hero's be,
To whom to be good subject I an oath did take,
Until my death I'd serve thee." Thus the man of cunning spake.
Alberich then bound he   as the giant before.
The mighty arm of Siegfried did trouble him full sore.
The Dwarf began to question: "Thy name, what may it be?"
Quoth he: "My name is Siegfried; I weened I well were known to thee."
"I joy to hear such tidings," Dwarf Alberich replied.
"Well now have I found thee in knightly prowess tried,
And with goodly reason lord o'er lands to be.
I'll do whate'er thou biddest, wilt thou only give me free."
Then spake his master Siegfried: "Quickly shalt thou go,
And bring me knights hither, the best we have to show,
A thousand Nibelungen, to stand before their lord."
Wherefore thus he wished it, spake he never yet a word.
The giant and Alberich straightway he unbound.
Then ran Alberich quickly where the knights he found.
The warriors of Nibelung he wakened full of fear.
Quoth he: "Be up, ye heroes, before Siegfried shall ye appear."
From their couches sprang they and ready were full soon,
Clothed well in armor a thousand warriors boon,
And went where they found standing Siegfried their lord.
Then was a mickle greeting courteously in act and word.
Candles many were lighted, and sparkling wine he drank.
That they came so quickly, therefor he all did thank.
Quoth he: "Now shall ye with me from hence across the flood."
Thereto he found full ready the heroes valiant and good.
Good thirty hundred warriors soon had hither pressed,
From whom were then a thousand taken of the best.
For them were brought their helmets and what they else did need.
For unto Brunhild's country would he straightway the warriors lead.
He spake: "Ye goodly nobles, that would I have you hear,

In full costly raiment shall ye at court appear,
For yonder must there see us full many a fair lady.
Therefore shall your bodies dight in good apparel be."
Upon a morning early went they on their way.
What host of brave companions bore Siegfried company!
Good steeds took they with them and garments rich to wear,
And did in courtly fashion unto Brunhild's country fare.
As gazed from lofty parapet women fair to see,
Spake the queen unto them: "Knows any who they be,
Whom I see yonder sailing upon the sea afar?
Rich sails their ships do carry, whiter than snow they are."
Then spake the king of Rhineland: "My good men they are,
That on my journey hither left I lying near.
I've sent to call them to me: now are they come, O Queen."
With full great amazing were the stately strangers seen.
There saw they Siegfried out on the ship's prow stand
Clad in costly raiment, and with him his good band.
Then spake Queen Brunhild: "Good monarch, let me know,
Shall I go forth to greet them, or shall I greetings high forego?"
He spake: "Thou shalt to meet them   before the palace go,
So that we see them gladly they may surely know."
Then did the royal lady fulfil the king's behest.
Yet Siegfried in the greeting was not honored with the rest.
Lodgings were made ready and their armor ta'en in hand.
Then was such host of strangers come into that land,
On all sides they jostled from the great company.
Then would the knights full valiant homeward fare to Burgundy.
Then spake Queen Brunhild: "In favor would I hold
Who might now apportion my silver and my gold
To my guests and the monarch's, for goodly store I have."
Thereto an answer Dankwart, Giselher's good warrior, gave:
"Full noble royal Lady, give me the keys to hold.
I trow I'll so divide it," spake the warrior bold,
"If blame there be about it, that shall be mine alone."
That he was not a niggard, beyond a doubt he soon had shown.
When now Hagen's brother   the treasure did command,
So many a lavish bounty   ealt out the hero's hand,
Whoso mark did covet, to him was given such store
That all who once were poor men might joyous live for evermore.
In sooth good pounds a hundred gave he to each and all.
A host in costly raiment were seen before the hall,
Who in equal splendor ne'er before were clad.
When the queen did hear it, verily her heart was sad.
Then spake the royal lady: "Good King, it little needs,
That now thy chamberlain of all my stately weeds
Leave no whit remaining, and squander clean my gold.
Would any yet prevent it, him would I aye in favor hold.

"He deals with hand so lavish, in sooth doth ween the thane
That death I've hither summoned; but longer I'll remain.
Eke trow I well to spend all my sire hath left to me."
Ne'er found queen a chamberlain of such passing generosity.
Then spake of Tronje Hagen: "Lady, be thou told,
That the king of Rhineland raiment hath and gold
So plenteous to lavish that we may well forego
To carry with us homeward aught that Brunhild can bestow."
"No; as high ye hold me," spake the queen again,
"Let me now have filled coffers twice times ten
Of gold and silken raiment, that may deal out my hand,
When that we come over into royal Gunther's land."
Then with precious jewels the coffers they filled for her.
The while her own chamberlain must be standing near:
For no whit would she trust it unto Giselher's man.
Whereat Gunther and Hagen heartily to laugh began.
Then spake the royal lady: "To whom leave I my lands?
First must they now be given in charge from out our hands."
Then spake the noble monarch: "Whomsoe'er it pleaseth thee,
Bid him now come hither, the same we'll let our Warden be."
One of her highest kindred near by the lady spied,
—He was her mother's brother— to him thus spake the maid:
"Now be to thee entrusted the castles and eke the land,
Until that here shall govern Gunther the king by his own hand."
Trusty knights two thousand from her company
Chose she to journey with her unto Burgundy,
Beyond those thousand warriors from Nibelungenland.
They made ready for the journey, and downward rode unto the strand.
Six and eighty ladies led they thence with her,
Thereto good hundred maidens that full beauteous were.
They tarried no whit longer, for they to part were fain.
Of those they left behind them, O how they all to weep began!
In high befitting fashion quitted she her land:
She kissed of nearest kindred all who round did stand.
After fair leave-taking they went upon the sea.
Back to her father's country came never more that fair lady.
Then heard you on the journey many a kind of play:
Every pleasant pastime in plenty had they.
Soon had they for their journey a wind from proper art:
So with full great rejoicing did they from that land depart.
Yet would she on the journey not be the monarch's spouse:
But was their pleasant pastime reserved for his own house
At Worms within his castle at a high festival,
Whither anon full joyous came they with their warriors all.

NINTH ADVENTURE

How Siegfried was sent to Worms

When that they had journeyed full nine days on their way,
Then spake of Tronje Hagen: "Now hear what I shall say.
We tarry with the tidings for Worms upon the Rhine.
At Burgundy already should now be messengers of thine."
Then outspake King Gunther: "There hast thou spoken true.
And this selfsame journey, none were so fit thereto
As thyself, friend Hagen. So do thou now ride on.
This our high court journey, none else can better make it known."
Thereto answered Hagen: "Poor messenger am I.
Let me be treasure-warden. Upon the ships I'll stay
Near by the women rather, their guardian to be,
Till that we bring them safely into the land of Burgundy.
"Now do thou pray Siegfried that he the message bear,
For he's a knight most fitting this thing to have in care.
If he decline the journey, then shalt thou courteously,
For kindness to thy sister, pray that he not unwilling be."
He sent for the good warrior who came at his command.
He spake: "Since we are nearing home in my own land,
So should I send a message to sister dear of mine
And eke unto my mother, that we are nigh unto the Rhine.
"Thereto I pray thee, Siegfried, now meet my wish aright,"
Spake the noble monarch: "I'll ever thee requite."
But Siegfried still refused it, the full valiant man,
Till that King Gunther sorely to beseech began.
He spake: "Now bear the message, in favor unto me
And eke unto Kriemhild a maiden fair to see,
That the stately maiden help me thy service pay."
When had heard it Siegfried, ready was the knight straightway.
"Now what thou wilt, command me: 'twill not be long delayed.
This thing will I do gladly for sake of that fair maid.
Why should I aught refuse her, who all my heart hath won?
What thou for her commandest, whate'er it be 'twill all be done."
"Then say unto my mother, Ute the queen,
That we on our journey in joyous mood have been.
Let know likewise my brothers what fortune us befell.
Eke unto all our kinsmen shalt thou then merry tidings tell.
"Unto my fair sister shalt thou all confide.
From me bring her fair compliment and from Brunhild beside,
And eke unto our household and all my warriors brave.
What my heart e'er did strive for, how well accomplished it I have!
"And say as well to Ortwein nephew dear of mine
That he do bid make ready at Worms beside the Rhine.
And all my other kindred, to them made known shall be,

With Brunhild I am minded to keep a great festivity.
"And say unto my sister, when that she hath learned
That I am to my country with many a guest returned,
She shall have care to welcome my bride in fitting way.
So all my thoughts of Kriemhild will be her service to repay."
Then did Sir Siegfried straightway in parting greet
High the Lady Brunhild, as 'twas very meet,
And all her company; then toward the Rhine rode he.
Nor in this world a better messenger might ever be.
With four and twenty warriors to Worms did he ride.
When soon it was reported the king came not beside,
Then did all the household of direst news have dread:
They feared their royal master were left in distant country dead.
Then sprang they from the saddle, full high they were of mood.
Full soon before them Giselher the prince so youthful stood,
And Gernot his brother. How quickly then spake he,
When he the royal Gunther saw not in Siegfried's company:
"Be thou welcome, Siegfried. Yet shalt thou tell to me,
Why the king my brother cometh not with thee.
Brunhild's prowess is it hath taken him, I ween;
And so this lofty wooing hath naught but our misfortune been."
"Now cease such ill foreboding. To you and friends hath sent
My royal companion his good compliment.
Safe and sound I left him; myself did he command
That I should be his herald with tidings hither to your land.
"Quickly shall ye see to it, how that it may be,
That I the queen and likewise your fair sister see.
From Gunther and Brunhild the message will I tell
That hath now been sent them: the twain do find them passing well."
Then spake the youthful Giselher: "So shalt thou go to her:
Here dost thou on my sister a favor high confer.
In sooth she's mickle anxious how't with my brother be.
The maid doth see thee gladly, —of that will I be surety."
Then outspake Sir Siegfried: "If serve her aught I can,
That same thing most willing in truth it shall be done.
Who now will tell the ladies I would with them confer?"
Then was therein Giselher the stately knight his messenger.
Giselher the valiant unto his mother kind
And sister spake the tidings when he the twain did find:
"To us returned is Siegfried, the hero of Netherlands
Unto the Rhine he cometh at my brother Gunther's command.
"He bringeth us the tidings how't with the king doth fare.
Now shall ye give permission that he 'fore you appear.
He'll tell the proper tidings from Isenland o'er the main."
Yet mickle sad forebodings did trouble still the ladies twain.
They sprang for their attire and donned it nothing slow.
Then bade they that Siegfried o court should thither go.

That did he right willing for he gladly them did see.
Kriemhild the noble maiden spake to him thus graciously.
"Welcome be, Sir Siegfried, thou knight right praiseworthy.
Yet where may King Gunther my noble brother be?
It is through Brunhild's prowess, I ween, he is forlorn.
Alack of me, poor maiden, that I into this world was born!"
The valiant knight then answered: "Give me news-bringer's meed
Know ye, fairest ladies, ye weep without a need.
I left him well and happy, that would I have you know;
They two have sent me hither to bear the tidings unto you.
"And offer thee good service both his bride and he,
My full noble lady, in love and loyalty.
Now give over weeping, for straight will they be here."
They had for many a season heard not a tale to them so dear.
With fold of snow-white garment then her eyes so bright
Dried she after weeping. She gan thank the knight
Who of these glad tidings had been the messenger.
Then was a mickle sorrow and cause of weeping ta'en from her.
She bade the knight be seated, which he did willingly.
Then spake the lovely maiden: "It were a joy to me,
Could I the message-bringer with gold of mine repay.
Thereto art thou too high-born; I'll serve thee then in other way."
"If I alone were ruler," spake he, "o'er thirty lands,
Yet gifts I'd take right gladly, came they from thy fair hands."
Then spake the virtuous maiden: "In truth it shall be so."
Then bade she her chamberlain forth for message-money go.
Four and twenty armlets with stones of precious kind,
These gave she him for guerdon. 'Twas not the hero's mind,
That he himself should keep them: he dealt them all around
Unto her fair attendants whom he within the chamber found.
Of service, too, her mother did kindly offer make.
"Then have I more to tell you," the keen warrior spake:
"Of what the king doth beg you, when comes he to the Rhine.
Wilt thou perform it, lady, then will he e'er to thee incline.
"The noble guests he bringeth, —this heard I him request,
That ye shall well receive them; and furthermore his hest,
That ye ride forth to meet him 'fore Worms upon the strand.
So have ye from the monarch faithfully his high command."
Then spake the lovely maiden: "Full ready there am I.
If I in aught can serve him, I'll never that deny.
In all good faith and kindness shall it e'er be done."
Then deeper grew her color that from increase of joy she won.
Never was royal message better received before.
The lady sheer had kissed him, if 'twere a thing to dare.
From those high ladies took he his leave in courteous wise.
Then did they there in Burgundy in way as Siegfried did advise.
Sindold and Hunold and Rumold the thane

In truth were nothing idle, but wrought with might and main
To raise the sitting-places 'fore Worms upon the strand.
There did the royal Steward busy 'mid the workers stand.
Ortwein and Gere thought longer not to bide,
But sent unto their kinsmen forth on every side.
They told of festive meeting there that was to be;
And deck themselves to meet them did the maidens fair to see.
The walls throughout the palace were dight full richly all,
Looking unto the strangers; and King Gunther's hall
Full well with seats and tables for many a noble guest.
And great was the rejoicing in prospect of the mighty feast.
Then rode from every quarter hither through the land
The three monarchs' kinsmen, who there were called to hand,
That they might be in waiting for those expected there.
Then from enfolding covers took they store of raiments rare.
Some watchers brought the tidings that Brunhild's followers were
Seen coming riding hither. Then rose a mickle stir
Among the folk so many in the land of Burgundy.
Heigh-ho! What valiant warriors alike on both parts might you see!
Then spake the fair Kriemhild: "Of my good maidens, ye
Who at this reception shall bear me company,
From out the chests now seek ye attire the very best.
So shall praise and honor be ours from many a noble guest."
Then came the knights also and bade bring forth to view
The saddles richly furnished of ruddy golden hue,
That ladies fair should ride on at Worms unto the Rhine.
Better horse-equipment could never artisan design.
Heigh-ho! What gold all glancing from the steeds there shone!
Sparkled from their bridles full many a precious stone.
Gold-wrought stools for mounting and shining carpets good
Brought they for the ladies: joyous were they all of mood.
Within the court the heroes bedight with trappings due
Awaited noble maidens, as I have told to you.
A narrow band from saddle went round each horse's breast,
Its beauty none could tell you: of silk it was the very best.
Six and eighty ladies came in manner meet
Wearing each a wimple. Kriemhild there to greet
They went, all fair to look on, in shining garments clad.
Then came eke well apparelled full many a fair and stately maid.
Four and fifty were they of the land of Burgundy,
And they were eke the noblest that ever you might see.
Adorned with shining hair-bands the fair-haired maids came on.
What now the king desired, that most carefully was done.
Made of stuffs all costly, the best you might desire,
Before the gallant strangers wore they such rich attire
As well did fit the beauty of many amid the throng.
He sure had lost his senses, who could have wished them any wrong.

Of sable and of ermine many a dress was worn.
Arms and hands a many did they full well adorn
With rings o'er silken dresses that there did clothe them well.
Of all the ready-making none might ever fully tell.
Full many a well-wrought girdle in long and costly braid
About the shining garments by many a hand was laid
On dress of precious ferrandine of silk from Araby.
And full of high rejoicing were those maids of high degree.
With clasps before her bosom was many a fair maid
Laced full beauteously. She might well be sad,
Whose full beaming color vied not with weeds she wore.
Such a stately company ne'er possessed a queen before.
When now the lovely maidens attired you might see,
Soon were those beside them should bear them company,
Of warriors high-hearted a full mickle band.
And with their shields they carried full many an ashen shaft in hand.

TENTH ADVENTURE

How Brunhild was received at Worms

On yonder side Rhine river they saw a stately band,
The king and host of strangers, ride down unto the strand,
And also many a lady sitting on charger led.
By those who should receive them was goodly preparation made.
Soon they of Isenland the ship had entered then,
And with them Siegfried's vassals the Nibelungen men;
They strained unto the shore with untiring hand
When they beheld the monarch's friends upon the farther strand.
Now list ye eke the story of the stately queen,
Ute, how at her bidding ladies fair were seen
Forth coming from the castle to ride her company.
Then came to know each other full many a knight and fair lady.
The Margrave Gere but to the castle gate
The bridle held for Kriemhild; the keen Siegfried did wait
Thenceforward upon her. She was a beauteous maid.
Well was the knight's good service by the lady since repaid.
Ortwein the valiant Queen Ute rode beside,
And many a knight full gallant was stately lady's guide.
At such a high reception, that may we say, I ween,
Was ne'er such host of ladies in company together seen.
With show of rider's talent the tilt was carried on,
For might the knights full gallant naught fitting leave undone,
As passed down to the river Kriemhild the lady bright.
Then helped was many a lady fair from charger to alight.
The king had then come over and many a stranger too.

Heigh-ho! What strong shafts splintered before the ladies flew!
Many a shaft go crashing heard you there on shield.
Heigh-ho! What din of costly arms resounded o'er the field.
The full lovely maidens upon the shore did stand,
As Gunther with the strangers stepped upon the land;
He himself did Brunhild by the hand lead on.
Then sparkled towards each other rich dress and many a shining stone.
Then went Lady Kriemhild with fullest courtesy due,
To greet the Lady Brunhild and her retinue.
And saw ye each the head-band with fair hand move aside
When they kissed each other: high courtesy did the ladies guide.
Then spake the maiden Kriemhild, a high-born lady she:
"Unto this our country shalt thou right welcome be,
To me and to my mother and each true friend of mine,
That we here have with us." Then each did unto each incline.
Within their arms the ladies oft-times clasped each other.
Like this fond reception heard ye of ne'er another,
As when both the ladies there the bride did greet,
Queen Ute and her daughter; oft-times they kissed her lips so sweet.
When all of Brunhild's ladies were come upon the strand,
Then was there taken full fondly by the hand
By the warriors stately many a fair lady.
Before the Lady Brunhild the train of fair maids might ye see.
Before their greetings ended a mickle time was gone,
For lips of rosy color were kissed there, many a one.
Long stood they together, the royal ladies high,
And so to look upon them pleased many a noble warrior's eye.
Then spied with probing eye, too, who before did hear
That till then was never aught beheld so fair,
As those two royal ladies: they found it was no lie.
In all their person might ye no manner of deceit espy.
Who there could spy fair ladies and judge of beauty rare,
They praised the wife of Gunther that she was passing fair;
Yet spake again the wise men who looked with keener gaze,
They rather would to Kriemhild before Brunhild award the praise.
Then went unto each other maid and fair lady.
Full many a fair one might ye in rich adornment see.
There stood rich tents a many, silken great and small,
Wherewith in every quarter 'fore Worms the field was covered all.
Of the king's high kindred a mighty press there was.
Then bade they Brunhild and Kriemhild on to pass,
And with them all the ladies, where they in shade might be.
Thither did bring them warriors of the land of Burgundy.
When now the strangers also on horse sat every one,
Plenteous knightly tilting at shield was there begun.
Above the field rose dust-clouds, as had the country been
All in flames a-burning; who bore the honors there was seen.

Looked on full many a maiden as the knights did sport them so.
Meseemeth that Sir Siegfried full many a to-and-fro
Did ride with his good followers along 'fore many a tent.
With him of Nibelungen a thousand stately men there went.
Then came of Tronje Hagen, whom the king did send;
He bade in pleasing manner the tourney have an end,
Before in dust be buried all the ladies fair.
And ready to obey him soon the courteous strangers were.
Then spake Sir Gernot: "Now let the chargers stand,
Until the air is cooler, for we must be at hand
As escort for fair ladies unto the stately hall;
And will the king take saddle, so let him find you ready all."
When now the sound of tourney o'er all the field was spent,
Then went for pleasant pastime 'neath many a lofty tent
The knights unto the ladies, and willing thither hied.
And there they passed the hours till such time as they thence should ride.
Just before the evening when the sun was in the west,
And the air grew cooler, no longer did they rest,
But both knights and ladies unto the castle passed.
And eyes in loving glances on many a beauteous maid were cast.
By hand of goodly warrior many a coat was rent,
For in the country's custom they tourneyed as they went,
Until before the palace the monarch did dismount.
They tended fairest ladies as knights high-spirited are wont.
After fairest greeting the queens did part again.
Dame Ute and her daughter, thither passed the twain
With train of fair attendants unto a hall full wide.
Din of merrymaking heard ye there on every side.
Arranged were sitting-places where the king would be
With his guests at table. By him might ye see
Standing the fair Brunhild. She wore a royal crown
In the monarch's country, the which might well such mistress own.
Seats for all the people at many a spacious board
There were, as saith the story, where victuals rich were stored.
How little there was lacking of all that makes a feast!
And by the monarch saw ye sitting many a stately guest.
The royal host's attendants in basins golden red
Carried water forward. And should it e'er be said
By any that a better service did receive
Ever guests of monarch, I never could such thing believe.
Before the lord of Rhineland with water was waited on,
Unto him Sir Siegfried, as fitting was, had gone;
He called to mind a promise that made by him had been
Ere that the Lady Brunhild afar in Isenland he'd seen.
He spake: "Thou shalt bethink thee what once did plight thy hand,
If that the Lady Brunhild should come unto this land,
Thou'dst give to me thy sister. Where now what thou hast sworn?

In this thy wooing journey not small the labor I have borne."
Then to his guest the monarch: "Well hast thou minded me,
And by this hand shall never false word plighted be.
To gain thy wish I'd help thee in the way as best I know."
Bidden then was Kriemhild forth unto the king to go.
With her full beauteous maidens unto the Hall she passed.
Then sprang the youthful Giselher adown the steps in haste
"Bid now these many maidens wend their way again;
None but my sister only unto the king shall enter in."
Then led they Kriemhild thither where the king was found,
With him were knights full noble from many a land around.
Within that Hall so spacious she waited the king's behest,
What time the Lady Brunhild betook her likewise to the feast.
Then spake the royal Gunther: "Sister mine full fair,
Redeem the word I've given, an hold'st thou virtue dear.
Thee to a knight I plighted: An tak'st thou him to man,
Thereby my wish full truly unto the warrior hast thou done."
Then spake the noble maiden: "Brother full dear to me,
Not long shalt thou entreat me. In truth I'll ever be
Obedient to thy bidding; that shall now be done,
And him I'll take full gladly, my Lord, whom thou giv'st me for man."
Before those fair eyes' glances grew Siegfried's color red.
The knight to Lady Kriemhild his service oferéd.
Within a ring together then were led the twain,
And they asked the maiden, if she to take the knight were fain.
Upon her face not little was the modest glow;
Nathless to joy of Siegfried did fortune will it so,
That the maiden would not refuse the knight her hand.
Eke swore his wife to make her the noble king of Netherland.
When he to her had plighted, and eke to him the maid,
Siegfried to embrace her nothing more delayed,
But clasped in arms full fondly and oft the lady fair,
And stately knights were witness how that he kissed the princess there.
When that the maids attendant from thence had ta'en their leave,
In place of honor seated Siegfried might ye perceive
And by him fairest Kriemhild; and many a knight at hand
Was seen of the Nibelungen at Siegfried's service ready stand.
There too was Gunther seated and with him Queen Brunhild.
At sight of Kriemhild sitting by Siegfried was she filled
With anger such as never before her heart did swell:
She wept, and tears in plenty adown her shining face there fell.
Then spake who ruled the country: "What aileth, lady mine,
That so thou let'st be dimméd thine eyes that brightly shine?
Be straight of joyous spirit, for now at thy command
My land and my good castles and host of stately warriors stand."
"Good cause to me for weeping," spake the lady fair.
"For sake of this thy sister sorrow now I bear,

Whom here behold I seated by one that serveth thee.
That must forever grieve me, shall she thus dishonored be."
Then answered her King Gunther: "But for the nonce be still.
At other time more fitting the thing to thee I'll tell,
Wherefore thus my sister to Siegfried I did give.
And truly with the hero may she ever joyous live."
She spake: "Her name and beauty thus lost it grieveth me.
An knew I only whither, from hence I'd surely flee,
This night nor e'er hereafter to share thy royal bed,
Say'st thou not truly wherefore Kriemhild thus hath Siegfried wed."
Then spake the noble monarch: "Then unto thee be known
That he as stately castles, lands wide as I, doth own.
And know thou that full surely a mighty monarch he;
Wherefore the fairest maiden I grant him thus his wife to be."
Whate'er the king did tell her, sad was she yet of mood.
Then hastened from the tables full many a warrior good,
And jousted that the castle walls gave back the din.
Amid his guests the monarch waiting longingly was seen.
He deemed 'twere better lying beside his fair lady.
Of thinking on that plaisance his mind he could not free,
And what her love would bring him before the night be past;
He many a glance full tender upon the Lady Brunhild cast.
The guests they bade give over in joust who combated,
For that with spouse new-wedded the monarch would to bed.
Leaving then the banquet, there together met
Kriemhild and Brunhild: their bitter hate was silent yet.
At hand were their attendants; they longer tarried not,
And chamberlains full lordly lights for them had brought.
Then parted eke the followers of the monarchs twain,
And bearing Siegfried company went full many a worthy thane.
The lords were both come thither where that they should lie.
As each one bethought him of loving victory
To win o'er winsome lady, merry he grew of mood.
The noble Siegfried's pastime it was beyond all measure good.
As there Sir Siegfried by fair Kriemhild lay
And to the maid devoted himself in such fond way
As noble knight beseemeth, they twain to him were one,
And not a thousand others had he then ta'en for her alone.
I'll tell you now no further how he the lady plied,
But list ye first the story what Gunther did betide
By Lady Brunhild lying. In sooth the noble thane
By side of other ladies a deal more happily had lain.
Withdrawn were now attendants, man and also maid;
Not long to lock the chamber within the king delayed.
He weened to have good pleasure of that fair lady,
Yet was the time still distant when that she his wife should be.
In gown of whitest linen unto the bed she passed.

Then thought the knight full noble: "Now have I here at last
All that I e'er desired as long as I can tell."
Perforce her stately beauty did please the monarch passing well.
That they should shine more dimly he placed the lights aside,
Then where did lie the lady the thane full eager hied.
He placed himself a-nigh her, his joy right great it was,
As in his arms the monarch the winsome maid did there embrace.
A loving plaisance had he with vigor there begun
If that the noble lady had let the same be done.
She then did rage so sorely that grieved was he thereat;
He weened to find who loved him, —instead he found him naught but hate.
Spake she: "Good knight and noble, from this thing give o'er.
That which thou here hast hope of, it may be nevermore.
A maid I still will keep me —well mayest thou know that—
Until I learn that story." Gunther wrathy grew thereat.
Her gown he wrought to ruin to win her maidenhead.
Whereat did seize a girdle the full stately maid,
A strong and silken girdle that round her sides she wore,
And with the same the monarch she soon had brought to pains full sore.
His feet and his hands also, together bound she all,
Unto a nail she bore him and hung him on the wall.
Him who disturbed her sleeping in his love she sorely let,
And from her mighty prowess, he full nigh his death had met.
Then gan he to entreat her, who master late had been.
"From these my bonds now loose me, my full noble queen.
Nor trow I e'er, fair lady, victor o'er thee to be,
And henceforth will I seldom seek to lie thus nigh to thee."
She recked not how 'twere with him, as she full softly lay.
There hung he, will he nill he, the night through unto day,
Until the light of morning through the windows shone.
Could he e'er boast of prowess, small now the measure he did own.
"Now tell me, lordly Gunther, wert thou thereat so sad,
If that in bonds should find thee" —spake the fairest maid—
"Thy royal men-in-waiting, bound by lady's hand?"
Then spake the knight full noble: "Thou should'st in case most evil stand.
"Eke had I little honor therefrom," continued he.
"For all thy royal honor let me then go to thee.
Since that my fond embracements do anger thee so sore,
With these my hands I pledge thee to touch thy garment nevermore."
Then she loosed him straightway and he once more stood free.
To the bed he went as erstwhile where rested his lady.
But far from her he laid him and well he now forebore
To stir the lady's anger by touching e'en the gown she wore.
At length came their attendants who garments fresh did bring,
Whereof was ready for them good store on that morning.
Yet merry as his folk were, a visage sad did own
The lord of that proud country, for all he wore that day a crown.

As was the country's custom, a thing folk do of right,
Gunther and Brunhild presently were dight
To go unto the minster where the mass was sung.
Thither eke came Siegfried, and in their trains a mighty throng.
As fitted royal honor for them was thither brought
The crown that each should carry and garments richly wrought.
There were they consecrated; and when the same was done,
Saw ye the four together happy stand and wearing crown.
There was knighted many a squire, —six hundred or beyond—
In honor of the crowning, that shall ye understand.
Arose full great rejoicing in the land of Burgundy
As hand of youthful warrior did shatter shaft right valiantly.
Then sat in castle casement maidens fair to see,
And many a shield beneath them gleamed full brilliantly.
Yet himself had sundered from all his men the king;
Though joyous every other, sad-visaged stood he sorrowing.
He and the doughty Siegfried, how all unlike their mood!
Well wist the thing did grieve him that noble knight and good.
He went unto the monarch and straight addressed him so:
"This night how hast thou fared? In friendship give thou me to know."
To his guest the king gave answer: "Than shame and scathe I've naught.
The devil's dam I surely into my house have brought.
When as I thought to have her she bound me like a thrall;
Unto a nail she bore me and hung me high upon the wall.
"There hung I sore in anguish the night through until day
Ere that she would unbind me, the while she softly lay!
And hast thou friendly pity know then the grief I bear."
Then spake the doughty Siegfried: "Such grieves me verily to hear.
"The which I'll show thee truly, wilt thou me not deny.
I'll bring it that to-night she so near to thee shall lie
That she to meet thy wishes shall tarry nevermore."
Thereat rejoice did Gunther to think perchance his trials o'er.
Then further spake Sir Siegfried: "With thee 'twill yet be right.
I ween that all unequal we twain have fared this night.
To me thy sister Kriemhild dearer is than life;
Eke shall the Lady Brunhild be yet this coming night thy wife."
"I'll come unto thy chamber this night all secretly,"
Spake he, "and wrapped in mantle invisible I'll be,
That of this my cunning naught shall any know;
And thy attendants shalt thou bid to their apartments go.
"The lights I'll all extinguish held by each page in hand,
By the which same token shalt thou understand
I present am to serve thee. I'll tame thy shrewish wife
That thou this night enjoy her, else forfeit be my caitiff life."
"An thou wilt truly leave me" —answered him the king—
'My lady yet a maiden, I joy o'er this same thing.
So do thou as thou willest; and takest thou her life,

E'en that I'll let pass o'er me, —to lose so terrible a wife."
"Thereto," spake then Siegfried, "plight I word of mine,
To leave her yet a maiden. A sister fair of thine
Is to me before all women I ever yet have seen."
Gunther believed right gladly what had by Siegfried plighted been.

Meanwhile the merry pastime with joy and zest went on.
But all the din and bustle bade they soon be done,
When band of fairest ladies would pass unto the hall
'Fore whom did royal chamberlains bid backward stand the people all.

The chargers soon and riders from castle court were sped.
Each of the noble ladies by bishop high was led,
When that before the monarchs they passed to banquet board,
And in their train did follow to table many a stately lord.

There sat the king all hopeful and full of merriment;
What him did promise Siegfried, thereon his mind was bent.
To him as long as thirty did seem that single day;
To plaisance with his lady, thither turned his thought alway.

And scarce the time he bided while that the feast did last.
Now unto her chamber the stately Brunhild passed,
And for her couch did Kriemhild likewise the table leave.
Before those royal ladies what host ye saw of warriors brave!

Full soon thereafter Siegfried sat right lovingly
With his fair wife beside him, and naught but joy had he.
His hand she clasped full fondly within her hand so white,
Until—and how she knew not— he did vanish from her sight.

When she the knight did fondle, and straightway saw him not,
Unto her maids attendant spake the queen distraught:
"Meseemeth a mickle wonder where now the king hath gone.
His hands in such weird fashion who now from out mine own hath drawn?"

Yet further not she questioned. Soon had he hither gone
Where with lights were standing attendants many a one.
The same he did extinguish in every page's hand;
That Siegfried then was present Gunther thereby did understand.

Well wist he what he would there; so bade he thence be gone
Ladies and maids-in-waiting. And when that was done,
Himself the mighty monarch fast did lock the door:
Two bolts all wrought securely he quickly shoved the same before.

The lights behind the curtains hid he presently.
Soon a play was started (for thus it had to be),
Betwixt the doughty Siegfried and the stately maid:
Thereat was royal Gunther joyous alike and sad.

Siegfried there laid him by the maid full near.
Spake she: "Let be, now, Gunther, an hast thou cause to fear
Those troubles now repeated which befell thee yesternight."
And soon the valiant Siegfried through the lady fell in sorry plight.

His voice did he keep under and ne'er a word spake he.
Intently listened Gunther, and though he naught could see,

Yet knew he that in secret nothing 'twixt them passed.
In sooth nor knight nor lady upon the bed had mickle rest.
He did there as if Gunther the mighty king he were,
And in his arms he pressed her, the maiden debonair.
Forth from the bed she hurled him where a bench there stood,
And head of valiant warrior against a stool went ringing loud.
Up sprang again undaunted the full doughty man,
To try for fortune better. When he anew began
Perforce to curb her fury, fell he in trouble sore.
I ween that ne'er a lady did so defend herself before.
When he would not give over, up the maid arose:
"My gown so white thou never thus shalt discompose.
And this thy villain's manner shall sore by thee be paid,
The same I'll teach thee truly," further spake the buxom maid.
Within her arms she clasped him, the full stately thane,
And thought likewise to bind him, as the king yestreen,
That she the night in quiet upon her couch might lie.
That her dress he thus did rumple, avenged the lady grievously.
What booted now his prowess and eke his mickle might?
Her sovereignty of body she proved upon the knight;
By force of arm she bore him, —'twixt wall and mighty chest
(For so it e'en must happen) him she all ungently pressed.
"Ah me!"—so thought the hero— "shall I now my life
Lose at hand of woman, then will every wife
Evermore hereafter a shrewish temper show
Against her lord's good wishes, who now such thing ne'er thinks to do."
All heard the monarch meanwhile and trembled for the man.
Sore ashamed was Siegfried, and a-raging he began.
With might and main he struggled again to make him free,
Ere which to sorest trouble 'neath Lady Brunhild's hand fell he.
Long space to him it seeméd ere Siegfried tamed her mood.
She grasped his hand so tightly that 'neath the nails the blood
Oozéd from the pressure, which made the hero wince.
Yet the stately maiden subdued he to obedience since.
Her unrestrainéd temper that she so late displayed,
All overheard the monarch, though ne'er a word he said.
'Gainst the bed did press her Siegfried that aloud she cried,
Ungentle was the treatment that he meted to the bride.
Then grasped she for a girdle that round her sides she wore,
And thought therewith to bind him; but her limbs and body o'er
Strained beneath the vigor that his strong arm displayed.
So was the struggle ended —Gunther's wife was vanquishéd.
She spake: "O noble monarch, take not my life away.
The harm that I have done thee full well will I repay.
No more thy royal embraces by me shall be withstood,
For now I well have seen it, thou canst be lord o'er woman's mood."
From the couch rose Siegfried, lying he left the maid,

As if that he would from him lay his clothes aside.
He drew from off her finger a ring of golden sheen
Without that e'er perceivéd his practice the full noble queen.
Thereto he took her girdle that was all richly wrought:
If from wanton spirit he did it, know I not.
The same he gave to Kriemhild: the which did sorrow bear.
Then lay by one another Gunther and the maiden fair.
Hearty were his embraces as such king became:
Perforce must she relinquish her anger and her shame.
In sooth not little pallid within his arms she grew,
And in that love-surrender how waned her mighty prowess too!
Then was e'en she not stronger than e'er another bride;
He lay with fond embraces the beauteous dame beside.
And had she struggled further, avail how could it aught?
Gunther, when thus he clasped her, such change upon her strength had wrought.
And with right inward pleasure she too beside him lay
In warmest love embracings until the dawn of day!
Meantime now had Siegfried departure ta'en from there,
And was full well receivéd by a lady debonair.
Her questioning he avoided and all whereon she thought,
And long time kept he secret what he for her had brought,
Until in his own country she wore a royal crown;
Yet what for her he destined, how sure at last it was her own.
Upon the morn was Gunther by far of better mood
Than he had been before it; joy thus did spread abroad
'Mid host of knights full noble that from his lands around
To his court had been invited, and there most willing service found.
The merry time there lasted until two weeks were spent,
Nor all the while did flag there the din of merriment
And every kind of joyance that knight could e'er devise;
With lavish hand expended the king thereto in fitting wise.
The noble monarch's kinsmen upon his high command
By gifts of gold and raiment told forth his generous hand,
By steed and thereto silver on minstrel oft bestowed.
Who there did gift desire departed thence in merry mood.
All the store of raiment afar from Netherland,
The which had Siegfried's thousand warriors brought to hand
Unto the Rhine there with them, complete 'twas dealt away,
And eke the steeds well saddled: in sooth a lordly life led they.
Ere all the gifts so bounteous were dealt the guests among,
They who would straightway homeward did deem the waiting long.
Ne'er had guests of monarch such goodly gifts before;
And so as Gunther willed it the merry feast at last was o'er.

ELEVENTH ADVENTURE

How Siegfried came home with his Wife

When that now the strangers all from thence were gone,
Spake unto his followers noble Siegmund's son:
"We shall eke make ready home to my land to fare."
Unto his spouse was welcome such news when she the same did hear.

She spake unto her husband: "When shall we hence depart?
Not hastily on the journey I pray thee yet to start.
With me first my brothers their wide lands shall share."
Siegfried yet it pleased not such words from Kriemhild to hear.

The princes went unto him and spake they there all three:
"Now know thou well, Sir Siegfried, for thee shall ever be
In faithfulness our service ready while yet we live."
The royal thanes then thanked he who thus did proof of friendship give.

"With thee further share we," spake young Giselher,
"The lands and eke the castles by us that ownéd are.
In wide lands whatsoever we rule o'er warriors brave,
Of the same with Kriemhild a goodly portion shalt thou have."

Then spake unto the princes the son of Siegmund
When he their lofty purpose did rightly understand:
"God grant your goodly heritage at peace may ever be,
And eke therein your people. The spouse in sooth so dear to me."

"May well forego the portion that ye to her would give.
For she a crown shall carry, if to such day I live,
And queen more rich than any that lives she then must be.
What else to her ye offer, therein I'll meet you faithfully."

Then spake the Lady Kriemhild: "If wealth thou wilt not choose,
Yet gallant thanes of Burgundy shalt thou not light refuse.
They're such as monarch gladly would lead to his own land.
Of these shall make division with me my loving brothers' hand."

Thereto spake noble Gernot: "Now take to please thy mind.
Who gladly will go with thee full many here thou'lt find.
Of thirty hundred warriors we give thee thousand men
To be thy royal escort." Kriemhild did summon then

Hagen of Tronje to her and Ortwein instantly:
And would they and their kinsmen make her good company?
To hear the same did Hagen begin to rage full sore.
Quoth he: "E'en royal Gunther may thus bestow us nevermore.

"Other men that serve thee, let them follow thee;
Thou know'st the men of Tronje and what their pledges be:
Here must we by the monarchs in service true abide;
Hereto as them we followed, so shall we henceforth keep their side."

And so the thing was ended: to part they ready make.
A high and noble escort did Kriemhild to her take,
Maidens two and thirty and five hundred men also.

In Lady Kriemhild's company the Margrave Eckewart did go.
Leave took they all together, squire and also knight,
Maidens and fair ladies, as was their wont aright.
There parted they with kisses and eke with clasp of hand:
Right merrily they journeyed forth from royal Gunther's land.
Their friends did give them escort upon the way full far.
Night-quarters at every station they bade for them prepare,
Where they might wish to tarry as on their way they went.
Then straightway was a messenger unto royal Siegmund sent,
To him and Siegelind bearing thereof the joyful sign
That his son was coming from Worms upon the Rhine
And with him Ute's daughter, Kriemhild the fair lady.
As this could other message nevermore so welcome be.
"Well is me!" quoth Siegmund, "that I the day have known,
When the fair Lady Kriemhild here shall wear a crown.
Thus higher shall my kingdom stand in majesty.
My son the noble Siegfried here himself the king shall be."
Then dealt the Lady Siegelind velvet red in store,
Silver and gold full heavy to them the news that bore:
She joyed to hear the story that there her ear did greet.
Then decked themselves her ladies all in rich attire meet.
'Twas told, with Siegfried coming whom they did expect.
Then bade they sitting-places straightway to erect,
Where he before his kinsmen a crown in state should wear.
Then men of royal Siegmund forward rode to meet him there.
Was e'er more royal greeting, news have I not to hand,
As came the knights full noble into Siegmund's land.
There the royal Siegelind to Kriemhild forth did ride
With ladies fair a many, and followed gallant knights beside
Out a full day's journey to welcome each high guest.
And little with the strangers did they ever rest
Until into a castle wide they came once more,
The same was called Xanten, where anon a crown they wore.
With smiling lips Dame Siegelind —and Siegmund eke did this—
To show the love they bore her full oft did Kriemhild kiss,
And eke the royal Siegfried: far was their sorrow gone.
And all the merry company, good welcome had they every one.
The train of strangers bade they 'fore Siegmund's Hall to lead,
And maidens fair a many down from gallant steed
Helped they there dismounting. Full many a man was there
To do them willing service as was meet for ladies fair.
How great soe'er the splendor erstwhile beside the Rhine,
Here none the less was given raiment yet more fine,
Nor were they e'er attired in all their days so well.
Full many a wonder might I of their rich apparel tell.
How there in state resplendent they sat and had full store,
And how each high attendant gold-broidered raiment wore,

With stones full rare and precious set with skill therein!
The while with care did serve them Siegelind the noble queen.
Then spake the royal Siegmund before his people so:
"To every friend of Siegfried give I now to know
That he before these warriors my royal crown shall wear."
And did rejoice that message the thanes of Netherland to hear.

His crown to him he tendered and rule o'er wide domain
Whereof he all was master. Where'er did reach his reign
Or men were subject to him bestowed his hand such care
That evil-doers trembled before the spouse of Kriemhild fair.

In such high honor truly he lived, as ye shall hear,
And judged as lofty monarch unto the tenth year,
What time his fairest lady to him a son did bear.
Thereat the monarch's kinsmen filled with mickle joyance were.

They soon the same did christen and gave to him a name,
Gunther, as hight his uncle, nor cause was that for shame:
Grew he but like his kinsmen then happy might he be.
As well he did deserve it, him fostered they right carefully.

In the selfsame season did Lady Siegelind die,
When was full power wielded by Ute's daughter high,
As meet so lofty lady should homage wide receive.
That death her thus had taken did many a worthy kinsman grieve.

Now by the Rhine yonder, as we likewise hear,
Unto mighty Gunther eke a son did bear
Brunhild his fair lady in the land of Burgundy.
In honor to the hero Siegfried naméd eke was he.

The child they also fostered with what tender care!
Gunther the noble monarch anon did masters rare
Find who should instruct him a worthy man to grow.
Alas! by sad misfortune to friends was dealt how fell a blow!

At all times the story far abroad was told,
How that in right worthy way the warriors bold
Lived there in Siegmund's country as noble knights should do.
Likewise did royal Gunther eke amid his kinsmen true.

Land of the Nibelungen Siegfried as well did own,
—Amid his lofty kindred a mightier ne'er was known—
And Schilbung's knights did serve him, with all that theirs had been.
That great was thus his power did fill with joy the knight full keen.

Hoard of all the greatest that hero ever won,
Save who erstwhile did wield it, now the knight did own,
The which before a mountain he seized against despite,
And for whose sake he further slew full many a gallant knight.

Naught more his heart could wish for; yet had his might been less,
Rightly must all people of the high knight confess,
One was he of the worthiest that e'er bestrode a steed.
Feared was his mickle prowess, and, sooth to say, thereof was need.

TWELFTH ADVENTURE

How Gunther bade Siegfried to the Feast

Now all time bethought her royal Gunther's wife:
"How now doth Lady Kriemhild lead so haughty life?
In sooth her husband Siegfried doth homage to us owe,
But now full long unto us little service he doth show."
That in her heart in secret eke she pondered o'er.
That they were strangers to her did grieve her heart full sore,
And so seldom sign of service came from Siegfried's land.
How it thus was fallen, that she fain would understand.
She probed then the monarch, if the thing might be,
That she the Lady Kriemhild once again might see.
She spake it all in secret whereon her heart did dwell;
The thing she then did speak of pleased the monarch passing well.
"How might we bring them hither"—spake the mighty king—
"Unto this my country? 'Twere ne'er to do, such thing.
They dwell too distant from us, the quest I fear to make."
Thereto gave answer Brunhild, and in full crafty wise she spake:
"How high soe'er and mighty king's man were ever one,
Whate'er should bid his master, may he not leave undone."
Thereat did smile King Gunther, as such words spake she:
Ne'er bade he aught of service, oft as Siegfried he did see.
She spake: "Full loving master, as thou hold'st me dear,
Help me now that Siegfried and thy sister fair
Come to this our country, that them we here may see;
In sooth no thing could ever unto me more welcome be.
"Thy sister's lofty bearing and all her courtesy,
Whene'er I think upon it, full well it pleaseth me,
How we did sit together when erst I was thy spouse!
Well in sooth with honor might she the valiant Siegfried choose."
She pleaded with the monarch so long till answered he:
"Know now that guests none other so welcome were to me.
To gain thy wish 'tis easy: straight messengers of mine
To both shall message carry, that hither come they to the Rhine."
Thereto the queen gave answer: "Now further shalt thou say,
When thou them wilt summon, or when shall be the day
That our dear friends come hither unto our country.
Who'll bear thy message thither, shalt thou eke make known to me."
"That will I," spake the monarch. "Thirty of my men
Shall thither ride unto them." The same he summoned then,
And bade them with the message to Siegfried's land to fare.
They joyed as gave them Brunhild stately raiment rich to wear.
Then further spake the monarch: "Ye knights from me shall bring

This message, nor withhold ye of it anything,
Unto the doughty Siegfried and eke my sister fair:
In the world could never any to them a better purpose bear.
"And pray them both that hither they come unto the Rhine.
With me will e'er my lady such grace to pay combine,
Ere turn of sun in summer he and his men shall know
That liveth here full many to them would willing honor show.
"Unto royal Siegmund bear greeting fair from me,
That I and my friends ever to him well-minded be.
And tell ye eke my sister she shall no wise omit
Hither to friends to journey: ne'er feast could better her befit."
Brunhild and Ute and ladies all at hand,
They sent a fairest greeting unto Siegfried's land
To winsome ladies many and many a warrior brave.
With godspeed from the monarch and friends the messengers took leave.
They fared with full equipment: their steeds did ready stand
And rich were they attired: so rode they from that land
They hastened on the journey whither they would fare;
Escort safe the monarch had bidden eke for them prepare.
Their journey had they ended e'er three weeks were spent.
At the Nibelungen castle, whither they were sent,
In the mark of Norway found they the knight they sought,
And weary were the horses the messengers so far had brought.
Then was told to Siegfried and to Kriemhild fair
How knights were there arrivéd who did raiment wear
Like as in land of Burgundy of wont the warriors dressed.
Thereat did hasten Kriemhild from couch where she did lying rest.
Then bade eke to a window one of her maids to go.
She saw the valiant Gere stand in the court below,
And with him his companions, who did thither fare.
To hear such joyous tidings, how soon her heart forgot its care.
She spake unto the monarch: "Look now thitherward
Where with the doughty Gere stand in the castle yard
Whom to us brother Gunther adown the Rhine doth send!"
Thereto spake doughty Siegfried: "With greeting fair we'll them attend."
Then hastened their retainers all the guests to meet,
And each of them in special manner then did greet
The messengers full kindly and warmest welcome bade.
Siegmund did likewise o'er their coming wax full glad.
In fitting way was harbored Gere and his men,
And steeds in charge were taken. The messengers went then
Where beside Sir Siegfried the Lady Kriemhild sat.
To court the guests were bidden, where them did greeting fair await.
The host with his fair lady, straightway up stood he,
And greeted fairly Gere of the land of Burgundy
And with him his companions King Gunther's men also.
Gere, knight full mighty, bade they to a settle go.

"Allow that first the message we give ere sit we down;
The while we'll stand, though weary upon our journey grown.
Tidings bring we to you what greetings high have sent
Gunther and Brunhild who live in royal fair content.
"Eke what from Lady Ute thy mother now we've brought.
The youthful Giselher and also Sir Gernot
And best among thy kinsmen have sent us here to thee:
A fairest greeting send they from the land of Burgundy."
"God give them meed," spake Siegfried; "Good will and faith withal
I trow full well they harbor, as with friends we shall;
Likewise doth eke their sister. Now further shall ye tell
If that our friends belovéd at home in high estate do dwell.
"Since that we from them parted hath any dared to do
Scathe to my lady's kinsmen? That shall ye let me know.
I'll help them ever truly all their need to bear
Till that their enemies have good cause my help to fear."
Then spake the Margrave Gere, a knight full good:
"In all that maketh knighthood right proud they stand of mood.
Unto the Rhine they bid you to high festivity:
They'd see you there full gladly, thereof may ye not doubtful be.
"And bid they eke my Lady Kriemhild that she too,
When ended is the winter, thither come with you.
Ere turn of sun in summer trust they you to see."
Then spake the doughty Siegfried: "That same thing might hardly be."
Thereto did answer Gere of the land of Burgundy:
"Your high mother Ute hath message sent by me,
Likewise Gernot and Giselher, that they plead not in vain.
That you they see so seldom daily hear I them complain.
"Brunhild my mistress and all her company
Of fair maids rejoice them; if the thing might be
That they again should see you, of merry mood they were."
Then joy to hear the tidings filled the Lady Kriemhild fair.
Gere to her was kinsman. The host did bid him rest,
Nor long were they in pouring wine for every guest.
Thither came eke Siegmund where the strangers he did see,
And in right friendly manner spake to the men of Burgundy:
"Welcome be, ye warriors, ye Gunther's men, each one.
Since that fair Kriemhild Siegfried my son
For spouse did take unto him, we should you ofter see
Here in this our country, an ye good friends to us would be."
They spake, whene'er he wished it, full glad to come were they.
All their mickle weariness with joy was ta'en away.
The messengers were seated and food to them they bore,
Whereof did Siegfried offer unto his guests a goodly store.
Until nine days were over must they there abide,
When did at last the valiant knights begin to chide
That they did not ride thither again unto their land.

Then did the royal Siegfried summon his good knights to hand.
He asked what they did counsel: should they unto the Rhine?
"Me unto him hath bidden Gunther, friend of mine,
He and his good kinsmen, to high festivity.
Thither went I full gladly, but that his land so far doth lie.
"Kriemhild bid they likewise that she with me shall fare.
Good friends, now give ye counsel how we therefor prepare.
And were it armies thirty to lead in distant land,
Yet must serve them gladly evermore Siegfried's hand."
Then answer gave his warriors. "An't pleaseth thee to go
Thither to the festival, we'll counsel what thou do.
Thou shalt with thousand warriors unto Rhine river ride.
So may'st thou well with honor in the land of Burgundy abide."
Then spake of Netherland Siegmund the king:
"Will ye to the festival, why hide from me the thing!
I'll journey with you thither, if it not displeasing be,
And lead good thanes a hundred wherewith to swell your company."
"And wilt thou with us journey, father full dear to me,"
Spake the valiant Siegfried, "full glad thereat I'll be.
Before twelve days are over from these my lands I fare."
To all who'd join the journey steeds gave they and apparel rare.
When now the lofty monarch was minded thus to ride
Bade he the noble messengers longer not to bide,
And to his lady's kinsmen to the Rhine a message sent,
How that he would full gladly join to make them merriment.
Siegfried and Kriemhild, this same tale we hear,
To the messengers gave so richly that the burden could not bear
Their horses with them homeward, such wealth in sooth he had.
The horses heavy-laden drove they thence with hearts full glad.
Siegfried and Siegmund their people richly clad.
Eckewart the Margrave, straightway he bade
For ladies choose rich clothing, the best that might be found,
Or e'er could be procuréd in all Siegfried's lands around.
The shields and the saddles gan they eke prepare,
To knights and fair ladies who with them should fare
Lacked nothing that they wished for, but of all they were possessed.
Then to his friends led Siegfried many a high and stately guest.
The messengers swift hasted homeward on their way,
And soon again came Gere to the land of Burgundy.
Full well was he receivéd, and there dismounted all
His train from off their horses before the royal Gunther's Hall.
Old knights and youthful squires crowded, as is their way,
To ask of them the tidings. Thus did the brave knight say:
"When to the king I tell them then shall ye likewise hear."
He went with his companions and soon 'fore Gunther did appear.
Full of joy the monarch did from the settle spring;
And did thank them also for their hastening

Brunhild the fair lady. Spake Gunther eagerly:
"How now liveth Siegfried, whose arm hath oft befriended me?"
Then spake the valiant Gere: "Joy o'er the visage went
Of him and eke thy sister. To friends was never sent
A more faithful greeting by good knight ever one,
Than now the mighty Siegfried and his royal sire have done."
Then spake unto the Margrave the noble monarch's wife:
"Now tell me, cometh Kriemhild? And marketh yet her life
Aught of the noble bearing did her erstwhile adorn?"
"She cometh to thee surely," Gere answer did return.
Ute straightway the messengers to her did command.
Then might ye by her asking full well understand
To her was joyous tidings how Kriemhild did betide.
He told her how he found her, and that she soon would hither ride.
Eke of all the presents did they naught withhold,
That had given them Siegfried: apparel rich and gold
Displayed they to the people of the monarchs three.
To him were they full grateful who thus had dealt so bounteously.
"Well may he," quoth Hagen, "of his treasure give,
Nor could he deal it fully, should he forever live:
Hoard of the Nibelungen beneath his hand doth lie.
Heigh-ho, if came it ever into the land of Burgundy!"
All the king's retainers glad they were thereat,
That the guests were coming. Early then and late
Full little were they idle, the men of monarchs three.
Seats builded they full many toward the high festivity.
The valiant knight Hunold and Sindold doughty thane
Little had of leisure. Meantime must the twain,
Stands erect full many, as their high office bade.
Therein did help them Ortwein, and Gunther's thanks therefor they had.
Rumold the High Steward busily he wrought
Among them that did serve him. Full many a mighty pot,
And spacious pans and kettles, how many might ye see!
For those to them were coming prepared they victuals plenteously.

THIRTEENTH ADVENTURE

How they fared to the Feast

Leave we now the ardor wherewith they did prepare,
And tell how Lady Kriemhild and eke her maidens fair
From land of Nibelungen did journey to the Rhine.
Ne'er did horses carry such store of raiment rich and fine.
Carrying-chests full many for the way they made ready.
Then rode the thane Siegfried with his friends in company
And eke the queen thither where joy they looked to find.

Where now was high rejoicing they soon in sorest grief repined.
At home behind them left they Lady Kriemhild's son
That she did bear to Siegfried —'twas meet that that be done.
From this their festive journey rose mickle sorrow sore:
His father and his mother their child beheld they never more.
Then eke with them thither Siegmund the king did ride.
Had he e'er had knowledge what should there betide
Anon from that high journey, such had he never seen:
Ne'er wrought upon dear kindred might so grievous wrong have been.
Messengers sent they forward that the tidings told should be.
Then forth did ride to meet them with gladsome company
Ute's friends full many and many a Gunther's man.
With zeal to make him ready unto his guests the king began.
Where he found Brunhild sitting, thither straight went he.
"How receivéd thee my sister, as thou cam'st to this country?
Like preparations shalt thou for Siegfried's wife now make."
"Fain do I that; good reason have I to love her well," she spake.
Then quoth the mighty monarch: "The morn shall see them here.
Wilt thou go forth to meet them, apace do thou prepare,
That not within the castle their coming we await.
Guests more welcome never greeted I of high estate."
Her maidens and her ladies straight did she command
To choose them rich apparel, the best within the land,
In which the stately company before the guests should go.
The same they did right gladly, that may ye full surely know.
Then eke to offer service the men of Gunther hied,
And all his doughty warriors saw ye by the monarch's side.
Then rode the queen full stately the strangers forth to meet,
And hearty was the welcome as she her loving guests did greet.
With what glad rejoicings the guests they did receive!
They deemed that Lady Kriemhild did unto Brunhild give
Ne'er so warm a welcome to the land of Burgundy.
Bold knights that yet were strangers rejoiced each other there to see.
Now come was also Siegfried with his valiant men.
The warriors saw ye riding thither and back again,
Where'er the plain extended, with huge company.
From the dust and crowding could none in all the rout be free.
When the monarch of the country Siegfried did see
And with him also Siegmund, spake he full lovingly:
"Be ye to me full welcome and to all these friends of mine.
Our hearts right glad they shall be o'er this your journey to the Rhine."
"God give thee meed," spake Siegmund, a knight in honor grown.
"Since that my son Siegfried thee for a friend hath known,
My heart hath e'er advised me that thee I soon should see."
Thereto spake royal Gunther: "Joy hast thou brought full great to me."
Siegfried was there receivéd, as fitted his high state,
With full lofty honors, nor one did bear him hate.

There joined in way right courteous Gernot and Giselher:
I ween so warm a welcome did they make for strangers ne'er.
The spouse of each high monarch greeted the other there.
Emptied was many a saddle, and many a lady fair
By hero's hand was lifted adown upon the sward.
By waiting on fair lady how many a knight sought high reward!
So went unto each other the ladies richly dight;
Thereat in high rejoicing was seen full many a knight,
That by both the greeting in such fair way was done.
By fair maidens standing saw ye warriors many a one.
Each took the hand of other in all their company;
In courteous manner bending full many might ye see
And loving kisses given by ladies debonair.
Rejoiced the men of Gunther and Siegfried to behold them there.
They bided there no longer but rode into the town.
The host bade to the strangers in fitting way be shown,
That they were seen full gladly in the land of Burgundy.
High knights full many tilting before fair ladies might ye see.
Then did of Tronje Hagen and eke Ortwein
In high feats of valor all other knights outshine.
Whate'er the twain commanded dared none to leave undone;
By them was many a service to their high guests in honor shown.
Shields heard ye many clashing before the castle gate
With din of lances breaking. Long in saddle sate
The host and guests there with him, ere that within they went.
With full merry pastime joyfully the hours they spent.
Unto the Hall so spacious rode the merry company.
Many a silken cover wrought full cunningly
Saw ye beyond the saddles of the ladies debonair
On all sides down hanging. King Gunther's men did meet them there.
Led by the same the strangers to their apartments passed.
Meanwhile oft her glances Brunhild was seen to cast
Upon the Lady Kriemhild, for she was passing fair.
In lustre vied her color with the gold that she did wear.
Within the town a clamor at Worms on every hand
Arose amid their followers. King Gunther gave command
To Dankwart his Marshal to tend them all with care.
Then bade he fitting quarters for the retinue prepare.
Without and in the castle the board for all was set:
In sooth were never strangers better tended yet.
Whatever any wished for did they straightway provide:
So mighty was the monarch that naught to any was denied.
To them was kind attention and all good friendship shown.
The host then at the table with his guests sat him down.
Siegfried they bade be seated where he did sit before.
Then went with him to table full many a stately warrior more.
Gallant knights twelve hundred in the circle there, I ween,

With him sat at table. Brunhild the lofty queen
Did deem that never vassal could more mighty be.
So well she yet was minded, she saw it not unwillingly.
There upon an evening, as the king with guests did dine,
Full many a rich attire was wet with ruddy wine,
As passed among the tables the butlers to and fro.
And great was their endeavor full honor to the guests to show.
As long hath been the custom at high festivity
Fit lodging there was given to maid and high lady.
From whence soe'er they came there they had the host's good care;
Unto each guest was meted of fitting honors fullest share.
When now the night was ended and came forth the dawn,
From chests they carried with them, full many a precious stone
Sparkled on costly raiment by hand of lady sought.
Stately robes full many forth to deck them then they brought.
Ere dawn was full appeared, before the Hall again
Came knights and squires many, whereat arose the din
E'en before the matins that for the king were sung.
Well pleaséd was the monarch at joust to see the warriors young.
Full lustily and loudly many a horn did blare,
Of flutes and eke of trumpets such din did rend the air
That loud came back the echo from Worms the city wide.
The warriors high-hearted to saddle sprung on every side.
Arose there in that country high a jousting keen
Of many a doughty warrior whereof were many seen,
Whom there their hearts more youthful did make of merry mood;
Of these 'neath shield there saw ye many a stately knight and good.
There sat within the casements many a high lady
And maidens many with them, the which were fair to see.
Down looked they where did tourney many a valiant man.
The host with his good kinsmen himself a-riding soon began.
Thus they found them pastime, and fled the time full well;
Then heard they from the minster the sound of many a bell.
Forth upon their horses the ladies thence did ride;
Many a knight full valiant the lofty queens accompanied.
They then before the minster alighted on the grass.
Unto her guests Queen Brunhild yet well-minded was.
Into the spacious minster they passed, and each wore crown.
Their friendship yet was broken by direst jealousy anon.
When the mass was ended went they thence again
In full stately manner. Thereafter were they seen
Joyous at board together. The pleasure full did last,
Until days eleven amid the merry-making passed.

FOURTEENTH ADVENTURE

How the Queens Berated Each Other

Before the time of vespers arose a mickle stir
On part of warriors many upon the courtyard there.
In knightly fashion made they the time go pleasantly;
Thither knights and ladies went their merry play to see.
There did sit together the queens, a stately pair,
And of two knights bethought them, that noble warriors were.
Then spake the fair Kriemhild: "Such spouse in sooth have I,
That all these mighty kingdoms might well beneath his sceptre lie."
Then spake the Lady Brunhild: "How might such thing be?
If that there lived none other but himself and thee,
So might perchance his power rule these kingdoms o'er;
The while that liveth Gunther, may such thing be nevermore."
Then again spake Kriemhild: "Behold how he doth stand
In right stately fashion before the knightly band,
Like as the bright moon beameth before the stars of heaven.
In sooth to think upon it a joyous mood to me is given."
Then spake the Lady Brunhild: "How stately thy spouse be,
Howe'er so fair and worthy, yet must thou grant to me
Gunther, thy noble brother, doth far beyond him go:
In sooth before all monarchs he standeth, shalt thou truly know."
Then again spake Kriemhild: "So worthy is my spouse,
That I not have praised him here without a cause.
In ways to tell full many high honor doth he bear:
Believe well may'st thou, Brunhild, he is the royal Gunther's peer."
"Now guard thee, Lady Kriemhild, my word amiss to take,
For not without good reason here such thing I spake.
Both heard I say together, when them I first did see,
When that erstwhile the monarch did work his royal will o'er me,
And when in knightly fashion my love for him he won,
Then himself said Siegfried he were the monarch's man.
For liegeman thus I hold him, since he the same did say."
Then spake fair Lady Kriemhild: "With me 'twere dealt in sorry way.
"And these my noble brothers, how could they such thing see,
That I of their own liegeman e'er the wife should be?
Thus will I beg thee, Brunhild, as friend to friend doth owe,
That thou, as well befits thee, shalt further here such words forego."
"No whit will I give over," spake the monarch's spouse.
"Wherefore should I so many a knight full valiant lose,
Who to us in service is bounden with thy man?"
Kriemhild the fair lady thereat sore to rage began.
"In sooth must thou forego it that he should e'er to thee
Aught of service offer. More worthy e'en is he
Than is my brother Gunther, who is a royal lord.

So shalt thou please to spare me what I now from thee have heard.
"And to me is ever wonder, since he thy liegeman is,
And thou dost wield such power over us twain as this,
That he so long his tribute to thee hath failed to pay.
'Twere well thy haughty humor thou should'st no longer here display."
"Too lofty now thou soarest," the queen did make reply.
"Now will I see full gladly if in such honor high
This folk doth hold thy person as mine own it doth."
Of mood full sorely wrathful were the royal ladies both.
Then spake the Lady Kriemhild: "That straightway shall be seen.
Since that thou my husband dost thy liegeman ween,
To-day shall all the followers of both the monarchs know,
If I 'fore wife of monarch dare unto the minster go.
"That I free-born and noble shalt thou this day behold,
And that my royal husband, as now to thee I've told,
'Fore thine doth stand in honor, by me shall well be shown.
Ere night shalt thou behold it, how wife of him thou call'st thine own
To court shall lead good warriors in the land of Burgundy.
And ne'er a queen so lofty as I myself shall be
Was seen by e'er a mortal, or yet a crown did wear."
Then mickle was the anger that rose betwixt the ladies there.
Then again spake Brunhild: "Wilt thou not service own,
So must thou with thy women hold thyself alone
Apart from all my following, as we to minster go."
Thereto gave answer Kriemhild: "In truth the same I fain will do."
"Now dress ye fair, my maidens," Kriemhild gave command.
"Nor shall shame befall me here within this land.
An have ye fair apparel, let now be seen by you.
What she here hath boasted may Brunhild have full cause to rue."
But little need to urge them: soon were they richly clad
In garments wrought full deftly, lady and many a maid.
Then went with her attendants he spouse of the monarch high;
And eke appeared fair Kriemhild, her body decked full gorgeously,
With three and forty maidens, whom to the Rhine led she,
All clad in shining garments wrought in Araby.
So came unto the minster the maidens fair and tall.
Before the hall did tarry for them the men of Siegfried all.
The people there did wonder how the thing might be,
That no more together the queens they thus did see,
And that beside each other they went not as before.
Thereby came thanes a many anon to harm and trouble sore.
Here before the minster the wife of Gunther stood.
And good knights full many were there of merry mood
With the fair ladies that their eyes did see.
Then came the Lady Kriemhild with a full stately company.
Whate'er of costly raiment decked lofty maids before,
'Twas like a windy nothing 'gainst what her ladies wore.

The wives of thirty monarchs —such riches were her own—
Might ne'er display together what there by Lady Kriemhild shown.
Should any wish to do so he could not say, I ween,
That so rich apparel e'er before was seen
As there by her maidens debonair was worn:
But that it grievéd Brunhild had Kriemhild that to do forborne.
There they met together before the minster high.
Soon the royal matron, through mickle jealousy,
Kriemhild to pass no further, did bid in rage full sore:
"She that doth owe her homage shall ne'er go monarch's wife before."
Then spake the Lady Kriemhild —angry was her mood:
"An could'st thou but be silent that for thee were good.
Thyself hast brought dishonor upon thy fair body:
How might, forsooth, a harlot ever wife of monarch be?"
"Whom mak'st thou now a harlot?" the king's wife answered her.
"That do I thee," spake Kriemhild, "for that thy body fair
First was clasped by Siegfried, knight full dear to me.
In sooth 'twas ne'er my brother won first thy maidenhead from thee.
"How did thy senses leave thee? Cunning rare was this.
How let his love deceive thee, since he thy liegeman is?
And all in vain," quoth Kriemhild, "the plaint I hear thee bring."
"In sooth," then answered Brunhild, "I'll tell it to my spouse the king."
"What reck I of such evil? Thy pride hath thee betrayed,
That thou deem'st my homage should e'er to thee be paid.
Know thou in truth full certain the thing may never be:
Nor shall I e'er be ready to look for faithful friend in thee."
Thereat did weep Queen Brunhild: Kriemhild waited no more,
But passed into the minster the monarch's wife before,
With train of fair attendants. Arose there mickle hate,
Whereby eyes brightly shining anon did grow all dim and wet.
However God they worshipped or there the mass was sung,
Did deem the Lady Brunhild the waiting all too long,
For that her heart was saddened and angry eke her mood.
Therefore anon must suffer many a hero keen and good.
Brunhild with her ladies 'fore the minster did appear.
Thought she: "Now must Kriemhild further give me to hear
Of what so loud upbraideth me this free-tongued wife.
And if he thus hath boasted, amend shall Siegfried make with life."
Now came the noble Kriemhild followed by warrior band.
Then spake the Lady Brunhild: "Still thou here shalt stand.
Thou giv'st me out for harlot: let now the same be seen.
Know thou, what thus thou sayest to me hath mickle sorrow been."
Then spake the Lady Kriemhild: "So may'st thou let me go.
With the ring upon my finger I the same can show:
That brought to me my lover when first by thee he lay."
Ne'er did Lady Brunhild know grief as on this evil day.
Quoth she: "This ring full precious some hand from me did steal,

And from me thus a season in evil way conceal:
Full sure will I discover who this same thief hath been."
Then were the royal ladies both in mood full angry seen.
Then gave answer Kriemhild: "I deem the thief not I.
Well hadst thou been silent, hold'st thou thine honor high.
I'll show it with this girdle that I around me wear,
That in this thing I err not: Siegfried hath lain by thee full near."
Wrought of silk of Nineveh a girdle there she wore,
That of stones full precious showed a goodly store.
When saw it Lady Brunhild straight to weep gan she:
Soon must Gunther know it and all the men of Burgundy.
Then spake the royal matron: "Bid hither come to me
Of Rhine the lofty monarch. Hear straightway shall he
How that his sister doth my honor stain.
Here doth she boast full open that I in Siegfried's arms have lain."
The king came with his warriors, where he did weeping find
His royal spouse Brunhild, then spake in manner kind:
"Now tell me, my dear lady, who hath done aught to thee?"
She spake unto the monarch: "Thy wife unhappy must thou see.
"Me, thy royal consort, would thy sister fain
Rob of all mine honor. To thee must I complain:
She boasts her husband Siegfried hath known thy royal bed."
Then spake the monarch Gunther: "An evil thing she then hath said."
"I did lose a girdle: here by her 'tis worn,
And my ring all golden. That I e'er was born,
Do I rue full sorely if thou wardest not from me
This full great dishonor: that will I full repay to thee."
Then spake the monarch Gunther: "Now shall he come near,
And hath he such thing boasted, so shall he let us hear:
Eke must full deny it the knight of Netherland."
Then straight the spouse of Kriemhild hither to bring he gave command.
When that angry-minded Siegfried them did see,
Nor knew thereof the reason, straightway then spake he:
"Why do weep these ladies? I'd gladly know that thing,
Or wherefore to this presence I am bidden by the king."
Then spake the royal Gunther: "Sore grieveth me this thing:
To me my Lady Brunhild doth the story bring,
How that thereof thou boastest that her fair body lay
First in thy embraces: this doth thy Lady Kriemhild say."
Thereto gave answer Siegfried: "An if she thus hath said,
Full well shall she repent it ere doth rest my head:
Before all thy good warriors of that I'll make me free,
And swear by my high honor such thing hath ne'er been told by me."
Then spake of Rhine the monarch: "That shalt thou let us see.
The oath that thou dost offer, if such performéd be,
Of all false accusation shalt thou delivered stand."
In ring to take their station did he the high-born thanes command.

The full valiant Siegfried in oath the hand did give.
Then spake the lordly monarch: "Well now do I perceive
How thou art all blameless, of all I speak thee free;
What here maintains my sister, the same hath ne'er been done by thee."
Thereto gave answer Siegfried: "If gain should e'er accrue
Unto my spouse, that Brunhild from her had cause to rue,
Know that to me full sorely 'twould endless sorrow be."
Then looked upon each other the monarchs twain right graciously.
"So should we govern women," spake the thane Siegfried,
"That to leave wanton babble they should take good heed.
Forbid it to thy wife now, to mine I'll do the same.
Such ill-becoming manner in sooth doth fill my heart with shame."
No more said many a lady fair, but thus did part.
Then did the Lady Brunhild grieve so sore at heart,
That it must move to pity all King Gunther's men.
To go unto his mistress Hagen of Tronje saw ye then.
He asked to know her worry, as he her weeping saw.
Then told she him the story. To her straight made he vow,
That Lady Kriemhild's husband must for the thing atone,
Else henceforth should never a joyous day by him be known.
Then came Ortwein and Gernot where they together spake,
And there the knights did counsel Siegfried's life to take.
Thither came eke Giselher, son of Ute high.
When heard he what they counselled, spake he free from treachery:
"Ye good knights and noble, wherefore do ye that?
Ne'er deserved hath Siegfried in such way your hate,
That he therefor should forfeit at your hands his life.
In sooth small matter is it that maketh cause for woman's strife."
"Shall we rear race of bastards?" Hagen spake again:
"Therefrom but little honor had many a noble thane.
The thing that he hath boasted upon my mistress high,
Therefor my life I forfeit, or he for that same thing shall die."
Then spake himself the monarch: "To us he ne'er did give
Aught but good and honor: let him therefore live.
What boots it if my anger I vent the knight upon?
Good faith he e'er hath shown us, and that full willingly hath done."
Then outspake of Metz Ortwein the thane:
"In sooth his arm full doughty may bring him little gain.
My vengeance full he'll suffer, if but my lord allow."
The knights—nor reason had they— against him mortal hate did vow.
None yet his words did follow, but to the monarch's ear
Ne'er a day failed Hagen the thought to whisper there:
If that lived not Siegfried, to him would subject be
Royal lands full many. The king did sorrow bitterly.
Then did they nothing further: soon began the play.
As from the lofty minster passed they on their way,
What doughty shafts they shattered Siegfried's spouse before!

Gunther's men full many saw ye there in rage full sore.
Spake the king: "Now leave ye such mortal enmity:
The knight is born our honor and fortune good to be.
Keen is he unto wonder, hath eke so doughty arm
That, were the contest open, none is who dared to work him harm."
"Naught shall he know," quoth Hagen. "At peace ye well may be:
I trow the thing to manage so full secretly
That Queen Brunhild's weeping he shall rue full sore.
In sooth shall he from Hagen have naught but hate for evermore."
Then spake the monarch Gunther: "How might such thing e'er be?"
Thereto gave answer Hagen: "That shalt thou hear from me.
We'll bid that hither heralds unto our land shall fare,
Here unknown to any, who shall hostile tidings bear.
"Then say thou 'fore the strangers that thou with all thy men
Wilt forth to meet the enemy. He'll offer service then
If that thus thou sayest, and lose thereby his life,
Can I but learn the story from the valiant warrior's wife."
The king in evil manner did follow Hagen's rede,
And the two knights, ere any man thereof had heed,
Had treachery together to devise begun.
From quarrel of two women died heroes soon full many a one.

FIFTEENTH ADVENTURE

How Siegfried was Betrayed

Upon the fourth morning two and thirty men
Saw ye to court a-riding. Unto King Gunther then
Were tidings borne that ready he should make for foe—
This lie did bring to women many, anon full grievous woe.
Leave had they 'fore the monarch's presence to appear,
There to give themselves out for men of Luedeger,
Him erstwhile was conquered by Siegfried's doughty hand
And brought a royal hostage bound unto King Gunther's land.
The messengers he greeted and to seat them gave command.
Then spake one amongst them: "Allow that yet we stand
Until we tell the tidings that to thee are sent.
Know thou that warriors many on thee to wreak their hate are bent.
"Defiance bids thee Luedegast and eke Luedeger
Who at thy hands full sorely erstwhile aggrievéd were:
In this thy land with hostile host they'll soon appear."
To rage begin the monarch when such tidings he did hear.
Those who did act thus falsely they bade to lodge the while.
How himself might Siegfried guard against such guile
As there they planned against him, he or ever one?
Unto themselves 'twas sorrow great anon that e'er 'twas done.

With his friends the monarch secret counsel sought.
Hagen of Tronje let him tarry not.
Of the king's men yet were many who fain would peace restore:
But nowise would Hagen his dark purpose e'er give o'er.
Upon a day came Siegfried when they did counsel take,
And there the knight of Netherland thus unto them spake:
"How goeth now so sorrowful amid his men the king?
I'll help you to avenge it, hath he been wronged in anything."
Then spake the monarch Gunther: "Of right do I lament,
Luedegast and Luedeger have hostile message sent:
They will in open manner now invade my land."
The knight full keen gave answer: "That in sooth shall Siegfried's hand,
"As doth befit thy honor, know well to turn aside.
As erstwhile to thy enemies, shall now from me betide:
Their lands and eke their castles laid waste by me shall be
Ere that I give over: thereof my head be surety.
"Thou and thy good warriors shall here at home abide,
And let me with my company alone against them ride.
That I do serve thee gladly, that will I let them see;
By me shall thy enemies, —that know thou— full requited be."
"Good tidings, that thou sayest," then the monarch said,
As if he in earnest did joy to have such aid.
Deep did bow before him the king in treachery.
Then spake Sir Siegfried: "Bring that but little care to thee."
Then serving-men full many bade they ready be:
'Twas done alone that Siegfried and his men the same might see.
Then bade he make them ready the knights of Netherland,
And soon did Siegfried's warriors for fight apparelled ready stand.
"My royal father Siegmund, here shalt thou remain,"
Spake then Sir Siegfried. "We come full soon again
If God but give good fortune, hither the Rhine beside;
Here shalt thou with King Gunther full merrily the while abide."
Then bound they on the banners as they thence would fare.
Men of royal Gunther were full many there,
Who naught knew of the matter, or how that thing might be:
There with Siegfried saw ye of knights a mickle company.
Their helms and eke their mail-coats bound on horse did stand:
And doughty knights made ready to fare from out that land.
Then went of Tronje Hagen where he Kriemhild found
And prayed a fair leave-taking, for that to battle they were bound.
"Now well is me, such husband I have," Kriemhild said,
"That to my loving kindred can bring so potent aid,
As my lord Siegfried doth now to friends of me.
Thereby," spake the high lady, "may I full joyous-minded be.
"Now full dear friend Hagen, call thou this to mind,
Good-will I e'er have borne thee, nor hate in any kind.
Let now therefrom have profit the husband dear to me.

If Brunhild aught I've injured may't not to him requited be.
"For that I since have suffered," spake the high lady.
"Sore punishment hath offered therefor the knight to me.
That I have aught e'er spoken to make her sad of mood,
Vengeance well hath taken on me the valiant knight and good."
"In the days hereafter shall ye be reconciled full well.
Kriemhild, belovéd lady, to me shalt thou tell
How that in Siegfried's person I may service do to thee.
That do I gladly, lady, and unto none more willingly."
"No longer were I fearful," spake his noble wife,
"That e'er in battle any should take from him his life,
Would he but cease to follow his high undaunted mood:
Secure were then forever the thane full valiant and good."
"Lady," spake then Hagen, "an hast thou e'er a fear
That hostile blade should pierce him, now shalt thou give to hear
With what arts of cunning I may the same prevent.
On horse and foot to guard him shall ever be my fair intent."
She spake: "Of my kin art thou, as I eke of thine.
In truth to thee commended be then dear spouse of mine,
That him well thou guardest whom full dear I hold."
She told to him a story 'twere better had she left untold.
She spake: "A valorous husband is mine, and doughty too.
When he the worm-like dragon by the mountain slew,
In its blood the stately knight himself then bathed,
Since when from cutting weapons in battle is he all unscathed.
"Nathless my heart is troubled when he in fight doth stand,
And full many a spear-shaft is hurled by hero's hand,
Lest that I a husband full dear should see no more.
Alack! How oft for Siegfried must I sit in sorrow sore!
"On thy good-will I rest me, dear friend, to tell to thee,
And that thy faith thou fully provest now to me,
Where that my spouse may smitten be by hand of foe.
This I now shall tell thee, and on thy honor this I do.
"When from the wounded dragon reeking flowed the blood,
And therein did bathe him the valiant knight and good,
Fell down between his shoulders full broad a linden leaf.
There may he be smitten; 'tis cause to me of mickle grief.'
Then spake of Tronje Hagen: "Upon his tunic sew
Thou a little token. Thereby shall I know
Where I may protect him when in the fight we strain."
She weened to save the hero, yet wrought she nothing save his bane.
She spake: "All fine and silken upon his coat I'll sew
A little cross full secret. There, doughty thane, shalt thou
From my knight ward danger when battle rageth sore,
And when amid the turmoil he stands his enemies before."
"That will I do," quoth Hagen, "lady full dear to me."
Then weenéd eke the lady it should his vantage be,

But there alone did Kriemhild her own good knight betray.
Leave of her took Hagen, and joyously he went away.
The followers of the monarch were all of merry mood.
I ween that knight thereafter never any could
Of treachery be guilty such as then was he
When that Queen Kriemhild did rest on his fidelity.
With his men a thousand upon the following day
Rode thence Sir Siegfried full joyously away.
He weened he should take vengeance for harm his friends did bear.
That he might view the tunic Hagen rode to him full near.
When he had viewed the token sent Hagen thence away
Two of his men in secret who did other tidings say:
How that King Gunther's country had nothing now to fear
And that unto the monarch had sent them royal Luedeger.
'Twas little joy to Siegfried that he must turn again
Ere for the hostile menace vengeance he had ta'en.
In sooth the men of Gunther could scarce his purpose bend.
Then rode he to the monarch, who thus began his thanks to lend:
"Now God reward thee for it, my good friend Siegfried,
That thou with mind so willing hast holpen me in need.
That shall I e'er repay thee, as I may do of right.
To thee before all other friends do I my service plight.
"Now that from battle-journey free we are once more,
So will I ride a-hunting the wild bear and the boar
Away to the Vosges forest, as I full oft have done."
The same had counselled Hagen, the full dark and faithless man.
"To all my guests here with me shall now be told
That we ride forth at daybreak: themselves shall ready hold,
Who will join the hunting; will any here remain
For pastime with fair ladies, the thing behold I eke full fain."
Then outspake Sir Siegfried as in manner due:
"If that thou rid'st a-hunting, go I gladly too.
A huntsman shalt thou grant me and good hound beside
That shall the game discover; so with thee to the green I'll ride."
Straightway spake the monarch: "Wilt thou but one alone?
And wilt thou, four I'll grant thee, to whom full well is known
The forest with the runways where most the game doth stray,
And who unto the camp-fires will help thee back to find thy way."
Unto his spouse then rode he, the gallant knight and bold.
Full soon thereafter Hagen unto the king had told
How he within his power would have the noble thane:
May deed so dark and faithless ne'er by knight be done again!

SIXTEENTH ADVENTURE

How Siegfried was slain

Gunther and Hagen, the knights full keen,
Proposed with evil forethought a hunting in the green:
The boar within the forest they'd chase with pointed spear,
And shaggy bear and bison. —What sport to valiant men more dear?
With them rode also Siegfried happy and light of heart:
Their load of rich refreshments was made in goodly part.
Where a spring ran cooling they took from him his life,
Whereto in chief had urged them Brunhild, royal Gunther's wife.
Then went the valiant Siegfried where he Kriemhild found;
Rich hunting-dress was laden and now stood ready bound
For him and his companions across the Rhine to go.
Than this a sadder hour nevermore could Kriemhild know.
The spouse he loved so dearly upon the mouth he kissed.
"God grant that well I find thee again, if so He list,
And thine own eyes to see me. 'Mid kin that hold thee dear
May now the time go gently, the while I am no longer near."
Then thought she of the story—but silence must she keep—
Whereof once Hagen asked her: then began to weep
The princess high and noble that ever she was born,
And wept with tears unceasing the valiant Siegfried's wife forlorn.
She spake unto her husband: "Let now this hunting be.
I dreamt this night of evil, how wild boars hunted thee,
Two wild boars o'er the meadow, wherefrom the flowers grew red.
That I do weep so sorely have I poor woman direst need.
"Yea, do I fear, Sir Siegfried, something treacherous,
If perchance have any of those been wronged by us
Who might yet be able to vent their enmity.
Tarry thou here, Sir Siegfried: let that my faithful counsel be."
Quoth he: "I come, dear lady, when some short days are flown.
Of foes who bear us hatred here know I never one.
All of thine own kindred are gracious unto me,
Nor know I aught of reason why they should other-minded be."
"But nay, belovéd Siegfried, thy death I fear 'twill prove.
This night I dreamt misfortune, how o'er thee from above
Down there fell two mountains: I never saw thee more.
And wilt thou now go from me, that must grieve my heart full sore."
The lady rich in virtue within his arms he pressed,
And with loving kisses her fair form caressed.
From her thence he parted ere long time was o'er:
Alas for her, she saw him alive thereafter nevermore.
Then rode from thence the hunters deep within a wold
In search of pleasant pastime. Full many a rider bold
Followed after Gunther in his stately train.

Gernot and Giselher, —at home the knights did both remain.
Went many a horse well laden before them o'er the Rhine,
That for the huntsmen carried store of bread and wine,
Meat along with fishes and other victualling,
The which upon his table were fitting for so high a king.
Then bade they make encampment before the forest green
Where game was like to issue, those hunters proud and keen,
Who there would join in hunting, on a meadow wide that spread.
Thither also was come Siegfried: the same unto the king was said.
By the merry huntsmen soon were watched complete
At every point the runways. The company then did greet
Siegfried the keen and doughty: "Who now within the green
Unto the game shall guide us, ye warriors so bold and keen?"
"Now part we from each other," answered Hagen then,
"Ere that the hunting we do here begin!
Thereby may be apparent to my masters and to me
Who on this forest journey of the hunters best may be.
"Let then hounds and huntsmen be ta'en in equal share,
That wheresoever any would go, there let him fare.
Who then is first in hunting shall have our thanks this day."
Not longer there together did the merry hunters stay.
Thereto quoth Sir Siegfried: "Of dogs have I no need,
More than one hound only of trusty hunting breed
For scenting well the runway of wild beast through the brake.
And now the chase begin we!" —so the spouse of Kriemhild spake.
Then took a practised hunter a good tracking-hound,
That did bring them where they game in plenty found,
Nor kept them long awaiting. Whate'er did spring from lair
Pursued the merry huntsmen, as still good hunters everywhere.
As many as the hound started slew with mighty hand
Siegfried the full doughty hero of Netherland.
So swiftly went his charger that none could him outrun;
And praise before all others soon he in the hunting won.
He was in every feature a valiant knight and true.
The first within the forest that with his hand he slew
Was a half-grown wild-boar that he smote to ground;
Thereafter he full quickly a wild and mighty lion found.
When it the hound had started, with bow he shot it dead,
Wherewith a pointed arrow he had so swiftly sped
That the lion after could forward spring but thrice.
All they that hunted with him cried Siegfried's praise with merry voice.
Soon fell a prey unto him an elk and bison more,
A giant stag he slew him and huge ure-oxen four.
His steed bore him so swiftly that none could him outrun;
Of stag or hind encountered scarce could there escape him one.
A boar full huge and bristling soon was likewise found,
And when the same bethought him to flee before the hound,

Came quick again the master and stood athwart his path.
The boar upon the hero full charged straightway in mickle wrath.
Then the spouse of Kriemhild, with sword the boar he slew,
A thing that scarce another hunter had dared to do.

When he thus had felled him they lashed again the hound,
And soon his hunting prowess was known to all the people round.
Then spake to him his huntsmen: "If that the thing may be,
So let some part, Sir Siegfried, of the forest game go free;
To-day thou makest empty hillside and forest wild."
Thereat in merry humor the thane so keen and valiant smiled.
Then they heard on all sides the din, from many a hound
And huntsmen eke the clamor so great was heard around
That back did come the answer from hill and forest tree—
Of hounds had four-and-twenty packs been set by hunter free.

Full many a forest denizen from life was doomed to part.
Each of all the hunters thereon had set his heart,
To win the prize in hunting. But such could never be,
When they the doughty Siegfried at the camping-place did see.
Now the chase was ended, —and yet complete 'twas not.
All they to camp who wended with them thither brought
Skin of full many an animal and of game good store.
Heigho! unto the table how much the king's attendants bore!

Then bade the king the noble hunters all to warn
That he would take refreshment, and loud a hunting-horn
In one long blast was winded: to all was known thereby
That the noble monarch   at camp did wait their company.
Spake one of Siegfried's huntsmen: "Master, I do know
By blast of horn resounding that we now shall go
Unto the place of meeting; thereto I'll make reply."
Then for the merry hunters blew the horn right lustily.

Then spake Sir Siegfried: "Now leave we eke the green."
His charger bore him smoothly, and followed huntsmen keen.
With their rout they started a beast of savage kind,
That was a bear untaméd. Then spake the knight to those behind
"For our merry party some sport will I devise.
Let slip the hound then straightway, a bear now meets my eyes,
And with us shall he thither unto the camp-fire fare.
Full rapid must his flight be shall he our company forbear."

From leash the hound was loosened, the bear sprang through the brake,
When that the spouse of Kriemhild did wish him to o'ertake.
He sought a pathless thicket, but yet it could not be,
As bruin fondly hoped it, that from the hunter he was free.
Then from his horse alighted the knight of spirit high,
And gan a running after. Bruin all unguardedly
Was ta'en, and could escape not. Him caught straightway the knight,
And soon all unwounded had him bound in fetters tight.
Nor claws nor teeth availed him for aught of injury,

But bound he was to saddle. Then mounted speedily
The knight, and to the camp-fire in right merry way
For pastime led he bruin, the hero valiant and gay.
In what manner stately unto the camp he rode!
He bore a spear full mickle, great of strength and broad.
A sword all ornamented hung down unto his spur,
And wrought of gold all ruddy at side a glittering horn he wore.
Of richer hunting-garments heard I ne'er tell before.
Black was the silken tunic that the rider wore,
And cap of costly sable did crown the gallant knight.
Heigho, and how his quiver with well-wrought hands was rich bedight!
A skin of gleaming panther covered the quiver o'er,
Prized for its pleasant odor. Eke a bow he bore,
The which to draw if ever had wished another man,
A lever he had needed: such power had Siegfried alone.
Of fur of costly otter his mantle was complete,
With other skins embroidered from head unto the feet.
And 'mid the fur all shining, full many a golden seam
On both sides of the valiant huntsman saw ye brightly gleam.
Balmung, a goodly weapon broad, he also wore,
That was so sharp at edges that it ne'er forbore
To cleave when swung on helmet: blade it was full good.
Stately was the huntsman as there with merry heart he rode.
If that complete the story to you I shall unfold,
Full many a goodly arrow did his rich quiver hold
Whereof were gold the sockets, and heads a hand-breadth each.
In sooth was doomed to perish whate'er in flight the same did reach.
Pricking like goodly huntsman the noble knight did ride
When him the men of Gunther coming thither spied.
They hasted out to meet him and took from him his steed,
As bruin great and mighty by the saddle he did lead.
When he from horse alighted he loosed him every band
From foot and eke from muzzle. Straight on every hand
Began the dogs a howling when they beheld the bear.
Bruin would to the forest: among the men was mickle stir.
Amid the clamor bruin through the camp-fires sped:
Heigho, how the servants away before him fled!
O'erturned was many a kettle and flaming brands did fly:
Heigho, what goodly victuals did scattered in the ashes lie!
Then sprang from out the saddle knights and serving-men.
The bear was wild careering: the king bade loosen then
All the dogs that fastened within their leashes lay.
If this thing well had ended, then had there passed a merry day.
Not longer then they waited but with bow and eke with spear
Hasted the nimble hunters to pursue the bear,
Yet none might shoot upon him for all the dogs around.
Such clamor was of voices that all the mountain did resound.

When by the dogs pursuéd the bear away did run,
None there that could o'ertake him but Siegfried alone.
With his sword he came upon him and killed him at a blow,
And back unto the camp-fire bearing bruin they did go.
Then spake who there had seen it, he was a man of might.
Soon to the table bade they come each noble knight,
And on a smiling meadow the noble company sat.
Heigho, with what rare victuals did they upon the huntsmen wait!
Ne'er appeared a butler wine for them to pour.
Than they good knights were never better served before,
And had there not in secret been lurking treachery,
Then were the entertainers from every cause of cavil free.
Then spake Sir Siegfried: "A wonder 'tis to me,
Since that from the kitchen so full supplied are we,
Why to us the butlers of wine bring not like store:
If such the huntsman's service a huntsman reckon me no more.
"Meseems I yet did merit some share of courtesy."
The king who sat at table spake then in treachery:
"Gladly shall be amended wherein we're guilty so.
The fault it is of Hagen, he'd willing see us thirsting go."
Then spake of Tronje Hagen: "Good master, hear me say,
I weened for this our hunting we did go to-day
Unto the Spessart forest: the wine I thither sent.
Go we to-day a-thirsting, I'll later be more provident."
Thereto replied Sir Siegfried: "Small merit here is thine.
Good seven horses laden with mead and sparkling wine
Should hither have been conducted. If aught the same denied,
Then should our place of meeting have nearer been the Rhine beside."
Then spake of Tronje Hagen: "Ye noble knights and bold,
I know here nigh unto us a spring that's flowing cold.
Be then your wrath appeaséd, and let us thither go."
Through that same wicked counsel came many a thane to grievous woe.
Sore was the noble Siegfried with the pangs of thirst:
To bid them rise from table was he thus the first.
He would along the hillside unto the fountain go:
In sooth they showed them traitors, those knights who there did counsel so.
On wagons hence to carry the game they gave command
Which had that day been slaughtered by Siegfried's doughty hand.
He'd carried off the honors, all who had seen did say.
Hagen his faith with Siegfried soon did break in grievous way.
When now they would go thither to where the linden spread,
Spake of Tronje Hagen: "To me hath oft been said,
That none could follow after Kriemhild's nimble knight
Or vie with him in running: would that he'd prove it to our sight!"
Then spake of Netherland bold Siegfried speedily:
"That may ye well have proof of, will ye but run with me
In contest to the fountain. When that the same be done,

To him be given honor who the race hath fairly won."
"Now surely make we trial," quoth Hagen the thane.
Thereto the doughty Siegfried: "I too will give you gain,
Afore your feet at starting to lay me in the grass."
When that he had heard it, thereat how joyous Gunther was!
And spake again the warrior: "And ye shall further hear:
All my clothing likewise will I upon me wear,
The spear and shield full heavy and hunting-dress I'll don."
His sword as well as quiver had he full quickly girded on.
Doffed they their apparel and aside they laid it then:
Clothed in white shirts only saw you there the twain.
Like unto two wild panthers they coursed across the green:
Yet first beside the fountain was the valiant Siegfried seen.
No man in feats of valor who with him had vied.
The sword he soon ungirded and quiver laid aside,
The mighty spear he leanéd against the linden-tree:
Beside the running fountain stood the knight stately to see.
To Siegfried naught was lacking that doth good knight adorn.
Down the shield then laid he where did flow the burn,
Yet howsoe'er he thirsted no whit the hero drank
Before had drunk the monarch: therefor he earned but evil thank.
There where ran clear the water and cool from out the spring,
Down to it did bend him Gunther the king.
And when his thirst was quenchéd rose he from thence again:
Eke the valiant Siegfried, how glad had he done likewise then.
For his courtesy he suffered. Where bow and sword there lay,
Both did carry Hagen from him thence away,
And again sprang quickly thither where the spear did stand:
And for a cross the tunic of the valiant knight he scanned.
As there the noble Siegfried to drink o'er fountain bent,
Through the cross he pierced him, that from the wound was sent
The blood nigh to bespatter the tunic Hagen wore.
By hand of knight such evil deed shall wrought be nevermore.
The spear he left projecting where it had pierced the heart.
In terror as that moment did Hagen never start
In flight from any warrior he ever yet had found.
Soon as the noble Siegfried within him felt the mighty wound,
Raging the knight full doughty up from the fountain sprang,
The while from 'twixt his shoulders stood out a spearshaft long.
The prince weened to find there his bow or his sword:
Then in sooth had Hagen found the traitor's meet reward.
When from the sorely wounded knight his sword was gone,
Then had he naught to 'venge him but his shield alone.
This snatched he from the fountain and Hagen rushed upon,
And not at all escape him could the royal Gunther's man.
Though he nigh to death was wounded he yet such might did wield
That out in all directions flew from off the shield

Precious stones a many: the shield he clave in twain.
Thus vengeance fain had taken upon his foe the stately thane.
Beneath his hand must Hagen stagger and fall to ground.
So swift the blow he dealt him, the meadow did resound.
Had sword in hand been swinging, Hagen had had his meed,
So sorely raged he stricken: to rage in sooth was mickle need.
Faded from cheek was color, no longer could he stand,
And all his might of body soon complete had waned,
As did a deathly pallor over his visage creep.
Full many a fairest lady for the knight anon must weep.
So sank amid the flowers Kriemhild's noble knight,
While from his wound flowed thickly the blood before the sight.
Then gan he reviling —for dire was his need—
Who had thus encompassed his death by this same faithless deed.
Then spake the sorely wounded: "O ye base cowards twain,
Doth then my service merit that me ye thus have slain?
To you I e'er was faithful and so am I repaid.
Alas, upon your kindred now have ye shame eternal laid.
"By this deed dishonored hereafter evermore
Are their generations. Your anger all too sore
Have ye now thus vented and vengeance ta'en on me.
With shame henceforth be parted from all good knights' company."
All the hunters hastened where he stricken lay,
It was in sooth for many of them a joyless day.
Had any aught of honor, he mourned that day, I ween,
And well the same did merit the knight high-spirited and keen.
As there the king of Burgundy mourned that he should die,
Spake the knight sore wounded: "To weep o'er injury,
Who hath wrought the evil hath smallest need, I trow.
Reviling doth he merit, and weeping may he well forego."
Thereto quoth grim Hagen: "Ye mourn, I know not why:
This same day hath ended all our anxiety.
Few shall we find henceforward for fear will give us need,
And well is me that from his mastery we thus are freed."
"Light thing is now thy vaunting," did Siegfried then reply.
"Had I e'er bethought me of this thy infamy
Well had I preservéd 'gainst all thy hate my life.
Me rueth naught so sorely as Lady Kriemhild my wife.
"Now may God have mercy that to me a son was born,
That him alack!, the people in times to come shall spurn,
That those he nameth kinsmen have done the murderer's deed.
An had I breath," spake Siegfried, "to mourn o'er this I well had need."
Then spake, in anguish praying, the hero doomed to die:
"An wilt thou, king, to any yet not good faith deny,
In all the world to any, to thee commended be
And to thy loving mercy the spouse erstwhile was wed to me.
"Let it be her good fortune that she thy sister is:

By all the princely virtues, I beg thee pledge me this.
For me long time my father and men henceforth must wait:
Upon a spouse was never wrought, as mine, a wrong so great."
All around the flowers were wetted with the blood
As there with death he struggled. Yet not for long he could,
Because the deadly weapon had cut him all too sore:
And soon the keen and noble knight was doomed to speak no more.
When the lords perceivéd how that the knight was dead,
Upon a shield they laid him that was of gold full red,
And counsel took together how of the thing should naught
Be known, but held in secret that Hagen the deed had wrought.
Then spake of them a many: "This is an evil day.
Now shall ye all conceal it and all alike shall say,
When as Kriemhild's husband the dark forest through
Rode alone a-hunting, him the hand of robber slew."
Then spake of Tronje Hagen: "Myself will bring him home.
In sooth I reck but little if to her ears it come,
Who my Lady Brunhild herself hath grieved so sore.
It maketh me small worry, an if she weep for evermore."

SEVENTEENTH ADVENTURE

How Kriemhild mourned for Siegfried, and How he was Buried

There till the night they tarried and o'er the Rhine they went.
By knights in chase might never more evil day be spent;
For the game that there they hunted wept many a noble maid.
In sooth by many a valiant warrior must it since be paid.
Of humor fierce and wanton list now and ye shall hear,
And eke of direst vengeance. Hagen bade to bear
Siegfried thus lifeless, of the Nibelung country,
Unto a castle dwelling where Lady Kriemhild found might be.
He bade in secret manner to lay him there before
Where she should surely find him when she from out the door
Should pass to matins early, ere that had come the day.
In sooth did Lady Kriemhild full seldom fail the hour to pray.
When, as was wont, in minster the bell to worship bade,
Kriemhild, fair lady, wakened from slumber many a maid:
A light she bade them bring her and eke her dress to wear.
Then hither came a chamberlain who Siegfried's corse found waiting there.
He saw him red and bloody, all wet his clothing too.
That it was his master, in sooth no whit he knew.
On unto the chamber the light in hand he bore,
Whereby the Lady Kriemhild did learn what brought her grief full sore.
When she with train of ladies would to the minster go,
Then spake the chamberlain: "Pause, I pray thee now:

Here before thy dwelling a noble knight lies slain."
Thereat gan Lady Kriemhild in grief unmeasured sore to plain.
Ere yet that 'twas her husband she did rightly find,
Had she Hagen's question begun to call to mind,
How might he protect him: then first did break her heart,
For all her joy in living did with his death from her depart.

Unto the earth then sank she ere she a word did say,
And reft of all her pleasure there the fair lady lay.
Soon had Kriemhild's sorrow all measure passed beyond:
She shrieked, when past the swooning, that did the chamber all resound.

Then spake her attendants: "What if't a stranger were?"
From out her mouth the heart-blood did spring from anguish sore.
Then spake she: "It is Siegfried my husband, other none:
This thing hath counselled Brunhild, and Hagen's hand the deed hath done."

The lady bade them lead her where did lie the knight,
And his fair head she raiséd with her hand full white.
Red though it was and bloody she knew him yet straightway,
As all forlorn the hero of Nibelungenland there lay.

Then cried the queen in anguish, whose hand such wealth might wield:
"O woe is me for sorrow! Yet is not thy shield
With blow of sword now battered, but murdered dost thou lie.
And knew I who hath done it, by my counsel should he die."

All of her attendants did weep and wail enow
With their belovéd mistress, for filled they were with woe
For their noble master whom they should see no more.
For anger of Queen Brunhild had Hagen wrought revenge full sore.

Then spake Kriemhild sorrowing: "Hence now the message take,
And all the men of Siegfried shall ye straightway awake.
Unto Siegmund likewise tell ye my sorrow deep,
If that he will help me for the doughty Siegfried weep."

Then ran straightway a messenger and soon he found at hand,
Siegfried's valiant warriors of Nibelungenland.
Of joy he all bereft him with tale that he did bear,
Nor would they aught believe it till sound of weeping met their ear.

The messenger came eke quickly where the king did lie,
Yet closed was not in sleeping the monarch Siegmund's eye:
I ween his heart did tell him the thing that there had been,
And that his dear son living might nevermore by him be seen.

"Awake, awake, Lord Siegmund. Hither hath sent for thee
Kriemhild my mistress. A wrong now beareth she,
A grief that 'fore all others unto her heart doth go:
To mourn it shalt thou help her, for sorely hast thou need thereto."

Up raised himself then Siegmund. He spake: "What may it be
Of wrong that grieveth Kriemhild, as thou hast told to me?"
The messenger spake weeping: "Now may I naught withhold:
Know thou that of Netherland Siegfried brave lies slain and cold."

Thereto gave answer Siegmund: "Let now such mocking be

And tale of such ill tidings —an thou regardest me—
As that thou say'st to any now he lieth slain:
An were it so, I never unto my end might cease to plain."
"Wilt thou now believe not the tidings that I bear,
So may'st thyself the Lady Kriemhild weeping hear,
And all of her attendants, that Siegfried lieth dead."
With terror filled was Siegmund: whereof in very sooth was need.
He and his men a hundred from their beds they sprang,
Then snatched in hand full quickly swords both sharp and long,
And toward the sound of weeping in sorrow sore did speed.
There came a thousand warriors eke of the valiant knight Siegfried.
When they heard the women weeping in such sore distress
Thought some, strict custom keeping, we first must don our dress.
In sooth for very sorrow their wits no more had they,
For on their hearts a burden of grief full deep and heavy lay.
Then came the monarch Siegmund where he Kriemhild espied.
He spake: "Alack that ever to this country I did ride!
Who in such wondrous manner, and while good friends are near,
Hath of my child bereft me and thee of spouse thou hold'st so dear?"
"Ah, might I him discover," spake the lady high,
"Evermore would mercy I to him deny.
Such meed of vengeance should he at my hands receive
That all who call him kinsman reason good should have to grieve."
Siegmund the monarch in arms the knight did press,
And of his friends there gathered so great was the distress,
That from the mighty wailing palace and wide hall
And Worms the city likewise with sound of woe re-echoed all.
None was who aught might comfort the wife of Siegfried there.
They drew the knight's attire from off his body fair,
From wounds the blood, too, washed they and laid him on the bier.
Then from all his people a mighty wailing might ye hear.
Then outspake his warriors of Nibelungenland:
"Until he be avengéd rest shall not our hand.
He is within this castle who the deed hath done."
Then rushed to find their weapons Siegfried's warriors every one.
The knights of chosen valor with shields did thither throng,
Eleven hundred warriors, that did to train belong
Of Siegmund the monarch. That his son lay dead,
Would he wreak dire vengeance, whereof in very sooth was need.
Yet knew they not whom should they beset in battle then,
If it were not Gunther and with him his men
With whom their lord Siegfried unto the hunting rode.
Yet filled with fear was Kriemhild when she beheld how armed they stood.
How great soe'er her sorrow and stern the grief she bore,
Yet for the Nibelungen feared she death full sore
From her brother's warriors, and bade them hold their wrath.
She gave them kindly warning as friend to friend beloved doth.

Then spake she rich in sorrow: "What thing beginnest thou,
Good my lord Siegmund? This case thou dost not know.
In sooth hath here King Gunther so many a valiant knight,
Lost are ye all together, will ye the thanes withstand in fight."
With shields upraised they ready for the fight did stand.
But the queen full noble did straightway give command
To those high knights, and prayed them, their purpose to give o'er.
That she might not dissuade them, in sooth to her was sorrow sore.
Spake she thus: "Lord Siegmund, thou shalt this thing let be
Until more fitting season. Seek will I e'er with thee
Full to avenge my husband. Who him from me hath ta'en,
An I shall know him guilty, in me shall surely find his bane.
"Of warriors proud and mighty are many here by Rhine,
Therefore will I advise not the struggle to begin.
For one that we can muster good thirty men have they;
As unto us their dealing, God them requite in equal way.
"Here shall ye bide with me and help my grief to bear;
Soon as dawns the morning, ye noble knights and rare,
Help me my loved husband prepare for burial."
"That shall be done full willing," spake the doughty warriors all.
To you could never any full the wonder say,
Of knights and noble ladies, so full of grief were they,
That the sound of wailing through the town was heard afar,
Whereat the noble burghers hastily did gather there.
With the guests they mourned together, for sore they grieved as well.
What was the guilt of Siegfried none to them might tell,
Wherefore the knight so noble thus his life should lose.
Then wept with the high ladies many a worthy burgher's spouse.
Smiths they bade a casket work full hastily
All of gold and silver that great and strong should be.
They bade them fast to weld it with bands of steel full good.
Then saw ye all the people stand right sorrowful of mood.
Now the night was over, for day, they said, drew near.
Then bade the noble lady unto the minster bear
Siegfried her lord full lovéd for whom she mourned so.
Whoe'er was friend unto him, him saw ye weeping thither go.
As they brought him to the minster bells full many rung.
On every hand then heard ye how priests did chant their song.
Thither with his followers came Gunther the king
And eke the grim knight Hagen where was sound of sorrowing.
He spake: "Full loving sister, alack for grief to thee,
And that from such great evil spared we might not be!
Henceforth must we ever mourn for Siegfried's sake."
"That do ye without reason," full of woe the lady spake.
"If that ye grievéd for it, befallen were it not.
For say I may full truly, me had ye all forgot
There where I thus was parted from my husband dear.

Would it God," spake Kriemhild, "that done unto myself it were!"
Fast they yet denied it. Kriemhild spake again:
"If any speak him guiltless, let here be seen full plain.
Unto the bier now shall he before the people go;
Thus the truth full quickly may we in this manner know."
It is a passing wonder that yet full oft is seen,
Where blood-bespotted slayer beside slain corse hath been,
That from the wounds come blood-drops, as here it eke befell.
Thereby the guilt of Hagen might they now full plainly tell.
Now ran the wounds all bloody like as they did before.
Who erstwhile wept full sorely now wept they mickle more.
Then spake the monarch Gunther: "To thee the truth be known:
Slain hath he been by robbers, nor is this deed by Hagen done."
"Of these same robbers," spake she, "full well I understand.
God give that yet may vengeance wreak some friendly hand.
Gunther and Hagen, yourselves have done this deed."
Then looked for bloody conflict the valiant thanes that served Siegfried.
Then spake unto them Kriemhild: "Now bear with me my need."
Knights twain came likewise hither and did find him dead,—
Gernot her brother and the young Giselher.
With upright hearts then joined they with the others grief to share.
They mourned for Kriemhild's husband with hearts all full of woe.
A mass should then be chanted: to the minster forth did go
Man and child and woman gathered from every side.
E'en they did likewise mourn him who little lost that Siegfried died.
Gernot and Giselher spake: "O Sister dear,
Now comfort thee in sorrow, for death is ever near.
Amends we'll make unto thee the while that we shall live."
In the world might never any unto her a comfort give.
His coffin was made ready about the middle day.
From off the bier they raised him whereupon he lay.
But yet would not the lady let him be laid in grave.
Therefor must all the people first a mickle trouble have.
In a shroud all silken they the dead man wound.
I ween that never any that wept not might be found.
There mournéd full of sorrow Ute the queen full high
And all of her attendants that such a noble knight did die.
When did hear the people how they in minster sung,
And that he there lay coffined, came then a mickle throng:
For his soul's reposing what offerings they bore!
E'en amid his enemies found he of good friends a store.
Kriemhild the poor lady to her attendants spake:
"Let them shun no trouble to suffer for my sake,
Who to him are friendly-minded and me in honor hold;
For the soul of Siegfried meted be to them his gold."
Child so small there was not, did it but reason have,
But offering carried thither. Ere he was laid in grave,

More than a hundred masses upon the day they sung,
Of all the friends of Siegfried was gathered there a mickle throng.
When were the masses over, the folk departed soon.
Then spake the Lady Kriemhild: "Leave ye me not alone
To pass the night in watching by this chosen thane now dead,
With whose passing from me all my joy of life hath fled.
"Three days and three nights further shall he lie on bier,
Until my heart find quiet that weeps for spouse so dear.
God perchance commandeth that death eke me do take:
That were for me poor Kriemhild fit end of all my woe to make."
Then of the town the people went to their homes again.
Priests and monks yet bade she longer there remain,
And all the hero's followers who willing served alway.
They watched a night all gruesome, and full of toil was eke the day.
Meat and drink forgetting abode there many a one.
If any were would take it 'twas unto all made known,
That have they might in plenty: thus did provide Siegmund.
Then for the Nibelungen did trouble and sore need abound.
The while the three days lasted —such the tale we hear—
All who could join the chanting, mickle must they bear
There of toil and trouble. What gifts to them they bore!
Rich were seen full many who did suffer need before.
As many poor as found they who themselves had naught,
By them yet an offering bade they there be brought,
Of gold of Siegfried's treasure. Though he no more might live,
Yet for his soul's reposing marks many thousand did they give.
Land of fruitful income bestowed Kriemhild around,
Wheresoever cloisters and worthy folk were found.
Silver and apparel to the poor she gave in store,
And in good manner showed she that truest love to him she bore.
Upon the third morning at the mass' tide
Was there beside the minster filled the church-yard wide
With country-folk a-weeping that came from far and near:
In death they yet did serve him as is meet for friend full dear.
And so it hath been told us, ere these four days were o'er,
Marks full thirty thousand, yea, in sooth, and more,
For his soul's reposing to the poor were given there:
The while that lay all broken his life and eke his body fair.
When ended was the service and full the masses sung,
In unrestrained sorrow there the flock did throng.
They bade that from the minster he to the grave be borne.
Them that fain had kept him there beheld ye weep and mourn.
Thence full loud lamenting did the people with him pass.
Unmoved there never any nor man nor woman was.
Ere that in grave they laid him chanted they and read.
What host of priests full worthy at his burial were gatheréd!
Ere that the wife of Siegfried was come unto the grave,

With water from the fountain full oft her face they lave,
So struggled with her sorrow the faithful lady fair.
Great beyond all measure was the grief that she did bear.
It was a mickle wonder that e'er her life she kept.
Many a lady was there that helped her as she wept.
Then spake the queen full noble: "Ye men that service owe
To Siegfried, as ye love me, now to me a mercy show.
"Upon this sorrow grant ye the little grace to me
That I his shining visage yet once more may see."
So filled she was with anguish and so long time she sought,
Perforce they must break open the casket all so fairly wrought.
Where she did see him lying they then the lady led.
With hand full white and spotless raised she his fair head;
Then kissed she there all lifeless the good and noble knight,—
And wept so that for sorrow ran blood from out her eyes so bright.
Mournful was the parting that then did rend the twain.
Thence away they bore her, nor might she walk again,
But in a swoon did senseless the stately lady lie.
In sooth her winsome body for sorrow sore was like to die.
When they the knight full noble now in the grave had laid,
Beheld ye every warrior beyond all measure sad
That with him was come hither from Nibelung country.
Full seldom joyous-hearted might ye royal Siegmund see.
And many were among them that for sorrow great
Till three days were over did nor drink nor eat.
Yet might they not their bodies long leave uncared-for so:
For food they turned from mourning as people still are wont to do.

EIGHTEENTH ADVENTURE

How Siegmund fared Home Again

Then went royal Siegmund where he Kriemhild found.
Unto the queen spake he: "Home must we now be bound.
We ween that guests unwelcome here are we by the Rhine.
Kriemhild, belovéd lady, come now to country that is mine.
"Though from us hath been taken by foul traitor's hand
Thy good spouse and noble here in stranger land,
Thine be it not to suffer: good friend thou hast in me
For sake of son belovéd: thereof shalt thou undoubting be.
"Eke shalt thou have, good lady, all the power to hold,
The which erstwhile hath shown thee Siegfried the thane full bold.
The land and the crown likewise, be they thine own to call,
And gladly eke shall serve thee Siegfried's doughty warriors all."
Then did they tell the servants that they thence would ride,
And straight to fetch the horses these obedient hied.
'Mid such as so did hate them it grieved them more to stay:

Ladies high and maidens were bidden dress them for the way.
When that for royal Siegmund stood ready horse and man,
Her kinsmen Lady Kriemhild to beseech began
That she from her mother would still forbear to go.
Then spake the lofty lady: "That might hardly yet be so.
"How might I for ever look with eyes upon
Him that to me, poor woman, such evil thing hath done?"
Then spake the youthful Giselher: "Sister to me full dear,
By thy goodness shalt thou tarry with thy mother here."
"Who in this wise have harmed thee and so grieved thy heart,
Thyself may'st spurn their service: of what is mine take part."
Unto the knight she answered: "Such thing may never be.
For die I must for sorrow when that Hagen I should see."
"From need thereof I'll save thee, sister full dear to me,
For with thy brother Giselher shalt thou ever be.
I'll help to still thy sorrow that thy husband lieth dead."
Then spake she sorrow-stricken: "Thereof in sooth had Kriemhild need."
When that the youthful Giselher such kindly offer made,
Then her mother Ute and Gernot likewise prayed,
And all her faithful kinsmen, that she would tarry there:
For that in Siegfried's country but few of her own blood there were.
"To thee they all are strangers," did Gernot further say.
Nor lived yet man so mighty but dead at last he lay.
Bethink thee that, dear sister, in comfort of thy mood.
Stay thou amid thy kinsmen, I counsel truly for thy good."
To Giselher she promised that she would tarry there.
For the men of Siegmund the horses ready were,
When they thence would journey to the Nibelungen land:
On carrying-horses laden the knights' attire did ready stand.
Went the royal Siegmund unto Kriemhild then;
He spake unto the lady: "Now do Siegfried's men
Await thee by the horses. Straight shall we hence away,
For 'mid the men of Burgundy unwilling would I longer stay."
Then spake the Lady Kriemhild: "My friends have counselled me,
That by the love I bear them, here my home shall be,
For that no kinsmen have I in the Nibelungen land."
Grieved full sore was Siegmund when he did Kriemhild understand.
Then spake the royal Siegmund: "To such give not thine ear,
A queen 'mid all my kinsmen, thou a crown shalt wear
And wield as lordly power as e'er till now thou hast.
Nor thou a whit shalt forfeit, that we the hero thus have lost.
"And journey with us thither, for child's sake eke of thine:
Him shalt thou never, lady, an orphan leave to pine.
When hath grown thy son to manhood, he'll comfort thee thy mood.
Meanwhile shall ready serve thee many a warrior keen and good."
She spake: "O royal Siegmund, I may not thither ride,
For I here must tarry, whate'er shall me betide,

'Mid them that are my kinsmen, who'll help my grief to share."
The knights had sore disquiet that such tidings they must hear.
"So might we say full truly," spake they every one,
"That unto us still greater evil now were done,
Would'st thou longer tarry here amid our foes:
In sooth were never journey of knights to court more full of woes."
"Now may ye free from trouble in God's protection fare:
I'll bid that trusty escort shall you have in care
Unto Siegmund's country. My child full dear to me,
Unto your knights' good mercy let it well commended be."
When that they well perceived how she would not depart,
Wept all the men of Siegmund and sad they were at heart.
In what right heavy sorrow Siegmund then took leave
Of the Lady Kriemhild! Full sore thereover must he grieve.
"Woe worth this journey hither," the lofty monarch spake.
"Henceforth from merry meeting shall nevermore o'ertake
King or his faithful kinsmen what here our meed hath been.
Here 'mid the men of Burgundy may we never be more seen."
Then spake the men of Siegfried in open words and plain:
"An might we right discover who our lord hath slain,
Warriors bent on vengeance shall yet lay waste this ground.
Among his kin in plenty may doughty foemen be found."
Anon he kissed Kriemhild and spake sorrowfully,
When she there would tarry, and he the same did see:
"Now ride we joy-forsaken home unto our land.
First now what 'tis to sorrow do I rightly understand."
From Worms away sans escort unto the Rhine they rode:
I ween that they full surely did go in such grim mood,
That had against them any aught of evil dared,
Hand of keen Nibelungen had known full well their life to guard.
Nor parting hand they offered to any that were there.
Then might ye see how Gernot and likewise Giselher
Did give him loving greeting. That as their very own
They felt the wrong he suffered, by the courteous knights and brave was shown.
Then spake in words full kindly the royal knight Gernot:
"God in heaven knoweth that of guilt I've naught
In the death of Siegfried, that e'er I e'en did hear
Who here to him were hostile. Well may I of thy sorrow share."
An escort safe did furnish the young knight Giselher:
Forth from out that country he led them full of care,
The monarch with his warriors, to Netherland their home.
How joyless is the greeting as thither to their kin they come!
How fared that folk thereafter, that can I nowise say.
Here heard ye Kriemhild plaining as day did follow day,
That none there was to comfort her heart and sorry mood,
Did Giselher not do it; he faithful was to her and good.
The while the fair Queen Brunhild in mood full haughty sat,

And weep howe'er did Kriemhild, but little recked she that,
Nor whit to her of pity displayed she evermore.
Anon was Lady Kriemhild eke cause to her of sorrow sore.

NINETEENTH ADVENTURE

How the Nibelungen Hoard was Brought to Worms

When that the noble Kriemhild thus did widowed stand,
Remained there with his warriors by her in that land
Eckewart the margrave, and served her ever true.
And he did help his mistress oft to mourn his master too.
At Worms a house they built her the minster high beside,
That was both rich and spacious, full long and eke full wide,
Wherein with her attendants joyless did she dwell.
She sought the minster gladly,—that to do she loved full well.
Seldom undone she left it, but thither went alway
In sorry mood where buried her loved husband lay.
God begged she in his mercy his soul in charge to keep,
And, to the thane right faithful, for him full often did she weep.
Ute and her attendants all times a comfort bore,
But yet her heart was stricken and wounded all so sore
That no whit might avail it what solace e'er they brought.
For lover taken from her with such grief her heart was fraught,
As ne'er for spouse belovéd a wife did ever show.
Thereby how high in virtue she stood ye well might know.
She mourned until her ending and while did last her life.
Anon a mighty vengeance wreaked the valiant Siegfried's wife.
And so such load of sorrow for her dead spouse she bore,
The story sayeth truly, for years full three or more,
Nor ever unto Gunther any word spake she,
And meantime eke her enemy Hagen never might she see.
Then spake of Tronje Hagen: "Now seek'st thou such an end,
That unto thee thy sister be well-disposéd friend?
Then Nibelungen treasure let come to this country:
Thereof thou much might'st win thee, might Kriemhild friendly-minded be."
He spake: "Be that our effort. My brothers' love hath she:
Them shall we beg to win her that she our friend may be,
And that she gladly see it that we do share her store."
"I trow it well," spake Hagen, "may such thing be nevermore."
Then did he Ortwein unto the court command
And the margrave Gere. When both were found at hand,
Thither brought they Gernot and eke young Giselher.
In friendly manner sought they to win the Lady Kriemhild there.
Then spake of Burgundy Gernot the warrior strong:
"Lady, the death of Siegfried thou mournest all too long.

Well will the monarch prove thee that him he ne'er hath slain.
'Tis heard how that right sorely thou dost for him unending plain."
She spake: "The king none chargeth: t'was Hagen's hand that slew.
When Hagen me did question where might one pierce him through,
How might e'er thought come to me that hate his heart did bear?
Then 'gainst such thing to guard me," spake she, "had I ta'en good care.

"And kept me from betraying to evil hands his life,
Nor cause of this my weeping had I his poor lorn wife.
My heart shall hate forever who this foul deed have done."
And further to entreat her young Giselher had soon begun.

When that to greet the monarch a willing mind spake she,
Him soon with noble kinsmen before her might ye see.
Yet dare might never Hagen unto her to go:
On her he'd wrought sore evil, as well his guilty mind did know.

When she no hatred meted unto Gunther as before,
By Hagen to be greeted were fitting all the more.
Had but by his counsel no ill to her been done,
So might he all undaunted unto Kriemhild have gone.

Nor e'er was peace new offered kindred friends among
Sealed with tears so many. She brooded o'er her wrong.
To all she gave her friendship save to one man alone.
Nor slain her spouse were ever, were not the deed by Hagen done.

Small time it was thereafter ere they did bring to pass
That with the Lady Kriemhild the mighty treasure was,
That from Nibelungen country she brought the Rhine unto.
It was her bridal portion and 'twas fairly now her due.

For it did journey thither Gernot and Giselher.
Warriors eighty hundred Kriemhild commanded there
That they should go and fetch it where hidden it did lie,
And where the good thane Alberich with friends did guard it faithfully.

When saw they coming warriors from Rhine the hoard to take,
Alberich the full valiant to his friends in this wise spake:
"We dare not of the treasure aught from them withhold:
It is her bridal portion, —thus the noble queen hath told.

"Yet had we never granted," spake Alberich, "this to do,
But that in evil manner   the sightless mantle too
With the doughty Siegfried we alike did lose,
The which did wear at all times the fair Kriemhild's noble spouse.

"Now alas hath Siegfried had but evil gain
That from us the sightless mantle the hero thus hath ta'en,
And so hath forced to serve him all these lands around."
Then went forth the porter where full soon the keys he found.

There stood before the mountain ready Kriemhild's men,
And her kinsmen with them. The treasure bore they then
Down unto the water where the ships they sought:
To where the Rhine flowed downward across the waves the hoard they brought.

Now of the treasure further may ye a wonder hear:

Heavy wains a dozen scarce the same might bear
In four days and nights together from the mountain all away,
E'en did each one of them thrice the journey make each day.
In it was nothing other than gold and jewels rare.
And if to every mortal on earth were dealt a share,
Ne'er 'twould make the treasure by one mark the less.
Not without good reason forsooth would Hagen it possess.
The wish-rod lay among them, of gold a little wand.
Whosoe'er its powers full might understand,
The same might make him master o'er all the race of men.
Of Alberich's kin full many with Gernot returned again.
When they did store the treasure in King Gunther's land,
And to royal Kriemhild 'twas given 'neath her hand,
Storing-rooms and towers could scarce the measure hold.
Nevermore such wonder might of wealth again be told.
And had it e'en been greater, yea a thousandfold,
If but again might Kriemhild safe her Siegfried hold,
Fain were she empty-handed of all the boundless store.
Spouse than she more faithful won a hero nevermore.
When now she had the treasure, she brought into that land
Knights many from far distance. Yea, dealt the lady's hand
So freely that such bounty ne'er before was seen.
High in honor held they for her goodly heart the queen.
Unto both rich and needy began she so to give
That fearful soon grew Hagen, if that she would live
Long time in such high power, lest she of warriors true
Such host might win to serve her, that cause would be her strength to rue.
Spake Gunther then: "The treasure is hers and freedom too.
Wherefore shall I prevent her, whate'er therewith she do?
Yea, nigh she did her friendship from me evermore withhold.
Now reck we not who shareth or her silver or her gold."
Unto the king spake Hagen: "No man that boasteth wit
Should to any woman such hoard to hold permit.
By gifts she yet will bring it that will come the day
When valiant men of Burgundy rue it with good reason may."
Then spake the monarch Gunther: "To her an oath I swore,
That I would cause of evil to her be nevermore,
Whereof henceforth I'll mind me: sister she is to me."
Then spake further Hagen: "Let me bear the guilt for thee."
Many they were that kept not there their plighted word:
From the widow took they all that mighty hoard:
Every key had Hagen known to get in hand.
Rage filled her brother Gernot when he the thing did understand.
Then spake the knight Giselher: "Hagen here hath wrought
Sore evil to my sister: permit this thing I'll not.
And were he not my kinsman, he'd pay it with his life."
Anew did fall aweeping then the doughty Siegfried's wife.

Then spake the knight Gernot: "Ere that forever we
Be troubled with this treasure, let first commanded be
Deep in the Rhine to sink it, that no man have it more."
In sad manner plaining Kriemhild stood Giselher before.
She spake: "Belovéd brother, be mindful thou of me:
What life and treasure toucheth shalt thou my protector be."
Then spake he to the lady: "That shall sure betide,
When we again come hither: now called we are away to ride."
The monarch and his kinsmen rode from out the land,
And in his train the bravest ye saw on any hand:
Went all save Hagen only, and there he stayed for hate,
That he did bear to Kriemhild, and full gladly did he that.
Ere that the mighty monarch was thither come again,
In that while had Hagen all that treasure ta'en.
Where Loch is by the river all in the Rhine sank he.
He weened thereof to profit, yet such thing might never be.
The royal knights came thither again with many a man.
Kriemhild with her maidens and ladies then began
To mourn the wrong they suffered, that pity was to hear.
Fain had the faithful Giselher been unto her a comforter.
Then spake they all together: "Done hath he grievous wrong."
But he the princes' anger avoided yet so long
At last to win their favor. They let him live sans scathe.
Then filled thereat was Kriemhild as ne'er before with mickle wrath.
Ere that of Tronje Hagen had hidden thus the hoard,
Had they unto each other given firm plighted word,
That it should lie concealéd while one of them might live.
Thereof anon nor could they to themselves nor unto other give.
With renewéd sorrows   heavy she was of heart
That so her dear-loved husband perforce from life must part,
And that of wealth they reft her. Therefor she mourned alway,
Nor ever ceased her plaining until was come her latest day.
After the death of Siegfried dwelt she in sorrow then,
—Saith the tale all truly— full three years and ten,
Nor in that time did ever for the knight mourn aught the less.
To him she was right faithful, must all the folk of her confess.

TWENTIETH ADVENTURE

How King Etzel sent to Burgundy for Kriemhild

In that same time when ended was Lady Helke's life,
And that the monarch Etzel did seek another wife,
To take a highborn widow of the land of Burgundy
Hun his friends did counsel: Lady Kriemhild hight was she.
Since that was ended the fair Helke's life,

Spake they: "Wilt thou ever win for thee noble wife,
The highest and the fairest that ever king did win,
Take to thee this same lady that doughty Siegfried's spouse hath been."
Then spake the mighty monarch: "How might that come to pass
Since that I am a heathen, nor named with sign of cross?
The lady is a Christian, thereto she'll ne'er agree.
Wrought must be a wonder, if the thing may ever be."
Then spake again his warriors: "She yet may do the same.
For sake of thy great power and thy full lofty name
Shalt thou yet endeavor such noble wife to gain.
To woo the stately lady might each monarch high be fain."
Then spake the noble monarch: "Who is 'mong men of mine,
That knoweth land and people dwelling far by Rhine?"
Spake then of Bechelaren the trusty Ruediger:
"I have known from childhood the noble queen that dwelleth there.
"And Gunther and Gernot, the noble knights and good,
And hight the third is Giselher: whatever any should
That standeth high in honor and virtue, doth each one:
Eke from eld their fathers have in like noble manner done."
Then spake again Etzel: "Friend, now shalt thou tell,
If she within my country crown might wear full well—
For be she fair of body as hath been told to me,
My friends for this their counsel shall ever full requited be."
"She likeneth in beauty well my high lady,
Helke that was so stately. Nor forsooth might be
In all this world a fairer spouse of king soe'er.
Whom taketh she for wooer, glad of heart and mind he were."
He spake: "Make trial, Ruediger, as thou hold'st me dear.
And if by Lady Kriemhild e'er I lie full near,
Therefor will I requite thee as in best mode I may:
So hast thou then fulfilled all my wish in fullest way.
"Stores from out my treasure I'll bid to thee to give,
That thou with thy companions merry long shalt live,
Of steeds and rich apparel what thou wilt have to share.
Thereof unto thy journey I'll bid in measure full prepare."
Thereto did give him answer the margrave Ruediger:
"Did I thy treasure covet unworthy thing it were.
Gladly will I thy messenger be unto the Rhine,
From my own store provided: all have I e'en from hand of thine."
Then spake the mighty monarch: "When now wilt thou fare
To seek the lovely lady? God of thee have care
To keep thee on thy journey and eke a wife to me.
Therein good fortune help me, that she to us shall gracious be."
Then again spake Ruediger: "Ere that this land we quit,
Must we first prepare us arms and apparel fit,
That we may thus in honor in royal presence stand.
To the Rhine I'll lead five hundred warriors, a doughty band.

"Wherever they in Burgundy me and my men may see,
Shall they all and single then confess of thee
That ne'er from any monarch so many warriors went
As now to bear thy message thou far unto the Rhine hast sent.
"May it not, O mighty monarch, thee from thy purpose move:
Erstwhile unto Siegfried she gave her noble love,
Who scion is of Siegmund: him thou here hast seen.
Worthy highest honor verily the knight had been."
Then answered him King Etzel: "Was she the warrior's wife,
So worthy was of honor the noble prince in life,
That I the royal lady therefor no whit despise.
'Tis her surpassing beauty that shall be joy unto mine eyes."
Then further spake the margrave: "Hear then what I do say:
After days four-and-twenty shall we from hence away.
Tidings to Gotelinde I'll send, my spouse full dear,
That I to Lady Kriemhild myself will be thy messenger."
Away to Bechelaren sent then Ruediger.
Both sad his spouse and joyous was the news to hear.
He told how for the monarch a wife he was to woo:
With love she well remembered the fair Lady Helke too.
When that the margravine did the message hear,
In part 'twas sorrow to her, and weep she must in fear
At having other mistress than hers had been before.
To think on Lady Helke did grieve her inmost heart full sore.
Ruediger from Hunland in seven days did part,
Whereat the monarch Etzel merry was of heart.
When at Vienna city all was ready for the way,
To begin the journey might he longer not delay.
At Bechelaren waited Gotelinde there,
And eke the young margravine, daughter of Ruediger,
Was glad at thought her father and all his men to see.
And many a lovely maiden looked to the coming joyfully.
Ere that to Bechelaren rode noble Ruediger
From out Vienna city, was rich equipment there
For them in fullest measure on carrying-horses brought,
That went in such wise guarded that robber hand disturbed them not.
When they at Bechelaren within the town did stand,
His fellows on the journey did the host command
To lead to fitting quarters and tend carefully.
The stately Gotelinde, glad she was her spouse to see.
Eke his lovely daughter the youthful margravine,—
To her had nothing dearer than his coming been.
The warriors too from Hunland, what joy for her they make!
With a laughing spirit to all the noble maiden spake:
"Be now to us right welcome, my father and all his men."
Fairest thanks on all sides saw ye offered then
Unto the youthful margravine by many a valiant knight.

How Ruediger was minded knew Gotelinde aright.
When then that night she by Ruediger lay,
Questioned him the margravine in full loving way,
Wherefore had sent him thither the king of Hunland.
He spake: "My Lady Gotelinde, that shalt thou gladly understand.
"My master now hath sent me to woo him other wife,
Since that by death was ended the fair Helke's life.
Now will I to Kriemhild ride unto the Rhine:
She shall here in Hunland be spouse to him and stately queen."
"God will it," spake Gotelinde, "and well the same might be,
Since that so high in honor ever standeth she.
The death of my good mistress we then may better bear;
Eke might we grant her gladly among the Huns a crown to wear."
Then spake to her the margrave: "Thou shalt, dear lady mine,
To them that shall ride with me thither unto the Rhine,
In right bounteous manner deal out a goodly share.
Good knights go lighter-hearted when they well provided fare."
She spake: "None is among them, an he would take from me,
But I will give whatever to him may pleasing be,
Ere that ye part thither, thou and thy good men."
Thereto spake the margrave: "So dost thou all my wishes then."
Silken stuffs in plenty they from her chamber bore,
And to the knights full noble dealt out in goodly store,
Mantles lined all richly from collar down to spur.
What for the journey pleased him did choose therefrom Sir Ruediger.
Upon the seventh morning from Bechelaren went
The knight with train of warriors. Attire and armament
Bore they in fullest measure through the Bavarian land,
And ne'er upon the journey dared assail them robber band.
Unto the Rhine then came they ere twelve days were flown,
And there were soon the tidings of their coming known.
'Twas told unto the monarch and with him many a man,
How strangers came unto him. To question then the king began,
If any was did know them, for he would gladly hear.
They saw their carrying-horses right heavy burdens bear:
That they were knights of power knew they well thereby.
Lodgings they made them ready in the wide city speedily.
When that the strangers had passed within the gate
Every eye did gaze on the knights that came in state,
And mickle was the wonder whence to the Rhine they came.
Then sent the king for Hagen, if he perchance might know the same.
Then spake he of Tronje: "These knights I ne'er have seen,
Yet when we now behold them I'll tell thee well, I ween,
From whence they now ride hither unto this country.
An I not straightway know them, from distant land in sooth they be."
For the guests fit lodgings now provided were.
Clad in rich apparel came the messenger,

And to the court his fellows did bear him company.
Sumptuous attire wore they, wrought full cunningly.
Then spake the doughty Hagen: "As far as goes my ken,
For that long time the noble knight I not have seen,
Come they in such manner as were it Ruediger,
The valiant thane from Hunland, that leads the stately riders here."
Then straightway spake the monarch: "How shall I understand
That he of Bechelaren should come unto this land?"
Scarce had King Gunther his mind full spoken there,
When saw full surely Hagen that 'twas the noble Ruediger.
He and his friends then hastened with warmest welcoming.
Then saw ye knights five hundred adown from saddle spring,
And were those knights of Hunland received in fitting way.
Messengers ne'er beheld ye attired in so fine array.
Hagen of Tronje, with voice full loud spake he:
"Unto these thanes full noble a hearty welcome be,
To the lord of Bechelaren and his men every one."
Thereat was fitting honor done to every valiant Hun.
The monarch's nearest kinsmen went forth the guests to meet.
Of Metz the knight Sir Ortwein Ruediger thus did greet:
"The while our life hath lasted, never yet hath guest
Here been seen so gladly: be that in very truth confessed."
For that greeting thanked they the brave knights one and all.
With train of high attendants they passed unto the hall,
Where valiant men a many stood round the monarch's seat.
The king arose from settle in courteous way the guests to greet.
Right courteously he greeted then the messenger.
Gunther and Gernot, full busy both they were
For stranger and companions a welcome fit to make.
The noble knight Sir Ruediger by the hand the king did take.
He led him to the settle where himself he sat:
He bade pour for the strangers (a welcome work was that)
Mead the very choicest and the best of wine,
That e'er ye might discover in all the lands about the Rhine.
Giselher and Gere joined the company too,
Eke Dankwart and Volker, when that they knew
The coming of the strangers: glad they were of mood,
And greeted 'fore the monarch fair the noble knights and good.
Then spake unto his master of Tronje the knight:
"Let our thanes seek ever fully to requite
What erstwhile the margrave in love to us hath done:
Fair Gotelinde's husband our gratitude full well hath won."
Thereto spake King Gunther: "Withhold it not I may.
How they both do bear them, tell me now, I pray,
Etzel and Helke afar in Hunland."
Then answered him the margrave: "Fain would I have thee understand."
Then rose he from the settle and his men every one.

He spake unto the monarch: "An may the thing be done,
And is't thy royal pleasure, so will I naught withhold,
But the message that I bring thee shall full willingly be told."
He spake: "What tale soever, doth this thy message make,
I grant thee leave to tell it, nor further counsel take.
Now shalt thou let us hear it, me and my warriors too,
For fullest leave I grant thee thy high purpose to pursue."
Then spake the upright messenger: "Hither to thee at Rhine
Doth faithful service tender master high of mine;
To all thy kinsmen likewise, as many as may be:
Eke is this my message borne in all good will to thee.
"To thee the noble monarch bids tell his tale of need.
His folk 's forlorn and joyless; my mistress high is dead,
Helke the full stately my good master's wife,
Whereby now is orphaned full many a fair maiden's life,
"Children of royal parents for whom hath cared her hand:
Thereby doth the country in plight full sorry stand.
Alack, nor is there other that them with love may tend.
I ween the time long distant eke when the monarch's grief shall end."
"God give him meed," spake Gunther, "that he so willingly
Doth offer thus good service to my kinsmen and to me—
I joy that I his greeting here have heard this day—
The which with glad endeavor my kinsmen and my men shall pay."
Thereto the knight of Burgundy, the valiant Gernot, said:
"The world may ever rue it that Helke fair lies dead,
So manifold the virtues that did her life adorn."
A willing testimony by Hagen to the words was borne.
Thereto again spake Ruediger the noble messenger:
"Since thou, O king, dost grant it, shalt thou now further hear
What message 'tis my master beloved hath hither sent,
For that since death of Helke his days he hath in sorrow spent.
"'Tis told my lord that Kriemhild doth widowed live alone,
And dead is doughty Siegfried. May now such thing be done,
And wilt thou grant that favor, a crown she then shall wear
Before the knights of Etzel: this message from my lord I bear."
Then spake the mighty monarch —a king he was of grace—
"My will in this same matter she'll hear, an so she please.
Thereof will I instruct thee ere three days are passed by—
Ere I her mind have sounded, wherefore to Etzel this deny?"
Meanwhile for the strangers bade they make cheer the best
In sooth so were they tended that Ruediger confessed
He had 'mong men of Gunther of friends a goodly store.
Hagen full glad did serve him, as he had Hagen served of yore.
Thus there did tarry Ruediger until the third day.
The king did counsel summon —he moved in wisest way—
If that unto his kinsmen seemed it fitting thing,
That Kriemhild take unto her for spouse Etzel the king.

Together all save Hagen did the thing advise,
And unto King Gunther spake he in this wise:
"An hast thou still thy senses, of that same thing beware,
That, be she ne'er so willing, thou lend'st thyself her will to share."
"Wherefore," spake then Gunther, "should I allow it not?
Whene'er doth fortune favor Kriemhild in aught,
That shall I gladly grant her, for sister dear is she.
Yea, ought ourselves to seek it, might it but her honor be."
Thereto gave answer Hagen: "Now such words give o'er.
Were Etzel known unto thee as unto me of yore,
And did'st thou grant her to him, as 'tis thy will I hear,
Then wouldst thou first have reason for thy later weal to fear."
"Wherefore?" spake then Gunther. "Well may I care for that,
E'er to thwart his temper that so I aught of hate
At his hands should merit, an if his wife she be."
Thereto gave answer Hagen: "Such counsel hast thou ne'er of me."
Then did they bid for Gernot and Giselher to go,
For wished they of the royal twain their mind to know,
If that the mighty monarch Kriemhild for spouse should take.
Yet Hagen and none other thereto did opposition make.
Then spake of Burgundy Giselher the thane:
"Well may'st thou now, friend Hagen, show upright mind again:
For sorrows wrought upon her may'st thou her well requite.
Howe'er she findeth fortune, ne'er should it be in thy despite."
"Yea, hast thou to my sister so many sorrows done,"
So spake further Giselher, the full noble thane,
"That fullest reason hath she to mete thee naught but hate.
In sooth was never lady than she bereft of joy more great."
"What I do know full certain, that known to all I make:
If e'er shall come the hour that she do Etzel take,
She'll work us yet sore evil, howe'er the same she plan.
Then in sooth will serve her full many a keen and doughty man."
In answer then to Hagen the brave Gernot said:
"With us doth lie to leave it until they both be dead,
Ere that we ride ever unto Etzel's land.
That we be faithful to her doth honor meantime sure command."
Thereto again spake Hagen: "Gainsay me here may none.
And shall the noble Kriemhild e'er sit 'neath Helke's crown,
Howe'er she that accomplish, she'll do us grievous hurt.
Good knights, therefrom to keep you doth better with your weal consort."
In anger spake then Giselher the son of Ute the fair:
"None shall yet among us himself like traitor bear.
What honor e'er befall her, rejoice thereat should we.
Whate'er thou sayest, Hagen, true helper shall she find in me."
When that heard it Hagen straightway waxed he wroth.
Gernot and Giselher the knights high-minded both,
And Gunther, mighty monarch, did counsel finally,

If that did wish it Kriemhild, by them 'twould unopposéd be.
Then spake the margrave Gere: "That lady will I tell
How that of royal Etzel she may think full well.
In fear are subject to him brave warriors many a one:
Well may he recompense her for wrong that e'er to her was done."
Then went the knight full valiant where he did Kriemhild find,
And straightway spake unto her upon her greeting kind:
"Me may'st thou gladly welcome with messengers high meed.
Fortune hath come to part thee now from all thy bitter need.
"For sake of love he bears thee, lady, doth seek thy hand
One of all the highest that e'er o'er monarch's land
Did rule in fullest honor, or ever crown might wear:
High knights do bring the message, which same thy brother bids thee hear."
Then spake she rich in sorrow: "Now God forbid to thee
And all I have of kinsmen that aught of mockery
They do on me, poor woman. What were I unto one,
Who e'er at heart the joyance of a noble wife hath known?"
Much did she speak against it. Anon as well came there
Gernot her brother and the young Giselher.
In loving wise they begged her her mourning heart to cheer:
An would she take the monarch, verily her weal it were.
Yet might not then by any the lady's mind be bent,
That any man soever to love she would consent.
Thereon the thanes besought her: "Now grant the thing to be,
An dost thou nothing further, that the messenger thou deign'st to see."
"That will I not deny you," spake the high lady,
"That the noble Ruediger I full gladly see,
Such knightly grace adorns him. Were he not messenger,
And came there other hither by him I all unspoken were."
She spake: "Upon the morrow bid him hither fare
Unto this my chamber. Then shall he fully hear
How that do stand my wishes, the which I'll tell him true."
Of her full grievous sorrow was she minded thus anew.
Eke not else desired the noble Ruediger
Than that by the lady leave thus granted were:
He knew himself so skilful, might he such favor earn,
So should he her full certain from her spoken purpose turn.
Upon the morrow early when that the mass was sung
Came the noble messengers, whereof a mickle throng.
They that should Sir Ruediger to court bear company,
Many a man full stately in rich apparel might ye see.
Kriemhild, dame high-stated, —full sad she was of mood—
There Ruediger awaited, the noble knight and good.
He found her in such raiment as daily she did wear:
The while were her attendants in dresses clad full rich and rare,
Unto the threshold went she the noble guest to meet,
And the man of Etzel did she full kindly greet.

Twelve knights there did enter, himself and eleven more,
And well were they received: to her such guests came ne'er before.
The messenger to seat him and his men they gave command.
The twain valiant margraves saw ye before her stand,
Eckewart and Gere, the noble knights and keen,
Such was the lady's sorrow, none saw ye there of cheerful mien.
They saw before her sitting full many a lady fair,
And yet the Lady Kriemhild did naught but sorrow there.
The dress upon her bosom was wet with tears that fell,
And soon the noble margrave perceived her mickle grief full well.
Then spake the lofty messenger: "Daughter of king full high,
To me and these my fellows that bear me company
Deign now the grace to grant us that we before thee stand
And tell to thee the tidings wherefore we rode unto thy land."
"That grace to thee is granted," spake the lofty queen;
"Whate'er may be thy message, I'll let it now be seen
That I do hear it gladly: thou'rt welcome messenger."
That fruitless was their errand deemed the others well to hear.
Then spake of Bechelaren the noble Ruediger:
"Pledge of true love unto thee from lofty king I bear,
Etzel who bids thee, lady, here royal compliment:
He hath to woo thy favor knights full worthy hither sent.
"His love to thee he offers full heartily and free:
Fidelity that lasteth he plighteth unto thee,
As erst to Lady Helke who o'er his heart held sway.
Yea, thinking on her virtues hath he full oft had joyless day."
Then spake the royal lady: "O Margrave Ruediger,
If that known to any my sharp sorrows were,
Besought then were I never again to take me spouse.
Such ne'er was won by lady as the husband I did lose."
"What is that sootheth sorrow," the valiant knight replied,
"An be't not loving friendship whene'er that may betide,
And that each mortal choose him who his delight shall be?
Naught is that so availeth to keep the heart from sorrow free.
"Wilt thou minded be to love him, this noble master mine,
O'er mighty crowns a dozen the power shall be thine.
Thereto of princes thirty my lord shall give thee land,
The which hath all subdued the prowess of his doughty hand.
"O'er many a knight full worthy eke mistress shalt thou be
That my Lady Helke did serve right faithfully,
And over many a lady that served amid her train,
Of high and royal lineage," spake the keen and valiant thane.
"Thereto my lord will give thee —he bids to thee make known—
If that beside the monarch thou deign'st to wear a crown,
Power in fullest measure that Helke e'er might boast:
The same in lordly manner shalt thou wield o'er Etzel's host."
Then spake the royal lady: "How might again my life

Have thereof desire to be a hero's wife?
Hath death in one already wrought me such sorrows sore,
That joyless must my days be from this time for evermore."
Then spake the men of Hunland: "O royal high lady,
Thy life shall there by Etzel so full of honor be
Thy heart 'twill ever gladden if but may be such thing:
Full many a thane right stately doth homage to the mighty king.
"Might but Helke's maidens and they that wait on thee
E'er be joined together in one royal company,
Well might brave knights to see them wax merry in their mood.
Be, lady, now persuaded —'tis verily thy surest good."
She spake in courteous manner: "Let further parley be
Until doth come the morrow. Then hither come to me.
So will I give my answer to bear upon your way."
The noble knights and worthy must straight therein her will obey.
When all from thence were parted and had their lodgings sought,
Then bade the noble lady that Giselher be brought,
And eke with him her mother. To both she then did tell
That meet for her was weeping, and naught might fit her mood so well.
Then spake her brother Giselher: "Sister, to me 'tis told—
And well may I believe it— that thy grief manifold
Etzel complete will scatter, an tak'st thou him for man.
Whate'er be other's counsel, meseems it were a thing well done."
Further eke spake Giselher: "Console thee well may he.
From Rhone unto Rhine river, from Elbe unto the sea,
King there is none other that holds so lordly sway.
An he for spouse do take thee, gladden thee full well he may."
"Brother loved full dearly, wherefore dost counsel it?
To mourn and weep forever doth better me befit.
How may I 'mid warriors appear in royal state?
Was ever fair my body, of beauty now 'tis desolate."
Then spake the Lady Ute her daughter dear unto:
"The thing thy brother counsels, my loving child, that do.
By thy friends be guided, then with thee well 'twill be.
Long time it now hath grieved me thee thus disconsolate to see."
Then prayed she God with fervor that he might her provide
With store of gold and silver and raiment rich beside,
As erstwhile when her husband did live a stately thane:
Since then so happy hour never had she known again.
In her own bosom thought she: "An shall I not deny
My body to a heathen —a Christian lady I—
So must I while life lasteth have shame to be my own.
An gave he realms unnumbered, such thing by me might ne'er be done."
And there withal she left it. The night through until day,
Upon her couch the lady with mind full troubled lay.
Nor yet her eyes full shining of tears at all were free,
Until upon the morrow forth to matins issued she.

When for mass was sounded, came there the kings likewise.
Again did they their sister by faithful word advise
To take for spouse unto her of Hunland the king.
All joyless was the visage they saw the lady thither bring.
They bade the men of Etzel thither lead again,
Who unto their country fain their leave had ta'en,
Their message won or fruitless, how that soe'er might be.
Unto the court came Ruediger. Full eager were his company
By the knight to be informéd how the thing befell,
And if betimes they knew it 'twould please them all full well,
For weary was the journey and long unto their land.
Soon did the noble Ruediger again in Kriemhild's presence stand.
In full earnest manner then the knight gan pray
The high royal lady that she to him might say
What were from her the message to Etzel he should bear.
Naught but denial only did he from the lady hear,
For that her love might never by man again be won.
Thereto spake the margrave: "Ill such thing were done.
Wherefore such fair body wilt thou to ruin give?
Spouse of knight full worthy may'st thou yet in honor live."
Naught booted how they besought her, till that Ruediger
Spake in secret manner in the high lady's ear,
How Etzel should requite her for ills she e'er did know.
Then gan her mickle sorrow milder at the thought to grow.
Unto the queen then spake he: "Let now thy weeping be.
If 'mong the Huns hadst thou other none than me
And my faithful kinsmen and my good men alone,
Sorely must he repay it who hath aught to thee of evil done."
Thereat apace all lighter the lady's sorrow grew,
She spake: "So swear thou truly, what any 'gainst me do,
That thou wilt be the foremost my sorrows to requite."
Thereto spake the margrave: "Lady, to thee my word I plight."
With all his men together sware then Ruediger
Faithfully to serve her, and in all things whatsoe'er
Naught would e'er deny her the thanes from Etzel's land,
Whereof she might have honor: thereto gave Ruediger his hand.
Then thought the faithful lady: "Since I thus have won
Band of friends so faithful, care now have I none
How shall speak the people in my sore need of me.
The death of my loved husband perchance shall yet avengéd be."
Thought she: "Since hath Etzel so many knights and true,
An shall I but command them, whate'er I will I do.
Eke hath he such riches that free may be my hand:
Bereft of all my treasure by Hagen's faithless art I stand."
Then spake she unto Ruediger: "Were it not, as I do know,
The king is yet a heathen, so were I fain to go
Whithersoe'er he willed it, and take him for my lord."

Thereto spake the margrave: "Lady, no longer hold such word.
"Such host he hath of warriors who Christians are as we,
That beside the monarch may care ne'er come to thee.
Yea, may he be baptized through thee to Christian life:
Well may'st thou then rejoice thee to be the royal Etzel's wife."
Then spake again her brother: "Sister, thy favor lend,
That now all thy sorrow thereby may have an end."
And so long they besought her that full of sadness she
Her word at length had plighted the monarch Etzel's wife to be.
She spake: "You will I follow, I most lorn lady,
That I fare to Hunland, as soon as it may be
That I friends have ready to lead me to his land."
Before the knights assembled fair Kriemhild pledged thereto her hand.
Then spake again the margrave: "Two knights do serve thee true,
And I thereof have many: 'tis easy thing to do,
That thee with fitting honor across the Rhine we guide.
Nor shalt thou, lady, longer here in Burgundy abide.
"Good men have I five hundred, and eke my kinsmen stand
Ready here to serve thee and far in Etzel's land,
Lady, at thy bidding. And I do pledge the same,
Whene'er thou dost admonish, to serve thee without cause for shame.
"Now bid with full equipment thy horses to prepare:
Ruediger's true counsel will bring thee sorrow ne'er;
And tell it to thy maidens whom thou wilt take with thee.
Full many a chosen warrior on the way shall join our company."
They had full rich equipment that once their train arrayed
The while that yet lived Siegfried, so might she many a maid
In honor high lead with her, as she thence would fare.
What steeds all rich caparisoned awaited the high ladies there!
If till that time they ever in richest dress were clad,
Thereof now for their journey full store was ready made,
For that they of the monarch had such tidings caught.
From chests longtime well bolted forth the treasures rich were brought.
Little were they idle until the fifth day,
But sought rich dress that folded secure in covers lay.
Kriemhild wide did open all her treasure there,
And largess great would give she unto the men of Ruediger.
Still had she of the treasure of Nibelungenland,
(She weened the same in Hunland to deal with bounteous hand)
So great that hundred horses ne'er the whole might bear.
How stood the mind of Kriemhild, came the tidings unto Hagen's ear.
He spake: "Since Kriemhild never may me in favor hold,
E'en so here must tarry Siegfried's store of gold.
Wherefore unto mine enemies such mickle treasure go?
What with the treasure Kriemhild intendeth, that full well I know.
"Might she but take it thither, in sooth believe I that,
'Twould be dealt out in largess to stir against me hate.

Nor own they steeds sufficient the same to bear away.
'Twill safe be kept by Hagen —so shall they unto Kriemhild say."
When she did hear the story, with grief her heart was torn.
Eke unto the monarchs all three the tale was borne.
Fain would they prevent it: yet when that might not be,
Spake the noble Ruediger in this wise full joyfully:
"Wherefore, queen full stately, weep'st thou o'er this gold?
For thee will King Etzel in such high favor hold
When but his eyes behold thee, to thee such store he'll give
That ne'er thou may'st exhaust it: that, lady, by my word believe."
Thereto the queen gave answer: "Full noble Ruediger,
Greater treasure never king's daughter had for share
Than this that Hagen from me now hath ta'en away."
Then went her brother Gernot to the chamber where the treasure lay.
With force he stuck the monarch's key into the door,
And soon of Kriemhild's treasure they from the chamber bore
Marks full thirty thousand or e'en more plenteously.
He bade the guests to take it, which pleased King Gunther well to see.
Then Gotelinde's husband of Bechelaren spake:
"An if my Lady Kriemhild with her complete might take
What treasure e'er came hither from Nibelungenland,
Ne'er a whit would touch it mine or my royal lady's hand.
"Now bid them here to keep it, for ne'er the same I'll touch.
Yea brought I from my country of mine own wealth so much,
That we upon our journey may be full well supplied,
And ne'er have lack in outlay as in state we homeward ride."
Chests well filled a dozen from the time of old
Had for their own her maidens, of the best of gold
That e'er ye might discover: now thence away 'twas borne,
And jewels for the ladies upon the journey to be worn.
Of the might she yet was fearful of Hagen grim and bold.
Still had she of mass-money a thousand marks in gold,
That gave she for the soul's rest of her husband dear.
Such loving deed and faithful did touch the heart of Ruediger.
Then spake the lady mournful: "Who now that loveth me,
And for the love they bear me may willing exiles be,
Who with me to Hunland now away shall ride?
Take they of my treasure and steeds and meet attire provide."
Then did the margrave Eckewart answer thus the queen:
"Since I from the beginning of thy train have been,
Have I e'er right faithful served thee," spake the thane,
"And to the end I'll ever thus faithful unto thee remain.
"Eke will I lead with me five hundred of my men,
Whom I grant to serve thee in faithful way again.
Nor e'er shall we be parted till that we be dead."
Low bowing thanked him Kriemhild, as verily might be his meed.
Forth were brought the horses, for that they thence would fare.

Then was a mickle weeping of friends that parted there.
Ute, queen full stately, and many a lady more
Showed that from Lady Kriemhild to part did grieve their hearts full sore.
A hundred stately maidens with her she led away,
And as for them was fitting, full rich was their array.
Many a bitter tear-drop from shining eye fell down:
Yet joys knew they full many eke in Etzel's land anon.
Thither came Sir Giselher and Gernot as well,
And with them train of followers, as duty did compel.
Safe escort would they furnish for their dear sister then,
And with them led of warriors a thousand brave and stately men.
Then came the valiant Gere, and Ortwein eke came he:
Rumold the High Steward might not absent be.
Unto the Danube did they night-quarters meet provide.
Short way beyond the city did the royal Gunther ride.
Ere from the Rhine they started had they forward sent
Messengers that full quickly unto Hunland went,
And told unto the monarch how that Ruediger
For spouse at length had won him the high-born queen beyond compare.

TWENTY-FIRST ADVENTURE

How Kriemhild fared to the Huns

The messengers leave we riding. Now shall ye understand
How did the Lady Kriemhild journey through the land,
And where from her were parted Gernot and Giselher.
Upon her had they waited as faithful unto her they were.
As far as to the Danube at Vergen did they ride,
Where must be the parting from their royal sister's side,
For that again they homeward would ride unto the Rhine.
No eye but wet from weeping in all the company was seen.
Giselher the valiant thus to his sister said:
"If that thou ever, lady, need hast of my aid,
And fronts thee aught of trouble, give me to understand,
And straight I'll ride to serve thee afar unto King Etzel's land."
Upon the mouth then kissed she all her friends full dear.
The escort soon had taken eke leave of Ruediger
And the margrave's warriors in manner lovingly.
With the queen upon her journey went many a maid full fair to see.
Four beyond a hundred there were, all richly clad
In silk of cunning pattern. Many a shield full broad
On the way did guard the ladies in hand of valiant thane.
Full many a stately warrior from thence did backward turn again.
Thence away they hastened down through Bavarian land.
Soon were told the tidings how that was at hand

A mickle host of strangers, where a cloister stands from yore
And where the Inn its torrent doth into Danube river pour.
At Passau in the city a lordly bishop bode.
Empty soon each lodging and bishop's palace stood:
To Bavarian land they hastened the high guests to meet,
And there the Bishop Pilgrim the Lady Kriemhild fair did greet.
The warriors of that country no whit grieved they were
Thus to see follow with her so many a maiden fair.
Upon those high-born ladies their eyes with joy did rest,
Full comfortable quarters prepared they for each noble guest.
With his niece the bishop unto Passau rode.
When among the burghers the story went abroad,
That thither was come Kriemhild, the bishop's niece full fair,
Soon did the towns-people reception meet for her prepare.
There to have them tarry was the bishop fain.
To him spake Sir Eckewart: "Here may we not remain.
Unto Ruediger's country must we journey down.
Thanes many there await us, to whom our coming well is known."
The tidings now knew likewise Lady Gotelinde fair.
Herself and noble daughter did them quick prepare.
Message she had from Ruediger that he well pleased would be,
Should she unto Lady Kriemhild show such courtesy,
That she ride forth to meet her, and bring his warriors true
Upward unto the Ense. When they the tidings knew,
Saw ye how on all sides they thronged the busy way.
Forth to meet the strangers rode and eke on foot went they.
As far as Everdingen meanwhile was come the queen:
In that Bavarian country on the way were never seen
Robbers seeking plunder, as e'er their custom was:
Of fear from such a quarter had the travellers little cause.
'Gainst that had well provided the noble margrave:
A band he led that numbered good thousand warriors brave.
There was eke come Gotelinde, spouse of Ruediger,
And bearing her high company full many noble knights there were.
When came they o'er the Traune by Ense on the green,
There full many an awning outstretched and tent was seen,
Wherein that night the strangers should find them welcome rest.
Well was made provision by Ruediger for each high guest.
Not long fair Gotelinde did in her quarters stay,
But left them soon behind her. Then coursed upon the way
With merry jingling bridle many a well-shaped steed.
Full fair was the reception: whereat was Ruediger right glad.
On one side and the other did swell the stately train
Knights that rode full gaily, many a noble thane.
As they in joust disported, full many a maid looked on,
Nor to the queen unwelcome was the riders' service done.
As rode there 'fore the strangers the men of Ruediger,

From shaft full many a splinter saw ye fly in air
In hand of doughty warrior that jousted lustily.
Them might ye 'fore the ladies pricking in stately manner see.
Anon therefrom they rested. Knights many then did greet
Full courteously each other. Then forth Kriemhild to meet
Went the fair Gotelinde, by gallant warriors led.
Those skilled in lady's service, —little there the rest they had.
The lord of Bechelaren unto his lady rode.
Soon the noble margravine her high rejoicing showed,
That all safe and sound he from the Rhine was come again.
The care that filled her bosom by mickle joy from her was ta'en.
When him she had receivéd, her on the green he bade
Dismount with all the ladies that in her train she led.
There saw ye all unidle many a knight of high estate,
Who with full ready service upon the ladies then did wait.
Then saw the Lady Kriemhild the margravine where she stood
Amid her fair attendants: nearer not she rode.
Upon the steed that bore her the rein she drew full tight,
And bade them straightway help her adown from saddle to alight.
The bishop saw ye leading his sister's daughter fair,
And with him eke went Eckewart to Gotelinde there.
The willing folk on all sides made way before their feet.
With kiss did Gotelinde the dame from land far distant greet.
Then spake in manner kindly the wife of Ruediger;
"Right glad am I, dear lady, that I thy visage fair
Have in this our country with mine own eyes seen.
In these times might never greater joy to me have been."
"God give thee meed," spake Kriemhild, "Gotelinde, for this grace.
If with son of Botelung happy may be my place,
May it henceforth be thy profit that me thou here dost see."
Yet all unknown to either was that which yet anon must be.
With curtsy to each other went full many a maid,
The knights a willing service unto the ladies paid.
After the greeting sat they adown upon the green;
Knew many then each other that hitherto had strangers been.
For the ladies they poured refreshment. Now was come mid-day,
And did those high attendants there no longer stay,
But went where found they ready many a spreading tent.
Full willing was the service unto the noble guests they lent.
The night through until morning did they rest them there.
They of Bechelaren meanwhile did prepare
That into fitting quarters each high guest be brought.
'Twas by the care of Ruediger that never one did want for aught.
Open ye saw the windows the castle walls along,
And the burgh at Bechelaren its gates wide open flung,
As through the guests went pricking, that there full welcome were.
For them the lord full noble had bidden quarters meet prepare.

Ruediger's fair daughter with her attendant train
Came forth in loving manner to greet the lofty queen.
With her was eke her mother the stately margravine;
There full friendly greeting of many a maiden fair was seen.
By the hand they took each other and thence did pass each pair
Into a Hall full spacious, the which was builded fair,
And 'neath its walls the Danube flowed down with rushing tide.
As breezes cool played round them, might they full happy there abide.
What they there did further, tell it not I can.
That they so long did tarry, heard ye the knights complain
That were of Kriemhild's company, who unwilling there abode.
What host of valiant warriors with them from Bechelaren rode!
Full kindly was the service did render Ruediger,
Likewise gave Lady Kriemhild twelve golden armbands rare
To Gotelinde's daughter, and dress so richly wrought
That finer was none other that into Etzel's land she brought.
Though Nibelungen treasure from her erstwhile was ta'en,
Good-will of all that knew her did she e'er retain
With such little portion as yet she did command.
Unto her host's attendants dealt she thereof with bounteous hand.
The Lady Gotelinde such honors high again
Did pay in gracious manner to the guests afar from Rhine
That of all the strangers found ye never one
That wore not rich attire from her, and many a precious stone.
When they their fast had broken and would thence depart,
The lady of the castle did pledge with faithful heart
Unto the wife of Etzel service true to bear.
Kriemhild caressed full fondly the margravine's young daughter fair.
To the queen then spake the maiden: "If e'er it pleaseth thee,
Well know I that my father dear full willingly
Unto thee will send me where thou livest in Hunland."
That faithful was the maiden, full well did Kriemhild understand.
Now ready were the horses the castle steps before,
And soon the queen full stately did take her leave once more
Of the lovely daughter and spouse of Ruediger.
Eke parted with fair greeting thence full many a maiden fair.
Each other they full seldom thereafter might behold.
From Medelick were carried beakers rich of gold
In hand and eke full many, wherein was sparkling wine:
Upon the way were greeted thus the strangers from the Rhine.
High there a lord was seated, Astold the name he bore,
Who that into Osterland did lead the way before
As far as to Mautaren adown the Danube's side.
There did they fitting service for the lofty queen provide.
Of his niece the bishop took leave in loving wise.
That she well should bear her, did he oft advise,
And that she win her honor as Helke erst had done.

Ah, how great the honor anon that 'mid the Huns she won!
Unto the Traisem brought they forth the strangers then.
Fair had they attendance from Ruediger's men,
Till o'er the country riding the Huns came them to meet.
With mickle honor did they then the royal lady greet.
For had the king of Hunland, Traisem's stream beside,
A full mighty castle, known afar and wide,
The same hight Traisenmauer: Dame Helke there before
Did sit, such bounteous mistress as scarce ye ever might see more.
An it were not Kriemhild who could such bounty show,
That after days of sorrow the pleasure she might know,
To be held in honor by Etzel's men each one:
That praise in fullest measure had she amid those thanes anon.
Afar the might of Etzel so well was known around,
That at every season within his court were found
Knights of all the bravest, whereof ye e'er did hear
In Christian lands or heathen: with him all thither come they were.
By him at every season, as scarce might elsewhere be,
Knights both of Christian doctrine and heathen use saw ye.
Yet in what mind soever did each and every stand,
To all in fullest measure dealt the king with bounteous hand.

TWENTY-SECOND ADVENTURE

How Etzel kept the Wedding-feast with Kriemhild

At Traisenmauer she tarried until the fourth day.
Upon the road the dust-clouds meanwhile never lay.
But rose like smoke of fire around on every side:
Onward then through Austria King Etzel's warriors did ride.
Then eke unto the monarch such tidings now were told,
That at the thought did vanish all his grief of old,
In what high manner Kriemhild should in his land appear.
Then gan the monarch hasten where he did find the lady fair.
Of many a tongue and varied upon the way were seen
Before King Etzel riding full many warriors keen,
Of Christians and of heathen a spreading company.
To greet their coming mistress forth they rode in fair array.
Of Reuss men and Greeks there great was the tale,
And rapid saw ye riding the Wallach and the Pole
On chargers full of mettle that they did deftly guide.
Their own country's custom did they in no wise lay aside.
From the land of Kief rode there full many a thane,
And the wild Petschenegers. Full many a bow was drawn,
As at the flying wild-fowl through air the bolt was sped.
With might the bow was bended as far as to the arrow's head.

A city by the Danube in Osterland doth stand,
Hight the same is Tulna: of many a distant land
Saw Kriemhild there the customs, ne'er yet to her were known.
To many there did greet her sorrow befell through her anon.
Before the monarch Etzel rode a company
Of merry men and mighty, courteous and fair to see,
Good four-and-twenty chieftains, mighty men and bold.
Naught else was their desire save but their mistress to behold.
Then the Duke Ramung from far Wallachia
With seven hundred warriors dashed forth athwart her way:
Their going might ye liken unto birds in flight.
Then came the chieftain Gibeke, with his host a stately sight.
Eke the valiant Hornbog with full thousand men
From the king went forward to greet his mistress then.
After their country's custom in joy they shouted loud;
The doughty thanes of Hunland likewise in merry tourney rode.
Then came a chief from Denmark, Hawart bold and keen,
And the valiant Iring, in whom no guile was seen,
And Irnfried of Thuringia, a stately knight to see:
Kriemhild they greeted that honor high therefrom had she,
With good knights twelve hundred whom led they in their train.
Thither with three thousand came Bloedel eke, the thane
That was King Etzel's brother out of Hunland:
Unto his royal mistress led he then his stately band.
Then did come King Etzel and Dietrich by his side
With all his doughty fellows. In state there saw ye ride
Many a knight full noble, valiant and void of fear.
The heart of Lady Kriemhild did such host of warriors cheer.
Then to his royal mistress spake Sir Ruediger:
"Lady, now give I greeting to the high monarch here.
Whom to kiss I bid thee, grant him such favor then:
For not to all like greeting may'st thou give 'mid Etzel's men."
They lifted then from saddle the dame of royal state.
Etzel the mighty monarch might then no longer wait,
But sprang from off his charger with many a warrior keen:
Unto Kriemhild hasting full joyously he then was seen.
As is to us related, did there high princes twain
By the lady walking bear aloft her train,
As the royal Etzel went forward her to meet,
And she the noble monarch with kiss in kindly wise did greet.
Aside she moved her wimple, whereat her visage fair
Gleamed 'mid the gold around it. Though many a knight stood there,
They deemed that Lady Helke did boast not fairer face.
Full close beside the monarch his brother Bloedel had his place.
To kiss him then Margrave Ruediger her did tell,
And eke the royal Gibeke and Sir Dietrich as well.
Of highest knights a dozen did Etzel's spouse embrace;

Other knights full many she greeted with a lesser grace.
All the while that Etzel stood by Kriemhild so,
Did the youthful riders as still they're wont to do:
In varied tourney saw ye each 'gainst the other pass,
Christian knights and heathen, as for each the custom was.
From men that followed Dietrich saw ye in kindly wise
Splinters from the lances flying high arise
Aloft above their bucklers, from hand of good knight sent!
By the German strangers pierced was many a shield and rent.
From shaft of lances breaking did far the din resound.
Together came the warriors from all the land around,
Eke the guests of the monarch and many a knight there was.
Thence did the mighty monarch then with Lady Kriemhild pass.
Stretched a fair pavilion beside them there was seen:
With tents as well was covered all around the green,
Where they now might rest them all that weary were.
By high-born knights was thither led full many a lady fair.
With their royal mistress, where in rich cushioned chair
Sat the queen full stately. 'Twas by the margrave's care
That well had been provided, with all that seeméd good,
A worthy seat for Kriemhild: thereat was Etzel glad of mood.
What was by Etzel spoken, may I not understand.
In his right hand resting lay her fair white hand.
They sat in loving fashion, nor Ruediger would let
The king have secret converse with Lady Kriemhild as yet.
'Twas bidden that the jousting on all sides they give o'er.
The din of stately tourney heard ye then no more.
All the men of Etzel unto their tents did go,
For every warrior present did they full spacious lodging show.
And now the day was ended and they did rest the night
Until beheld they shining once more the morning light.
Soon on charger mounted again was many a man:
Heigho, what merry pastime, the king to honor, they began!
By the Huns the monarch bade honors high be shown.
Soon rode they forth from Tulna unto Vienna town,
Where found they many a lady decked out in fair array:
The same the monarch Etzel's wife received in stately way.
In very fullest measure upon them there did wait
Whate'er they might desire. Of knights the joy was great,
Looking toward the revel. Lodging then sought each one.
The wedding of the monarch was in merry wise begun.
Yet not for all might lodging within the town be had.
All that were not strangers, Ruediger them bade
That they find them lodgings beyond the city's bound.
I ween that at all seasons by Lady Kriemhild's side was found
The noble Sir Dietrich and many another thane,
Who amid their labors but little rest had ta'en,

That the guests they harbored of merry mood should be.
For Ruediger and his companions went the time full pleasantly.
The wedding time was fallen upon a Whitsuntide,
When the monarch Etzel lay Kriemhild beside
In the town at Vienna. So many men I ween
Through her former husband had not in her service been.
Many that ne'er had seen her did her rich bounty take,
And many a one among them unto the strangers spake:
"We deemed that Lady Kriemhild of wealth no more had aught
Now hath she by her giving here full many a wonder wrought."
The wedding-feast it lasted for days full seventeen.
Ne'er of other monarch hath any told, I ween,
That wedded with more splendor: of such no tale we hear.
All that there were present, new-made apparel did they wear.
I ween that far in Netherland sat she ne'er before
Amid such host of warriors. And this believe I more:
Was Siegfried rich in treasure, that yet he ne'er did gain,
As here she saw 'fore Etzel, so many a high and noble thane.
Nor e'er gave any other at his own wedding-tide
So many a costly mantle flowing long and wide,
Nor yet so rich apparel —so may ye well believe—
As here from hand of Kriemhild did they one and all receive.
Her friends and eke the strangers were of a single mind,
That they would not be sparing of treasure in any kind:
What any from them desired, they gave with willing hand.
Many a thane from giving himself of clothing reft did stand.
How by her noble husband at the Rhine a queen she sat,
Of that she still was minded, and her eye grew wet thereat.
Yet well she kept it hidden that none the same might mark.
Now had she wealth of honor after long years of sorrow dark.
What any did with bounty, 'twas but an idle wind
By side of Dietrich's giving: what Etzel's generous mind
Before to him had given, complete did disappear.
Eke wrought there many a wonder the hand of bounteous Ruediger.
Bloedelein the chieftain that came from Hunland,
Full many a chest to empty did he then command,
Of gold and eke of silver. That did they freely give.
Right merrily the warriors of the monarch saw ye live.
Likewise the monarch's minstrels Werbel and Schwemmelein,
Won they at the wedding each alone, I ween,
Marks a good thousand or even more than that,
Whenas fair Lady Kriemhild 'neath crown by royal Etzel sat.
Upon the eighteenth morning from Vienna town they went.
Then in knightly pastime many a shield was rent
By spear full well directed by doughty rider's hand.
So came the royal Etzel riding into Hunland.
At Heimburg's ancient castle they tarried over night.

Tell the tale of people no mortal ever might,
And the number of good warriors did o'er the country come.
Ah, what fairest women were gathered unto Etzel's home!
By Miesenburg's majestic towers did they embark.
With horses eke and riders the water all was dark,
As if 'twere earth they trod on, as far as eye might see.
The way-worn ladies rested now on board right pleasantly.
Now was lashed together many a boat full good,
That no harm they suffered from the waves and flood.
Many a stately awning likewise above them spread,
Just as if beneath them had they land and flowery mead.
When to Etzelburg the tidings soon were borne along,
Therein of men and women were seen a merry throng.
Who once the Lady Helke as mistress did obey,
Anon by Lady Kriemhild lived they many a gladsome day.
There did stand expectant full many a maid high-born,
That since the death of Helke had pined all forlorn.
Daughters of seven monarchs Kriemhild there waiting found,
That were the high adornment of all King Etzel's country round.
Herrat, a lofty princess, did all the train obey,
Sister's child to Helke, in whom high virtues lay,
Betrothéd eke of Dietrich, of royal lineage born,
Daughter of King Nentwein; her did high honors eft adorn.
Against the strangers' coming her heart with joy flowed o'er:
Eke was thereto devoted of wealth a mickle store.
Who might e'er give the picture, how the king eft sat on throne?
Nor had with any mistress the Huns such joyous living known.
As with his spouse the monarch up from the river came,
Unto the noble Kriemhild of each they told the name
'Mong them that she did find there: she fairer each did greet.
Ah, how mighty mistress she long did sit in Helke's seat!
Ready and true the service to her was offered there.
The queen dealt out in plenty gold and raiment rare,
Silver eke and jewels. What over Rhine she brought
With her unto Hunland, soon thereof retained she naught.
Eke in faithful service she to herself did win
All the king's warriors and all his royal kin,
—So that ne'er did Lady Helke so mighty power wield
As until death to Kriemhild such host did willing service yield.
Thus stood so high in honor the court and country round,
That there at every season was pleasant pastime found
By each, whithersoever his heart's desire might stand:
That wrought the monarch's favor and the queen's full bounteous hand.

TWENTY-THIRD ADVENTURE

How Kriemhild thought to avenge her Wrong

In full lordly honor, —truth is that ye hear—
Dwelt they with each other until the seventh year.
Meanwhile Lady Kriemhild a son to Etzel bore,
Nor gladder might the monarch be o'er aught for evermore.
Yet would she not give over, nor with aught be reconciled,
But that should be baptizéd the royal Etzel's child
After Christian custom: Ortlieb they did him call.
Thereat was mickle joyance over Etzel's borders all.
Whate'er of highest virtues in Lady Helke lay,
Strove the Lady Kriemhild to rival her each day.
Herrat the stranger maiden many a grace she taught,
Who yet with secret pining for her mistress Helke was distraught.
To stranger and to native full well she soon was known,
Ne'er monarch's country, said they, did royal mistress own
That gave with freer bounty, that held they without fear.
Such praise she bore in Hunland, until was come the thirteenth year.
Now had she well perceivéd how all obeyed her will,
As service to royal mistress king's knights do render still,
And how at every season twelve kings 'fore her were seen.
She thought of many a sorrow that wrought upon her once had been.
Eke thought she of lordly power in Nibelungenland
That she erstwhile had wielded, and how that Hagen's hand
Of it all had reft her with her lord Siegfried dead;
She thought for so great evil how might he ever be repaid.
"'Twould be, might I but bring him hither into this land."
She dreamed that fondly led her full often by the hand
Giselher her brother, full oft in gentle sleep
Thought she to have kissed him, wherefrom he sorrow soon must reap.
I ween the evil demon was Kriemhild's counsellor
That she her peace with Gunther should sacred keep no more,
Whom she kissed in friendly token in the land of Burgundy.
Adown upon her bosom the burning tears fell heavily.
On her heart both late and early lay the heavy thought,
How that, herself all guiltless, thereto she had been brought,
That she must share in exile a heathen monarch's bed.
Through Hagen eke and Gunther come she was to such sore need.
From her heart such longing seldom might she dismiss.
Thought she: "A queen so mighty I am o'er wealth like this,
That I upon mine enemies may yet avenge me well.
Fain were I that on Hagen of Tronje yet my vengeance fell.
"For friends that once were faithful full oft my heart doth long.
Were they but here beside me that wrought on me such wrong,
Then were in sooth avengéd my lover reft of life;

Scarce may I bide that hour," spake the royal Etzel's wife.
Kriemhild they loved and honored, the monarch's men each one,
As they that came there with her: well might the same be done.
The treasure wielded Eckewart, and won good knights thereby.
The will of Lady Kriemhild might none in all that land deny.
She mused at every season: "The king himself I'll pray,"—
That he to her the favor might grant in friendly way,
To bring her kinsmen hither unto Hunland.
What vengeful thought she cherished might none soever understand.
As she in stillest night-time by the monarch lay
(In his arms enclosed he held her, as he was wont alway
To caress the noble lady: she was to him as life),
Again unto her enemies turned her thoughts his stately wife.
She spake unto the monarch: "My lord full dear to me,
Now would I pray a favor, if with thy grace it be,
That thou wilt show unto me if merit such be mine
That unto my good kinsmen truly doth thy heart incline."
The mighty monarch answered (from guile his heart was free):
"Of a truth I tell thee, if aught of good may be
The fortune of thy kinsmen,—of that I were full fain,
For ne'er through love of woman might I friends more faithful gain."
Thereat again spake Kriemhild: "That mayst thou well believe,
Full high do stand my kinsmen; the more it doth me grieve
That they deign so seldom hither to take their way.
That here I live a stranger, oft I hear the people say."
Then spake the royal Etzel: "Beloved lady mine,
Seemed not too far the journey, I'd bid from yond the Rhine
Whom thou wouldst gladly welcome hither unto my land."
Thereat rejoiced the lady when she his will did understand.
Spake she: "Wilt thou true favor show me, master mine,
Then shalt thou speed thy messengers to Worms across the Rhine.
Were but my friends acquainted what thing of them I would,
Then to this land came hither full many a noble knight and good."
He spake: "Whene'er thou biddest, straight the thing shall be.
Thyself mightst ne'er thy kinsmen here so gladly see,
As I the sons of Ute, high and stately queen.
It grieveth me full sorely that strangers here so long they've been.
"If this thing doth please thee, beloved lady mine,
Then gladly send I thither unto those friends of thine
As messengers my minstrels to the land of Burgundy."
He bade the merry fiddlers lead before him presently.
Then hastened they full quickly to where they found the king
By side of Kriemhild sitting. He told them straight the thing,
How they should be his messengers to Burgundy to fare.
Full stately raiment bade he for them straightway eke prepare.
Four and twenty warriors did they apparel well.
Likewise did the monarch to them the message tell,

How that they King Gunther and his men should bid aright.
Them eke the Lady Kriemhild to secret parley did invite.
Then spake the mighty monarch: "Now well my words attend.
All good and friendly greeting unto my friends I send,
That they may deign to journey hither to my country.
Few be the guests beside them that were so welcome unto me.

"And if they be so minded to meet my will in aught,
Kriemhild's lofty kinsmen, that they forego it not
To come upon the summer here where I hold hightide,
For that my joy in living doth greatly with my friends abide."
Then spake the fiddle-player, Schwemmelein full bold:
"When thinkst thou in this country such high feast to hold,
That unto thy friends yonder tell the same we may?"
Thereto spake King Etzel: "When next hath come midsummer day."
"We'll do as thou commandest," spake then Werbelein.
Unto her own chamber commanded then the queen
To bring in secret manner the messengers alone.
Thereby did naught but sorrow befall full many a thane anon.
She spake unto the messengers: "Mickle wealth I give to you,
If my will in this matter right faithfully ye do,
And bear what tidings send I home unto our country.
I'll make you rich in treasure and fair apparelled shall ye be.

"And friends of mine so many as ever see ye may
At Worms by Rhine river, to them ye ne'er shall say
That any mood of sorrow in me ye yet have seen.
Say ye that I commend me unto the knights full brave and keen."
"Pray them that to King Etzel's message they give heed,
Thereby to relieve me of all my care and need,
Else shall the Huns imagine that I all friendless am.
If I but a knight were, oft would they see me at their home.

"Eke say ye unto Gernot, brother to me full dear,
To him might never any disposéd be more fair;
Pray him that he bring hither unto this country
All our friends most steadfast, that we thereby shall honored be.

"Say further eke to Giselher that he do have in mind,
That by his guilt I never did cause for sorrow find;
Him therefore would I gladly here with mine own eyes see,
And give him warmest welcome, so faithful hath he been to me.

"How I am held in honor, to my mother eke make plain.
And if of Tronje Hagen hath mind there to remain,
By whom might they in coming through unknown lands be shown?
The way to Hunland hither from youth to him hath well been known."
No whit knew the messengers wherefore she did advise
That they of Tronje Hagen should not in any wise
Leave by the Rhine to tarry. That was anon their bane:
Through him to dire destruction was doomed full many a doughty thane.
Letters and kindly greeting now to them they give;

They fared from thence rich laden, and merrily might live.
Leave then they took of Etzel and eke his lady fair,
And parted on their journey dight in apparel rich and rare.

TWENTY-FOURTH ADVENTURE

How Werbel and Schwemmel brought the Message

When to the Rhine King Etzel his messengers had sent,
With hasty flight fresh tidings from land to land there went:
With messengers full quickly to his high festival
He bade them, eke and summoned. To many thereby did death befall.
The messengers o'er the borders of Hunland thence did fare
Unto the land of Burgundy; thither sent they were
Unto three lordly monarchs and eke their mighty men.
To Etzel's land to bid them hastily they journeyed then.
Unto Bechelaren rode they on their way,
Where found they willing service. Nor did aught delay
Ruediger to commend him and Gotelinde as well
And eke their fairest daughter to them that by the Rhine did dwell.
They let them not unladen with gifts from thence depart,
So did the men of Etzel fare on with lighter heart.
To Ute and to her household sent greeting Ruediger,
That never margrave any to them more well disposéd were.
Unto Brunhild also did they themselves commend
With willing service offered and steadfast to the end.
Bearing thus fair greeting the messengers thence did fare,
And prayed the noble margravine that God would have them in his care.
Ere the messengers had fully passed o'er Bavarian ground,
Had the nimble Werbel the goodly bishop found.
What greetings to his kinsmen unto the Rhine he sent,
That I cannot tell you; the messengers yet from him went
Laden with gold all ruddy, to keep his memory.
Thus spake the Bishop Pilgrim: "'Twere highest joy to me
Might I my sister's children here see in home of mine,
For that I may but seldom go unto them to the Rhine."
What were the ways they followed as through the lands they fared,
That can I nowise tell you. Yet never any dared
Rob them of wealth or raiment, for fear of Etzel's hand:
A lofty king and noble, mighty in sooth was his command.
Before twelve days were over came they unto the Rhine,
And rode into Worms city Werbel and Schwemmelein.
Told were soon the tidings to the kings and their good men,
How that were come strange messengers. Gunther the king did question then.
And spake the monarch further: "Who here may understand
Whence do come these strangers riding unto our land?"

Yet was never any might answer to him make,
Until of Tronje Hagen thus unto King Gunther spake:
"To us hath come strange tidings to hand this day, I ween,
For Etzel's fiddlers riding hither have I seen.
The same have by thy sister unto the Rhine been sent:
For sake of their high master now give we them fair compliment."
E'en then did ride the messengers unto the castle door,
And never royal minstrels more stately went before.
By the monarch's servants well received they were:
They gave them fitting lodging and for their raiment had a care.
Rich and wrought full deftly was the travelling-dress they wore,
Wherein they well with honor might go the king before;
Yet they at court no longer would the same garments wear.
The messengers inquired if any were might wish them there.
In sooth in such condition many eke were found,
Who would receive them gladly; to such they dealt around.
Then decked themselves the strangers in garments richer far,
Such as royal messengers beseemeth well at court to wear.
By royal leave came forward to where the monarch sat
The men that came from Etzel, and joy there was thereat.
Hagen then to meet them in courteous manner went,
And heartily did greet them, whereat they gave fair compliment.
To know what were the tidings,   to ask he then began
How did find him Etzel   and each valiant man.
Then answer gave the fiddler: "Ne'er higher stood the land,
Nor the folk so joyous: that shall ye surely understand."
They went unto the monarch. Crowded was the hall.
There were received the strangers as of right men shall
Kindly greeting offer in other monarch's land.
Many a valiant warrior saw Werbel by King Gunther stand.
Right courteously the monarch began to greet them then:
"Now be ye both right welcome, Hunland's merry men,
And knights that give you escort. Hither sent are ye
By Etzel mighty monarch unto the land of Burgundy?"
They bowed before the monarch; then spake Werbelein:
"My dear lord and master, and Kriemhild, sister thine,
Hither to thy country give fairest compliment.
In faith of kindly welcome us unto you they now have sent."
Then spake the lofty ruler: "I joy o'er this ye bring.
How liveth royal Etzel," further spake the king,
"And Kriemhild, my sister, afar in Hunland?"
Then answered him the fiddler: "That shalt thou straightway understand.
"That never any people more lordly life might show
Than they both do joy in, —that shalt thou surely know,—
Wherein do share their kinsmen and all their doughty train.
When from them we parted, of our journey were they fain."
"My thanks for these high greetings ye bring at his command

And from my royal sister. That high in joy they stand,
The monarch and his kinsmen, rejoiceth me to hear.
For, sooth to say, the tidings asked I now in mickle fear."
The twain of youthful princes were eke come thitherward,
As soon as they the tidings from afar had heard.
Right glad were seen the messengers for his dear sister's sake
By the young Giselher, who in such friendly manner spake:
"Right hearty were your welcome from me and brother mine,
Would ye but more frequent ride hither to the Rhine;
Here found ye friends full many whom glad ye were to see,
And naught but friendly favors the while that in this land ye be."
"To us how high thy favor," spake Schwemmel, "know we well;
Nor with my best endeavor might I ever tell
How kindly is the greeting we bear from Etzel's hand
And from your noble sister, who doth in highest honor stand.
"Your sometime love and duty recalleth Etzel's queen,
And how to her devoted in heart we've ever been,
But first to royal Gunther do we a message bear,
And pray it be your pleasure unto Etzel's land to fare.
"To beg of you that favor commanded o'er and o'er
Etzel mighty monarch and bids you know the more,
An will ye not your sister your faces give to see,
So would he know full gladly wherein by him aggrieved ye be,
"That ye thus are strangers to him and all his men.
If that his spouse so lofty to you had ne'er been known,
Yet well he thought to merit that him ye'd deign to see;
In sooth could naught rejoice him more than that such thing might be."
Then spake the royal Gunther: "A sennight from this day
Shall ye have an answer, whereon decide I may
With my friends in counsel. The while shall ye repair
Unto your place of lodging, and right goodly be your fare."
Then spake in answer Werbel: "And might such favor be
That we the royal mistress should first have leave to see,
Ute, the lofty lady, ere that we seek our rest?"
To him the noble Giselher in courteous wise these words addressed.
"That grace shall none forbid you. Will ye my mother greet,
Therein do ye most fully her own desire meet.
For sake of my good sister fain is she you to see,
For sake of Lady Kriemhild ye shall to her full welcome be."
Giselher then led him unto the lofty dame,
Who fain beheld the messengers from Hunland that came.
She greeted them full kindly as lofty manner taught,
And in right courteous fashion told they to her the tale they brought.
"Pledge of loyal friendship sendeth unto thee
Now my lofty mistress," spake Schwemmel. "Might it be,
That she should see thee often, then shalt thou know full well,
In all the world there never a greater joy to her befell."

Replied the royal lady: "Such thing may never be.
Gladly as would I oft-times my dearest daughter see,
Too far, alas, is distant the noble monarch's wife.
May ever yet full happy with King Etzel be her life.
"See that ye well advise me, ere that ye hence are gone,
What time shall be your parting; for messengers I none
Have seen for many seasons as glad as greet I you."
The twain gave faithful promise such courtesy full sure to do.
Forthwith to seek their lodgings the men of Hunland went,
The while the mighty monarch for trusted warriors sent,
Of whom did noble Gunther straightway question make,
How thought they of the message. Whereupon full many spake
That he might well with honor to Etzel's land be bound,
The which did eke advise him the highest 'mongst them found,
All save Hagen only, whom sorely grieved such rede.
Unto the king in secret spake he: "Ill shall be thy meed.
"What deed we twain compounded art thou full well aware,
Wherefor good cause we ever shall have Kriemhild to fear,
For that her sometime husband I slew by my own hand.
How dare we ever journey then unto King Etzel's land?"
Replied the king: "My sister no hate doth harbor more.
As we in friendship kissed her, vengeance she forswore
For evil that we wrought her, ere that from hence she rode,—
Unless this message, Hagen, ill for thee alone forebode."
"Now be thou not deceived," spake Hagen, "say what may
The messengers from Hunland. If thither be thy way,
At Kriemhild's hands thou losest honor eke and life,
For full long-avenging is the royal Etzel's wife."
Added then his counsel the princely Gernot there:
"Though be it thou hast reason thine own death to fear
Afar in Hunnish kingdom, should we for that forego
To visit our high sister, that were in sooth but ill to do."
Unto that thane did likewise Giselher then say:
"Since well thou know'st, friend Hagen, what guilt on thee doth weigh,
Then tarry here behind us and of thyself have care,
And let who dares the journey with us unto my sister fare."
Thereat did rage full sorely Tronje's doughty thane:
"So shall ye ne'er find any that were to go more fain,
Nor who may better guide you than I upon your way.
And will ye not give over, know then my humor soon ye may."
Then spake the Kitchen Master, Rumold a lofty thane:
"Here might ye guests and kinsmen in plenty long maintain
After your own pleasure, for ye have goodly store.
I ween ye ne'er found Hagen traitor to you heretofore.
"If heed ye will not Hagen, still Rumold doth advise
—For ye have faithful service from me in willing wise—
That here at home ye tarry for the love of me,

And leave the royal Etzel afar with Kriemhild to be.
"Where in the world might ever ye more happy be
Than here where from danger of every foeman free,
Where ye may go as likes you in goodliest attire,
Drink wine the best, and stately women meet your heart's desire.
"And daily is your victual the best that ever knew
A king of any country. And were the thing not true,
At home ye yet should tarry for sake of your fair wife
Ere that in childish fashion ye thus at venture set your life.
"Thus rede I that ye go not. Mighty are your lands,
And at home more easy may ye be freed from hostile hands
Than if ye pine in Hunland. How there it is, who knows?
O Master, go not thither, —such is the rede that Rumold owes."
"We'll ne'er give o'er the journey," Gernot then did say,
"When thus our sister bids us in such friendly way
And Etzel, mighty monarch. Wherefore should we refrain?
Who goes not gladly thither, here at home may he remain."
Thereto gave answer Hagen: "Take not amiss, I pray,
These my words outspoken, let befall what may.
Yet do I counsel truly, as ye your safety prize,
That to the Huns ye journey armed full well in warlike guise.
"Will ye then not give over, your men together call,
The best that ye may gather from districts one and all.
From out them all I'll choose you a thousand knights full good,
Then may ye reck but little the vengeful Kriemhild's angry mood."
"I'll gladly heed thy counsel," straight the king replied,
And bade the couriers traverse his kingdom far and wide.
Soon they brought together three thousand men or more,
Who little weened what mickle sorrow was for them in store.
Joyful came they riding to King Gunther's land.
Steeds and equipment for them all he did command,
Who should make the journey thence from Burgundy.
Warriors many were there to serve the king right willingly.
Hagen then of Tronje to Dankwart did assign
Of their warriors eighty to lead unto the Rhine.
Equipped in knightly harness were they soon at hand.
Riding in gallant fashion unto royal Gunther's land.
Came eke the doughty Volker, a noble minstrel he,
With thirty goodly warriors to join the company,
Who wore so rich attire 'twould fit a monarch well.
That he would fare to Hunland, bade he unto Gunther tell.
Who was this same Volker that will I let you know:
He was a knight full noble, to him did service owe
Many a goodly warrior in the land of Burgundy.
For that he well could fiddle, named the Minstrel eke was he.
Thousand men chose Hagen, who well to him were known.
What things in storm of battle their doughty arm had done,

Or what they wrought at all times, that knew he full well.
Nor of them might e'er mortal aught but deeds of valor tell.
The messengers of Kriemhild, full loath they were to wait,
For of their master's anger stood they in terror great.

Each day for leave to journey more great their yearning grew,
But daily to withhold it crafty Hagen pretext knew.
He spake unto his master: "Well shall we beware
Hence to let them journey ere we ourselves prepare

In seven days thereafter to ride to Etzel's land:
If any mean us evil, so may we better understand.
"Nor may the Lady Kriemhild ready make thereto,
That any by her counsel scathe to us may do.

Yet if such wish she cherish, evil shall be her meed,
For many a chosen warrior with us shall we thither lead."
Shields well-wrought and saddles, with all the mickle gear
That into Etzel's country the warriors should wear,

The same was now made ready for many a knight full keen.
The messengers of Kriemhild before King Gunther soon were seen.
When were come the messengers, Gernot them addressed:
"King Gunther now is minded to answer Etzel's quest.

Full gladly go we thither with him to make high-tide
And see our lofty sister, —of that set ye all doubt aside."
Thereto spake King Gunther: "Can ye surely say
When shall be the high-tide, or upon what day

We shall there assemble?" Spake Schwemmel instantly:
"At turn of sun in summer shall in sooth the meeting be."
The monarch leave did grant them, ere they should take their way,
If that to Lady Brunhild they would their homage pay,

His high pleasure was it they unto her should go.
Such thing prevented Volker, and did his mistress' pleasure so.
"In sooth, my Lady Brunhild hath scarce such health to-day
As that she might receive you," the gallant knight did say.

"Bide ye till the morrow, may ye the lady see."
When thus they sought her presence, might their wish not granted be.
To the messengers right gracious was the mighty king,
And bade he from his treasure on shields expansive bring

Shining gold in plenty whereof he had great store.
Eke richest gifts received they from his lofty kinsmen more.
Giselher and Gernot, Gere and Ortwein,
That they were free in giving soon full well was seen.

So costly gifts were offered unto each messenger
That they dared not receive them, for Etzel's anger did they fear.
Then unto King Gunther Werbel spake again:
Sire, let now thy presents in thine own land remain.

The same we may not carry, my master hath decreed
That we accept no bounty. Of that in sooth we've little need."
Thereat the lord of Rhineland was seen in high displeasure,

That they should thus accept not so mighty monarch's treasure?
In their despite yet took they rich dress and gold in store,
The which moreover with them home to Etzel's land they bore.
Ere that they thence departed they Lady Ute sought,
Whereat the gallant Giselher straight the minstrels brought
Unto his mother's presence. Kind greetings sent the dame,
And wish that high in honor still might stand her daughter's name.
Then bade the lofty lady embroidered silks and gold
For the sake of Kriemhild, whom loved she as of old,
And eke for sake of Etzel, unto the minstrels give.
What thus so free was offered might they in sooth right fain receive.
Soon now had ta'en departure the messengers from thence,
From knight and fairest lady, and joyous fared they hence
Unto Suabian country; Gernot had given behest
Thus far for armed escort, that none their journey might molest.
When these had parted from them, safe still from harm were they,
For Etzel's might did guard them wherever led their way.
Nor ever came there any that aught to take would dare,
As into Etzel's country they in mickle haste did fare.
Where'er they friends encountered, to all they straight made known
How that they of Burgundy should follow after soon
From Rhine upon their journey unto the Huns' country.
The message brought they likewise unto Bishop Pilgrim's see.
As down 'fore Bechelaren they passed upon their way,
The tidings eke to Ruediger failed they not to say,
And unto Gotelinde, the margrave's wife the same.
At thought so soon to see them was filled with joy the lofty dame.
Hasting with the tidings each minstrel's courser ran,
Till found they royal Etzel within his burgh at Gran.
Greeting upon greeting, which they must all bestow,
They to the king delivered; with joy his visage was aglow.
When that the lofty Kriemhild did eke the tidings hear,
How that her royal brothers unto the land would fare,
In sooth her heart was gladdened; on the minstrels she bestowed
Richest gifts in plenty, as she to her high station owed.
She spake: "Now shall ye, Werbel and Schwemmel, tell to me
Who cometh of my kinsmen to our festivity,
Who of all were bidden this our land to seek?
Now tell me, when the message heard he, what did Hagen speak?"
Answered: "He came to council early upon a day,
But little was of pleasant in what he there did say.
When learned he their intention, in wrath did Hagen swear,
To death 'twere making journey, to country of the Huns to fare.
"Hither all are coming, thy royal brothers three,
And they right high in spirit. Who more shall with them be,
The tale to tell entire were more than I might do.
To journey with them plighted Volker the valiant fiddler too."

"'Twere little lost, full truly," answered then the queen,
"If by my eyes never Volker here were seen.
'Tis Hagen hath my favor, a noble knight is he,
And mickle is my pleasure that him full soon we here may see."
Her way the Lady Kriemhild then to the king did take,
And in right joyous manner unto her consort spake:
"How liketh thee the tidings, lord full dear to me?
What aye my heart hath yearned for, that shall now accomplished be."
"Thy will my joy was ever," the lofty monarch said.
"In sooth for my own kinsmen I ne'er have been so glad,
To hear that they come hither unto my country.
To know thy friends are coming, hath parted sadness far from me."
Straight did the royal provosts give everywhere decree
That hall and stately palace well prepared should be
With seats, that unprovided no worthy guest be left.
Anon by them the monarch should be of mickle joy bereft.

TWENTY-FIFTH ADVENTURE

How the Knights all fared to the Huns

Tell we now no further how they here did fare.
Knights more high in spirit saw ye journey ne'er
In so stately fashion to the land of e'er a king.
Of arms and rich attire lacked they never anything.
At Rhine the lordly monarch equipped his warriors well,
A thousand knights and sixty, as I did hear tell,
And eke nine thousand squires toward the festivity.
Whom they did leave behind them anon must mourn full grievously.
As at Worms across the courtyard equipment full they bore
Spake there of Speyer a bishop old and hoar
Unto Lady Ute: "Our friends have mind to fare
Unto the festivity; may God their honor have in care."
Then spake unto her children Ute the noble dame:
"At home ye here should tarry, ye knights full high in fame.
Me dreamt but yester even a case of direst need,
How that in this country all the feathered fowl were dead."
"Who recketh aught of dreamings," Hagen then replied,
"Distraught is sure his counsel when trouble doth betide,
Or he would of his honor have a perfect care.
I counsel that my master straight to take his leave prepare.
"Gladly shall we journey into Etzel's land;
There at their master's service may good knights ready stand,
For that we there shall witness Kriemhild's festivity."
That Hagen gave such counsel, rue anon full sore did he.
Yet in sooth far other than this had been his word,

Had not with bitter mocking Gernot his anger stirred.
He spake to him of Siegfried whom Kriemhild loved so,
And said: "Therefore the journey would Hagen willingly forego."
Then spake of Tronje Hagen: "Through fear I nothing do.
Whenever will ye, Masters, set straight your hand thereto,
With you I'll gladly journey unto Etzel's land."
Many a shield and helmet there hewed anon his mighty hand.
The ships stood ready waiting, whereunto ample store
Of clothing for the journey men full many bore,
Nor had they time for resting till shades of even fell.
Anon in mood full joyous bade they friends at home farewell.
Tents full large and many arose upon the green,
Yonder side Rhine river. But yet the winsome queen
Caressed the doughty monarch that night, and still did pray
That far from Etzel's country among his kinsmen might he stay.
When sound of flute and trumpet arose at break of day,
A signal for their parting, full soon they took their way.
Each lover to his bosom did friend more fondly press:
King Etzel's wife full many did part anon in dire distress.
The sons of stately Ute, a good knight had they,
A brave man and a faithful. When they would thence away,
Apart unto the monarch did he his mind reveal,
And spake: "That ye will journey, may I naught but sorrow feel."
Hight the same was Rumold, a man of doughty hand.
He spake: "To whom now leave ye people here and land?
O that never any might alter your intent!
Small good, methinks, may follow message e'er by Kriemhild sent."
"The land to thee entrusted and eke my child shall be,
And tender care of ladies, —so hast command from me.
Whene'er thou seest weeping, do there thy comfort give.
Yea, trust we free from sorrow at hand of Etzel's wife to live."
For knight and royal master the chargers ready were,
As with fond embracing parted many there,
Who long in joy together a merry life had led.
By winsome dame full many therefor must bitter tear be shed.
As did those doughty warriors into the saddle spring,
Might full many a lady be seen there sorrowing;
For told them well their spirit that thus so long to part
Did bode a dire peril, the which must ever cloud the heart.
As mounted stood the valiant thanes of Burgundy,
Might ye a mickle stirring in that country see,
Both men and women weeping on either riverside.
Yet pricked they gaily forward, let what might their folk betide.
The Nibelungen warriors in hauberks bright arrayed
Went with them, a thousand, while at home behind them stayed
Full many a winsome lady, whom saw they nevermore.
The wounds of doughty Siegfried still grieved the Lady Kriemhild sore.

Their journey they directed onward to the Main,
Up through East Frankish country, the men of Gunther's train
Thither led by Hagen, who well that country knew;
Marshal to them was Dankwart, a knight of Burgundy full true.
On from East Frankish country to Schwanefeld they went,
A train of valiant warriors of high accomplishment,
The monarchs and their kinsmen, all knights full worthy fame.
Upon the twelfth morning the king unto the Danube came.
The knight of Tronje, Hagen, the very van did lead,
Ever to the Nibelungen a surest help in need.
First the thane full valiant down leapt upon the ground,
And straightway then his charger fast unto a tree he bound.
Flooded were the waters and ne'er a boat was near,
Whereat began the Nibelungen all in dread to fear
They ne'er might cross the river, so mighty was the flood.
Dismounted on the shore, full many a stately knight then stood.
"Ill may it," spake then Hagen, "fare here with thee,
Lord of Rhine river. Now thyself mayst see
How flooded are the waters, and swift the current flows.
I ween, before the morrow here many a goodly knight we lose."
"How wilt reproach me, Hagen?" the lofty monarch spake.
I pray thee yet all comfort not from our hearts to take.
The ford shalt thou discover whereby we may pass o'er,
Horse and equipment bringing safely unto yonder shore."
"In sooth, not I," quoth Hagen, "am yet so weary grown
Of life, that in these waters wide I long to drown.
Ere that, shall warriors sicken in Etzel's far country
Beneath my own arm stricken: —'tis my intent full certainly.
"Here tarry by the water, ye gallant knights and good,
The while I seek the boatmen myself along the flood,
Who will bring us over into Gelfrat's land."
With that the doughty Hagen took his trusty shield in hand.
He cap-a-pie was arméd, as thus he strode away,
Upon his head a helmet that gleamed with brilliant ray,
And o'er his warlike harness a sword full broad there hung,
That on both its edges did fiercely cut, in battle swung.
He sought to find the boatmen if any might be near,
When sound of falling waters full soon upon his ear.
Beside a rippling fountain, where ran the waters cool,
A group of wise mermaidens did bathe themselves within the pool.
Ware of them soon was Hagen and stole in secret near,
But fast away they hurried when they the sound did hear.
That they at all escaped him, filled they were with glee.
The knight did take their clothing, yet wrought none other injury.
Then spake the one mermaiden, Hadburg that hight:
"Hagen, knight full noble, tell will we thee aright,
An wilt thou, valiant warrior, our garments but give o'er,

What fortune may this journey to Hunland have for thee in store."
They hovered there before him like birds above the flood,
Wherefore did think the warrior that tell strange things they could,
And all the more believed he what they did feign to say,
As to his eager question in ready manner answered they.
Spake one: "Well may ye journey to Etzel's country.
Thereto my troth I give thee in full security
That ne'er in any kingdom might high guests receive
Such honors as there wait you,—this may ye in sooth believe."
To hear such speech was Hagen in sooth right glad of heart;
He gave to them their garments, and straightway would depart.
But when in strange attire they once more were dight,
Told they of the journey into Etzel's land aright.
Spake then the other mermaid, Siegelind that hight:
"I warn thee, son of Aldrian, Hagen valiant knight,
'Twas but to gain her clothing my cousin falsely said,
For, comest thou to Hunland, sorely shalt thou be betrayed.
"Yea, that thou turnest backward is fitter far, I ween;
For but your death to compass have all ye warriors keen
Receivéd now the bidding unto Etzel's land.
Whose doth thither journey, death leadeth surely by the hand."
Thereto gave answer Hagen: "False speech hath here no gain.
How might it ever happen that we all were slain
Afar in Etzel's country through hate of any man?"
To tell the tale more fully unto him she then began.
Spake again the other: "The thing must surely be,
That of you never any his home again shall see,
Save only the king's chaplain; well do we understand
That he unscathed returneth unto royal Gunther's land."
Then spake the valiant Hagen again in angry way:
"Unto my royal masters 'twere little joy to say
That we our lives must forfeit all in Hunland.
Now show us, wisest woman, how pass we safe to yonder strand."
She spake: "Since from thy purposed journey thou wilt not turn,
Where upward by the water a cabin stands, there learn
Within doth dwell a boatman, nor other find thou mayst."
No more did Hagen question, but strode away from there in haste.
As went he angry-minded one from afar did say:
"Now tarry still, Sir Hagen; why so dost haste away?
Give ear yet while we tell thee how thou reachest yonder strand.
Master here is Else, who doth rule this borderland.
"Hight is his brother Gelfrat, and is a thane full rare,
Lord o'er Bavarian country. Full ill with you 'twill fare,
Will ye pass his border. Watchful must ye be,
And eke with the ferryman 'twere well to walk right modestly.
"He is so angry-minded that sure thy bane 'twill be,
Wilt thou not show the warrior all civility.

Wilt thou that he transport thee, give all the boatman's due.
He guardeth well the border and unto Gelfrat is full true.
"If he be slow to answer, then call across the flood
That thy name is Amelrich. That was a knight full good,
Who for a feud did sometime go forth from out this land.
The ferryman will answer, when he the name doth understand.
Hagen high of spirit before those women bent,
Nor aught did say, but silent upon his way he went.
Along the shore he wandered till higher by the tide
On yonder side the river a cabin standing he espied.
He straight began a calling across the flood amain.
"Now fetch me over, boatman," cried the doughty thane.
"A golden armband ruddy I'll give to thee for meed.
Know that to make this crossing I in sooth have very need."
Not fitting 'twas high ferryman his service thus should give,
And recompense from any seldom might he receive;
Eke were they that served him full haughty men of mood.
Still alone stood Hagen on the hither side the flood.
Then cried he with such power the wave gave back the sound,
For in strength far-reaching did the knight abound:
"Fetch me now, for Amelrich, Else's man, am I,
That for feud outbroken erstwhile from this land did fly."
Full high upon his sword-point an armband did he hold,
Fair and shining was it made of ruddy gold,
The which he offered to him for fare to Gelfrat's land.
The ferryman high-hearted himself did take the oar in hand.
To do with that same boatman was ne'er a pleasant thing;
The yearning after lucre yet evil end doth bring.
Here where thought he Hagen's gold so red to gain,
Must he by the doughty warrior's fierce sword be slain.
With might across the river his oar the boatman plied,
But he who there was naméd might nowhere be espied.
His rage was all unbounded when he did Hagen find,
And loud his voice resounded as thus he spake his angry mind:
"Thou mayst forsooth be calléd Amelrich by name:
Whom I here did look for, no whit art thou the same.
By father and by mother brother he was to me.
Since me thou thus hast cozened, so yet this side the river be."
"Nay, by highest Heaven," Hagen did declare.
"Here am I a stranger that have good knights in care.
Now take in friendly manner here my offered pay,
And guide me o'er the ferry; my favor hast thou thus alway."
Whereat replied the boatman: "The thing may never be.
There are that to my masters do bear hostility;
Wherefore I never stranger do lead into this land.
As now thy life thou prizest, step straightway out upon the strand."
"Deny me not," quoth Hagen, "for sad in sooth my mood.

Take now for remembrance this my gold so good,
And carry men a thousand and horses to yonder shore."
Quoth in rage the boatman: "Such thing will happen nevermore."
Aloft he raised an oar that mickle was and strong,
And dealt such blow on Hagen, (but rued he that ere long,)
That in the boat did stumble that warrior to his knee.
In sooth so savage boatman ne'er did the knight of Tronje see.
With thought the stranger's anger the more to rouse anew,
He swung a mighty boat-pole that it in pieces flew
Upon the crown of Hagen;— he was a man of might.
Thereby did Else's boatman come anon to sorry plight.
Full sore enraged was Hagen, as quick his hand he laid
Upon his sword where hanging he found the trusty blade.
His head he struck from off him and flung into the tide.
Known was soon the story to the knights of Burgundy beside.
While the time was passing that he the boatman slew,
The waters bore him downward, whereat he anxious grew.
Ere he the boat had righted began his strength to wane,
So mightily was pulling royal Gunther's doughty thane.
Soon he yet had turned it, so rapid was his stroke,
Until the mighty oar beneath his vigor broke.
As strove he his companions upon the bank to gain,
No second oar he found him. Yet soon the same made fast again.
With quickly snatched shield-strap, a fine and narrow band.
Downward where stood a forest he sought again the land,
And there his master found he standing upon the shore.
In haste came forth to meet him many a stately warrior more.
The gallant knight they greeted with right hearty mood.
When in the boat perceived they reeking still the blood
That from the wound had issued where Hagen's sword did swing,
Scarce could his companions bring to an end their questioning.
When that royal Gunther the streaming blood did see
Within the boat there running, straightway then spake he:
"Where is now the ferryman, tell me, Hagen, pray?
By thy mighty prowess his life, I ween, is ta'en away."
Thereto replied he falsely: "When the boat I found
Where slopeth a wild meadow, I the same unbound.
Hereabout no ferryman I to-day have seen,
Nor ever cause of sorrow unto any have I been."
The good knight then of Burgundy, the gallant Gernot, spake:
"Dear friends full many, fear I, the flood this day will take,
Since we of the boatmen none ready here may find
To guide us o'er the current. 'Tis mickle sorrow to my mind."
Full loudly cried then Hagen: "Lay down upon the grass,
Ye squires, the horse equipments. I ween a time there was,
Myself was best of boatmen that dwelt the Rhine beside.
To Gelfrat's country trow I to bring you safely o'er the tide."

That they might come the sooner across the running flood,
Drove they in the horses. Their swimming, it was good,
For of them never any beneath the waves did sink,
Though many farther downward must struggle sore to gain the brink.
Their treasure and apparel unto the boat they bore,
Since by no means the journey thought they to give o'er.
Hagen was director, and safely reached the strand
With many a stalwart warrior bound unto the unknown land.
Gallant knights a thousand first he ferried o'er,
Whereafter came his own men. Of others still were more,
For squires full nine thousand he led unto that land.
That day no whit was idle that valiant knight of Tronje's hand.
When he them all in safety o'er the flood had brought,
Of that strange story the valiant warrior thought,
Which erstwhile had told him those women of the sea.
Lost thereby the chaplain's life well-nigh was doomed to be.
Beside his priestly baggage he saw the chaplain stand,
Upon the holy vestments resting with his hand.
No whit was that his safety; when Hagen him did see,
Must the priest full wretched suffer sorest injury.
From out the boat he flung him ere might the thing be told,
Whereat they cried together: "Hold, O Master, hold!"
Soon had the youthful Giselher to rage thereat begun,
And mickle was his sorrow that Hagen yet the thing had done.
Then outspake Sir Gernot, knight of Burgundy:
"What boots it thee, Sir Hagen, that thus the chaplain die?
Dared any else to do it, thy wrath 'twould sorely stir.
Wherein the priest's offending, thus thy malice to incur?"
To swim the chaplain struggled. He thought him yet to free,
If any but would help him. Yet such might never be,
For that the doughty Hagen full wrathful was of mood,
He sunk him to the bottom, whereat aghast each warrior stood.
When that no help forthcoming the wretched priest might see,
He sought the hither shore, and fared full grievously.
Though failed his strength in swimming, yet helped him God's own hand,
That he came securely back again unto the land.
Safe yonder stood the chaplain and shook his dripping dress.
Thereby perceived Hagen how true was none the less
The story that did tell him the strange women of the sea.
Thought he: "Of these good warriors soon the days must ended be."
When that the boat was emptied, and complete their store
All the monarch's followers had borne upon the shore,
Hagen smote it to pieces and cast it on the flood,
Whereat in mickle wonder the valiant knights around him stood.
"Wherefore dost this, brother," then Sir Dankwart spake;
"How shall we cross the river when again we make
Our journey back from Hunland, riding to the Rhine?"

Behold how Hagen bade him all such purpose to resign.
Quoth the knight of Tronje: "This thing is done by me,
That if e'er coward rideth in all our company,
Who for lack of courage from us away would fly,
He beneath these billows yet a shameful death must die."
One there journeyed with them from the land of Burgundy,
That was a knight of valor, Volker by name was he.
He spake in cunning manner whate'er might fill his mind,
And aught was done by Hagen did the Fiddler fitting find.
Ready stood their chargers, the carriers laden well;
At passage of the river was there naught to tell
Of scathe to any happened, save but the king's chaplain.
Afoot must he now journey back unto the Rhine again.

TWENTY-SIXTH ADVENTURE

How Gelfrat was Slain by Dankwart

When now they all were gathered upon the farther strand,
To wonder gan the monarch: "Who shall through this land
On routes aright direct us, that not astray we fare?"
Then spake the doughty Volker: "Thereof will I alone have care."
"Now hark ye all," quoth Hagen, "knight and squire too,
And list to friendly counsel, as fitting is to do.
Full strange and dark the tidings now ye shall hear from me:
Home nevermore return we unto the land of Burgundy.
"Thus mermaids twain did tell me, who spake to me this morn,
That back we come not hither. You would I therefore warn
That arméd well ye journey and of all ills beware.
To meet with doughty foemen well behooveth us prepare.
"I weened to turn to falsehood what those wise mermaids spake,
Who said that safe this journey none again should make
Home unto our country save the chaplain alone:
Him therefore was I minded to-day beneath the flood to drown."
From company to company quickly flew the tale,
Whereon grew many a doughty warrior's visage pale,
As gan he think in sorrow how death should snatch away
All ere the journey ended; and very need for grief had they.
By Moeringen was it they had the river crossed,
Where also Else's boatman thus his life had lost.
There again spake Hagen: "Since in such wise by me
Wrath hath been incurréd, assailed full surely shall we be.
"Myself that same ferryman did this morning slay.
Far bruited are the tidings. Now arm ye for the fray,
That if Gelfrat and Else be minded to beset
Our train to-day, they surely with sore discomfiture be met.

"So keen they are, well know I the thing they'll not forego.
Your horses therefore shall ye make to pace more slow,
That never man imagine we flee away in fear."
"That counsel will I follow," spake the young knight Giselher.
"Who will guide our vanguard through this hostile land?"
"Volker shall do it," spake they, "well doth he understand
Where leadeth path and highway, a minstrel brave and keen."
Ere full the wish was spoken, in armor well equipped was seen
Standing the doughty Fiddler. His helmet fast he bound,
And from his stately armor shot dazzling light around.
Eke to a staff he fastened a banner, red of hue.
Anon with royal masters came he to sorest sorrow too.
Unto Gelfrat meanwhile had sure tidings flown,
How that was dead his boatman; the story eke was known
Unto the doughty Else, and both did mourn his fate.
Their warriors they summoned, nor must long time for answer wait.
But little space it lasted —that would I have you know—
Ere that to them hasted who oft a mickle woe
Had wrought in stress of battle and injury full sore;
To Gelfrat now came riding seven hundred knights or more.
When they their foes to follow so bitterly began,
Led them both their masters. Yet all too fast they ran
After the valiant strangers vengeance straight to wreak.
Ere long from those same leaders did death full many a warrior take.
Hagen then of Tronje the thing had ordered there,
—How of his friends might ever knight have better care?—
That he did keep the rearguard with warriors many a one,
And Dankwart eke, his brother; full wisely the thing was done.
When now the day was over and light they had no more,
Injury to his followers gan he to dread full sore.
They shield in hand rode onward through Bavarian land,
And ere they long had waited beset they were by hostile band.
On either side the highway and close upon their rear
Of hoofs was heard the clatter; too keen the chasers were.
Then spake the valiant Dankwart: "The foe is close at hand.
Now bind we on the helmet, —wisdom doth the same command."
Upon the way they halted, nor else they safe had been.
Through the gloom perceived they of gleaming shields the sheen.
Thereupon would Hagen longer not delay:
"Who rideth on the highway?"— That must Gelfrat tell straight-way.
Of Bavaria the margrave thereupon replied:
"Our enemies now seek we, and swift upon them ride.
Fain would I discover who hath my boatman slain.
A knight he was of valor, whose death doth cause me grievous pain."
Then spake of Tronje Hagen: "And was the boatman thine
That would not take us over? The guilt herein is mine.
Myself did slay the warrior, and had, in sooth, good need,

For that beneath his valor I myself full nigh lay dead.
"For pay I rich attire did bid, and gold a store,
Good knight, that to thy country he should us ferry o'er.
Thereat he raged full sorely and on me swung a blow
With a mighty boat-pole, whereat I eke did angry grow.
"For my sword then reached I and made his rage to close
With a wound all gaping: so thou thy knight didst lose.
I'll give thee satisfaction as to thee seemeth good."
Straightway began the combat, for high the twain in valor stood.
"Well know I," spake Gelfrat, "when Gunther with his train
Rode through this my country that we should suffer bane
From Hagen, knight of Tronje. No more shall he go free,
But for my boatman's slaying here a hostage must he be."
Against their shields then lowered for the charge the spear
Gelfrat and Hagen; eager to close they were.
Else and Dankwart spurred eke in stately way,
Scanning each the other; then both did valorous arm display.
How might ever heroes show doughty arm so well?
Backward from off his charger from mighty tilt there fell
Hagen the valiant, by Gelfrat's hand borne down.
In twain was rent the breast-piece: to Hagen thus a fall was known.
Where met in charge their followers, did crash of shafts resound.
Risen eke was Hagen, who erst unto the ground
Was borne by mighty lance-thrust, prone upon the grass.
I ween that unto Gelfrat nowise of gentle mood he was.
Who held their horses' bridles can I not recount,
But soon from out their saddles did they all dismount.
Hagen and Gelfrat straightway did fierce engage,
And all their men around them did eke a furious combat wage.
Though with fierce onslaught Hagen upon Gelfrat sprung,
On his shield the noble margrave a sword so deftly swung
That a piece from off the border 'mid flying sparks it clave.
Well-nigh beneath its fury fell dead King Gunther's warrior brave.
Unto Dankwart loudly thereat he gan to cry:
"Help! ho! my good brother! Encountered here have I
A knight of arm full doughty, from whom I come not free."
Then spake the valiant Dankwart: "Myself thereof the judge will be."
Nearer sprang the hero and smote him such a blow
With a keen-edged weapon that he in death lay low.
For his slain brother Else vengeance thought to take,
But soon with all his followers 'mid havoc swift retreat must make.
Slain was now his brother, wound himself did bear,
And of his followers eighty eke had fallen there,
By grim death snatched sudden. Then must the doughty knight,
From Gunther's men to save him, turn away in hasty flight.
When that they of Bavaria did from the carnage flee,
The blows that followed after resounded frightfully;

For close the knights of Tronje upon their enemies chased,
Who to escape the fury did quit the field in mickle haste.
Then spake upon their fleeing Dankwart the doughty thane:
"Upon our way now let us backward turn again,
And leave them hence to hasten all wet with oozing blood.
Unto our friends return we, this verily meseemeth good."
When back they were returnéd where did the scathe befall,
Outspake of Tronje Hagen: "Now look ye, warriors all,
Who of our tale is lacking, or who from us hath been
Here in battle riven through the doughty Gelfrat's spleen."
Lament they must for warriors four from them were ta'en.
But paid for were they dearly, for roundabout lay slain
Of their Bavarian foemen a hundred or more.
The men of Tronje's bucklers with blood were wet and tarnished o'er.
From out the clouds of heaven a space the bright moon shone.
Then again spake Hagen: "Bear report let none
To my beloved masters how we here did fare.
Let them until the morrow still be free from aught of care."
When they were back returnéd who bore the battle's stress,
Sore troubled was their company from very weariness.
"How long shall we keep saddle?" was many a warrior's quest.
Then spake the valiant Dankwart: "Not yet may we find place of rest,
"But on ye all must journey till day come back again."
Volker, knight of prowess, who led the foremost train,
Bade to ask the marshal: "This night where shall we be,
That rest them may our chargers, and eke my royal masters three?"
Thereto spake valiant Dankwart: "The same I ne'er can say,
Yet may we never rest us before the break of day.
Where then we find it fitting we'll lay us on the grass."
When they did hear his answer, what source of grief to all it was!
Still were they unbetrayéd by reeking blood and red,
Until the sun in heaven its shining beams down shed
At morn across the hill-tops, that then the king might see
How they had been in battle. Spake he then full angrily:
"How may this be, friend Hagen? Scorned ye have, I ween,
That I should be beside you, where coats of mail have been
Thus wet with blood upon you. Who this thing hath done?"
Quoth he: "The same did Else, who hath this night us set upon.
"To avenge his boatman did they attack our train.
By hand of my brother hath Gelfrat been slain.
Then fled Else before us, and mickle was his need.
Ours four, and theirs a thousand, remained behind in battle dead."
Now can we not inform you where resting-place they found.
But cause to know their passing had the country-folk around,
When there the sons of Ute to court did fare in state.
At Passau fit reception did presently the knights await.
The noble monarchs' uncle, Bishop Pilgrim that was,

Full joyous-hearted was he that through the land did pass
With train of lusty warriors his royal nephews three.
That willing was his service, waited they not long to see.
To greet them on their journey did friends lack no device,
Yet not to lodge them fully might Passau's bounds suffice.
They must across the water where spreading sward they found,
And lodge and tent erected soon were stretching o'er the ground.
Nor from that spot they onward might journey all that day,
And eke till night was over, for pleasant was their stay.
Next to the land of Ruediger must they in sooth ride on,
To whom full soon the story of their coming eke was known.
When fitting rest had taken the knights with travel worn,
And of Etzel's country they had reached the bourn,
A knight they found there sleeping that ne'er should aught but wake,
From whom of Tronje Hagen in stealth a mighty sword did take.
Hight in sooth was Eckewart that same valiant knight.
For what was there befallen was he in sorry plight,
That by those heroes' passing he had lost his sword.
At Ruediger's marches found they meagre was the guard.
"O, woe is me dishonored," Eckewart then cried;
"Yea, rueth me fully sorely, this Burgundian ride.
What time was taken Siegfried, did joy depart from me.
Alack, O Master Ruediger, how ill my service unto thee!"
Hagen, full well perceiving the noble warrior's plight,
Gave him again his weapon and armbands six full bright.
"These take, good knight, in token that thou art still my friend.
A valiant warrior art thou, though dost thou lone this border tend."
"May God thy gifts repay thee," Eckewart replied,
"Yet rueth me full sorely that to the Huns ye ride.
Erstwhile slew ye Siegfried and vengeance have to fear;
My rede to you is truly: "Beware ye well of danger here."
"Now must God preserve us," answered Hagen there.
"In sooth for nothing further have these thanes a care
Than for place of shelter, the kings and all their band,
And where this night a refuge we may find within this land.
"Done to death our horses with the long journey are,
And food as well exhausted," Hagen did declare.
"Nor find we aught for purchase; a host we need instead,
Who would in kindness give us, ere this evening, of his bread."
Thereto gave answer Eckewart: "I'll show you such a one,
That so warm a welcome find ye never none
In country whatsoever as here your lot may be,
An if ye, thanes full gallant, the noble Ruediger will see.
He dwelleth by the highway and is most bounteous host
That house e'er had for master. His heart may graces boast,
As in the lovely May-time the flowrets deck the mead.
To do good thanes a service is for his heart most joyous deed."

Then spake the royal Gunther: "Wilt thou my messenger be,
If will my dear friend Ruediger, as favor done to me,
His hospitable shelter with all my warriors share,
Therefor full to requite thee shall e'er hereafter be my care."
"Thy messenger am I gladly," Eckewart replied,
And in right willing manner straight away did ride,
The message thus receivéd to Ruediger to bear.
Nor did so joyous tidings for many a season greet his ear.
Hasting to Bechelaren was seen a noble thane.
The same perceivéd Ruediger, and spake: "O'er yonder plain
Hither hastens Eckewart, who Kriemhild's might doth own."
He weened that by some foemen to him had injury been done.
Then passed he forth the gateway where the messenger did stand.
His sword he loosed from girdle and laid from out his hand.
The message that he carried might he not long withhold
From the master and his kinsmen; full soon the same to them was told.
He spake unto the margrave: "I come at high command
Of the lordly Gunther of Burgundian land,
And Giselher and Gernot, his royal brothers twain.
In service true commends him unto thee each lofty thane.
"The like hath Hagen bidden and Volker as well
With homage oft-times proffered. And more have I to tell,
The which King Gunther's marshal to thee doth send by me:
How that the valiant warriors do crave thy hospitality."
With smiling visage Ruediger made thereto reply:
"Now joyeth me the story that the monarchs high
Do deign to seek my service, that ne'er refused shall be.
Come they unto my castle, 'tis joy and gladness unto me."
"Dankwart the marshal hath bidden let thee know
Who seek with them thy shelter as through thy land they go:
Three score of valiant leaders and thousand knights right good,
With squires eke nine thousand." Thereat was he full glad of mood.
"To me 'tis mickle honor," Ruediger then spake,
"That through my castle's portals such guests will entry make,
For ne'er hath been occasion my service yet to lend.
Now ride ye, men and kinsmen, and on these lofty knights attend."
Then to horse did hasten knight and willing squire,
For glad they were at all times to do their lord's desire,
And keen that thus their service should not be rendered late.
Unwitting Lady Gotelinde still within her chamber sate.

TWENTY-SEVENTH ADVENTURE

How they came to Bechelaren

Then went forth the margrave where two ladies sate,
His wife beside his daughter, nor longer did he wait
To tell the joyful tidings that unto him were brought,
How Kriemhild's royal brothers his hospitality had sought.
"Dearly lovéd lady," spake then Ruediger,
"Full kind be thy reception to lordly monarchs here,
That now with train of warriors to court do pass this way.
Fair be eke thy greeting to Hagen, Gunther's man, this day.
"One likewise with them cometh, Dankwart by name,
Volker hight the other, a knight of gallant fame.
Thyself and eke thy daughter with kiss these six shall greet;
Full courteous be your manner as ye the doughty thanes shall meet."
Gave straight their word the ladies, and willing were thereto.
From out great chests they gorgeous attire in plenty drew,
Which they to meet the lofty strangers thought to wear,
Mickle was the hurry there of many a lady fair.
On ne'er a cheek might any but nature's hue be seen.
Upon their head they carried band of golden sheen,
That was a beauteous chaplet, that so their glossy hair
By wind might not be ruffled: that is truth as I declare.
At such employment busy leave we those ladies now.
Here with mickle hurry across the plain did see
Friends of noble Ruediger the royal guests to meet,
And them with warmest welcome unto the margrave's land did greet.
When coming forth the margrave saw their forms appear,
How spake with heart full joyous the valiant Ruediger!
"Welcome be ye, Sires, and all your gallant band.
Right glad am I to see you hither come unto my land."
Then bent the knights before him each full courteously.
That he good-will did bear them might they full quickly see.
Hagen had special greeting, who long to him was known;
To Volker eke of Burgundy was like highest honor shown.
Thus Dankwart eke he greeted, when spake the doughty thane:
"While we thus well are harbored, who then for all the train
Of those that follow with us shall meet provision make?"
"Yourselves this night right easy shall rest," the noble margrave spake.
"And all that follow with you, with equipment whatsoe'er
Ye bring into my country of steed or warlike gear,
So sure shall it be guarded that of all the sum,
E'en to one spur's value, to you shall never damage come.
"Now stretch aloft, my squires, the tents upon the plain.
What here ye have of losses will I make good again.
Unbridle now the horses and let them wander free."

Upon their way they seldom did meet like hospitality.
Thereat rejoiced the strangers. When thus it ordered was,
Rode the high knights forward. All round upon the grass
Lay the squires attendant and found a gentle rest.
I ween, upon their journey was here provision costliest.
Out before the castle the noble margravine
Had passed with her fair daughter. In her train were seen
A band of lovely women and many a winsome maid,
Whose arms with bracelets glittered, and all in stately robes arrayed.
The costly jewels sparkled with far-piercing ray
From out their richest vestments, and buxom all were they.
Now came the strangers thither and sprang upon the ground.
How high in noble courtesy the men of Burgundy were found!
Six and thirty maidens and many a fair lady,
—Nor might ye ever any more winsome wish to see—
Went then forth to meet them with many a knight full keen.
At hands of noble ladies fairest greeting then was seen.
The margrave's youthful daughter did kiss the kings all three
As eke had done her mother. Hagen stood thereby.
Her father bade her kiss him; she looked the thane upon,
Who filled her so with terror, she fain had left the thing undone.
When she at last must do it, as did command her sire,
Mingled was her color, both pale and hue of fire.
Likewise kissed she Dankwart and the Fiddler eke anon:
That he was knight of valor to him was such high favor shown.
The margrave's youthful daughter took then by the hand
The royal knight Giselher of Burgundian land.
E'en so led forth her mother the gallant Gunther high.
With those guests so lofty walked they there full joyfully.
The host escorted Gernot to a spacious hall and wide,
Where knights and stately ladies sate them side by side.
Then bade they for the strangers pour good wine plenteously:
In sooth might never heroes find fuller hospitality.
Glances fond and many saw ye directed there
Upon Ruediger's daughter, for she was passing fair.
Yea, in his thoughts caressed her full many a gallant knight;
A lady high in spirit, well might she every heart delight.
Yet whatsoe'er their wishes, might none fulfilléd be.
Hither oft and thither glanced they furtively
On maidens and fair ladies, whereof were many there.
Right kind the noble Fiddler disposéd was to Ruediger.
They parted each from other as ancient custom was,
And knights and lofty ladies did separating pass
When tables were made ready within the spacious hall.
There in stately manner they waited on the strangers all.
To do the guests high honor likewise the table sought
With them the lofty margravine. Her daughter led she not,

But left among the maidens, where fitting was she sat.
That they might not behold her, grieved were the guests in sooth thereat.
The drinking and the feasting, when 'twas ended all,
Escorted was the maiden again into the hall.
Then of merry jesting they nothing lacked, I ween,
Wherein was busy Volker, a thane full gallant and keen.
Then spake the noble Fiddler to all in lofty tone:
"Great mercy, lordly margrave, God to thee hath shown,
For that he hath granted unto thee a wife
Of so surpassing beauty, and thereto a joyous life.
"If that I were of royal birth," the Fiddler spake,
"And kingly crown should carry, to wife I'd wish to take
This thy lovely daughter, —my heart thus prompteth me.
A noble maid and gentle and fair to look upon is she."
Then outspake the margrave: "How might such thing be,
That king should e'er desire daughter born to me?
Exiled from my country here with my spouse I dwell:
What avails the maiden, be she favored ne'er so well?"
Thereto gave answer Gernot, a knight of manner kind:
"If to my desire I ever spouse would find,
Then would I of such lady right gladly make my choice."
In full kindly manner added Hagen eke his voice:
"Now shall my master Giselher take to himself a spouse.
The noble margrave's daughter is of so lofty house,
That I and all his warriors would glad her service own,
If that she in Burgundy should ever wear a royal crown."
Glad thereat full truly was Sir Ruediger,
And eke Gotelinde: they joyed such words to hear.
Anon arranged the heroes that her as bride did greet
The noble knight Giselher, as was for any monarch meet.
What thing is doomed to happen, who may the same prevent?
To come to the assembly they for the maidens sent,
And to the knight they plighted the winsome maid for wife,
Pledge eke by him was given, his love should yet endure with life.
They to the maid allotted castles and spreading land,
Whereof did give assurance the noble monarch's hand
And eke the royal Gernot, 'twould surely so be done.
Then spake to them the margrave: "Lordly castles have I none,
"Yet true shall be my friendship the while that I may live.
Unto my daughter shall I of gold and silver give
What hundred sumpter-horses full laden bear away,
That her husband's lofty kinsmen find honor in the fair array."
They bade the knight and maiden within a ring to stand,
As was of old the custom. Of youths a goodly band,
That all were merry-hearted, did her there confront,
And thought they on her beauty as mind of youth is ever wont.
When they began to question then the winsome maid,

Would she the knight for husband, somewhat she was dismayed,
And yet forego she would not to have him for her own.
She blushed to hear the question, as many another maid hath done.
Her father Ruediger prompted   that Yes her answer be,
And that she take him gladly. Unto her instantly
Sprang the young Sir Giselher, and in his arm so white
He clasped her to his bosom. —Soon doomed to end was her delight.
Then spake again the margrave: "Ye royal knights and high,
When that home ye journey again to Burgundy
I'll give to you my daughter, as fitting is to do,
That ye may take her with you." They gave their plighted word thereto.
What jubilation made they yet at last must end.
The maiden then was bidden unto her chamber wend,
And guests to seek their couches and rest until the day.
For them the host provided a feast in hospitable way.
When they had feasted fully and to the Huns' country
Thence would onward journey, "Such thing shall never be,"
Spake the host full noble, "but here ye still shall rest.
Seldom hath my good fortune welcomed yet so many a guest."
Thereto gave answer Dankwart: "In sooth it may not be.
Bread and wine whence hast thou and food sufficiently,
Over night to harbor of guests so great a train?"
When the host had heard it, spake he: "All thy words are vain.
"Refuse not my petition, ye noble lords and high.
A fortnight's full provision might I in sooth supply,
For you and every warrior that journeys in your train.
Till now hath royal Etzel small portion of my substance ta'en."
Though fain they had declined it, yet they there must stay
E'en to the fourth morning. Then did the host display
So generous hand and lavish that it was told afar.
He gave unto the strangers horses and apparel rare.
The time at last was over and they must journey thence.
Then did the valiant Ruediger with lavish hand dispense
Unto all his bounty, refused he unto none
Whate'er he might desire. Well-pleased they parted every one.
His courteous retainers to castle gateway brought
Saddled many horses, and soon the place was sought
Eke by the gallant strangers each bearing shield in hand,
For that they thence would journey onward into Etzel's land.
The host had freely offered rich presents unto all,
Ere that the noble strangers passed out before the hall.
High in honor lived he, a knight of bounty rare.
His fair daughter had he given unto Giselher.
Eke gave he unto Gunther, a knight of high renown,
What well might wear with honor the monarch as his own,
—Though seldom gift received he— a coat of harness rare.
Thereat inclined King Gunther before the noble Ruediger.

Then gave he unto Gernot a good and trusty blade,
Wherewith anon in combat was direst havoc made.
That thus the gift was taken rejoiced the margrave's wife:
Thereby the noble Ruediger was doomed anon to lose his life.

Gotelinde proffered Hagen, as 'twas a fitting thing,
Her gifts in kindly manner. Since scorned them not the king,
Eke he without her bounty to the high festivity
Should thence not onward journey. Yet loath to take the same was he.

"Of all doth meet my vision," Hagen then spake,
"Would I wish for nothing with me hence to take
But alone the shield that hanging on yonder wall I see.
The same I'd gladly carry into Etzel's land with me."

When the stately margravine Hagen's words did hear,
Brought they to mind her sorrow, nor might she stop a tear.
She thought again full sadly how her son Nudung fell,
Slain by hand of Wittich; and did her breast with anguish swell.

She spake unto the hero: "The shield to thee I'll give.
O would to God in heaven that he still did live,
Whose hand erstwhile did wield it! In battle fell he low,
And I, a wretched mother, must weep with never-ending woe.

Thereat the noble lady up from the settle rose,
And soon her arms all snow-white did the shield enclose.
She bore it unto Hagen, who made obeisance low;
The gift she might with honor upon so valiant thane bestow.

O'er it, to keep its color, a shining cover lay
With precious stones all studded, nor ever shone the day
Upon a shield more costly; if e'er a longing eye
Did covet to possess it, scarce thousand marks the same might buy.

The shield in charge gave Hagen thence away to bear.
Before his host then Dankwart himself presented there,
On whom the margrave's daughter did costly dress bestow.
Wherein anon in Hunland arrayed full stately he did go.

Whate'er of gifts by any was accepted there,
Them had his hand ne'er taken, but that intent all were
To do their host an honor who gave with hand so free.
By his guests in combat soon doomed was he slain to be.

Volker the valiant to Gotelinde came
And stood in courteous manner with fiddle 'fore the dame.
Sweet melodies he played her and sang his songs thereby,
For thought he from Bechelaren to take departure presently.

The margravine bade to her a casket forth to bear.
And now of presents given full freely may ye hear.
Therefrom she took twelve armbands and drew them o'er his hand.
"These shall thou with thee carry, as ridest thou to Etzel's land,

"And for my sake shalt wear them when at court thou dost appear,
That when thou hither comest I may the story hear
How thou hast done me honor at the high festival."

What did wish the lady, faithfully performed he all.
Thus to his guests the host spake: "That ye more safely fare,
Myself will give you escort and bid them well beware
That upon the highway no ill on you be wrought."
Thereat his sumpter horses straightway laden forth were brought
The host was well prepared with five hundred men
With horse and rich attire. These led he with him then
In right joyous humor to the high festival.
Alive to Bechelaren again came never one of all.
Thence took his leave Sir Ruediger with kiss full lovingly;
As fitting was for Giselher, likewise the same did he.
With loving arms enfolding caressed they ladies fair.
To many a maid the parting did bring anon full bitter tear.
On all sides then the windows were open wide flung,
As with his train of warriors the host to saddle sprung.
I ween their hearts did tell them how they should sorrow deep.
For there did many a lady and many a winsome maiden weep.
For dear friends left behind him grieved many a knight full sore.
Whom they at Bechelaren should behold no more.
Yet rode they off rejoicing down across the sand
Hard by the Danube river on their way to Etzel's land.
Then spake to the Burgundians the gallant knight and bold,
Ruediger the noble: "Now let us not withhold
The story of our coming unto the Hun's country.
Unto the royal Etzel might tidings ne'er more welcome be."
Down in haste through Austria the messenger did ride,
Who told unto the people soon on every side,
From Worms beyond Rhine river were high guests journeying.
Nor unto Etzel's people gladder tidings might ye bring.
Onward spurred the messengers who did the message bear,
How now in Hunnish country the Nibelungen were.
"Kriemhild, lofty lady, warm thy welcome be;
In stately manner hither come thy loving brothers three."
Within a lofty casement the Lady Kriemhild stood,
Looking for her kinsmen, as friend for friend full good.
From her father's country saw she many a knight;
Eke heard the king the tidings, and laughed thereat for sheer delight.
"Now well my heart rejoiceth," spake Lady Kriemhild.
"Hither come my kinsmen with many a new-wrought shield
And brightly shining hauberk: who gold would have from me,
Be mindful of my sorrow; to him I'll ever gracious be."

TWENTY-EIGHTH ADVENTURE

How the Burgundians came to Etzel's Castle

When that the men of Burgundy were come into the land,
He of Bern did hear it, the agéd Hildebrand.
He told it to his master, who sore thereat did grieve;
The knight so keen and gallant bade he in fitting way receive.
Wolfhart the valiant bade lead the heroes forth.
In company with Dietrich rode many a thane of worth,
As out to receive them across the plain he went,
Where might ye see erected already many a stately tent.
When that of Tronje Hagen them far away espied,
Unto his royal masters full courteously he said:
"Now shall ye, doughty riders, down from the saddle spring,
And forward go to meet them that here to you a welcome bring.
"A train there cometh yonder, well knew I e'en when young.
Thanes they are full doughty of the land of Amelung.
He of Bern doth lead them, and high of heart they are;
To scorn their proffered greeting shall ye in sooth full well beware."
Dismounted then with Dietrich, (as was meet and right,)
Attended by his squire many a gallant knight.
They went unto the strangers and greeted courteously
The knights that far had ridden from the land of Burgundy.
When then Sir Dietrich saw them coming near,
What words the thane delivered, now may ye willing hear,
Unto Ute's children. Their journey grieved him sore.
He weened that Ruediger knowing had warned what lay for them in store.
"Welcome be ye, Masters, Gunther and Giselher,
Gernot and Hagen, welcome eke Volker
And the valiant Dankwart. Do ye not understand?
Kriemhild yet sore bemoaneth the hero of Nibelungen land."
"Long time may she be weeping," Hagen spake again;
"In sooth for years a many dead he lies and slain.
To the monarch now of Hunland should she devoted be:
Siegfried returneth never, buried now long time is he."
"How Siegfried's death was compassed, let now the story be:
While liveth Lady Kriemhild, look ye for injury."
Thus did of Bern Sir Dietrich unto them declare:
"Hope of the Nibelungen, of her vengeance well beware."
"Whereof shall I be fearful?" the lofty monarch spake:
"Etzel hath sent us message, (why further question make?)
That we should journey hither into his country.
Eke hath my sister Kriemhild oft wished us here as guests to see.
"I give thee honest counsel," Hagen then did say,
"Now shalt thou here Sir Dietrich and his warriors pray
To tell thee full the story, if aught may be designed,

And let thee know more surely how stands the Lady Kriemhild's mind."
Then went to speak asunder the lordly monarchs three,
Gunther and Gernot, and Dietrich went he.
"Now tell us true, thou noble knight of Bern and kind,
If that perchance thou knowest how stands thy royal mistress' mind."
The lord of Bern gave answer: "What need to tell you more?
I hear each day at morning weeping and wailing sore
The wife of royal Etzel, who piteous doth complain
To God in heaven that Siegfried her doughty spouse from her was ta'en."
"Then must we e'en abide it," was the fearless word
Of Volker the Fiddler, "what we here have heard.
To court we yet shall journey and make full clear to all,
If that to valiant warriors may aught amid the Huns befall."
The gallant thanes of Burgundy unto court then rode,
And went in stately manner as was their country's mode.
Full many a man in Hunland looked eagerly to see
Of what manner Hagen, Tronje's doughty thane, might be.
For that was told the story (and great the wonder grew)
How that of Netherland Siegfried he slew,
That was the spouse of Kriemhild, in strength without a peer,
Hence a mickle questioning after Hagen might ye hear.
Great was the knight of stature, may ye know full true,
Built with breast expansive; mingled was the hue
Of his hair with silver; long he was of limb;
As he strode stately forward might ye mark his visage grim.
Then were the thanes of Burgundy unto quarters shown,
But the serving-man of Gunther by themselves alone.
Thus the queen did counsel, so filled she was with hate.
Anon where they were harbored the train did meet with direst fate.
Dankwart, Hagen's brother, marshal was he.
To him the king his followers commended urgently,
That he provide them plenty and have of them good care.
The noble knight of Burgundy their safety well in mind did bear.
By her train attended, Queen Kriemhild went
To greet the Nibelungen, yet false was her intent.
She kissed her brother Giselher and took him by the hand:
Thereat of Tronje Hagen did tighter draw his helmet's band.
"After such like greeting," the doughty Hagen spake,
"Let all watchful warriors full precaution take:
Differs wide the greeting on masters and men bestowed.
Unhappy was the hour when to this festival we rode."
She spake: "Now be ye welcome to whom ye welcome be.
For sake of friendship never ye greeting have from me.
Tell me now what bring ye from Worms across the Rhine,
That ye so greatly welcome should ever be to land of mine?"
"An I had only known it," Hagen spake again,
"That thou didst look for present from hand of every thane,

I were, methinks, so wealthy —had I me bethought—
That I unto this country likewise to thee my gift had brought."
"Now shall ye eke the story to me more fully say:
The Nibelungen treasure, where put ye that away?
My own possession was it, as well ye understand.
That same ye should have brought me hither unto Etzel's land."
"In sooth, my Lady Kriemhild, full many a day hath flown
Since of the Nibelungen hoard I aught have known.
Into the Rhine to sink it my lords commanded me:
Verily there must it until the day of judgment be."
Thereto the queen gave answer: "Such was e'en my thought.
Thereof right little have ye unto me hither brought,
Although myself did own it and once o'er it held sway.
'Tis cause that I for ever have full many a mournful day."
"The devil have I brought thee," Hagen did declare.
"My shield it is so heavy that I have to bear,
And my plaited armor; my shining helmet see,
And sword in hand I carry, —so might I nothing bring for thee."
Then spake the royal lady unto the warriors all:
"Weapon shall not any bear into the hall.
To me now for safe keeping, ye thanes shall give them o'er."
"In sooth," gave answer Hagen, "such thing shall happen nevermore.
"Such honor ne'er I covet, royal lady mild,
That to its place of keeping thou shouldst bear my shield
With all my other armor, —for thou art a queen.
Such taught me ne'er my sire: myself will be my chamberlain."
"Alack of these my sorrows!" the Lady Kriemhild cried;
"Wherefore will now my brother and Hagen not confide
To me their shields for keeping? Some one did warning give.
Knew I by whom 'twas given, brief were the space that he might live."
Thereto the mighty Dietrich in wrath his answer gave:
"'Tis I who now these noble lords forewarnéd have,
And Hagen, knight full valiant of the land of Burgundy.
Now on! thou devil's mistress, let not the deed my profit be."
Great shame thereat did Kriemhild's bosom quickly fill;
She feared lest Dietrich's anger should work her grievous ill.
Naught she spake unto them as thence she swiftly passed,
But fierce the lightning glances that on her enemies she cast.
By hand then grasped each, other doughty warriors twain:
Hight the one was Dietrich, with Hagen, noble thane.
Then spake in courteous manner that knight of high degree:
"That ye are come to Hunland, 'tis very sorrow unto me;
"For what hath here been spoken by the lofty queen."
Then spake of Tronje Hagen: "Small cause to grieve, I ween."
Held converse thus together those brave warriors twain,
King Etzel which perceiving thus a questioning began:
"I would learn full gladly," —in such wise spake he—

"Who were yonder warrior, to whom so cordially
Doth greeting give Sir Dietrich. Meseemeth high his mood.
Whosoe'er his sire, a thane he is of mettle good."
Unto the king gave answer of Kriemhild's train a knight:
"Born he was of Tronje, Aldrian his sire hight.
How merry here his bearing, a thane full grim is he.
That I have spoken truly, shalt thou anon have cause to see."
"How may I then perceive it that fierce his wrath doth glow?"
Naught of basest treachery yet the king did know,
That anon Queen Kriemhild 'gainst her kinsmen did contrive,
Whereby returned from Hunland not one of all their train alive.
"Well knew I Aldrian, he once to me was thane:
Praise and mickle honor he here by me did gain.
Myself a knight did make him, and gave him of my gold.
Helke, noble lady, did him in highest favor hold.
"Thereby know I fully what Hagen since befell.
Two stately youths as hostage at my court did dwell,
He and Spanish Walter, from youth to manhood led.
Hagen sent I homeward; Walter with Hildegunde fled."
He thought on ancient story that long ago befell.
His doughty friend of Tronje knew he then right well,
Whose youthful valor erstwhile did such assistance lend.
Through him in age he must be bereft of many a dearest friend.

TWENTY-NINTH ADVENTURE

How He arose not before Her

Then parted from each other the noble warriors twain,
Hagen of Tronje   and Dietrich, lofty thane.
Then did King Gunther's warrior cast a glance around,
Seeking a companion the same he eke full quickly found.
As standing there by Giselher he did Volker see,
He prayed the nimble Fiddler to bear him company,
For that full well he knew it how grim he was of mood,
And that in all things was he a knight of mettle keen and good.
While yet their lords were standing there in castle yard
Saw ye the two knights only walking thitherward
Across the court far distant before the palace wide.
The chosen thanes recked little what might through any's hate betide.
They sate them down on settle over against a hall,
Wherein dwelt Lady Kriemhild, beside the palace wall.
Full stately their attire on stalwart bodies shone.
All that did look upon them right gladly had the warriors known.
Like unto beasts full savage were they gaped upon,
The two haughty heroes, by full many a Hun.

Eke from a casement Etzel's wife did them perceive:
Once more to behold them must fair Lady Kriemhild grieve.
It called to mind her sorrow, and she to weep began,
Whereat did mickle wonder many an Etzel's man,
What grief had thus so sudden made her sad of mood.
Spake she: "That hath Hagen, ye knights of mettle keen and good."
They to their mistress answered: "Such thing, how hath it been?
For that thee right joyous we but now have seen.
Ne'er lived he so daring that, having wrought thee ill,
His life he must not forfeit, if but to vengeance point thy will."
"I live but to requite him that shall avenge my wrong;
Whate'er be his desire shall unto him belong.
Prostrate I beseech you," —so spake the monarch's wife—
"Avenge me upon Hagen, and forfeit surely be his life."
Three score of valiant warriors made ready then straightway
To work the will of Kriemhild and her best obey
By slaying of Sir Hagen, the full valiant thane,
And eke the doughty Fiddler; by shameful deed thus sought they gain.
When the queen beheld there so small their company,
In full angry humor to the warriors spake she:
"What there ye think to compass, forego such purpose yet:
So small in numbers never dare ye Hagen to beset.
"How doughty e'er be Hagen, and known his valor wide,
A man by far more doughty that sitteth him beside,
Volker the Fiddler: a warrior grim is he.
In sooth may not so lightly the heroes twain confronted be."
When that she thus had spoken, ready soon were seen
Four hundred stalwart warriors; for was the lofty queen
Full intent upon it to work them evil sore.
Therefrom for all the strangers was mickle sorrow yet in store.
When that complete attiréd were here retainers seen,
Unto the knights impatient in such wise spake the queen:
"Now bide ye yet a moment and stand ye ready so,
While I with crown upon me unto my enemies shall go.
"And list while I accuse him how he hath wrought me bane,
Hagen of Tronje, Gunther's doughty thane.
I know his mood so haughty, naught he'll deny of all.
Nor reck I what of evil therefrom may unto him befall."
Then saw the doughty Fiddler —he was a minstrel keen—
Adown the steps descending the high and stately queen
Who issued from the castle. When he the queen espied,
Spake the valiant Volker to him was seated by his side:
"Look yonder now, friend Hagen, how that she hither hies
Who to this land hath called us in such treacherous wise.
No monarch's wife I ever saw followed by such band
Of warriors armed for battle, that carry each a sword in hand.
"Know'st thou, perchance, friend Hagen, if hate to thee they bear?

Then would I well advise thee of them full well beware
And guard both life and honor. That methinks were good,
For if I much mistake not, full wrathful is the warriors' mood.
"Of many eke among them so broad the breasts do swell,
That who would guard him 'gainst them betimes would do it well.
I ween that 'neath their tunics they shining mail-coats wear:
Yet might I never tell thee, 'gainst whom such evil mind they bear."
Then spake all wrathful-minded Hagen the warrior keen:
"On me to vent their fury is their sole thought, I ween,
That thus with brandished weapons their onward press we see.
Despite them all yet trow I to come safe home to Burgundy.
"Now tell me, friend Volker, wilt thou beside me stand,
If seek to work me evil here Kriemhild's band?
That let me hear right truly, as I am dear to thee.
By thy side forever shall my service faithful be."
"Full surely will I help thee," the minstrel straight replied;
"And saw I e'en a monarch with all his men beside
Hither come against us, the while a sword I wield
Not fear shall ever prompt me from thy side one pace to yield."
"Now God in heaven, O Volker, give thy high heart its meed.
Will they forsooth assail me, whereof else have I need?
Wilt thou thus stand beside me as here is thy intent,
Let come all armed these warriors, on whatsoever purpose bent."
"Now rise we from this settle," the minstrel spake once more,
"While that the royal lady passeth here before.
To her be done this honor as unto lady high.
Ourselves in equal manner shall we honor eke thereby."
"Nay, nay! as me thou lovest," Hagen spake again,
"For so would sure imagine here each hostile thane
That 'twere from fear I did it, should I bear me so.
For sake of never any will I from this settle go.
"Undone we both might leave it in sooth more fittingly.
Wherefore should I honor who bears ill-will to me?
Such thing will I do never, the while I yet have life.
Nor reck I aught how hateth me the royal Etzel's wife."
Thereat defiant Hagen across his knee did lay
A sword that shone full brightly, from whose knob did play
The light of glancing jasper greener than blade of grass.
Well perceivéd Kriemhild that it erstwhile Siegfried's was.
When she the sword espiéd, to weep was sore her need.
The hilt was shining golden, the sheath a band of red.
As it recalled her sorrow, her tears had soon begun;
I ween for that same purpose 'twas thus by dauntless Hagen done.
Eke the valiant Volker a fiddle-bow full strong
Unto himself drew nearer; mickle it was and long,
Like unto a broad-sword full sharp that was and wide.
So sat they all undaunted the stately warriors side by side.

There sat the thanes together in such defiant wise
That would never either from the settle rise
Through fear of whomsoever. Then strode before their feet
The lofty queen, and wrathful did thus the doughty warriors greet.
Quoth she: "Now tell me, Hagen, upon whose command
Barest thou thus to journey hither to this land,
And knowest well what sorrow through thee my heart must bear.
Wert thou not reft of reason, then hadst thou kept thee far from here."
"By none have I been summoned," Hagen gave reply.
"Three lofty thanes invited were to this country:
The same I own as masters and service with them find.
Whene'er they make court journey 'twere strange should I remain behind."
Quoth she: "Now tell me further, wherefore didst thou that
Whereby thou hast deservéd my everlasting hate?
'Twas thou that slewest Siegfried, spouse so dear to me,
The which, till life hath ended, must ever cause for weeping be."
Spake he: "Why parley further, since further word were vain?
E'en I am that same Hagen by whom was Siegfried slain,
That deft knight of valor. How sore by him 'twas paid
That the Lady Kriemhild dared the fair Brunhild upbraid!
"Beyond all cavil is it, high and royal dame,
Of all the grievous havoc I do bear the blame.
Avenge it now who wisheth, woman or man tho't be.
An I unto thee lie not, I've wrought thee sorest injury."
She spake: "Now hear, ye warriors, how denies he not at all
The cause of all my sorrow. Whate'er may him befall
Reck I not soever, that know ye, Etzel's men."
The overweening warriors blank gazed upon each other then.
Had any dared the onset, seen it were full plain
The palm must be awarded to the companions twain,
Who had in storm of battle full oft their prowess shown.
What that proud band designed through fear must now be left undone.
Outspake one of their number: "Wherefore look thus to me?
What now I thought to venture left undone shall be,
Nor for reward of any think I my life to lose;
To our destruction lures us here the royal Etzel's spouse."
Then spake thereby another: "Like mind therein have I.
Though ruddy gold were offered like towers piléd high,
Yet would I never venture to stir this Fiddler's spleen.
Such are the rapid glances that darting from his eyes I've seen.
"Likewise know I Hagen from youthful days full well,
Nor more about his valor to me need any tell.
In two and twenty battles I the knight have seen,
Whereby sorest sorrow to many a lady's heart hath been.
"When here they were with Etzel, he and the knight of Spain
Bore storm of many a battle in many a warlike train
For sake of royal honor, so oft thereof was need.

Wherefore of right are honors high the valiant Hagen's meed.
"Then was yet the hero but a child in years;
Now how hoary-headed who were his youthful feres,
To wisdom now attainéd, a warrior grim and strong,
Eke bears he with him Balmung, the which he gained by mickle wrong."
Therewith the matter ended, and none the fight dared start,
Whereat the Lady Kriemhild full heavy was of heart.
Her warriors thence did vanish, for feared they death indeed
At hands of the Fiddler, whereof right surely was there need.
Outspake then the Fiddler: "Well we now have seen,
That enemies here do greet us, as we forewarned have been.
Back unto the monarchs let us straight repair,
That none against our masters to raise a hostile hand may dare.
"How oft from impious purpose doth fear hold back the hand,
Where friend by friend doth only firm in friendship stand,
Until right sense give warning to leave the thing undone.
Thus wisdom hath prevented the harm of mortals many a one."
"Heed I will thy counsel," Hagen gave reply.
Then passed they where the monarchs found they presently
In high state received within the palace court.
Loud the valiant Volker straight began after this sort
Unto his royal masters: "How long will ye stand so,
That foes may press upon you? To the king ye now shall go,
And from his lips hear spoken how is his mind to you."
The valiant lords and noble consorted then by two and two.
Of Bern the lofty Dietrich took by the hand
Gunther the lordly monarch of Burgundian land;
Irnfried escorted Gernot, a knight of valor keen,
And Ruediger with Giselher going unto the court was seen.
Howe'er with fere consorted there any thane might be,
Volker and Hagen ne'er parted company,
Save in storm of battle when they did reach life's bourne,
'Twas cause that highborn ladies anon in grievous way must mourn.
Unto the court then passing with the kings were seen.
Of their lofty retinue a thousand warriors keen,
And threescore thanes full valiant that followed in their train;
The same from his own country had doughty Hagen with him ta'en.
Hawart and eke Iring, chosen warriors twain,
Saw ye walk together in the royal train.
By Dankwart and Wolfhart, a thane of high renown,
Was high courtly bearing there before the others shown.
When the lord of Rhineland passed into the hall,
Etzel mighty monarch waited not at all,
But sprang from off his settle when he beheld him nigh.
By monarch ne'er was given greeting so right heartily.
"Welcome be, Lord Gunther, and eke Sir Gernot too,
And your brother Giselher. My greetings unto you

I sent with honest purpose to Worms across the Rhine;
And welcome all your followers shall be unto this land of mine.
"Right welcome be ye likewise, doughty warriors twain,
Volker the full valiant, and Hagen dauntless thane,
To me and to my lady here in my country.
Unto the Rhine to greet you many a messenger sent she."
Then spake of Tronje Hagen: "Thereof I'm well aware,
And did I with my masters not thus to Hunland fare,
To do thee honor had I ridden unto thy land."
Then took the lofty monarch the honored strangers by the hand.
He led them to the settle whereon himself he sat,
Then poured they for the strangers —with care they tended that—
In goblets wide and golden mead and mulberry wine,
And bade right hearty welcome unto the knights afar from Rhine.
Then spake the monarch Etzel: "This will I freely say:
Naught in this world might happen to bring my heart more joy,
Than that ye lofty heroes thus are come to me.
The queen from mickle sadness thereby make ye likewise free.
"To me 'twas mickle wonder wherein had I transgressed,
That I for friends had won me so many a noble guest,
Yet ye had never deignéd to come to my country.
'Tis now turned cause of gladness that you as guests I here may see."
Thereto gave answer Ruediger, a knight of lofty mind:
"Well mayst thou joy to see them; right honor shalt thou find
And naught but noble bearing in my high mistress' kin.
With them for guest thou likewise many a stately thane dost win."
At turn of sun in summer were the knights arrived
At mighty Etzel's palace. Ne'er hath monarch lived
That lordly guests did welcome with higher compliment.
When come was time of eating, the king with them to table went.
Amid his guests more stately a host was seated ne'er.
They had in fullest measure of drink and goodly fare;
Whate'er they might desire, they ready found the same.
Tales of mickle wonder had spread abroad the heroes' fame.

THIRTIETH ADVENTURE

How they kept Guard

And now the day was ended and nearing was the night.
Came then the thought with longing unto each way-worn knight,
When that they might rest them and to their beds be shown.
'Twas mooted first by Hagen and straight was answer then made known.
To Etzel spake then Gunther: "Fair days may God thee give!
To bed we'll now betake us, an be it by thy leave;
We'll come betimes at morning, if so thy pleasure be."

From his guests the monarch parted then full courteously.
Upon the guests on all sides the Huns yet rudely pressed,
Whereat the valiant Volker these words to them addressed:
"How dare ye 'fore these warriors thus beset the way?
If that ye desist not, rue such rashness soon ye may.
"Let fall will I on some one such stroke of fiddle-bow,
That eyes shall fill with weeping if he hath friend to show.
Why make not way before us, as fitting were to do!
Knights by name ye all are, but knighthood's ways unknown to you."
When outspake the Fiddler thus so wrathfully
Backward glanced bold Hagen to see what this might be.
Quoth he: "He redes you rightly, this keen minstrel knight.
Ye followers of Kriemhild, now pass to rest you for the night.
"The thing whereof ye're minded will none dare do, I ween.
If aught ye purpose 'gainst us, on the morrow be that seen,
And let us weary strangers the night in quiet pass;
I ween, with knights of honor such evermore the custom was."
Then were led the strangers into a spacious hall
Where they found prepared for the warriors one and all
Beds adorned full richly, that were both wide and long.
Yet planned the Lady Kriemhild to work on them the direst wrong.
Rich quilted mattress covers of Arras saw ye there
Lustrous all and silken, and spreading sheets there were
Wrought of silk of Araby, the best might e'er be seen.
O'er them lay rich embroidered stuffs that cast a brilliant sheen.
Coverlets of ermine full many might ye see,
With sullen sable mingled, whereunder peacefully
They should rest the night through till came the shining day.
A king with all retinue ne'er, I ween, so stately lay.
"Alack for these night-quarters!" quoth young Giselher,
"Alack for my companions who this our journey share!
How kind so e'er my sister's hospitality,
Dead by her devising, I fear me, are we doomed to be."
"Let now no fears disturb you," Hagen gave reply;
"Through the hours of sleeping keep the watch will I.
I trust full well to guard you until return the day,
Thereof be never fearful; let then preserve him well who may."
Inclined they all before him thereat to give him grace.
Then sought they straight their couches; in sooth 'twas little space
Until was softly resting every stately man.
But Hagen, valiant hero, the while to don his armor gan.
Spake then to him the Fiddler, Volker a doughty thane:
"I'll be thy fellow, Hagen, an wilt thou not disdain,
While watch this night thou keepest, until do come the morn."
Right heartily the hero to Volker then did thanks return.
"God in heaven requite thee, Volker, trusty fere.
In all my time of trouble wished I none other near,

None other but thee only, when dangers round me throng.
I'll well repay that favor, if death withhold its hand so long."
Arrayed in glittering armor both soon did ready stand;
Each did take unto him a mighty shield in hand,
And passed without the portal there to keep the way.
Thus were the strangers guarded, and trusty watchers eke had they.
Volker the valiant, as he sat before the hall,
Leaned his trusty buckler meanwhile against the wall,
Then took in hand his fiddle as he was wont to do:
All times the thane would render unto his friends a service true.
Beneath the hall's wide portal he sat on bench of stone;
Than he a bolder fiddler was there never none.
As from his chords sweet echoes resounded through the hall,
Thanks for glad refreshment had Volker from the warriors all.
Then from the strings an echo the wide hall did fill,
For in his fiddle-playing the knight had strength and skill.
Softer then and sweeter to fiddle he began
And wiled to peaceful slumber many an anxious brooding man.
When they were wrapped in slumber and he did understand,
Then took again the warrior his trusty shield in hand
And passed without the portal to guard the entrance tower,
And safe to keep his fellows where Kriemhild's crafty men did lower.
About the hour of midnight, or earlier perchance,
The eye of valiant Volker did catch a helmet's glance
Afar from out the darkness: the men of Kriemhild sought
How that upon the strangers might grievous scathe in stealth be wrought.
Quoth thereat the Fiddler: "Friend Hagen, 'tis full clear
That we do well together here this watch to share.
I see before us yonder men arméd for the fight;
I ween they will attack us, if I their purpose judge aright."
"Be silent, then," spake Hagen, "and let them come more nigh.
Ere that they perceive us shall helmets sit awry,
By good swords disjointed that in our hands do swing.
Tale of vigorous greeting shall they back to Kriemhild bring."
Amid the Hunnish warriors one full soon did see,
That well the door was guarded; straightway then cried he:
"The thing we here did purpose 'tis need we now give o'er,
For I behold the Fiddler standing guard before the door.
"Upon his head a helmet of glancing light is seen,
Welded strong and skilful, dintless, of clearest sheen.
The mail-rings of his armor do sparkle like the fire,
Beside him stands eke Hagen; safe are the strangers from our ire."
Straightway they back returned. When Volker that did see,
Unto his companion wrathfully spake he:
"Now let me to those caitiffs across the court-yard go;
What mean they by such business, from Kriemhild's men I fain would know."
"No, as thou dost love me," Hagen straight replied;

"If from this hall thou partest, such ill may thee betide
At hands of these bold warriors and from the swords they bear,
That I must haste to help thee, though here our kinsmen's bane it were.
"Soon as we two together have joined with them in fight,
A pair or two among them will surely hasten straight
Hither to this hall here, and work such havoc sore
Upon our sleeping brethren, as must be mournéd evermore."
Thereto gave answer Volker: "So much natheless must be,
That they do learn full certain how I the knaves did see,
That the men of Kriemhild hereafter not deny
What they had wrought full gladly here with foulest treachery."
Straightway then unto them aloud did Volker call:
"How go ye thus in armor, ye valiant warriors all?
Or forth, perchance, a-robbing, Kriemhild's men, go ye?
Myself and my companion shall ye then have for company."
Thereto no man gave answer. Wrathful grew his mood:
"Fie, ye caitiff villains," spake the hero good,
"Would ye us so foully have murdered while we slept?
With knights so high in honor full seldom thus hath faith been kept."
Then unto Queen Kriemhild were the tidings borne,
How her men did fail their purpose: 'twas cause for her to mourn.
Yet otherwise she wrought it, for grim she was of mood:
Anon through her must perish full many a valorous knight and good.

THIRTY-FIRST ADVENTURE

How they went to Mass

"So cool doth grow my armor," Volker made remark,
"I ween but little longer will endure the dark.
By the air do I perceive it, that soon will break the day."
Then waked they many a warrior who still in deepest slumber lay.
When brake the light of morning athwart the spacious hall,
Hagen gan awaken the stranger warriors all,
If that they to the minster would go to holy mass.
After the Christian custom, of bells a mickle ringing was.
There sang they all uneven, that plainly might ye see
How Christian men and heathen did not full well agree.
Each one of Gunther's warriors would hear the service sung,
So were they all together up from their night-couches sprung.
Then did the warriors lace them in so goodly dress,
That never heroes any, that king did e'er possess,
More richly stood attired; that Hagen grieved to see.
Quoth he: "Ye knights, far other here must your attire be.
"Yea, know among you many how here the case doth stand.
Bear ye instead of roses your good swords in hand,

For chaplets all bejewelled your glancing helmets good,
Since we have well perceivéd how is the angry Kriemhild's mood.
"To-day must we do battle, that will I now declare.
Instead of silken tunic shall ye good hauberks wear,
And for embroidered mantle a trusty shield and wide,
That ye may well defend you, if ye must others' anger bide.
"My masters well belovéd, knights and kinsmen true,
'Tis meet that ye betake you unto the minster too,
That God do not forsake you in peril and in need,
For certain now I make you that death is nigh to us indeed.
"Forget ye not whatever wrong ye e'er have done,
But there 'fore God right meekly all your errors own;
Thereto would I advise you, ye knights of high degree,
For God alone in heaven may will that other mass ye see."
Thus went they to the minster, the princes and their men.
Within the holy churchyard bade them Hagen then
Stand all still together that they part not at all.
Quoth he: "Knows not any what may at hands of Huns befall.
"Let stand, good friends, all ready, your shields before your feet,
That if ever any would you in malice greet,
With deep-cut wound ye pay him; that is Hagen's rede,
That from men may never aught but praises be your meed."
Volker and Hagen, the twain thence did pass
Before the broad minster. Therein their purpose was
That the royal Kriemhild must meet them where they stood
There athwart her pathway. In sooth full grim she was of mood.
Then came the royal Etzel and eke his spouse full fair.
Attired were the warriors all in raiment rare
That following full stately with her ye might see;
The dust arose all densely round Kriemhild's mickle company.
When the lofty monarch thus all armed did see
The kings and their followers, straightway then cried he:
"How see I in this fashion my friends with helm on head?
By my troth I sorrow if ill to them have happenéd.
"I'll gladly make atonement as doth to them belong.
Hath any them affronted or done them aught of wrong,
To me 'tis mickle sorrow, well may they understand.
To serve them am I ready, in whatsoever they command."
Thereto gave answer Hagen: "Here hath wronged us none.
'Tis custom of my masters to keep their armor on
Till full three days be over, when high festival they hold.
Did any here molest us, to Etzel would the thing be told."
Full well heard Kriemhild likewise how Hagen gave reply.
Upon him what fierce glances flashed furtively her eye!
Yet betray she would not the custom of her country,
Though well she long had known it in the land of Burgundy.
How grim soe'er and mighty the hate to them she bore,

Had any told to Etzel how stood the thing before,
Well had he prevented what there anon befell.
So haughty were they minded that none to him the same would tell.
With the queen came forward there a mighty train,
But no two handbreadths yielded yet those warriors twain
To make way before her. The Huns did wrathful grow,
That their mistress passing should by them be jostled so.
Etzel's highborn pages were sore displeased thereat,
And had upon the strangers straightway spent their hate,
But that they durst not do it their high lord before.
There was a mickle pressing, yet naught of anger happened more.
When they thence were parting from holy service done,
On horse came quickly prancing full many a nimble Hun.
With the Lady Kriemhild went many a maiden fair,
And eke to make her escort seven thousand knights rode there.
Kriemhild with her ladies within the casement sat
By Etzel, mighty monarch, —full pleased he was thereat.
They wished to view the tourney of knights beyond compare.
What host of strangers riding thronged the court before them there!
The marshal with the squires not in vain ye sought,
Dankwart the full valiant: with him had he brought
His royal master's followers of the land of Burgundy.
For the valiant Nibelungen the steeds well saddled might ye see.
When their steeds they mounted, the kings and all their men,
Volker thane full doughty, gave his counsel then,
That after their country's fashion they ride a mass mellay.
His rede the heroes followed and tourneyed in full stately way.
The knight had counsel given in sooth that pleased them well;
The clash of arms in mellay soon full loud did swell.
Many a valiant warrior did thereto resort,
As Etzel and Kriemhild looked down upon the spacious court.
Came there unto the mellay six hundred knights of those
That followed Dietrich's bidding, the strangers to oppose.
Pastime would they make them with the men of Burgundy,
And if he leave had granted had done the same right willingly.
In their company rode there how many a warrior bold!
When unto Sir Dietrich then the thing was told,
Forbade he that 'gainst Gunther's men they join the play.
He feared lest harm befall them, and well his counsel did he weigh.
When of Bern the warriors thence departed were,
Came they of Bechelaren, the men of Ruediger,
Bearing shield five hundred, and rode before the hall;
Rather had the margrave that they came there not at all.
Prudently then rode he amid their company
And told unto his warriors how they might plainly see,
That the men of Gunther were in evil mood:
Did they forego the mellay, please him better far it would.

When they were thence departed, the stately knights and bold,
Came they of Thuringia, as hath to us been told,
And of them of Denmark a thousand warriors keen.
From crash of spear up-flying full frequent were the splinters seen.
Irnfried and Hawart rode into the mellay,
Whom the gallant men of Rhineland received in knightly play:
Full oft the men of Thuringia they met in tournament,
Whereby the piercing lance-point through many a stately shield was sent.
Eke with three thousand warriors came Sir Bloedel there.
Etzel and Kriemhild were of his coming ware,
As this play of chivalry before them they did see.
Now hoped the queen that evil befall the men of Burgundy.
Schrutan and Gibecke rode into the mellay,
Eke Ramung and Hornbog after the Hunnish way;
Yet must they come to standstill 'fore the thanes of Burgundy.
High against the palace wall the splintered shafts did fly.
How keen soe'er the contest, 'twas naught but knightly sport.
With shock of shields and lances heard ye the palace court
Loud give back the echo where Gunther's men rode on.
His followers in the jousting on every side high honor won.
So long they held such pastime and with so mickle heat
That through the broidered trappings oozed clear drops of sweat
From the prancing chargers whereon the knights did ride.
In full gallant manner their skill against the Huns they tried.
Then outspake the Fiddler, Volker deft of hand:
"These knights, I ween, too timid are 'gainst us to stand.
Oft did I hear the story what hate to us they bore;
Than this a fairer season to vent it, find they nevermore."
"Lead back unto the stables," once more spake Volker then,
"Now our weary chargers; we'll ride perchance again
When comes the cool of evening, if fitting time there be.
Mayhap the queen will honor award to men of Burgundy."
Beheld they then prick hither one dressed in state so rare
That of the Huns none other might with him compare.
Belike from castle tower did watch his fair lady;
So gay was his apparel as it some knight's bride might be.
Then again quoth Volker: "How may I stay my hand?
Yonder ladies' darling a knock shall understand.
Let no man here deter me, I'll give him sudden check.
How spouse of royal Etzel thereat may rage, I little reck."
"Nay, as thou dost love me," straight King Gunther spake;
"All men will but reproach us if such affront we make.
The Huns be first offenders, for such would more befit."
Still did the royal Etzel in casement by Queen Kriemhild sit.
"I'll add unto the mellay," Hagen did declare;
"Let now all these ladies and knights be made aware
How we can ride a charger; 'twere well we make it known,

For, come what may, small honor shall here to Gunther's men be shown."
Once more the nimble Volker into the mellay spurred,
Whereat full many a lady soon to weep was heard.
His lance right through the body of that gay Hun he sent:
'Twas cause that many a woman and maiden fair must sore lament.
Straight dashed into the mellay Hagen and his men.
With three score of his warriors spurred he quickly then
Forward where the Fiddler played so lustily.
Etzel and Kriemhild full plainly might the passage see.
Then would the kings their minstrel —that may ye fairly know—
Leave not all defenceless there amid the foe.
With them a thousand heroes rode forth full dexterously,
And soon had gained their purpose with show of proudest chivalry.
When in such rude fashion the stately Hun was slain,
Might ye hear his kinsmen weeping loud complain.
Then all around did clamor: "Who hath the slayer been?"
"None but the Fiddler was it, Volker the minstrel keen."
For swords and for shields then called full speedily
That slain margrave's kinsmen of the Hun's country.
To avenge him sought they Volker in turn to slay.
In haste down from the casement royal Etzel made his way.
Arose a mighty clamor from the people all;
The kings and men of Burgundy dismounted 'fore the hall,
And likewise their chargers to the rear did send.
Came then the mighty Etzel and sought to bring the strife to end.
From one of that Hun's kinsmen who near by him did stand
Snatched he a mighty weapon quick from out his hand,
And therewith backward smote them, for fierce his anger wrought.
"Shall thus my hospitality unto these knights be brought to naught?"
"If ye the valiant minstrel here 'fore me should slay,"
Spake the royal Etzel, "it were an evil day.
When he the Hun impaléd I did observe full well,
That not through evil purpose but by mishap it so befell.
"These my guests now must ye ne'er disturb in aught."
Himself became their escort. Away their steeds were brought
Unto the stables by many a waiting squire,
Who ready at their bidding stood to meet their least desire.
The host with the strangers into the palace went,
Nor would he suffer any further his wrath to vent.
Soon were the tables ready and water for them did wait.
Many then had gladly on them of Rhineland spent their hate.
Not yet the lords were seated till some time was o'er.
For Kriemhild o'er her sorrow meantime did trouble sore.
She spake: "Of Bern, O Master, thy counsel grant to me,
Thy help and eke thy mercy, for here in sorry plight I be."
To her gave answer Hildebrand, a thane right praiseworthy:
"Who harms the Nibelungen shall ne'er have help of me,

How great soe'er the guerdon. Such deed he well may rue,
For never yet did any these gallant doughty knights subdue."
Eke in courteous manner Sir Dietrich her addressed:
"Vain, O lofty mistress, unto me thy quest.
In sooth thy lofty kinsmen have wronged me not at all,
That I on thanes so valorous should thus with murderous purpose fall.

"Thy prayer doth thee small honor, O high and royal dame,
That upon thy kinsmen thou so dost counsel shame.
Thy grace to have they deeméd when came they to this land.
Nevermore shall Siegfried avengéd be by Dietrich's hand."
When she no guile discovered in the knight of Bern,
Unto Bloedel straightway did she hopeful turn
With promise of wide marches that Nudung erst did own.
Slew him later Dankwart that he forgot the gift full soon.

Spake she: "Do thou help me, Sir Bloedel, I pray.
Yea, within the palace are foes of mine this day,
Who erstwhile slew Siegfried, spouse full dear to me.
Who helps me to avenge it, to him I'll e'er beholden be."
Thereto gave answer Bloedel: "Lady, be well aware,
Ne'er to do them evil 'fore Etzel may I dare,
For to thy kinsmen, lady, beareth he good will.
Ne'er might the king me pardon, wrought I upon them aught of ill."

"But nay, Sir Bloedel, my favor shalt thou have evermore.
Yea, give I thee for guerdon silver and gold in store,
And eke a fairest lady, that Nudung erst should wed:
By her fond embraces may'st thou well be comforted.
"The land and eke the castles, all to thee I'll give;
Yea, may'st thou, knight full noble, in joyance ever live,
Call'st thou thine the marches, wherein did Nudung dwell.
Whate'er this day I promise, fulfil it all I will full well."

When understood Sir Bloedel what gain should be his share,
And pleased him well the lady for that she was so fair,
By force of arms then thought he to win her for his wife.
Thereby the knight aspirant was doomed anon to lose his life.
"Unto the hall betake thee," quoth he unto the queen,
"Alarum I will make thee ere any know, I ween.
Atone shall surely Hagen where he hath done thee wrong:
To thee I'll soon give over King Gunther's man in fetters strong."

"To arms, to arms!" quoth Bloedel, "my good warriors all:
In their followers' quarters upon the foe we'll fall.
Herefrom will not release me royal Etzel's wife.
To win this venture therefore fear not each one to lose his life."
When at length Queen Kriemhild found Bloedel well content
To fulfil her bidding, she to table went
With the monarch Etzel and eke a goodly band.
Dire was the treason she against the guests had planned.

Since in none other manner she knew the strife to start,

(Kriemhild's ancient sorrow still rankled in her heart),
Bade she bring to table Etzel's youthful son:
By woman bent on vengeance how might more awful deed be done?
Went upon the instant four of Etzel's men,
And soon came bearing Ortlieb, the royal scion, then
Unto the princes' table, where eke grim Hagen sate.
The child was doomed to perish by reason of his deadly hate.
When the mighty monarch then his child did see,
Unto his lady's kinsmen in manner kind spake he:
"Now, my good friends, behold ye here my only son,
And child of your high sister: may it bring you profit every one.
"Grow he but like his kindred, a valiant man he'll be,
A mighty king and noble, doughty and fair to see.
Live I but yet a little, twelve lands shall he command;
May ye have faithful service from the youthful Ortlieb's hand.
"Therefore grant me favor, ye good friends of mine;
When to your country ride ye again unto the Rhine,
Shall ye then take with you this your sister's son,
And at your hands may ever by the child full fair be done.
"Bring him up in honor until to manhood grown.
If then in any country hath wrong to you been done,
He'll help you by his valor vengeance swift to wreak."
Eke heard the Lady Kriemhild royal Etzel thus to speak.
"Well might these my masters on his faith rely,
Grew he e'er to manhood," Hagen made reply:
"Yet is the prince, I fear me, more early doomed of fate.
'Twere strange did any see me ever at court on Ortlieb wait."
The monarch glanced at Hagen, sore grieved at what he heard;
Although the king full gallant thereto spake ne'er a word,
Natheless his heart was saddened and heavy was his mind.
Nowise the mood of Hagen was to merriment inclined.
It grieved all the princes and the royal host
That of his child did Hagen make such idle boast.
That they must likewise leave it unanswered, liked they not:
They little weaned what havoc should by the thane anon be wrought.

THIRTY-SECOND ADVENTURE

How Bloedel was Slain

The knights by Bloedel summoned soon armed and ready were,
A thousand wearing hauberks straightway did repair
Where Dankwart sat at table with many a goodly squire.
Soon knight on knight was seeking in fiercest way to vent his ire.
When there Sir Bloedel strode unto the board,
Dankwart the marshal thus spoke courteous word:

"Unto this hall right welcome good Sir Bloedel be.
What business hast thou hither is cause of wonder yet to me."
"No greeting here befits thee," spake Bloedel presently,
"For that this my coming now thy end must be,
Through Hagen's fault, thy brother, who Siegfried erstwhile slew
To the Huns thou mak'st atonement, and many another warrior too."
"But nay, but nay, Sir Bloedel," Dankwart spake thereto,
"For so should we have reason our coming here to rue.
A child I was and little when Siegfried lost his life,
Nor know I why reproacheth me the royal Etzel's wife."
"In sooth I may the story never fully tell.
Gunther and Hagen was it by whom the deed befell.
Now guard you well, ye strangers, for doomed in sooth are ye,
Unto Lady Kriemhild must your lives now forfeit be."
"An so thou wilt desist not," Dankwart declared,
"Regret I my entreaty, my toil were better spared."
The nimble thane and valiant up from the table sprung,
And drew a keen-edged weapon, great in sooth that was and long.
Then smote he with it Bloedel such a sudden blow
That his head full sudden before his feet lay low.
"Be that thy wedding-dower," the doughty Dankwart spake,
"Along with bride of Nudung whom thou would'st to thy bosom take.
"To-morrow may she marry, but some other one:
Will he have bridal portion, e'en so to him be done."
A Hun that liked not treason had given him to know
How that the queen upon him thought to work so grievous woe.
When the men of Bloedel saw thus their master slain,
To fall upon the strangers would they longer not refrain.
With swords swung high above them upon the squires they flew
In a grimmest humor. Soon many must that rashness rue.
Full loudly cried then Dankwart to all his company:
"Behold ye, noble squires, the fate that ours must be.
Now quit yourselves with valor, for evil is our pass,
Though fair to us the summons hither from Lady Kriemhild was!"
They, too, reached down before them, who no weapons bore,
And each a massive footstool snatched from off the floor,
For the Burgundian squires no whit were they dismayed;
And by the selfsame weapons was many a dint in helmet made.
How fierce they fought to shield them the strangers one and all!
E'en their arméd foemen drove they from the hall.
Or smote dead within it hundreds five or more;
All the valiant fighters saw ye drenched with ruddy gore.
Ere long the wondrous tidings some messenger did tell
Unto Etzel's chieftain—fierce did their anger swell—
How that slain was Bloedel and knights full many a one;
The which had Hagen's brother with his lusty squires done.
The Huns, by anger driven, ere Etzel was aware,

Two thousand men or over, did quick themselves prepare.
They fell upon those squires —e'en so it had to be—
And never any living they left of all that company.
A mickle host they faithless unto those quarters brought,
But lustily the strangers 'gainst their assailants fought.
What booted swiftest valor? Soon must all lie dead.
A dire woe thereafter on many a man was visited.
Now may ye hear a wondrous tale of honor told:
Of squires full nine thousand soon in death lay cold,
And eke good knights a dozen there of Dankwart's band.
Forlorn ye saw him only the last amid his foemen stand.
The din at last was ended and lulled the battle-sound,
When the valiant Dankwart did cast a glance around.
"Alack for my companions," cried he, "now from me reft.
Alack that I now only forlorn amid my foes am left."
The swords upon his body fell full thick and fast,
Which rashness many a warrior's widow mourned at last.
His shield he higher lifted and drew the strap more low:
Down coats of ring-made armor made he the ebbing blood to flow.
"O woe is me!" spake Dankwart, the son of Aldrian.
"Now back, ye Hunnish fighters, let me the open gain,
That the air give cooling to me storm-weary wight."
In splendid valor moving strode forward then anew the knight.
As thus he battle-weary through the hall's portal sprang,
What swords of new-come fighters upon his helmet rang!
They who not yet had witnessed what wonders wrought his hand,
Rashly rushed they forward to thwart him of Burgundian land.
"Now would to God," quoth Dankwart, "I found a messenger
Who to my brother Hagen might the tidings bear,
That 'fore host of foemen in such sad case am I!
From hence he'd surely help me, or by my side he slain would lie."
Then Hunnish knights gave answer: "Thyself the messenger
Shalt be, when to thy brother thee a corse we bear.
So shall that thane of Gunther first true sorrow know.
Upon the royal Etzel here hast thou wrought so grievous woe."
Quoth he: "Now leave such boasting and yield me passage free,
Else shall mail-rings a many with blood bespattered be.
Myself will tell the tidings soon at Etzel's court,
And eke unto my masters of this my travail make report."
Etzel's men around him belabored he so sore
That they at sword-point durst not withstand him more.
Spears shot into his shield he so many there did stop
That he the weight unwieldy must from out his hand let drop.
Then thought they to subdue him thus of his shield bereft,
But lo! the mighty gashes wherewith he helmets cleft!
Must there keen knights full many before him stagger down,
High praise the valiant Dankwart thereby for his valor won.

On right side and on left side they still beset his way,
Yet many a one too rashly did mingle in the fray.
Thus strode he 'mid the foemen as doth in wood the boar
By yelping hounds beleaguered; more stoutly fought he ne'er before.
As there he went, his pathway with reeking blood was wet.
Yea, never any hero more bravely battled yet
When by foes surrounded, than he did might display.
To court did Hagen's brother with splendid valor make his way.
When stewards and cup-bearers heard how sword-blades rung,
Many a brimming goblet from their hands they flung
And eke the viands ready that they to table bore;
Thus many doughty foemen withstood him where he sought the door.
"How now, ye stewards?" cried the weary knight;
"'Twere better that ye tended rather your guests aright,
Bearing to lords at table choice food that fitteth well,
And suffered me these tidings unto my masters dear to tell."
Whoe'er before him rashly athwart the stairway sprung,
On him with blow so heavy his mighty sword he swung,
That soon faint heart gave warning before his path to yield.
Mickle wonder wrought he where sword his doughty arm did wield.

THIRTY-THIRD ADVENTURE

How the Burgundians fought with the Huns

Soon as the valiant Dankwart stood beneath the door,
Bade he Etzel's followers all make way before.
With blood from armor streaming did there the hero stand;
A sharp and mighty weapon bore he naked in his hand.
Into the hall then Dankwart cried with voice full strong:
"At table, brother Hagen, thou sittest all too long.
To thee and God in heaven must I sore complain:
Knights and squires also lie within their lodging slain."
Straight he cried in answer: "Who hath done such deed?"
"That hath done Sir Bloedel and knights that he did lead.
Eke made he meet atonement, that may'st thou understand:
His head from off his body have I struck with mine own hand."
"'Tis little cause for sorrow," Hagen spake again,
"When they tell the story of a valiant thane,
That he to death was smitten by knight of high degree.
The less a cause for weeping to winsome women shall it be.
"Now tell me, brother Dankwart, how thou so red may'st be;
From thy wounds thou sufferest, I ween, full grievously.
Lives he within this country who serves thee in such way,
Him must the devil shelter, or for the deed his life shall pay."
"Behold me here all scatheless. My gear is wet with blood,

From wounds of others, natheless, now hath flowed that flood,
Of whom this day so many beneath my broadsword fell:
Must I make solemn witness, ne'er knew I full the tale to tell."
He answered: "Brother Dankwart, now take thy stand before,
And Huns let never any make passage by the door.
I'll speak unto these warriors, as needs must spoken be:
Dead lie all our followers, slain by foulest treachery."
"Must I here be chamberlain," replied the warrior keen,
"Well know I such high monarchs aright to serve, I ween.
So will I guard the stairway as sorts with honor well."
Ne'er to the thanes of Kriemhild so sorry case before befell.
"To me 'tis mickle wonder," Hagen spake again,
"What thing unto his neighbor whispers each Hunnish thane.
I ween they'd forego the service of him who keeps the door,
And who such high court tidings to his friends of Burgundy bore.
"Long since of Lady Kriemhild the story I did hear,
How unavenged her sorrow she might no longer bear.
A memory-cup now quaff we and pay for royal cheer!
The youthful lord of Hunland shall make the first instalment here."
Thereat the child Ortlieb doughty Hagen slew,
That from the sword downward the blood to hand-grip flew,
And into lap of Kriemhild the severed head down rolled.
Then might ye see 'mid warriors a slaughter great and grim unfold.
By both hands swiftly wielded, his blade then cut the air
And smote upon the tutor who had the child in care,
That down before the table his head that instant lay:
It was a sorry payment wherewith he did the tutor pay.
His eye 'fore Etzel's table a minstrel espied:
To whom in hasty manner did wrathful Hagen stride,
Where moved it on the fiddle his right hand off smote he;
"Have that for thy message unto the land of Burgundy."
"Alack my hand!" did Werbel that same minstrel moan;
"What, Sir Hagen of Tronje, have I to thee done?
I bore a faithful message unto thy master's land.
How may I more make music thus by thee bereft of hand?"
Little in sooth recked Hagen, fiddled he nevermore.
Then in the hall all wrathful wrought he havoc sore
Upon the thanes of Etzel whereof he many slew;
Ere they might find exit, to death then smote he not a few.
Volker the full valiant up sprang from board also:
In his hand full clearly rang out his fiddle-bow,
For mightily did fiddle Gunther's minstrel thane.
What host of foes he made him because of Hunnish warriors slain!
Eke sprang from the table the lofty monarchs three,
Who glad had stilled the combat ere greater scathe might be.
Yet all their art availed not their anger to assuage,
When Volker and Hagen so mightily began to rage.

When the lord of Rhineland saw how his toil was vain,
Gaping wounds full many himself did smite amain
Through rings of shining mail-coats there upon the foe.
He was a valiant hero, as he full gallantly did show.
Strode eke into the combat Gernot a doughty thane;
By whom of Hunnish warriors full many a one was slain
With a sword sharp-edgéd he had of Ruediger;
Oft sent to dire ruin by him the knights of Etzel were.
The youthful son of Ute eke to the combat sprang,
And merrily his broadsword upon the helmets rang
Of many a Hunnish warrior there in Etzel's land;
Feasts of mickle wonder wrought Giselher with dauntless hand.
How bold soe'er was any, of kings and warrior band,
Saw ye yet the foremost Giselher to stand
There against the foemen, a knight of valor good;
Wounded deep full many made he to fall in oozing blood.
Eke full well defend them did Etzel's warriors too.
There might ye see the strangers their gory way to hew
With swords all brightly gleaming adown that royal hall;
Heard ye there on all sides loudly ring the battle-call.
Join friends within beleaguered would they without full fain,
Yet might they at the portal but little vantage gain.
Eke they within had gladly gained the outer air;
Nor up nor down did Dankwart suffer one to pass the stair.
There before the portal surged a mighty throng,
And with a mickle clangor on helm the broadsword rung.
Thus on the valiant Dankwart his foes did sorely press,
And soon his trusty brother was anxious grown o'er his distress.
Full loudly cried then Hagen unto Volker:
"Trusty fere, behold'st thou my brother standing there,
Where on him Hunnish warriors their mighty blows do rain?
Good friend, save thou my brother ere we do lose the valiant thane."
"That will I do full surely," thereat the minstrel spake.
Adown the hall he fiddling gan his way to make;
In his hand full often a trusty sword rang out,
While grateful knights of Rhineland acclaimed him with a mickle shout.
Soon did the valiant Volker Dankwart thus address:
"Hard this day upon thee hath weighed the battle's stress.
That I should come to help thee thy brother gave command;
Keep thou without the portal, I inward guarding here will stand."
Dankwart, thane right valiant, stood without the door
And guarded so the stairway that none might pass before.
There heard ye broadswords ringing, swung by warrior's hand,
While inward in like manner wrought Volker of Burgundian land.
There the valiant Fiddler above the press did call:
"Securely now, friend Hagen, closed is the hall.
Yea, so firmly bolted is King Etzel's door

By hands of two good warriors, as thousand bars were set before,"
When Hagen thus of Tronje the door did guarded find,
The warrior far renownéd swung his shield behind;
He first for harm receivéd revenge began to take,
Whereat all hope of living did soon his enemies forsake.
When of Bern Sir Dietrich rightly did perceive
How the doughty Hagen did many a helmet cleave,
The king of Amelungen upon a bench leaped up;
Quoth he: "Here poureth Hagen for us exceeding bitter cup."
Great fear fell eke on Etzel, as well might be the case,
(What trusty followers snatched they to death before his face!)
For well nigh did his enemies on him destruction bring.
There sat he all confounded. What booted him to be a king?
Cried then aloud to Dietrich Kriemhild, the high lady:
"Now help me, knight so noble, that hence with life I flee,
By princely worth, I pray thee, thou lord of Amelung's land;
If here do reach me Hagen, straight find I death beneath his hand."
"How may my help avail thee, noble queen and high?"
Answered her Sir Dietrich, "Fear for myself have I.
Too sorely is enraged each knight in Gunther's band,
To no one at this season may I lend assisting hand."
"But nay, but nay, Sir Dietrich, full noble knight and keen,
What maketh thy bright chivalry, let it this day be seen,
And bring me hence to safety, else am I death's sure prey."
Good cause was that on Kriemhild's bosom fear so heavy lay.
"So will I here endeavor to help thee as I may;
Yet shalt thou well believe me, hath passed full many a day
Since saw I goodly warriors of so bitter mood.
'Neath swords behold I flowing through helmets plenteously the blood."
Lustily then cried he, the warrior nobly born,
That his voice rang loudly like blast from bison's horn,
That all around the palace gave back the lusty sound;
Unto the might of Dietrich never limit yet was found.
When did hear King Gunther how called the doughty man
Above the storm of combat, to hearken he began.
Quoth he: "The voice of Dietrich hath fallen upon mine ear;
I ween some of his followers before our thanes have fallen here.
"High on the board I see him; he beckons with the hand.
Now my good friends and kinsmen of Burgundian land,
Stay ye your hands from conflict, let us hear and see
If done upon the chieftain aught by my men of scathe there be."
When thus King Gunther did beg and eke command,
With swords in stress of battle stayed they all the hand.
'Twas token of his power that straight the strife did pause.
Then him of Bern he questioned what of his outcry were the cause.
He spake: "Full noble Dietrich, what here on thee is wrought
By any of my warriors? For truly is my thought

To make a full atonement and amends to thee.
If here hath wronged thee any, 'twere cause of mickle grief to me."
Then answered him Sir Dietrich: "Myself do nothing grieve.
Grant me with thy protection but this hall to leave
And quit the dire conflict, with them that me obey.
Then surely will I ever seek thy favor to repay."
"How plead'st thou thus so early?" Wolfhart was heard;
"The Fiddler so securely the door not yet hath barred,
But it so wide we'll open to pass it through, I trow."
"Now hold thy peace," quoth Dietrich, "wrought but little here hast thou."
Then spake the royal Gunther: "That grant I thee to do,
Forth from the hall lead many or lead with thee few,
An if my foes it be not; here stay they every one.
Upon me here in Hunland hath grievous wrong by them been done."
When heard he Gunther's answer he took beneath his arm
The noble Queen Kriemhild, who dreaded mickle harm.
On the other side too led he Etzel with him away;
Eke went thence with Dietrich six hundred knights in fair array.
Then outspake the margrave, the noble Ruediger:
"If leave to any others be granted forth to fare,
Of those who glad would serve you, give us the same to see.
Yea, peace that's never broken 'twixt friends 'tis meet should ever be."
Thereto gave answer Giselher of the land of Burgundy:
"Peace and unbroken friendship wish we e'er with thee,
With thee and all thy kinsmen, as true thou ever art.
We grant thee all untroubled with thy friends from hence to part."
When thus Sir Ruediger from the hall did pass,
A train of knights five hundred or more with him there was,
Of them of Bechelaren, kinsmen and warriors true,
Whose parting gave King Gunther anon full mickle cause to rue.
When did a Hunnish warrior Etzel's passing see
'Neath the arm of Dietrich, to profit him thought he.
Smote him yet the Fiddler such a mighty blow,
That 'fore the feet of Etzel sheer on the floor his head fell low.
When the country's monarch had gained the outer air,
Turned he looking backward and gazed on Volker.
"Alack such guests to harbor! Ah me discomfited!
That all the knights that serve me shall before their might lie dead.
"Alack their coming hither!" spake the king once more.
"Within, a warrior fighteth like to wild forest boar;
Hight the same is Volker, and a minstrel is also;
To pass the demon scatheless I to fortune's favor owe.
"Evil sound his melodies, his strokes of bow are red,
Yea, beneath his music full many a knight lies dead.
I know not what against us hath stirred that player's ire,
For guests ne'er had I any whereby to suffer woe so dire."
None other would they suffer to pass the door than those.

Then 'neath the hall's high roof-tree a mighty din arose.
For evil wrought upon them those guests sore vengeance take.
Volker the doughty Fiddler, what shining helmets there he brake!
Gunther, lofty monarch, thither turned his ear.
"Hear'st thou the music, Hagen, that yonder Volker
Doth fiddle for the Hun-men, when near the door they go?
The stroke is red of color, where he doth draw the fiddle-bow."
"Mickle doth it rue me," Hagen spake again,
"That in the hall far severed I am from that bold thane.
I was his boon companion and he sworn friend to me:
Come we hence ever scatheless, trusty feres we yet shall be.
"Behold now, lofty sire, the faith of Volker bold!
With will he seeks to win him thy silver and thy gold.
With fiddle-bow he cleaveth e'en the steel so hard,
Bright-gleaming crests of helmets are scattered by his mighty sword.
"Never saw I fiddler so dauntless heart display,
As the doughty Volker here hath done this day.
Through shield and shining helmet his melodies ring clear;
Give him to ride good charger and eke full stately raiment wear."
Of all the Hunnish kindred that in the hall had been,
None now of all their number therein to fight was seen.
Hushed was the din of battle and strife no more was made:
From out their hands aweary their swords the dauntless warriors laid.

THIRTY-FOURTH ADVENTURE

How they cast out the Dead

From toil of battle weary rested the warriors all.
Volker and Hagen passed out before the hall,
And on their shields did lean them, those knights whom naught could daunt.
Then with full merry converse gan the twain their foes to taunt.
Spake meanwhile of Burgundy Giselher the thane:
"Not yet, good friends, may ye think to rest again.
Forth from the hall the corses shall ye rather bear.
Again we'll be assailéd, that would I now in sooth declare.
"Beneath our feet no longer here the dead must lie.
But ere in storm of battle at hand of Huns to die,
We'll deal such wounds around us as 'tis my joy to see.
Thereon," spake Giselher, "my heart is fixed right steadfastly."
"I joy in such a master," Hagen spake again:
"Such counsel well befitteth alone so valiant thane
As my youthful master hath shown himself this day.
Therefor, O men of Burgundy, every one rejoice ye may."
Then followed they his counsel and from the hall they bore
Seven thousand bodies and cast them from the door.

Adown the mounting stairway all together fell,
Whereat a sound of wailing did from mourning kinsmen swell.
Many a man among them so slight wound did bear
That he were yet recovered had he but gentle care,
Who yet falling headlong now surely must be dead.
Thereat did grieve their kinsmen as verily was sorest need.
Then outspake the Fiddler, Volker a hero bold:
"Now do I find how truly hath to me been told
That cowards are the Hun-men who do like women weep.
Rather should be their effort their wounded kin alive to keep."
These words deemed a margrave spoken in kindly mood.
He saw one of his kinsmen weltering in his blood.
In his arms he clasped him and thought him thence to bear,
But as he bent above him pierced him the valiant minstrel's spear.
When that beheld the others all in haste they fled,
Crying each one curses on that same minstrel's head.
From the ground then snatched he a spear with point full keen,
That 'gainst him up the stairway by a Hun had hurléd been.
Across the court he flung it with his arm of might
Far above the people. Then did each Hunnish knight
Seek him safer quarters more distant from the hall.
To see his mighty prowess did fill with fear his foemen all.
As knights full many thousand far 'fore the palace stood,
Volker and Hagen gan speak in wanton mood
"Unto King Etzel, nor did they aught withhold;
Wherefrom anon did sorrow o'ertake those doughty warriors bold.
"'Twould well beseem," quoth Hagen, "the people's lofty lord
Foremost in storm of battle to swing the cutting sword,
As do my royal masters each fair example show.
Where hew they through the helmets their swords do make the blood to flow."
To hear such words brave Etzel snatched in haste his shield.
"Now well beware of rashness," cried Lady Kriemhild,
"And offer to thy warriors gold heaped on shield full high:
If yonder Hagen reach thee, straightway shalt thou surely die."
So high was the king's mettle that he would not give o'er,
Which case is now full seldom seen in high princes more;
They must by shield-strap tugging him perforce restrain.
Grim of mood then Hagen began him to revile again.
"It was a distant kinship," spake Hagen, dauntless knight,
"That Etzel unto Siegfried ever did unite,
And husband he to Kriemhild was ere thee she knew.
Wherefore, O king faint-hearted, seek'st thou such thing 'gainst me to do?"
Thereto eke must listen the noble monarch's spouse,
And grievously to hear it did Kriemhild's wrath arouse.
That he 'fore men of Etzel durst herself upbraid;
To urge them 'gainst the strangers she once more her arts essayed.
Cried she: "Of Tronje Hagen whoso for me will slay,

And his head from body severed here before me lay,
For him the shield of Etzel I'll fill with ruddy gold,
Eke lands and lordly castles I'll give him for his own to hold."
"I wot not why they tarry," —thus the minstrel cried;
"Ne'er saw I heroes any so their courage hide,
When to them was offered, like this, reward so high.
'Tis cause henceforth that Etzel for aye to them goodwill deny."
"Who in such craven manner do eat their master's bread,
And like caitiffs fail him in time of greatest need,
Here see I standing many of courage all forlorn,
Yet would be men of valor; all time be they upheld to scorn."

THIRTY-FIFTH ADVENTURE

How Iring was Slain

Cried then he of Denmark, Iring the margrave:
"Fixed on things of honor my purpose long I have,
And oft in storm of battle, where heroes wrought, was I.
Bring hither now my armor, with Hagen I'll the combat try."
"I counsel thee against it," Hagen then replied,
"Or bring a goodly company of Hun-men by thy side.
If peradventure any find entrance to the hall,
I'll cause that nowise scatheless down the steps again they fall."
"Such words may not dissuade me," Iring spake once more;
"A thing of equal peril oft have I tried before.
Yea, will I with my broadsword confront thee all alone.
Nor aught may here avail thee thus to speak in haughty tone."
Soon the valiant Iring armed and ready stood,
And Irnfried of Thuringia a youth of mettle good,
And eke the doughty Hawart, with thousand warriors tried.
Whate'er his purpose, Iring should find them faithful by his side.
Advancing then with Iring did the Fiddler see
All clad in shining armor a mighty company,
And each a well-made helmet securely fastened wore.
Thereat the gallant Volker began to rail in anger sore.
"Seest thou, friend Hagen, yonder Iring go,
Who all alone to front thee with his sword did vow?
Doth lying sort with honor? Scorned the thing must be.
A thousand knights or over here bear him arméd company."
"Now make me not a liar," cried Hawart's man aloud,
"For firm is still my purpose to do what now I vowed,
Nor will I turn me from it through any cause of fear.
Alone I'll stand 'fore Hagen, awful howsoe'er he were."
On ground did throw him Iring before his warriors' feet,
That they leave might grant him alone the knight to meet.

Loath they were to do it; well known to them might be
The haughty Hagen's prowess of the land of Burgundy.
Yet so long besought he that granted was their leave;
When they that followed with him did his firm mind perceive,
And how 'twas bent on honor, they not restrained him.
Then closed the two chieftains together in a combat grim.
Iring of Denmark raised his spear on high,
And with the shield he covered himself full skilfully;
He upward rushed on Hagen unto the hall right close,
When round the clashing fighters soon a mighty din arose.
Each hurled upon the other the spear with arm of might,
That the firm shields were piercéd e'en to their mail-coats bright,
And outward still projecting the long spear-shafts were seen.
In haste then snatched their broadswords both the fighters grim and keen.
In might the doughty Hagen and prowess did abound,
As Iring smote upon him the hall gave back the sound.
The palace all and towers re-echoed from their blows,
Yet might that bold assailant with victory ne'er the combat close.
On Hagen might not Iring wreak aught of injury.
Unto the doughty Fiddler in haste then turnéd he.
Him by his mighty sword-strokes thought he to subdue,
But well the thane full gallant to keep him safe in combat knew.
Then smote the doughty Fiddler so lustily his shield
That from it flew its ornaments where he the sword did wield.
Iring must leave unconquered there the dauntless man;
Next upon King Gunther of Burgundy in wrath he ran.
There did each in combat show him man of might;
Howe'er did Gunther and Iring yet each the other smite,
From wounds might never either make the blood to flow,
So sheltered each his armor, well wrought that was and strong enow.
Gunther left he standing, upon Gernot to dash,
And when he smote ring-armor the fire forth did flash.
But soon had he of Burgundy, Gernot the doughty thane,
Well nigh his keen assailant Iring of Denmark slain.
Yet from the prince he freed him, for nimble was he too.
Four of the men of Burgundy the knight full sudden slew
Of those that followed with them from Worms across the Rhine.
Thereupon might nothing the wrath of Giselher confine.
"God wot well, Sir Iring," young Giselher then cried,
"Now must thou make requital for them that here have died
'Neath thy hand so sudden." He rushed upon him so
And smote the knight of Denmark that he might not withstand the blow.
Into the blood down fell he staggering 'neath its might,
That all who there beheld it might deem the noble knight
Sword again would never wield amid the fray.
Yet 'neath the stroke of Giselher Iring all unwounded lay.
Bedazed by helmet's sounding where ringing sword swung down,

Full suddenly his senses so from the knight were flown:
That of his life no longer harbored he a thought.
That the doughty Giselher by his mighty arm had wrought.
When somewhat was subsided the din within his head
From mighty blow so sudden on him was visited,
Thought he: "I still am living and bear no mortal wound.
How great the might of Giselher, till now unwitting, have I found."
He hearkened how on all sides his foes around did stand;
Knew they what he did purpose, they had not stayed their hand.
He heard the voice of Giselher eke in that company,
As cunning he bethought him how yet he from his foes might flee.
Up from the blood he started with fierce and sudden bound;
By grace alone of swiftness he his freedom found.
With speed he passed the portal where Hagen yet did stand,
And swift his sword he flourished and smote him with his doughty hand.
To see such sight quoth Hagen: "To death thou fall'st a prey;
If not the Devil shield thee, now is thy latest day."
Yet Iring wounded Hagen e'en through his helmet's crown.
That did the knight with Waske, a sword that was of far renown.
When thus Sir Hagen the smart of wound did feel,
Wrathfully he brandished on high his blade of steel.
Full soon must yield before him Hawart's daring man,
Adown the steps pursuing Hagen swiftly after ran.
O'er his head bold Iring his shield to guard him swung,
And e'en had that same stairway been full three times as long,
Yet had he found no respite from warding Hagen's blows.
How plenteously the ruddy sparks above his helm arose!
Unscathed at last came Iring where waited him his own.
Soon as was the story unto Kriemhild known,
How that in fight on Hagen he had wrought injury,
Therefor the Lady Kriemhild him gan to thank full graciously.
"Now God requite thee, Iring, thou valiant knight and good,
For thou my heart hast comforted and merry made my mood.
Red with blood his armor, see I yonder Hagen stand."
For joy herself did Kriemhild take his shield from out his hand.
"Small cause hast thou to thank him," thus wrathful Hagen spake;
"For gallant knight 'twere fitting trial once more to make.
If then returned he scatheless, a valiant man he were.
The wound doth boot thee little that now from his hand I bear.
"That here from wound upon me my mail-coat see'st thou red,
Shall bring woful reprisal on many a warrior's head.
Now is my wrath aroused in full 'gainst Hawart's thane.
As yet in sooth hath Iring wrought on me but little bane."
Iring then of Denmark stood where fanned the wind.
He cooled him in his armor and did his helm unbind.
Then praised him all the people and spoke him man of might,
Whereat the margrave's bosom swelled full high with proud delight.

"Now hearken friends unto me," Iring once more spake;
"Make me straightway ready, new trial now to make
If I this knight so haughty may yet perchance subdue."
New shield they brought, for Hagen did his erstwhile asunder hew.
Soon stood again the warrior in armor all bedight.
In hand a spear full massy took the wrathful knight,
Wherewith on yonder Hagen he thought to vent his hate.
With grim and fearful visage on him the vengeful thane did wait.
Yet not abide his coming might Hagen longer now.
Adown he rushed upon him with many a thrust and blow,
Down where the stairway ended for fierce did burn his ire.
Soon the might of Iring must 'neath his furious onset tire,
Their shields they smote asunder that the sparks began
To fly in ruddy showers. Hawart's gallant man
Was by sword of Hagen wounded all so sore
Through shield and shining cuirass, that whole he found him never more.
When how great the wound was Iring fully knew,
Better to guard his helm-band his shield he higher drew.
The scathe he first receivéd he deemed sufficient quite,
Yet injury far greater soon had he from King Gunther's knight.
From where it lay before him Hagen a spear did lift
And hurled it upon Iring with aim so sure and swift,
It pierced his head, and firmly fixed the shaft did stand;
Full grim the end that met him 'neath the doughty Hagen's hand.
Backward Iring yielded unto his Danish men.
Ere for the knight his helmet they undid again,
From his head they drew the spear-point; to death he was anigh.
Wept thereat his kinsmen, and sore need had verily.
Came thereto Queen Kriemhild and o'er the warrior bent,
And for the doughty Iring gan she there lament.
She wept to see him wounded, and sorely grieved the queen.
Then spake unto his kinsmen the warrior full brave and keen.
"I pray thee leave thy moaning, royal high lady.
What avails thy weeping? Yea, soon must ended be
My life from wounds outflowing that here I did receive.
To serve thyself and Etzel will death not longer grant me leave."
Eke spake he to them of Thuringia and to them of Danish land:
"Of you shall never any receive the gift in hand
From your royal mistress of shining gold full red.
Whoe'er withstandeth Hagen death calleth down upon his head."
From cheek the color faded, death's sure token wore
Iring the gallant warrior: thereat they grieved full sore.
Nor more in life might tarry Hawart's valiant knight:
Enraged the men of Denmark again did arm them for the fight.
Irnfried and Hawart before the hall then sprang
Leading thousand warriors. Full furious a clang
Of weapons then on all sides loud and great ye hear.

Against the men of Burgundy how hurled they many a mighty spear!
Straight the valiant Irnfried the minstrel rushed upon,
But naught but grievous injury 'neath his hand he won:
For the noble Fiddler did the landgrave smite
E'en through the well-wrought helmet; yea, grim and savage was the knight.
Sir Irnfried then in answer the valiant minstrel smote,
That must fly asunder the rings of his mailed coat
Which showered o'er his cuirass like sparks of fire red.
Soon must yet the landgrave fall before the Fiddler dead.
Eke were come together Hawart and Hagen bold,
And saw he deeds of wonder who did the sight behold.
Swift flew the sword and fiercely swung by each hero's hand.
But soon lay Hawart prostrate before him of Burgundian land.
When Danish men and Thuringians beheld their masters fall,
Fearful was the turmoil that rose before the hall
As to the door they struggled, on dire vengeance bent.
Full many a shield and helmet was there 'neath sword asunder rent.
"Now backward yield," cried Volker "and let them pass within;
Thus only are they thwarted of what they think to win.
When but they pass the portals are they full quickly slain.
With death shall they the bounty of their royal mistress gain."
When thus with pride o'erweening they did entrance find,
The head of many a warrior was so to earth inclined,
That he must life surrender 'neath blows that thickly fell.
Well bore him valiant Gernot and eke Sir Giselher as well.
Four knights beyond a thousand were come into the house;
The light from sword-blades glinted, swift swung with mighty souse.
Not one of all their number soon might ye living see;
Tell might ye mickle wonders of the men of Burgundy.
Thereafter came a stillness, and ceased the tumult loud.
The blood in every quarter through the leak-holes flowed,
And out along the corbels from men in death laid low.
That had the men of Rhineland wrought with many a doughty blow.
Then sat again to rest them they of Burgundian land,
Shield and mighty broadsword they laid from out the hand.
But yet the valiant Fiddler stood waiting 'fore the door,
If peradventure any would seek to offer combat more.
Sorely did King Etzel and eke his spouse lament,
Maidens and fair ladies did sorrow sore torment.
Death long since upon them, I ween, such ending swore.
To fall before the strangers was doomed full many a warrior more.

THIRTY-SIXTH ADVENTURE

How the Queen bade set fire to the Hall

"Now lay ye off the helmets," the words from Hagen fell:
"I with a boon companion will be your sentinel.
And seek the men of Etzel to work us further harm,
For my royal masters full quickly will I cry alarm."
Then freed his head of armor many a warrior good.
They sate them on the corses, that round them in the blood
Of wounds themselves had dealt them, prostrate weltering lay.
Now to his guests so lofty scant courtesy did Etzel pay.
Ere yet was come the even, King Etzel did persuade,
And eke the Lady Kriemhild, that once more essayed
The Hunnish knights to storm them. Before them might ye see
Good twenty thousand warriors, who soon for fight must ready be.
Then with a furious onset the strangers they attacked.
Dankwart, Hagen's brother, who naught of courage lacked,
Sprang out 'mid the besiegers to ward them from the door.
'Twas deemed a deadly peril, yet scatheless stood he there before.
Fierce the struggle lasted till darkness brought an end.
Themselves like goodly heroes the strangers did defend
Against the men of Etzel all the long summer day.
What host of valiant warriors before them fell to death a prey!
At turn of sun in summer that havoc sore was wrought,
When the Lady Kriemhild revenge so dire sought
Upon her nearest kinsmen and many a knight beside,
Wherefore with royal Etzel never more might joy abide.
As day at last was ending sad they were of heart.
They deemed from life 'twere better in sudden death to part
Than be thus long tormented by great o'erhanging dread.
That respite now be granted, the knights so proud and gallant prayed.
They prayed to lead the monarch hither to them there.
As heroes blood-bespotted, and stained from battle-gear,
Forth from the hall emergéd the lofty monarchs three.
They wist not to whom complainéd might their full grievous sorrows be.
Etzel and Kriemhild they soon before them found,
And great was now their company from all their lands around.
Spake Etzel to the strangers: "What will ye now of me?
Ye hope for end of conflict, but hardly may such favor be.
"This so mighty ruin that ye on me have wrought,
If death thwart not my purpose, shall profit you in naught.
For child that here ye slew me and kinsmen dear to me,
Shall peace and reconcilement from you withheld forever be."
Thereto gave answer Gunther: "To that drove sorest need.
Lay all my train of squires before thy warriors dead

Where they for night assembled. How bore I so great blame?
Of friendly mind I deemed thee, as trusting in thy faith I came."
Then spake eke of Burgundy the youthful Giselher:
"Ye knights that still are living of Etzel, now declare
Whereof ye may reproach me! How hath you harmed my hand?
For in right friendly manner came I riding to this land."
Cried they: "Well is thy friendship in burgh and country known
By sorrow of thy making. Gladly had we foregone
The pleasure of thy coming from Worms across the Rhine.
Our country hast thou orphaned, thou and brother eke of thine."
In angry mood King Gunther unto them replied:
"An ye this mighty hatred appeased would lay aside,
Borne 'gainst us knights here homeless, to both a gain it were
For Etzel's wrath against us we in sooth no guilt do bear."
The host then to the strangers: "Your sorrow here and mine
Are things all unequal. For now must I repine
With honor all bespotted and 'neath distress of woe.
Of you shall never any hence from my country living go."
Then did the doughty Gernot unto King Etzel say:
"God then in mercy move thee to act in friendly way.
Slay us knights here homeless, yet grant us down to go
To meet thee in the open: thine honor biddeth thus to do.
"Whate'er shall be our portion, let that straightway appear.
Men hast thou yet so many that, should they banish fear,
Not one of us storm-weary might keep his life secure.
How long shall we here friendless this woeful travail yet endure?"
By the warriors of Etzel their wish nigh granted was,
And leave well nigh was given that from the hall they pass.
When Kriemhild knew their purpose, high her anger swelled,
And straightway such a respite was from the stranger knights withheld.
"But nay, ye Hunnish warriors! what ye have mind to do,
Therefrom now desist ye, —such is my counsel true;
Nor let foes so vengeful pass without the hall,
Else must in death before them full many of your kinsmen fall.
"If of them lived none other but Ute's sons alone,
My three noble brothers, and they the air had won
Where breeze might cool their armor, to death ye were a prey.
In all this world were never born more valiant thanes than they."
Then spake the youthful Giselher: "Full beauteous sister mine,
When to this land thou bad'st me from far beside the Rhine,
I little deemed such trouble did here upon me wait.
Whereby have I deservéd from the Huns such mortal hate?
"To thee I ever faithful was, nor wronged thee e'er.
In such faith confiding did I hither fare,
That thou to me wert gracious, O noble sister mine.
Show mercy now unto us, we must to thee our lives resign."
"No mercy may I show you, —unmerciful I'll be.

By Hagen, knight of Tronje, was wrought such woe to me,
That ne'er is reconcilement the while that I have life.
That must ye all atone for," —quoth the royal Etzel's wife.
"Will ye but Hagen only to me as hostage give,
Then will I not deny you to let you longer live.
Born are ye of one mother and brothers unto me,
So wish I that compounded here with these warriors peace may be."
"God in heaven forfend it," Gernot straightway said;
"E'en though we were a thousand, lay we all rather dead,
We who are thy kinsmen, ere that warrior one
Here we gave for hostage. Never may such thing be done."
"Die must we all," quoth Giselher, "for such is mortal's end.
Till then despite of any, our knighthood we'll defend.
Would any test our mettle, here may he trial make.
For ne'er, when help he needed, did I a faithful friend forsake."
Then spake the valiant Dankwart, a knight that knew no fear;
"In sooth stands not unaided my brother Hagen here.
Who here have peace denied us may yet have cause to rue.
I would that this ye doubt not, for verily I tell you true."
The queen to those around her: "Ye gallant warriors, go
Now nigher to the stairway and straight avenge my woe.
I'll ever make requital therefor, as well I may.
For his haughty humor will I Hagen full repay.
"To pass without the portal let not one at all,
For at its four corners I'll bid ignite the hall.
So will I fullest vengeance take for all my woe."
Straightway the thanes of Etzel ready stood her hest to do.
Who still without were standing were driven soon within
By sword and spear upon them, that made a mighty din.
Yet naught might those good warriors from their masters take,
By their faith would never each the other's side forsake.
To burn the hall commanded Etzel's wife in ire,
And tortured they those warriors there with flaming fire;
Full soon with wind upon it the house in flames was seen.
To any folk did never sadder plight befall, I ween.
Their cries within resounded: "Alack for sorest need!
How mickle rather lay we in storm of battle dead.
'Fore God 'tis cause for pity, for here we all must die!
Now doth the queen upon us vengeance wreak full grievously."
Among them spake another: "Our lives we here must end.
What now avails the greeting the king to us did send?
So sore this heat oppresseth and parched with thirst my tongue,
My life from very anguish I ween I must resign ere long."
Then quoth of Tronje Hagen: "Ye noble knights and good,
Whoe'er by thirst is troubled, here let him drink the blood.
Than wine more potent is it where such high heat doth rage,
Nor may we at this season find us a better beverage."

Where fallen knight was lying, thither a warrior went.
Aside he laid his helmet, to gaping wound he bent,
And soon was seen a-quaffing therefrom the flowing blood.
To him though all unwonted, yet seemed he there such drinking good.
"Now God reward thee, Hagen," the weary warrior said,
"That I so well have drunken, thus by thy teaching led.
Better wine full seldom hath been poured for me,
And live I yet a season I'll ever faithful prove to thee."
When there did hear the others how to him it seeméd good,
Many more beheld ye eke that drank the blood.
Each thereby new vigor for his body won,
And eke for lover fallen wept many a buxom dame anon.
The flaming brands fell thickly upon them in the hall,
With upraised shields they kept them yet scatheless from their fall,
Though smoke and heat together wrought them anguish sore.
Beset were heroes never, I ween, by so great woe before.
Then spake of Tronje Hagen: "Stand nigh unto the wall,
Let not the brands all flaming upon your helmets fall.
Into the blood beneath you tread them with your feet.
In sooth in evil fashion us doth our royal hostess greet."
In trials thus enduréd ebbed the night away.
Still without the portal did the keen Fiddler stay
And Hagen his good fellow, o'er shield their bodies leant;
They deemed the men of Etzel still on further mischief bent.
Then was heard the Fiddler: "Pass we into the hall,
For so the Huns shall fondly deem we are perished all
Amid the mickle torture we suffer at their hand.
Natheless shall they behold us bound for fight before them stand."
Spake then of Burgundy the young Sir Giselher:
"I ween 'twill soon be dawning, for blows a cooler air.
To live in fuller joyance now grant us God in heaven.
To us dire entertainment my sister Kriemhild here hath given."
Spake again another: "Lo! how I feel the day.
For that no better fortune here await us may,
So don, ye knights, your armor, and guard ye well your life.
Full soon, in sooth, we suffer again at hands of Etzel's wife."
Fondly Etzel fancied the strangers all were dead,
From sore stress of battle and from the fire dread;
Yet within were living six hundred men so brave,
That never thanes more worthy a monarch for liegemen might have.
The watchers set to watch them soon full well had seen
How still lived the strangers, spite what wrought had been
Of harm and grievous evil, on the monarchs and their band.
Within the hall they saw them still unscathed and dauntless stand.
Told 'twas then to Kriemhild how they from harm were free.
Whereat the royal lady quoth, such thing ne'er might be
That any still were living from that fire dread.

"Nay, believe I rather that within they all lie dead."
Gladly yet the strangers would a truce compound,
Might any grace to offer amid their foes be found.
But such appeared not any in them of Hunnish land.
Well to avenge their dying prepared they then with willing hand.
About the dawn of morning greeted they were again
With a vicious onslaught, that paid full many a thane.
There was flung upon them many a mighty spear,
While gallantly did guard them the lofty thanes that knew not fear.
The warriors of Etzel were all of eager mood,
And Kriemhild's promised bounty win for himself each would;
To do the king's high bidding did likewise urge their mind.
'Twas cause full soon that many were doomed swift death in fight to find.
Of store of bounty promised might wonders great be told,
She bade on shields to carry forth the ruddy gold,
And gave to him that wished it or would but take her store;
In sooth a greater hire ne'er tempted 'gainst the foe before.
A mickle host of warriors went forth in battle-gear.
Then quoth the valiant Volker: "Still may ye find us here.
Ne'er saw I move to battle warriors more fain,
That to work us evil the bounty of the king have ta'en."
Then cried among them many: "Hither, ye knights, more nigh!
Since all at last must perish, 'twere better instantly;
And here no warrior falleth but who fore-doomed hath been."
With well-flung spears all bristling full quickly then their shields were seen.
What need of further story? Twelve hundred stalwart men,
Repulsed in onset gory, still returned again;
But dealing wounds around them the strangers cooled their mood,
And there stood all unvanquished. Flowing might ye see the blood
From deep wounds and mortal, whereof were many slain.
For friends in battle fallen heard ye loud complain;
Slain were all those warriors that served the mighty king,
Whereat from loving kinsmen arose a mickle sorrowing.

THIRTY-SEVENTH ADVENTURE

How the Margrave Ruediger was Slain

At morning light the strangers had wrought high deed of fame,
When the spouse of Gotelinde unto the courtyard came.
To behold on both sides such woe befallen there,
Might not refrain from weeping sorely the faithful Ruediger.
"O woe is me!" exclaimed he, "that ever I was born.
Alack that this great sorrow no hand from us may turn!
Though I be ne'er so willing, the king no peace will know,
For he beholds his sorrow ever great and greater grow."

Then did the kindly Ruediger unto Dietrich send,
If to the lofty monarchs they yet might truce extend.
The knight of Bern gave message: "How might such thing be?
For ne'er the royal Etzel granteth to end it peacefully."

When a Hunnish warrior saw standing Ruediger
As from eyes sore weeping fell full many a tear,
To his royal mistress spake he: "Behold how stands he there
With whom here by Etzel none other may in might compare,

"And who commandeth service of lands and people all.
How many lordly castles Ruediger his own doth call,
That unto him hath given the bounty of the king!
Not yet in valorous conflict saw'st thou here his sword to swing.

"Methinks, but little recks he, what may here betide,
Since now in fullest measure his heart is satisfied.
'Tis told he is, surpassing all men, forsooth, so keen,
But in this time of trials his valor ill-displayed hath been."

Stood there full of sorrow the brave and faithful man,
Yet whom he thus heard speaking he cast his eyes upon.
Thought he: "Thou mak'st atonement, who deem'st my mettle cold.
Thy thought here all too loudly hast thou unto the people told."

His fist thereat he doubled and upon him ran,
And smote with blow so mighty there King Etzel's man
That prone before him straightway fell that mocker dead.
So came but greater sorrow on the royal Etzel's head.

"Hence thou basest caitiff," cried then Ruediger;
"Here of pain and sorrow enough I have to bear.
Wherefore wilt thou taunt me that I the combat shun?
In sooth had I the utmost of harm upon the strangers done,

"For that good reason have I to bear them hate indeed,
But that myself the warriors as friends did hither lead.
Yea, was I their safe escort into my master's land;
So may I, man most wretched, ne'er raise against them hostile hand."

Then spake the lofty Etzel unto the margrave:
"What aid, O noble Ruediger, here at thy hands we have!
Our country hath so many already doomed to die,
We need not any other: now hast thou wrought full wrongfully."

Returned the knight so noble: "My heart he sore hath grieved,
And reproached me for high honors at thy hand received
And eke for gifts unto me by thee so freely made;
Dearly for his slander hath the base traducer paid."

When had the queen come hither and had likewise seen
How on the Hunnish warrior his wrath had vented been,
Incontinent she mourned it, and tears bedimmed her sight.
Spake she unto Ruediger: "How dost thou now our love requite,

"That for me and thy master thou bring'st increase of woe?
Now hast thou, noble Ruediger, ever told us so,
How that thou life and honor for our sake wouldst dare.

Eke heard I thanes full many proclaim thee knight beyond compare.
"Of the oath I now remind thee that thou to me didst swear,
When counsel first thou gavest to Etzel's land to fare,
That thou wouldst truly serve me till one of us were dead:
Of that I wretched woman never stood so sore in need."
"Nor do I, royal mistress, deny that so I sware
That I for thy well-being would life and honor dare:
But eke my soul to forfeit, —that sware I not indeed.
'Tis I thy royal brothers hither to this land did lead."
Quoth she: "Bethink thee, Ruediger, of thy fidelity
And oath once firmly plighted that aught of harm to me
Should ever be avengéd, and righted every ill."
Replied thereto the margrave: "Ne'er have I failed to work thy will."
Etzel the mighty monarch to implore him then began,
And king and queen together down knelt before their man,
Whereat the good margrave was seen in sorest plight,
And gan to mourn his station in piteous words the faithful knight.
"O woe is me most wretched," he sorrow-stricken cried,
"That forced I am my honor thus to set aside,
And bonds of faith and friendship God hath imposed on me.
O Thou that rul'st in heaven! come death, I cannot yet be free.
"Whate'er it be my effort to do or leave undone,
I break both faith and honor in doing either one;
But leave I both, all people will cry me worthy scorn.
May He look down in mercy who bade me wretched man be born!"
With many a prayer besought him the king and eke his spouse,
Wherefore was many a warrior soon doomed his life to lose
At hand of noble Ruediger, when eke did die the thane.
Now hear ye how he bore him, though filled his heart with sorest pain.
He knew how scathe did wait him and boundless sorrowing,
And gladly had refuséd to obey the king
And eke his royal mistress. Full sorely did he fear,
That if one stranger slew he, the scorn of all the world he'd bear.
Then spake unto the monarch the full gallant thane:
"O royal sire, whatever thou gavest, take again,
The land and every castle, that naught remain to me.
On foot a lonely pilgrim I'll wander to a far country."
Thereto replied King Etzel: "Who then gave help to me?
My land and lordly castles give I all to thee,
If on my foes, O Ruediger, revenge thou wilt provide.
A mighty monarch seated, shalt thou be by Etzel's side."
Again gave answer Ruediger: "How may that ever be?
At my own home shared they my hospitality.
Meat and drink I offered to them in friendly way,
And gave them of my bounty: how shall I seek them here to slay?
"The folk belike will fancy that I a coward be.
Ne'er hath faithful service been refused by me

Unto the noble princes and their warriors too;
That e'er I gained their friendship, now 'tis cause for me to rue.
"For spouse unto Sir Giselher gave I a daughter mine,
Nor into fairer keeping might I her resign,
Where truth were sought and honor and gentle courtesy:
Ne'er saw I thane so youthful virtuous in mind as he."
Again gave answer Kriemhild: "O noble Ruediger,
To me and royal Etzel in mercy now give ear
For sorrows that o'erwhelm us. Bethink thee, I implore,
That monarch never any harbored so evil guests before."
Spake in turn the margrave unto the monarch's wife:
"Ruediger requital must make to-day with life
For that thou and my master did me so true befriend.
Therefore must I perish; now must my service find an end.
"E'en this day, well know I, my castles and my land
Must surely lose their master beneath a stranger's hand.
To thee my wife and children commend I for thy care,
And with all the lorn ones that wait by Bechelaren's towers fair."
"Now God reward thee, Ruediger," thereat King Etzel quoth.
He and the queen together, right joyful were they both.
"To us shall all thy people full commended be;
Eke trow I by my fortune no harm shall here befall to thee."
For their sake he ventured soul and life to lose.
Thereat fell sore to weeping the royal Etzel's spouse.
He spake: "I must unto you my plighted word fulfil.
Alack! beloved strangers, whom to assail forbids my will."
From the king there parting ye saw him, sad of mood,
And passed unto his warriors who at small distance stood.
"Don straightway now your armor, my warriors all," quoth he.
"Alas! must I to battle with the valiant knights of Burgundy."
Then straightway for their armor did the warriors call.
A shining helm for this one, for that a shield full tall
Soon did the nimble squires before them ready hold.
Anon came saddest tidings unto the stranger warriors bold.
With Ruediger there saw ye five hundred men arrayed,
And noble thanes a dozen that came unto his aid,
Thinking in storm of battle to win them honor high.
In sooth but little knew they how death awaited them so nigh.
With helm on head advancing saw ye Sir Ruediger.
Swords that cut full keenly the margrave's men did bear,
And eke in hand each carried a broad shield shining bright.
Boundless was the Fiddler's sorrow to behold the sight.
When saw the youthful Giselher his bride's sire go
Thus with fastened helmet, how might he ever know
What he therewith did purpose if 'twere not only good?
Thereat the noble monarchs right joyous might ye see of mood.
"I joy for friends so faithful," spake Giselher the thane,

"As on our journey hither we for ourselves did gain.
Full great shall be our vantage that I found spouse so dear,
And high my heart rejoiceth that plighted thus to wed we were."
"Small cause I see for comfort," thereto the minstrel spake.
"When saw ye thanes so many come a truce to make
With helmet firmly fastened and bearing sword in hand?
By scathe to us will Ruediger service do for tower and land."
The while that thus the Fiddler had spoken to the end,
His way the noble Ruediger unto the hall did wend.
His trusty shield he rested on the ground before his feet,
Yet might he never offer his friends in kindly way to greet.
Loudly the noble margrave cried into the hall:
"Now guard you well, ye valiant Nibelungen all.
From me ye should have profit: now have ye harm from me.
But late we plighted friendship: broken now these vows must be."
Then quailed to hear such tidings those knights in sore distress,
For none there was among them but did joy the less
That he would battle with them for whom great love they bore.
At hand of foes already had they suffered travail sore.
"Now God in heaven forfend it," there King Gunther cried,
"That from mercy to us thou so wilt turn aside,
And the faithful friendship whereof hope had we.
I trow in sooth that never may such thing be done by thee."
"Desist therefrom I may not," the keen knight made reply,
"But now must battle with you, for vow thereto gave I.
"Now guard you, gallant warriors, as fear ye life to lose:
From plighted vow release me will nevermore King Etzel's spouse."
"Too late thou turnst against us," spake King Gunther there.
"Now might God requite thee, O noble Ruediger,
For the faith and friendship thou didst on us bestow,
If thou a heart more kindly even to the end wouldst show.
"We'd ever make requital for all that thou didst give,—
I and all my kinsmen, wouldst thou but let us live,—
For thy gifts full stately, as faithfully thou here
To Etzel's land didst lead us: know that, O noble Ruediger."
"To me what pleasure were it," Ruediger did say,
"With full hand of my treasure unto you to weigh
And with a mind right willing as was my hope to do!
Thus might no man reproach me with lack of courtesy to you."
"Turn yet, O noble Ruediger." Gernot spake again,
"For in so gracious manner did never entertain
Any host the stranger, as we were served by thee;
And live we yet a little, shalt thou well requited be."
"O would to God, full noble Gernot," spake Ruediger,
"That ye were at Rhine river and that dead I were
With somewhat saved of honor, since I must be your foe!
Upon good knights was never wrought by friends more bitter woe."

"Now God requite thee, Ruediger," Gernot gave reply,
"For gifts so fair bestowéd. I rue to see thee die,
For that in thee shall perish knight of so gentle mind.
Here thy sword I carry, that gav'st thou me in friendship kind.
"It never yet hath failed me in this our sorest need,
And 'neath its cutting edges many a knight lies dead.
'Tis strong and bright of lustre, cunning wrought and well.
I ween, whate'er was given by knight it doth in worth excel.
"An wilt thou not give over upon us here to fall,
And if one friend thou slayest here yet within this hall,
With this same sword thou gavest, I'll take from thee thy life.
I sorrow for thee Ruediger, and eke thy fair and stately wife."
"Would God but give, Sir Gernot, that such thing might be,
That thou thy will completely here fulfilled mightst see,
And of thy friends not any here his life should lose!
Yea, shalt thou live to comfort both my daughter and my spouse."
Then out spake of Burgundy the son of Ute fair:
"How dost thou so, Sir Ruediger? All that with me are
To thee are well disposéd. Thou dost an evil thing,
And wilt thine own fair daughter to widowhood too early bring.
"If thou with arméd warriors wilt thus assail me here,
In what unfriendly manner thou makest to appear
How that in thee I trusted beyond all men beside,
When thy fairest daughter erstwhile I won to be my bride."
"Thy good faith remember, O Prince of virtue rare,
If God from hence do bring thee," —so spake Ruediger:
"Forsake thou not the maiden when bereft of me,
But rather grant thy goodness be dealt to her more graciously."
"That would I do full fairly," spake Giselher again.
"But if my lofty kinsmen, who yet do here remain,
Beneath thy hand shall perish, severed then must be
The friendship true I cherish eke for thy daughter and for thee."
"Then God to us give mercy," the knight full valiant spake.
Their shields in hand then took they, as who perforce would make
Their passage to the strangers into Kriemhild's hall.
Adown the stair full loudly did Hagen, knight of Tronje, call:
"Tarry yet a little, O noble Ruediger,
For further would we parley," —thus might ye Hagen hear—
"I and my royal masters, as presseth sorest need.
What might it boot to Etzel that we strangers all lay dead.
"Great is here my trouble," Hagen did declare:
"The shield that Lady Gotelinde gave to me to bear
Hath now been hewn asunder by Hun-men in my hand.
With friendly thought I bore it hither into Etzel's land.
"Would that God in heaven might grant in kindliness,
That I a shield so trusty did for my own possess
As in thy hand thou bearest, O noble Ruediger!

In battle-storm then need I never hauberk more to wear."
"Full glad I'd prove my friendship to thee with mine own shield,
Dared I the same to offer before Lady Kriemhild.
But take it, natheless, Hagen, and bear it in thy hand.
Would that thou mightst take it again unto Burgundian land!"
When with mind so willing he offered him his shield,
Saw ye how eyes full many with scalding tears were filled;
For the last gift was it that was offered e'er
Unto any warrior by Bechelaren's margrave, Ruediger.
How grim soe'er was Hagen and stern soe'er of mind,
That gift to pity moved him that there the chieftain kind,
So near his latest moment, did on him bestow.
From eyes of many another began likewise the tears to flow.
"Now God in heaven requite thee, O noble Ruediger!
Like unto thee none other warrior was there e'er,
Unto knights all friendless so bounteously to give.
God grant in his mercy thy virtue evermore to live.
"Woe's me to hear such tiding," Hagen did declare.
"Such load of grief abiding already do we bear,
If we with friends must struggle, to God our plaint must be."
Thereto replied the margrave: "'Tis cause of sorrow sore to me."
"To pay thee for thy favor, O noble Ruediger,
Howe'er these lofty warriors themselves against thee bear,
Yet never thee in combat here shall touch my hand,
E'en though complete thou slayest them from out Burgundian land."
Thereat the lofty Ruediger 'fore him did courteous bend.
On all sides was lamenting that no man might end
These so great heart-sorrows that sorely they must bear.
The father of all virtue fell with noble Ruediger.
Then eke the minstrel Volker from hall down glancing said:
"Since Hagen thus, my comrade, peace with thee hath made,
Lasting truce thou likewise receivest from my hand.
Well hast thou deserved it as fared we hither to this land.
"Thou, O noble margrave, my messenger shalt be.
These arm-bands ruddy golden thy lady gave to me,
That here at this high festival I the same should wear.
Now mayst thyself behold them and of my faith a witness bear."
"Would God but grant," spake Ruediger, "who ruleth high in heaven,
That to thee by my lady might further gift be given!
I'll gladly tell thy tidings to spouse full dear to me,
An I but live to see her: from doubt thereof thou mayst be free."
When thus his word was given, his shield raised Ruediger.
Nigh to madness driven bode he no longer there,
But ran upon the strangers like to a valiant knight.
Many a blow full rapid smote the margrave in his might.
Volker and Hagen made way before the thane,
As before had promised to him the warriors twain.

Yet found he by the portal so many a valiant man
That Ruediger the combat with mickle boding sore began.
Gunther and Gernot with murderous intent
Let him pass the portal, as knights on victory bent.
Backward yielded Giselher, with sorrow all undone;
He hoped to live yet longer, and therefore Ruediger would shun.
Straight upon their enemies the margrave's warriors sprung,
And following their master was seen a valiant throng.
Swords with cutting edges did they in strong arm wield,
'Neath which full many a helmet was cleft, and many a fair wrought shield.
The weary strangers likewise smote many a whirring slash,
Wherefrom the men of Bechelaren felt deep and long the gash
Through the shining ring-mail e'en to their life's core.
In storm of battle wrought they glorious deeds a many more.
All his trusty followers now eke had gained the hall,
On whom Volker and Hagen did soon in fury fall,
And mercy unto no man save Ruediger they showed.
The blood adown through helmets, where smote their swords, full plenteous flowed.
How right furiously were swords 'gainst armor driven!
On shields the well-wrought mountings from their wards were riven,
And fell their jewelled facings all scattered in the blood.
Ne'er again might warriors show in fight so grim a mood.
The lord of Bechelaren through foemen cut his way,
As doth each doughty warrior in fight his might display.
On that day did Ruediger show full plain that he
A hero was undaunted, full bold and eke full praiseworthy.
Stood there two knights right gallant, Gunther and Gernot,
And in the storm of battle to death full many smote.
Eke Giselher and Dankwart, never aught recked they
How many a lusty fighter saw 'neath their hand his latest day.
Full well did show him Ruediger a knight of mettle true,
Doughty in goodly armor. What warriors there he slew!
Beheld it a Burgundian, and cause for wrath was there.
Not longer now was distant the death of noble Ruediger.
Gernot, knight full doughty, addressed the margrave then,
Thus speaking to the hero: "Wilt thou of all my men
Living leave not any, O noble Ruediger?
That gives me grief unmeasured; the sight I may not longer bear.
"Now must thy gift unto me prove thy sorest bane,
Since of my friends so many thou from me hast ta'en.
Now hither turn to front me, thou bold and noble knight:
As far as might may bear me I trust to pay thy gift aright."
Ere that full the margrave might make his way to him,
Must rings of glancing mail-coats with flowing blood grow dim.
Then sprang upon each other those knights on honor bent,
And each from wounds deep cutting sought to keep him all unshent.

Their swords cut so keenly that might withstand them naught.
With mighty arm Sir Ruediger Gernot then smote
Through the flint-hard helmet, that downward flowed the blood.
Therefor repaid him quickly the knight of keen and valiant mood.
The gift he had of Ruediger high in hand he swung,
And though to death was wounded he smote with blow so strong
That the good shield was cloven and welded helmet through.
The spouse of fair Gotelinde, then his latest breath he drew.
In sooth so sad requital found rich bounty ne'er.
Slain fell they both together, Gernot and Ruediger,
Alike in storm of battle, each by the other's hand.
Sore was the wrath of Hagen when he the harm did understand.
Cried there the lord of Tronje: "Great is here our loss.
In death of these two heroes such scathe befalleth us,
Wherefor land and people shall repine for aye.
The warriors of Ruediger must now to us the forfeit pay."
"Alack for this my brother, snatched by death this day!
What host of woes unbidden encompass me alway!
Eke must I moan it ever that noble Ruediger fell.
Great is the scathe to both sides and great the sorrowing as well."
When then beheld Sir Giselher his lover's sire dead,
Must all that with him followed suffer direst need.
There Death was busy seeking to gather in his train,
And of the men of Bechelaren came forth not one alive again.
Gunther and Giselher and with them Hagen too,
Dankwart and Volker, doughty thanes and true,
Went where found they lying the two warriors slain,
Nor at the sight the heroes might their grief and tears restrain.
"Death robbeth us right sorely," spake young Sir Giselher:
"Yet now give o'er your weeping and let us seek the air,
That the ringed mail grow cooler on us storm-weary men.
God in sooth will grant us not longer here to live, I ween."
Here sitting, and there leaning was seen full many a thane,
Resting once more from combat, the while that all lay slain
The followers of Ruediger. Hushed was the battle's din.
At length grew angry Etzel, that stillness was so long within.
"Alack for such a service!" spake the monarch's wife;
"For never 'tis so faithful that our foes with life
Must to us make payment at Ruediger's hand.
He thinks in sooth to lead them again unto Burgundian land.
"What boots it, royal Etzel, that we did ever share
With him what he desired? The knight doth evil there.
He that should avenge us, the same a truce doth make."
Thereto the stately warrior Volker in answer spake:
"Alas 'tis no such case here, O high and royal dame.
Dared I but give the lie to one of thy lofty name,
Thou hast in fiendish manner Ruediger belied.

He and all his warriors have laid all thoughts of truce aside.
"With so good heart obeyed he his royal master's will
That he and all his followers here in death lie still.
Look now about thee, Kriemhild, who may thy hests attend.
Ruediger the hero hath served thee faithful to the end.
"Wilt thou my words believe not, to thee shall clear be shown."
To cause her heart a sorrow, there the thing was done.
Wound-gashed they bore the hero where him the king might see.
Unto the thanes of Etzel ne'er might so great sorrow be.
When did they the margrave a corse on bier behold,
By chronicler might never written be nor told
All the wild lamenting of women and of men,
As with grief all stricken out-poured they their hearts' sorrow then.
Royal Etzel's sorrow there did know no bound.
Like to the voice of lion echoing rang the sound
Of the king's loud weeping, wherein the queen had share.
Unmeasured they lamented the death of noble Ruediger.

THIRTY-EIGHTH ADVENTURE

How all Sir Dietrich's Knights were Slain

On all sides so great sorrow heard ye there around,
That palace and high tower did from the wail resound.
Of Bern a man of Dietrich eke the same did hear,
And speedily he hastened the tidings to his lord to bear.
Spake he unto his master: "Sir Dietrich give me ear.
What yet hath been my fortune, never did I hear
Lamenting past all measure, as at this hour hath been.
Scathe unto King Etzel himself hath happenéd, I ween.
"Else how might they ever all show such dire need?
The king himself or Kriemhild, one of them lieth dead,
By the doughty strangers for sake of vengeance slain.
Unmeasured is the weeping of full many a stately thane."
Then spake of Bern Sir Dietrich: "Ye men to me full dear,
Now haste ye not unduly. The deeds performéd here
By the stranger warriors show sore necessity.
That peace with them I blighted, let it now their profit be."
Then spake the valiant Wolfhart: "Thither will I run
To make question of it what they now have done,
And straight will tidings bring thee, master full dear to me,
When yonder I inform me, whence may so great lamenting be."
Answer gave Sir Dietrich: "Fear they hostility,
The while uncivil questioning of their deed there be,
Lightly are stirred to anger good warriors o'er the thing.
Yea, 'tis my pleasure, Wolfhart, thou sparest them all such questioning.

Helfrich he then commanded thither with speed to go
That from men of Etzel he might truly know,
Or from the strangers straightway, what thing there had been.
As that, so sore lamenting of people ne'er before was seen.
Questioned then the messenger: "What hath here been wrought?"
Answered one among them: "Complete is come to naught
What of joy we cherished here in Hunnish land.
Slain here lieth Ruediger, fallen 'neath Burgundian hand.
"Of them that entered with him not one doth longer live."
Naught might ever happen Helfrich more to grieve,
Nor ever told he tidings so ruefully before.
Weeping sore the message unto Dietrich then he bore.
"What the news thou bringst us?" Dietrich spake once more;
"Yet, O doughty Helfrich, wherefore dost weep so sore?"
Answered the noble warrior: "With right may I complain:
Yonder faithful Ruediger lieth by the Burgundians slain."
The lord of Bern gave answer: "God let not such thing be!
That were a mighty vengeance, and eke the Devil's glee.
Whereby had ever Ruediger from them deserved such ill?
Well know I to the strangers was ever well disposed his will."
Thereto gave answer Wolfhart: "In sooth have they this done,
Therefor their lives shall forfeit surely, every one.
And make we not requital, our shame for aye it were;
Full manifold our service from hand of noble Ruediger."
Then bade the lord of Amelungen the case more full to learn.
He sat within a casement and did full sadly mourn.
He prayed then that Hildebrand unto the strangers go,
That he from their own telling of the case complete might know.
The warrior keen in battle, Master Hildebrand,
Neither shield nor weapon bore he in his hand,
But would in chivalrous manner unto the strangers go.
His sister's son reviled him that he would venture thus to do.
Spake in anger Wolfhart: "Goest thou all weaponless,
Must I of such action free my thought confess:
Thou shalt in shameful fashion hither come again;
Goest thou arméd thither, will all from harm to thee refrain."
So armed himself the old man at counsel of the young.
Ere he was ware of it, into their armor sprung
All of Dietrich's warriors and stood with sword in hand.
Grieved he was, and gladly had turned them Master Hildebrand.
He asked them whither would they. "Thee company we'll bear,
So may, perchance, less willing Hagen of Tronje dare,
As so oft his custom, to give thee mocking word."
The thane his leave did grant them at last when he their speech had heard.
Keen Volker saw approaching, in armor all arrayed,
Of Bern the gallant warriors that Dietrich's word obeyed,
With sword at girdle hanging and bearing shield in hand.

Straight he told the tidings to his masters of Burgundian land.
Spake the doughty Fiddler: "Yonder see I come near
The warriors of Dietrich all clad in battle gear
And decked their heads with helmets, as if our harm they mean.
For us knights here homeless approacheth evil end, I ween."
Meanwhile was come anigh them Master Hildebrand.
Before his foot he rested the shield he bore in hand,
And soon began to question the men of Gunther there:
"Alack, ye gallant warriors, what harm hath wrought you Ruediger?
"Me did my master Dietrich hither to you command:
If now the noble margrave hath fallen 'neath the hand
Of any knight among you, as word to us is borne,
Such a mighty sorrow might we never cease to mourn."
Then spake of Tronje Hagen: "True is the tale ye hear.
Though glad I were, if to you had lied the messenger,
And if the faithful Ruediger still his life might keep,
For whom both man and woman must ever now in sorrow weep!"
When they for sooth the passing of the hero knew,
Those gallant knights bemoaned him like faithful friends and true;
On Dietrich's lusty warriors saw ye fall the tear
Adown the bearded visage, for sad of heart in truth they were.
Of Bern then a chieftain, Siegstab, further cried:
"Of all the mickle comfort now an end is made,
That Ruediger erst prepared us after our days of pain.
The joy of exiled people here lieth by you warriors slain."
Then spake of Amelungen the thane Wolfwein:
"If that this day beheld I dead e'en sire of mine,
No more might be my sorrow than for this hero's life.
Alack! who bringeth comfort now to the noble margrave's wife?"
Spake eke in angry humor Wolfhart a stalwart thane:
"Who now shall lead our army on the far campaign,
As full oft the margrave of old hath led our host?
Alack! O noble Ruediger, that in such manner thee we've lost!"
Wolfbrand and Helfrich and Helmnot with warriors all
Mournéd there together that he in death must fall.
For sobbing might not further question Hildebrand.
He spake: "Now do, ye warriors, according to my lord's command.
"Yield unto us Ruediger's corse from out the hall,
In whose death to sorrow hath passed our pleasure all;
And let us do him service for friendship true of yore
That e'er for us he cherished and eke for many a stranger more.
"We too from home are exiles like unto Ruediger.
Why keep ye us here waiting? Him grant us hence to bear,
That e'en though death hath reft him our service he receive,
Though fairer had we paid it the while the hero yet did live."
Thereto spake King Gunther: "No service equal may
That which, when death hath reft him, to friend a friend doth pay.

Him deem I friend right faithful, whoe'er the same may do.
Well make ye here requital for many a service unto you."
"How long shall we beseech you," spake Wolfhart the thane;
"Since he that best consoled us by you now lieth slain,
And we, alas, no longer his living aid may have,
Grant us hence to bear him and lay the hero in his grave."
Thereto answered Volker: "Thy prayer shall all deny.
From out the hall thou take him, where doth the hero lie
'Neath deep wounds and mortal in blood now smitten down.
So may by thee best service here to Ruediger be shown."
Answered Wolfhart boldly: "Sir Fiddleman, God wot
Thou shalt forbear to stir us, for woe on us thou'st wrought.
Durst I despite my master, uncertain were thy life;
Yet must we here keep silence, for he did bid us shun the strife."
Then spake again the Fiddler: "'Tis all too much of fear,
For that a thing's forbidden, meekly to forbear.
Scarce may I deem it valor worthy good knight to tell."
What said his faithful comrade, did please the doughty Hagen well.
"For proof be not o'er-eager," Wolfhart quick replied,
"Else so I'll tune thy fiddle that when again ye ride
Afar unto Rhine river, sad tale thou tellest there.
Thy haughty words no longer may I now with honor bear."
Spake once more the Fiddler: "If e'er the harmony
Of my fiddle-strings thou breakest, thy helmet's sheen shall be
Made full dim of lustre by stroke of this my hand,
Howe'er fall out my journey homeward to Burgundian land."
Then would he rush upon him but that him did restrain
Hildebrand his uncle who seizéd him amain.
"I ween thou would'st be witless, by youthful rage misled.
My master's favor had'st thou evermore thus forfeited."
"Let loose the lion, Master, that doth rage so sore.
If but my sword may reach him," spake Volker further more,
"Though he the world entire by his own might had slain,
I'll smite him that an answer never may he chant again."
Thereat with anger straightway the men of Bern were filled.
Wolfhart, thane right valiant, grasped in haste his shield,
And like to a wild lion out before them sped.
By friends a goodly number full quickly was he followéd.
Though by the hall went striding ne'er so swift the thane,
O'ertook him Master Hildebrand ere he the steps might gain,
For nowise would he let him be foremost in the fray.
In the stranger warriors worthy foemen soon found they.
Straight saw ye upon Hagen rush Master Hildebrand,
And sword ye heard give music in each foeman's hand.
Sore they were enragéd, as ye soon were ware,
For from their swinging broadswords whirred the ruddy sparks in air.
Yet soon the twain were parted in the raging fight:

The men of Bern so turned it by their dauntless might.
Ere long then was Hildebrand from Hagen turned away,
While that the doughty Wolfhart the valiant Volker sought to slay.
Upon the helm the Fiddler he smote with blow so fierce
That the sword's keen edges unto the frame did pierce.
With mighty stroke repaid him the valiant minstrel too,
And so belabored Wolfhart that thick the sparks around him flew.
Hewing they made the fire from mail-rings scintillate,
For each unto the other bore a deadly hate.
Of Bern the thane Wolfwein at length did part the two,—
Which thing might none other than man of mickle prowess do.
Gunther, knight full gallant, received with ready hand
There the stately warriors of Amelungen land.
Eke did young Giselher of many a helmet bright,
With blood all red and reeking, cause to grow full dim the light.
Dankwart, Hagen's brother, was a warrior grim.
What erstwhile in combat had been wrought by him
Against the men of Etzel seemed now as toying vain,
As fought with flaming ire the son of valiant Aldrian.
Ritschart and Gerbart, Helfrich and Wichart
Had oft in storm of battle with valor borne their part,
As now 'fore men of Gunther they did clear display.
Likewise saw ye Wolfbrand glorious amid the fray.
There old Master Hildebrand fought as he were wode.
Many a doughty warrior was stricken in the blood
By the sword that swinging in Wolfhart's hand was seen.
Thus took dire vengeance for Ruediger those knights full keen.
Havoc wrought Sir Siegstab there with might and main.
Ho! in the hurly-burly what helms he cleft in twain
Upon the crowns of foemen, Dietrich's sister's son!
Ne'er in storm of battle had he more feats of valor done.
When the doughty Volker there aright had seen
How many a bloody rivulet was hewn by Siegstab keen
From out the well-wrought mail-rings, the hero's ire arose.
Quick he sprang toward him, Siegstab then his life must lose.
Ere long time was over, 'neath the Fiddler's hand,
Who of his art did give him such share to understand
That beneath his broadsword smitten to death he lay.
Old Hildebrand avenged him as bade his mighty arm alway.
"Alack that knight so loved," spake Master Hildebrand,
"Here should thus lie fallen 'neath Volker's hand.
Now lived his latest hour in sooth this Fiddler hath."
Filled was the hero Hildebrand straightway with a mighty wrath.
With might smote he Volker that severed flew the band
E'en to the hall's wide limit far on either hand
From shield and eke from helmet borne by the Fiddler keen;
Therewith the doughty Volker reft of life at last had been.

Pressed eager to the combat Dietrich's warriors true,
Smiting that the mail-rings afar from harness flew,
And that the broken sword-points soaring aloft ye saw,
The while that reeking blood-stains did they from riven helmets draw.
There of Tronje Hagen beheld Volker dead.
In that so bloody carnage 'twas far the sorest need
Of all that did befall him in death of friend and man.
Alack! for him what vengeance Hagen then to wreak began!
"Therefrom shall profit never Master Hildebrand.
Slain hath been here my helper 'neath the warrior's hand,
The best of feres in battle that fortune ever sent."
His shield upraised he higher and hewing through the throng he went.
Next saw ye Dankwart by doughty Helfrich slain,
Gunther and Giselher did full sorely plain,
When they beheld him fallen where fiercely raged the fray.
For his death beforehand dearly did his foemen pay.
The while coursed Wolfhart thither and back again,
Through Gunther's men before him hewing wide a lane.
Thrice in sooth returning strode he down the hall,
And many a lusty warrior 'neath his doughty hand must fall.
Soon the young Sir Giselher cried aloud to him:
"Alack, that I should ever find such foeman grim!
Sir knight, so bold and noble, now turn thee here to me.
I trow to end thy coursing, the which will I no longer see."
To Giselher then turned him Wolfhart in the fight,
And gaping wounds full many did each the other smite.
With such a mighty fury he to the monarch sped
That 'neath his feet went flying the blood e'en high above his head.
With rapid blows and furious the son of Ute fair
Received the valiant Wolfhart as came he to him there.
How strong soe'er the thane was, his life must ended be.
Never king so youthful might bear himself more valiantly.
Straight he smote Wolfhart through well-made cuirass,
That from the wound all gaping the flowing blood did pass.
Unto death he wounded Dietrich's liegeman true,
Which thing in sooth might never any save knight full gallant do.
When the valiant Wolfhart of the wound was ware,
His shield flung he from him and high with hand in air
Raised he a mighty weapon whose keen edge failéd not.
Through helmet and through mail-rings Giselher with might he smote.
Grimly each the other there to death had done.
Of Dietrich's men no longer lived there ever one.
When old Master Hildebrand Wolfhart's fall had seen,
In all his life there never such sorrow him befell, I ween.
Fallen now were Gunther's warriors every one,
And eke the men of Dietrich. Hildebrand the while had gone
Where Wolfhart had fallen down in pool of blood.

In his arms then clasped he the warrior of dauntless mood.
Forth from the hall to bear him vainly did he try:
But all too great the burden and there he still must lie.
The dying knight looked upward from his bloody bed
And saw how that full gladly him his uncle thence had led.
Spake he thus mortal wounded: "Uncle full dear to me,
Now mayst thou at such season no longer helpful be.
To guard thee well from Hagen indeed me seemeth good,
For bears he in his bosom a heart in sooth of grimmest mood.
"And if for me my kinsmen at my death would mourn,
Unto the best and nearest by thee be message borne
That for me they weep not, —of that no whit is need.
At hand of valiant monarch here lie I gloriously dead.
"Eke my life so dearly within this hall I've sold,
That have sore cause for weeping the wives of warriors bold.
If any make thee question, then mayst thou freely say
That my own hand nigh hundred warriors hath slain to-day."
Now was Hagen mindful of the minstrel slain,
From whom the valiant Hildebrand erstwhile his life had ta'en.
Unto the Master spake he: "My woes shalt thou repay.
Full many a warrior gallant thou hast ta'en from us hence away."
He smote upon Hildebrand that loud was heard the tone
Of Balmung resounding that erst did Siegfried own,
But Hagen bold did seize it when he the hero slew.
The old warrior did guard him, as he was knight of mettle true.
Dietrich's doughty liegeman with broadsword did smite
That did cut full sorely, upon Tronje's knight;
Yet had the man of Gunther never any harm.
Through his cuirass well-jointed Hagen smote with mighty arm.
Soon as his wound percevéd the aged Hildebrand,
Feared he more of damage to take from Hagen's hand;
Across his back full deftly his shield swung Dietrich's man,
And wounded deep, the hero in flight 'fore Hagen's fury ran.
Now longer lived not any of all that goodly train
Save Gunther and Hagen, doughty warriors twain.
With blood from wound down streaming fled Master Hildebrand,
Whom soon in Dietrich's presence, saw ye with saddest tidings stand.
He found the chieftain sitting with sorrow all distraught,
Yet mickle more of sadness unto him he brought.
When Dietrich saw how Hildebrand cuirass all blood-red wore,
With fearful heart he questioned, what the news to him he bore.
"Now tell me, Master Hildebrand, how thus wet thou be
From thy life-blood flowing, or who so harmeth thee.
In hall against the strangers thou'st drawn thy sword, I ween.
'Twere well my straight denial here by these had honored been."
Replied he to his master: "From Hagen cometh all.
This deep wound he smote me there within the hall

When I from his fury thought to turn away.
'Tis marvel that I living saved me from the fiend this day."
Then of Bern spake Dietrich: "Aright hast thou thy share,
For thou didst hear me friendship unto these knights declare,
And now the peace hast broken, that I to them did give.
If my disgrace it were not, by this hand no longer shouldst thou live."
"Now be not, Master Dietrich, so sorely stirred to wrath.
On me and on my kinsmen is wrought too great a scathe.
Thence sought we Ruediger to bear all peacefully,
The which by men of Gunther to us no whit would granted be."
"Ah, woe is me for sorrow! Is Ruediger then dead,
In all my need there never such grief hath happenéd.
The noble Gotelinde is cousin fair to me.
Alack for the poor orphans that there in Bechelaren must be!"
Grief and anguish filled him o'er Ruediger thus slain,
Nor might at all the hero the flowing tears restrain.
"Alack for faithful helper that death from me hath torn.
King Etzel's trusty liegeman never may I cease to mourn.
"Canst thou, Master Hildebrand, true the tidings say,
Who might be the warrior that Ruediger did slay?"
"That did the doughty Gernot with mighty arm," he said:
"Eke at hand of Ruediger lieth the royal hero dead."
Spake he again to Hildebrand: "Now let my warriors know,
That straightway they shall arm them, for thither will I go.
And bid to fetch hither my shining mail to me.
Myself those knights will question of the land of Burgundy."
"Who here shall do thee service?" spake Master Hildebrand;
"All that thou hast yet living, thou seest before thee stand.
Of all remain I only; the others, they are dead."
As was in sooth good reason, filled the tale his soul with dread,
For in his life did never such woe to him befall.
He spake: "Hath death so reft me of my warriors all,
God hath forsaken Dietrich, ah me, a wretched wight!
Sometime a lofty monarch I was, high throned in wealth and might."
"How might it ever happen?" Dietrich spake again,
"That so worthy heroes   here should all be slain
By the battle-weary strangers thus beset?
Ill fortune me hath chosen, else death had surely spared them yet.
"Since that fate not further to me would respite give,
Then tell me, of the strangers doth any longer live?"
Answered Master Hildebrand: "God wot, never one
Save Hagen, and beside him Gunther lofty king alone."
"Alack, O faithful Wolfhart, must I thy death now mourn,
Soon have I cause to rue me   that ever I was born.
Siegstab and Wolfwein and eke Wolfbrand!
Who now shall be my helpers in the Amelungen land?
"Helfrich, thane full valiant, and is he likewise slain?

For Gerbart and Wichart when shall I cease to plain?
Of all my life's rejoicing is this the latest day.
Alack that die for sorrow never yet a mortal may!"

THIRTY-NINTH ADVENTURE

How Gunther and Hagen and Kriemhild were Slain

Himself did then Sir Dietrich his armor take in hand,
To don the which did help him Master Hildebrand.
The doughty chieftain meanwhile must make so loud complain
That from high palace casement oft came back the sound again.
Natheless his proper humor soon he did regain,
And arméd full in anger stood the worthy thane;
A shield all wrought full firmly took he straight in hand,
And forth they strode together, he and Master Hildebrand.
Spake then of Tronje Hagen: "Lo, where doth hither wend
In wrath his way Sir Dietrich. 'Tis plain he doth intend
On us to wreak sore vengeance for harm befallen here.
To-day be full decided who may the prize for valor bear!
"Let ne'er of Bern Sir Dietrich hold him so high of might
Nor deem his arm so doughty and terrible in fight
That, will he wreak his anger on us for sorest scathe,"—
Such were the words of Hagen, —"I dare not well withstand his wrath."
Upon these words defiant left Dietrich Hildebrand,
And to the warriors hither came where both did stand
Without before the palace, and leaning respite found.
His shield well proved in battle Sir Dietrich lowered to the ground.
Addressed to them Sir Dietrich these words of sorrowing:
"Wherefore hast thou such evil, Gunther mighty king,
Wrought 'gainst me a stranger? What had I done to thee,
Of my every comfort in such manner reft to be?
"Seemed then not sufficient the havoc unto you
When from us the hero Ruediger ye slew,
That now from me ye've taken my warriors one and all?
Through me did so great sorrow ne'er to you good knights befall.
"Of your own selves bethink you and what the scathe ye bore,
The death of your companions and all your travail sore,
If not your hearts, good warriors, thereat do heavy grow.
That Ruediger hath fallen, —ah me! how fills my heart with woe!
"In all this world to any more sorrow ne'er befell,
Yet have ye minded little my loss and yours as well.
Whate'er I most rejoiced in beneath your hands lies slain;
Yea, for my kinsmen fallen never may I cease to plain."
"No guilt lies here upon us," Hagen in answer spake.
"Unto this hall hither your knights their way did take,

With goodly train of warriors full arméd for the fight.
Meseemeth that the story hath not been told to thee aright."
"What shall I else believe in? To me told Hildebrand
How, when the knights that serve me of Amelungenland
Did beg the corse of Ruediger to give them from the hall,
Nought offered ye but mockings unto the valiant warriors all."
Then spake the King of Rhineland: "Ruediger to bear away
Came they in company hither; whose corse to them deny
I bade, despiting Etzel, nor with aught malice more,
Whereupon did Wolfhart begin to rage thereat full sore."
Then spake of Bern the hero: "'Twas fated so to be.
Yet Gunther, noble monarch, by thy kingly courtesy
Amends make for the sorrow thou here on me hast wrought,
That so thy knightly honor still unsullied be in aught.
"Then yield to me as hostage thyself and eke thy man;
So will I surely hinder, as with best might I can,
That any here in Hunland harm unto thee shall do:
Henceforward shalt thou find me ever well disposed and true."
"God in heaven forfend it," Hagen spake again,
"That unto thee should yield them ever warriors twain
Who in their strength reliant all armed before thee stand,
And yet 'fore foes defiant may freely swing a blade in hand."
"So shall ye not," spake Dietrich, "proffered peace forswear,
Gunther and Hagen. Misfortune such I bear
At both your hands, 'tis certain ye did but do aright,
Would ye for so great sorrow now my heart in full requite.
"I give you my sure promise and pledge thereto my hand
That I will bear you escort home unto your land;
With honors fit I'll lead you, thereon my life I set,
And for your sake sore evil suffered at your hands forget."
"Ask thou such thing no longer," Hagen then replied.
"For us 'twere little fitting the tale be bruited wide,
That twain of doughty warriors did yield them 'neath thy hand.
Beside thee is none other now but only Hildebrand."
Then answered Master Hildebrand: "The hour may come, God wot,
Sir Hagen, when thus lightly disdain it thou shalt not
If any man such offer of peace shall make to thee.
Welcome might now my master's reconciliation be."
"I'd take in sooth his friendship," Hagen gave reply,
"Ere that I so basely forth from a hall would fly.
As thou hast done but lately, O Master Hildebrand.
I weened with greater valor couldst thou 'fore a foeman stand."
Thereto gave answer Hildebrand: "From thee reproach like that?
Who was then on shield so idle 'fore the Waskenstein that sat,
The while that Spanish Walter friend after friend laid low?
Such valor thou in plenty hast in thine own self to show."
Outspake then Sir Dietrich: "Ill fits it warriors bold

That they one another like old wives should scold.
Thee forbid I, Hildebrand, aught to parley more.
Ah me, most sad misfortune weigheth on my heart full sore.
"Let me hear, Sir Hagen," Dietrich further spake,
"What boast ye doughty warriors did there together make,
When that ye saw me hither come with sword in hand?
Thought ye then not singly me in combat to withstand?"
"In sooth denieth no one," bold Sir Hagen spake,
"That of the same with sword-blow I would trial make,
An but the sword of Niblung burst not within my hand.
Yea, scorn I that to yield us thus haughtily thou mak'st demand."
When Dietrich now perceivéd how Hagen raged amain,
Raise his shield full quickly did the doughty thane.
As quick upon him Hagen adown the perron sprang,
And the trusty sword of Niblung full loud on Dietrich's armor rang.
Then knew full well Sir Dietrich that the warrior keen
Savage was of humor, and best himself to screen
Sought of Bern the hero from many a murderous blow,
Whereby the valiant Hagen straightway came he well to know.
Eke fear he had of Balmung, a strong and trusty blade.
Each blow meanwhile Sir Dietrich with cunning art repaid,
Till that he dealt to Hagen a wound both deep and long,
Whereat give o'er the struggle must the valiant knight and strong.
Bethought him then Sir Dietrich: "Through toil thy strength has fled,
And little honor had I shouldst thou lie before me dead.
So will I yet make trial if I may not subdue
Thee unto me as hostage." Light task 'twas not the same to do.
His shield down cast he from him and with what strength he found
About the knight of Tronje fast his arms he wound.
In such wise was subduéd by him the doughty knight;
Gunther the noble monarch did weep to see his sorry plight.
Bind Hagen then did Dietrich, and led him where did stand
Kriemhild the royal lady, and gave into her hand
Of all the bravest warrior that ever weapon bore.
After her mickle sorrow had she merry heart once more.
For joy before Sir Dietrich bent royal Etzel's wife:
"Blessed be thou ever in heart while lasteth life.
Through thee is now forgotten all my dire need;
An death do not prevent me, from me shall ever be thy meed."
Then spake to her Sir Dietrich, "Take not his life away,
High and royal lady, for full will he repay
Thee for the mickle evil on thee have wrought his hands.
Be it not his misfortune that bound before thee here he stands."
Then bade she forth lead Hagen to dungeon keep near by,
Wherein he lay fast bolted and hid from every eye.
Gunther, the noble monarch, with loudest voice did say:
"The knight of Bern who wrongs me, whither hath he fled away?"

Meanwhile back towards him the doughty Dietrich came,
And found the royal Gunther a knight of worthy name.
Eke he might bide longer but down to meet him sprang,
And soon with angry clamor their swords before the palace rang.
How famed soe'er Sir Dietrich and great the name he bore,
With wrath was filled King Gunther, and eke did rage full sore
At thought of grievous sorrow suffered at his hand:
Still tell they as high wonder how Dietrich might his blows withstand.
In store of doughty valor each did nothing lack.
From palace and from tower the din of blows came back
As on well-fastened helmets the lusty swords came down,
And royal Gunther's valor in the fight full clear was shown.
The knight of Bern yet tamed him as Hagen erst befell,
And oozing through his armor the blood was seen to swell
From cut of sharpest weapon in Dietrich's arm that swung.
Right worthily King Gunther had borne him after labors long.
Bound was then the monarch by Sir Dietrich's hand,
Albeit bonds should suffer ne'er king of any land.
But deemed he, if King Gunther and Hagen yet were free,
Secure might never any from their searching vengeance be.
When in such manner Dietrich the king secure had bound
By the hand he led him where Kriemhild he found.
At sight of his misfortune did sorrow from her flee:
Quoth she: "Welcome Gunther from out the land of Burgundy."
He spake: "Then might I thank thee, sister of high degree,
When that some whit more gracious might thy greeting be.
So angry art thou minded ever yet, O queen,
Full spare shall be thy greeting to Hagen and to me, I ween."
Then spake of Bern the hero: "Ne'er till now, O queen,
Given o'er as hostage have knights so worthy been,
As I, O lofty lady, in these have given to thee:
I pray thee higher evils to spare them now for sake of me."
She vowed to do it gladly. Then forth Sir Dietrich went
With weeping eyes to see there such knights' imprisonment.
In grimmest ways thereafter wreaked vengeance Etzel's wife:
Beneath her hand those chosen warriors twain must end their life.
She let them lie asunder the less at ease to be,
Nor did each the other thenceforward ever see
Till that unto Hagen her brother's head she bore.
In sooth did Kriemhild vengeance wreak upon the twain full sore.
Forth where she should find Hagen the queen her way did take,
And in right angry manner she to the warrior spake:
"An thou wilt but restore me that thou hast ta'en from me,
So may'st thou come yet living home to the land of Burgundy."
Answered thereto grim Hagen: "'Twere well thy breath to save,
Full high and royal lady. Sworn by my troth I have
That I the hoard will tell not; the while that yet doth live

Of my masters any, the treasure unto none I'll give."
"Then ended be the story," the noble lady spake.
She bade them from her brother straightway his life to take.
His head they struck from off him, which by the hair she bore
Unto the thane of Tronje. Thereat did grieve the knight full sore.
When that he in horror his master's head had seen,
Cried the doughty warrior unto Kriemhild the queen:
"Now is thy heart's desire at length accomplishéd.
And eke hath all befallen as my foreboding heart hath said.
"Dead lieth now the noble king of Burgundy,
Also youthful Giselher and Sir Gernot eke doth he.
The treasure no one knoweth but God and me alone,
Nor e'er by thee, she-devil, shall its hiding-place be known."
Quoth she: "But ill requital hast thou made to me.
Yet mine the sword of Siegfried now henceforth shall be,
The which when last I saw him, my loved husband bore,
In whom on me such sorrow through guilt of thine doth weigh full sore."
She drew it from the scabbard, nor might he say her nay,
Though thought she from the warrior his life to take away.
With both hands high she raised it and off his head struck she,
Whereat did grieve King Etzel full sore the sorry sight to see.
"To arms!" cried then the monarch: "here lieth foully slain
Beneath the hand of woman of all the doughtiest thane
That e'er was seen in battle or ever good shield bore!
Though foeman howsoever, yet grieveth this my heart full sore."
Quoth then the aged Hildebrand: "Reap no gain she shall,
That thus she dared to slay him. Whate'er to me befall,
And though myself in direst need through him have been,
By me shall be avengéd the death of Tronje's knight full keen."
In wrathful mood then Hildebrand unto Kriemhild sprung,
And 'gainst the queen full swiftly his massy blade he swung.
Aloud she then in terror 'fore Hildebrand did wail,
Yet that she shrieked so loudly, to save her what might that avail?
So all those warriors fated by hand of death lay strewn,
And e'en the queen full lofty in pieces eke was hewn.
Dietrich and royal Etzel at length to weep began,
And grievously they mournéd kinsmen slain and many a man.
Who late stood high in honor now in death lay low,
And fate of all the people weeping was and woe.
To mourning now the monarch's festal tide had passed,
As falls that joy to sorrow turneth ever at the last.
Nor can I tell you further what later did befall,
But that good knights and ladies saw ye mourning all,
And many a noble squire, for friends in death laid low.
Here hath the story ending, —that is the Nibelungen woe.

THE SAGA OF THORSTEIN, VIKING'S SON

By Rasmus Bjorn Anderson

I

A KING named Loge ruled that country which is north of Norway. Loge was larger and stronger than any other man in that country. His name was lengthened from Loge to Haloge, and after him the country was called Halogeland.

Loge was the fairest of men, and his strength and stature was like unto that of his kinsmen, the giants, from whom he descended. His wife was Glod, a daughter of Grim of Grimsgard, which is situated in Jotunheim in the north; and Jotunheim was at that time called Elivags (Elivagar in the north). Grim was a very great berserk; his wife was Alvor, a sister of Alf the Old. He ruled that kingdom which lies between two rivers, both of which were called Elfs, taking their name from him (Alf). The river south of his kingdom, dividing it from Gautland, the country of King Gaut, was called Gaufs Elf; the one north of it was called Raum's Elf, named after King Raum, and the kingdom of the latter was called Raum's-ric. The land governed by King Alf was called Alfheim, and all his offspring are related to the Elves.

They were fairer than any other people save the giants. King Alf was married to Bryngerd, a daughter of king Raum of Raum's-ric; she was a large woman, but she was not beautiful, because her father, king Raum, was ugly-looking, and hence ugly-looking and large men are called great 'raums.' King Haloge and his wife, queen Glod, had two daughters, named Eisa ('glowing embers') and Eimyrja ('embers'). These maids were the fairest in the land, on account of their parentage, for their father and mother were both very fair. But as fire and light make dark things bright, so these things took their names from the above-named maids. There lived with Haloge two jarls, named Vifil and Vesete, both of whom were large and strong men, and they were the warders of the king's land. One day the jarls went to the king, Vifil to woo Eimyrja and Vesete to woo Eisa; but the king refused both, on which account they grew so angry that they soon afterward carried the maids off, fleeing with them out of the land, and thus putting themselves out of his reach. But the king declared them outlaws in his kingdom, hindered them by witchcraft from ever again becoming dwellers in his land, and, moreover, enchanted their kinsmen, making these also outlaws, and deprived them of the benefit of their estates forever. Vesete settled in an island or holm, which hight Borgund's holm (Bornholm), and became the father of Bue and Sigurd, nicknamed Cape. Vifil sailed further to the east and established himself in an island called Vifil's Isle. With his wife, Eimyrja, he got a son, Viking by name, who in his early youth became a man of great stature and extraordinary strength.

II

THERE WAS a king who ruled folk of Sweden. With his queen he had an only child, a daughter, by name Hunvor, a maiden of unrivaled beauty and education. She had a magnificent bower, and was attended by a suite of maidens. Ingeborg hight the maiden, who was next to her in position, and she was a daughter of Herfinn, jarl of Woolen Acre. Most people said that Ingeborg was not inferior to the daughter of the king in any respect, excepting in strength and wisdom, which Hunvor possessed in a higher degree than all others in the land. Many kings and princes wooed Ingeborg, but she refused them all. She was thought to be a woman of boundless pride and insolence, and it was also talked by many that her pride and insolence might some day receive a check in some way or other.

Thus time passed on for a while. There was a mountain back of the king's residence so high that no human paths traversed it. One day a man — if he might be so called — came down from the mountain. He was larger and more fierce-looking than any person that had before been seen, and he looked more like a giant than like a human being. In his hand he held a bayonet-like two-pointed pike. This happened while the king was sitting at the table. This 'raum' came to the door of the hall and requested to be permitted to enter, but the porters refused to admit him. Then he smote the porters with his pike and pierced both of them from breast to back, one being pierced by one point of the pike and the other by the other: whereupon he lifted both of them over his head and threw their corpses down upon the ground behind him.

Then, entering the door, he approached the king's throne, and thus addressed him: As I, king Ring, have honored you so much as to visit you, I think it your duty to grant my request. The king asked what the request might be, and what his name was.

He answered: My name is Harek, the Ironhead, and I am a son of king Eol Kroppinbak (the humpback) of India; but my errand is that I wish you to place your daughter, your country, and your subjects in my hands. And, I think, most people will say that it is better for the kingdom that I rule it instead of you, who are destitute of strength and manhood, and moreover, enfeebled by age. But, as it may seem humiliating to you to surrender your kingdom, I will agree, on my part, to marry your daughter, Hunvor. But, if this is not satisfactory to you, I will kill you, take possession of your kingdom, and make Hunvor my concubine. Now the king felt sorely perplexed, for all the people were grieved at their conversation. Then said the king: It seems to me that we ought to know what she will answer. To this Harek assented. Then Hunvor was sent for, and the matter was explained to her.

She said: I like the looks of this man very well, although he seems likely to treat me with severity; but I consider him perfectly worthy of me, if I marry him; nevertheless, I wish to ask whether no ransom can be paid and I be free.

Yes, there can, answered Harek. If the king will try a holm-gang with me within four nights, or procure another man in his stead, then all powers shall be surrendered to the one slaying the other in the duel. Certainly, answered Hunvor, none can be found who is able to subdue you in a duel; nevertheless, I will agree to your proposition.

After this, Harek went out, but Hunvor betook herself to her bower, weeping bitterly. Then the king asked his men if there was nobody among them who regarded his daughter Hunvor a sufficient prize for which to risk his life in a holm-gang with Harek. But, although all wished to marry her, yet nobody was willing to risk the duel, looking upon it as certain death. Many also said that this fate was deserved by her, since she had refused so many, and marrying Harek would be a check to her pride. She had a manservant, by name Eymund, a fellow faithful to her and to be trusted in all matters. This man she sent for straightway on the same day, saying to him: It will not prove advisable to keep quiet; I want to send you away; take a boat and row to the island, which lies outside of Woolen Acre, and is called Vifil's Isle. On the island there is a byre; thither you must go and arrive there to-morrow at nightfall. You are to enter the western door of the byre, and when you have entered you will see a sprightly old man and an elderly woman; any other persons you will not see. They have a son by name Viking, who is now fifteen years old and a man of great ability, but he will not be present, I hope he will be able to help us out of our troubles; if not, I fear there will scarcely be any help for us. You must keep out of sight, but if you happen to see a third person, then throw this letter on his lap and hurry home.

Without delay, Eymund, with a company of eleven men, went on board a ship and sailed to Vifil's Isle. He goes ashore alone and proceeds to the byre, where he finds the fire-house and places himself behind the door. The bonde was sitting by the fire with his wife, and he seemed to Eymund a man of brave countenance. The fire was almost burnt out and the house was but faintly lighted by the embers.

Said the woman: I think, my dear Vifil, that it would prove to our advantage if our son Viking should present himself, for no one seems to be offering himself for combat, and the time for the duel with Harek is close at hand. I do not think it advisable, Eimyrja, answered he, for our son is yet young and rash, ambitious and careless. It will be his sudden death if he should be induced to fight with Harek; nevertheless, it is for you to manage this matter as you think best. Presently, a door opened back of the bonde, and a man of wonderful stature entered, taking his seat by the side of his mother. Eymund threw the letter on the lap of Viking, ran to the ship, came to Hunvor and told her how he had done his errand. Fate will now have to settle the matter, says Hunvor.

Viking took the letter, in which he found a greeting from the king's daughter, and, moreover, a promise that she would be his wife if he would fight with Harek, the Ironhead. At this Viking turned pale, observing which, Vifil asked him what letter that was. Viking showed him the letter. This I knew, said Vifil, and it would have been better, Eimyrja, if I had decided this matter myself, when we talked about it a little while ago, but what do you propose to do?

Says Viking: Would it not be well to save the princess?

Replied Vifil: It will be sudden death to you if you fight with Harek.

I will run the risk, answered Viking.

Then there is no remedy, says Vifil, but I will give you an account of his family and of himself.

III

TIRUS THE GREAT was king of India. He was an excellent ruler in every respect, and his queen was a very superior woman, with whom he had an only daughter, who hight Trona. She was the fairest among the fair, and, unlike the majority of her sex, she excelled all other princesses in wisdom. The Saga must also mention a man by name Kol, of whom a great many good things are told: first, that he was large as a giant, ugly-looking as the devil, and so well skilled in the black art that he could pass through the earth as well as walk upon it, could glue together steeds and stars; furthermore, he was so great a ham-leaper that he could burst into the shape of various kinds of animals; he would sometimes ride on the winds or pass through the sea, and he had so large a hump on his back that, although he stood upright, the hump would reach above his head.

This Kol went to India with a great army, slew Tirus, married Trona, and subjugated the land and the people. He begot many children with Trona, all of whom were more like their father than like their mother. Kol was nicknamed Kroppinbak (i.e. Humpback). He had three rare treasures. These were: a sword so mighty that none better was wielded at that time, and the name of this sword was Angervadil; another of the treasures was a gold ring, called Gleser; the third was a horn, and such was the nature of the beverage contained in the lower part of it that all who drank therefrom were attacked by an illness called leprosy, and became so forgetful that they remembered nothing of the past; but by drinking from the upper part of the horn their health and memory were restored.

Their eldest child was Bjorn, the Blue-tooth. His tooth was of a blue color, and extended an ell and a half out of his mouth; with this tooth he often, in battles or when he was violently in rage, put people to death. A daughter of Kol was Dis. The third child of Kol and Trona hight Harek, whose head at the age of seven was perfectly bald, and whose skull was as hard as steel, wherefore he was called Ironhead. Their fourth child hight Ingjald, whose upper lip measured an ell from the nose, whence he was called Ingjald Trana (the snout).

It was the pastime of the brothers when at home that Bjorn the Blue-tooth cut his tooth into the skull of his brother Harek with all his might without hurting him. No weapon could be made to stick in the lip of Ingjald Snout. By incantations Kol the Hump-back brought it about, that none of his offspring could be killed by any other weapon than by the sword Angervadil; no other iron can scathe them. But when Kol had become old enough he died a horrible death. At the time of his death Trona was pregnant, and gave birth to a son, called Kol after his father, and he was as like his father as he was akin to him. One year old, Kol was so ugly to children that he was nicknamed Kol Krappe (the crafty). Dis married Jokul Ironback, a blue berserk. She and her brothers divided their father's heritage betwixt themselves, so that Dis got the horn, but Bjorn Blue-tooth the sword, Harek the ring, Ingjald the kingdom, and Kol the personal property. Three winters after the death of king Kol, Trona married jarl Herfinn, a son of king Rodmar of Marseraland, and the first winter after they were married she bore him a son, named Framar, who was a man of great possibilities and unlike his brothers.

Now it seems to me, continued Vifil, that you ought not to risk your life in a duel with this Hel-strong man, whom no iron can scathe. Not so, answered Viking; I shall run the risk, whatsoever may be the result. And Vifil, seeing that Viking was in real earnest when he insisted on fighting with Harek, said: I can tell you still more about the sons of Kol. Vesete and I were wardens of king Haloge's country; during the summer seasons we used to wage wars, and once we met Bjorn Blue-tooth in Grening's Sound (the present Gronsund, between the Isle of Man and Palster in Denmark), and in such a manner did we fight that Vesete smote Bjorn's hand with his club, so that the sword fell from his hand, and then I caught it, flung it through him, and he lost his life. From that time I have worn the sword, and now I give it to you, my son.

Vifil then brought forth the sword and gave it to Viking, who liked it very much. Viking then prepared himself, went on board a boat, and came to the hall of the king on the day appointed for the duel. There everything was sad and dreary. Viking went before the king and greeted him. The king asked him his name. Viking told him the truth. Hunvor was sitting on one side of the king. Then Viking asked her whether she had requested him to come. She replied in the affirmative. Viking asked what terms he offered him for venturing a holm-gang with Harek. Replied the king: I will give you my daughter in marriage, and a suitable dowry besides. Viking gave his consent to this, and then he was betrothed to Hunvor; but it was the common opinion that it would be certain death to him if he should fight with Harek.

IV

THEN VIKING went to the holm, accompanied by the king and his courtiers. Thither came Harek, too, and asked who was appointed to fight with him.

Viking stepped forward and said: I am the man.

Whereto Harek made reply: I suppose it will be an easy matter to strike you to the ground, for I know it will be the end of you if I smite you with my fist.

But I suppose, answered Viking, that you consider it no trifling matter to fight with me, since you tremble at the very sight of me.

Harek replies: Not so, and I must save your life, since you go willingly into the open jaws of death; and do you smite first, according to the laws of holm-gang, for I am the challenger in this duel; but, in the meantime, I shall stand perfectly still, for I am not afraid of any danger.

At this time Viking drew his sword, Angervadil, from which lightning seemed to flash. Harek seeing this, said: I would never have fought with you had I known that you were in possession of Angervadil, and most likely it will turn out as my father said, namely, that I and my brothers and my sister would all be short-lived, excepting the one bearing his own name, and it was a great misfortune that Angervadil passed out of the hands of our family.

At this moment Viking struck Harek's skull and split his trunk from one end to the other, so that the sword stood in the ground to the hilt. Then the men of the king burst out in loud triumphant shouting, and the king went home to his hall with great joy.

Now they began to talk about preparing the wedding-feast, but Viking said he was not willing to be married yet; she shall remain betrothed, he said, and not be wedded till after three years, meanwhile I am going to wage war. So was done, and Viking went abroad with two ships. He was very successful, gaining victory in every battle; and after having spent two years as a viking, he landed at an island in the autumn at a time when the weather was fair and very warm.

V

THE SAME day as Viking landed at the island, he went ashore to amuse himself. He turned his steps to a forest and then he grew very hot. Having come to an open place in the forest, he sat down, and saw a woman of exquisite beauty walking along. She came up to him, greeted him very courteously, and he received her very kindly. They talked together a long time, and their conversation was very friendly. He asked her her name, and she said it was Solbjort (sun-bright). She then asked him if he was not thirsty, as he had walked so far, but Viking said he was not. She then took a horn, which she had kept under her cloak, offered him a drink from it, and he accepting it, and drinking therefrom, became sleepy, and bending his body into the lap of Solbjort, he fell asleep. But when he woke up again she had entirely disappeared. The drink had made him feel somewhat strange, and his whole body was shivering; the weather was gusty and cold, and he had forgotten nearly everything of the past, and least of all did he recollect Hunvor. He then went to his ship and departed from that place, and now he was confined to his bed by the disease called leprosy. He and his men frequently sailed near land, but were unwilling to go ashore and remain there.

After having suffered twelve months from this sickness it grew still more severe, and his body was covered with many sores. One day sailing to land, they saw three ships passing the harbor, and at their meeting they asked for each other's names. Viking told his name, but the other chieftain said his name was Halfdan, and that he was a son of Ulf. Halfdan was a large and strong-looking man, and when he had learned the condition of Viking he set on board his ship, where he found him very weak. Halfdan asked him the cause of his illness, and Viking told him everything that had happened.

Halfdan answered: Here the ham-leaper, Dis, Kol's daughter, has succeeded in her tricks, and I think it will be difficult to get any assistance from her in righting this matter, for she undoubtedly thinks she has avenged her brother, Harek Ironhead. Now I will offer you foster-brotherhood, and we will try whether we cannot revenge ourselves on Dis.

Answered Viking to this: Owing to my weakness, I have no hope at all of being able to kill Dis and her husband, Jokul Ironback, but such is my opinion of you, that even though I were in the best circumstances, your valor makes your offer very flattering to me.

And thus it was agreed that they should become foster-brothers. Halfdan had a great dragon, called Iron-ram; all of this ship that stood out of the water was ironclad; it rose high out of the sea, and was a very costly treasure. Having spent a short time there they left the place and went home to Svafe. Then Viking's strength diminished so that he became sick unto death. But when they had landed, Halfdan left the ships alone and proceeded until he came into an open space in a forest, where there stood a large rock, which he went up to and knocked at with his rod, and out of the rock there came a dwarf, who lived there and hight Lit (color), a warm friend of Halfdan, whom the dwarf greeted kindly and asked what his errand was. Replied Halfdan: It is now of great importance to me, foster-father, that you do my errand. What is it, my foster-son? asked Lit. I want you to procure for me the good horn of Dis, Kol's daughter, said Halfdan. Risk that yourself, said Lit, for it will be my death if I attempt it; and even the sacrifice of myself would be in vain, for you know there does not exist such a troll in the whole world as Dis. Replied Halfdan: I am sure you will do as well as you can. Upon this they parted, Halfdan returning to his ships and remaining there for some time.

VI

NOW IT must be told of king Ring that he and his daughter Hunvor dwelt in his kingdom after the slaying of Harek Ironhead, which seemed to all a deed of great daring. This event was heard of in India, and Ingjald Snout was startled by the tidings of Harek's death. He began to cut the war-arrow, and dispatched it throughout the whole country, thus collecting an army containing a crowd of people, among whom there were many of the rabble, and with this army he marched toward Sweden. He came there unexpected, and offered the king battle. The challenge was accepted without delay, although the king had but a few men, and the result of this battle was soon decided. King Ring fell, together with all his courtiers; but Ingjald took Hunvor and Ingeborg and carried them away to India. Jokul Ironback went to seek after the foster-brothers, wishing to revenge the death of his brother-in-law, Harek.

Now the story goes on to tell about Viking and Halfdan staying at Svafe. Seven nights had passed away when Lit met Halfdan and brought the horn to him. This made Halfdan very glad, and he went to Viking, whom almost everybody then thought to be not far from death, Halfdan put a drop of fluid from the upper part of the horn on Viking's lips. This brought Viking to his senses; he began to grow stronger and was like unto a person awakening from a slumber; and the uncleanness fell from him as scales fall from a fish. Thus he, day by day, grew better and was restored. After this they got ready to depart from Svafe, and directed their course north of Balegard-side. There they saw eighteen ships, all of large size and covered with black tents.

Said Halfdan: Here I think Jokul Ironback and his wife, the ham-leaper, are lying before us, and I do not know how Lit has parted with them, he being so exhausted that he could not speak. But now I think there is good reason for going to battle. Let everything of value be taken away from the ships, and let stones be put in instead. This was done. Then after a quick rowing to the strangers, they asked who the chieftains were. Jokul gave them his name and asked for their names in return. They said they hight Halfdan, and Viking. Then we need not ask what came to pass. A very hot battle took place, and the foster-brothers lost more men than Jokul, for the latter dealt heavy blows. Then Viking, followed by Halfdan, made an attempt to board Jokul's dragon, after which a great number of the crew of the dragon were slain. Jokul and Halfdan met and exchanged blows with each other; but although Jokul was the stronger, Halfdan succeeded in giving him a blow across the back with his sword; yet, in spite of his being without his coat-of-mail, the sword did not scathe him.

Meanwhile Viking came to Halfdan's assistance. He smote Jokul's shoulder and split his side, thus separating one arm and both feet, the one above the knee, from the trunk. Then Jokul fell, but was not yet dead, and said: I knew that when Dis had been forsaken by luck, much of evil was in store; the first of all was that the villain Lit betrayed her, and thus succeeded by tricks in stealing the horn from her and at the same time hurt her, so that she is still confined to her bed from the encounter; but I should also be inclined to think that he has not escaped without some injury himself either. Had she been on foot, the matter would not have resulted thus. But I am glad you have not got the princess Hunvor from my brother-in-law, Ingjald Snout. After this he soon died, and then a cry of victory was shouted and quarter was given to the wounded who could be cured. They got much booty there, and on shore they found Dis almost lifeless from the encounter with Lit. Her they seized, put a belg (whole skin) over her head, and stoned her to death. Hereupon they went back to Svafe and cured the wounds of their men. And having equipped twenty-four ships, all well furnished with men and weapons, they announced that they were bound for India.

VII

INGJALD SNOUT made great preparations, fortifying the walls of his burg and collecting a great number of people, some of which were rabble of the worst kind. As soon as the foster-brothers had landed they harried the country with fire and sword; everybody was in fear of them, and before Ingjald was aware of it they had made a great plunder.

Now he goes against them; they met, and a battle was fought. Halfdan and Viking thought they had never before been in so great danger as in this battle. The foster-brothers showed great bravery, and toward the end of the battle more men began to fall in Ingjald's army. The battle lasted four days, and at last none but Ingjald remained on his feet. He could not be wounded at all, and seemed to move through the air as easily as on the ground. Finally, by surrounding him with shields, they succeeded in getting him captive, put him in chains, and bound his hands with a bow-string. It was then so dark that they did not think it convenient to kill him on the spot, Viking being unwilling to slay a man at night-time.

They ran into the burg and carried Hunvor and Ingeborg away to their ships. Here they lay during the night; but in the morning the warders were dead, and Ingjald was not to be found, his chains lying unbroken and the bow-string not untied. No mark of iron could be found on the warders, and thus it was clear that Ingjald had made use of troll-craft. Now they hoisted their sails, left this country, and directed their course homeward to Sweden. Then Viking made preparations for the wedding, and married Hunvor. At the same time Halfdan began his suit and asked for the hand of Ingeborg, the daughter of the jarl. Word was sent to jarl Herfinn of Woolen Acre. He came and gave a favorable answer, and it was agreed that Halfdan should marry Ingeborg. Arrangements for the wedding were made, and the marriage ceremony was performed. The foster-brothers stayed there during the winter. The following summer they went abroad with ten ships, waged wars in the Baltic, and having got great booty they returned home in the fall.

Thus they lived as vikings three years, spending only the winters at home; and none were more famous than they. One summer they sailed to Denmark; here they harried and entered the Limfjord, where they saw nine ships and a dragon lying at anchor. They immediately directed their fleet toward these ships, and asked for the name of the commander. He said he hight Njorfe, and added: I am the ruler of the Uplands In Norway, and I have just gotten my paternal heritage; but what is the name of those who have just come? They told him this.

Said Halfdan: I will offer to you, as to other vikings two conditions: the one that you give up your fee, ships and weapons, and go ashore free; and the other, that you fight a battle with us.

Answered Njorfe: This seems to me hard terms, and I choose rather to defend my fee, and, if need be, fall with bravery, than to flee feeless and dishonored, although you have a larger army and ships of greater size and number than mine.

Said Viking: We shall not be so mean as to attack you with more ships than you have; five of our ships shall therefore be idle during the battle.

Answered Njorfe: This is bravely spoken.

And so they got ready for the battle, which then began. They fought with their ships stem to stem. The attack was very violent on both sides, for Njorfe fought with great daring, and the foster-brothers also showed great bravery.

Three days they fought, but still they did not seem to know who would win. Asked then Viking: Is there much fee in your ships?

Answered Njorfe: No, for from those places where we have been harrying this summer the bondes fled with their fee, and hence but little booty has been taken. Said Viking: Unwise it seems to me to fight only for the sake of outdoing each other, and thus spill the blood of many men; but are you willing to form a league with us?

Answered Njorfe: It will be good for me to form a league with you, although you are not a king's son, for I know that your father was a jarl, and an excellent man; and I am willing to have a foster-brotherhood formed between us on the condition that you hight jarl and I king, according to our birth-right, which must remain unchanged whether we are in my kingdom or in any other.

During this talk Halfdan was silent. Viking asked why he had so little to say in this matter. Answered Halfdan: It seems to me that it may be good to make such an agreement betwixt you; but I shall not be surprised if you should get to feel that some or other of Njorfe's relatives become burdensome to you. I will, however, have nothing to do with this matter — will neither dissuade nor encourage you.

The result was, that Njorfe and Viking came to terms and formed a foster-brotherhood, giving oaths mutually on the terms which have before been stated. They waged wars during the summer and took much booty; but in the fall they parted, Njorfe going to Norway, and Viking, accompanied by Halfdan, to Sweden. But soon after Viking had come home, Hunvor was taken sick and died. They had a son, who hight Ring. He was brought up in Sweden until he was full-grown, and became a king of that country. He did not live long, but had a great many descendants. The foster-brothers kept on waging wars every summer and became very famous: during their warfares they gathered so many ships that they had fifty in all.

VIII

IT MUST be told of Ingjald Snout, that he gathered an innumerable army and went to search for the foster-brothers, Viking and Halfdan.

And one Summer they met in the Baltic, Ingjald having forty ships. It came straightway to a fight, and they fought in such a manner that it was not easy to see which side would win. At last Viking, immediately followed by Njorfe and Halfdan, tried to board Ingjald's dragon.

They made a great havoc, killing one man after the other. Then Ingjald rushed toward the stern of the dragon, with a great atgeir (javelin) ready for slaughter. Now the foster-brothers attacked Ingjald, and although they fought a large part of the day with him they did not wound him, and when the fight seemed to Ingjald to grow very hot, he sprang overboard, followed by Njorfe and Halfdan, both swimming as fast as they could. Viking did not stop fighting before he had slain every man on the dragon, after which he jumped into a boat and rowed ashore. Ingjald kept swimming till he reached the land, and then Halfdan and Njorfe were drawing near to the surf. Ingjald took a stone and threw it at Halfdan, but he dodged under the water. Meanwhile Njorfe landed, and Halfdan soon after him, in another place. They attacked Ingjald mightily, and having fought thus for a long time, they heard a great crash, and looked thither whence they heard the crash, but on turning their faces back, Ingjald was out of sight, and instead of him there was a grim-looking boar, that left nothing undone as he attacked them, so they could do nothing but defend themselves. When this had been done for some time, the boar turned upon Halfdan, bearing away the whole calf of his leg.

Straightway came Viking and smote the bristles of the boar, so that his back was cut in two. Then seeing that Ingjald lay dead on the spot, they kindled a fire and burned him to ashes. Now they went back to their ships and bound up the wounds of Halfdan. After this they sailed away from this place north to an isle called Thruma, and ruled by a man who hight Betil a son of the sea-king Meli. He had a daughter who hight Finna, a maid of surpassing fairness and accomplishments. Viking courted her, and with king Njorfe's help, and Halfdan's bravery, the marriage was agreed to. Then the foster-brothers ended their warfaring. King Njorfe established himself in his kingdom, and Viking took his abode with him and became his jarl, but Halfdan was made a great herser and dwelt on his byre, called Vags. His land was separated by a mountain from that which was ruled by jarl Viking. They held to their friendship as long as they lived, but it was more cold between Halfdan and Njorfe.

IX

A KING, hight Olaf, ruled Fjord-fylke (the county of the fjords). He was a son of Eystein and a brother of Onund, who was the father of Ingjald the Wicked. They were all unsafe and wicked in their dealings. King Olaf had a daughter who hight Bryngerd, whom Njorfe married, took her with him, and got with her nine sons: Jokul hight the eldest of these brothers; the rest hight Olaf, Grim, Geiter, Teit, Tyrfing, Bjorn, Geir, Grane and Toke. They were all promising men, though Jokul far surpassed them all in all accomplishments.

He was so haughty that he thought everything below himself. Olaf stood next to him, as a man skillful in all deeds; but he was of a noisy, troublesome and overbearing temperament, and the same might be said of all his brothers, and they boasted very much. Viking had nine sons, the eldest of whom was Thorstein, and the others hight Thorer, Finn, Ulf, Stein, Bomund, Finnboge, Eystein and Thorgeir. They were hopeful men, of great skill in action, though Thorstein held the highest rank among them in everything. He was the largest and strongest of men; he was popular, steadfast in his friendship, faithful and reliable in all things. He could not easily be provoked to do harm, but when attacked he revenged himself grimly. If he was insulted, it could scarcely be seen in his daily life whether he liked it or not, but long afterward he would act as if he had just been injured. Thorer was of a most sanguine and vehement temperament; if injured or affronted he would suddenly be seized by an irresistible rage, and, no matter whom he had to do with, or what the result might be, he never hesitated to do whatsoever came into his mind. He was a most adroit man in all kinds of games, and a man of uncommon strength. He was second only to his brother Thorstein. These young men grew up together in the kingdom. In the mountain separating Viking's and Halfdan's lands, there was a chasm of fearful depth and of a breadth of thirty ells at the narrowest, so that it was perfectly impassable for human beings, and hence the mountain was not crossed by any paths. It had been tried by king Njorfe and jarl Viking and Halfdan how easily they might leap over the chasm. The result was, that Viking had leaped over it in full armor, Njorfe had done it in his lightest clothes, but Halfdan had only done it by being received on the other side by Viking. Now they all kept quiet for a long time, and the friendship of jarl Viking and king Njorfe remained unimpaired.

X

NJORFE AND Viking became old, and their sons were rapidly advancing in growth. Jokul became in all things a violent and restless man. The sons of Njorfe were of nearly the same age as the sons of Viking, the youngest ones being at this point of our Saga about twelve years old, while Thorstein and Jokul were at the age of twenty.

The sons of Njorfe used to play with the sons of Viking, and the latter were in no way below the former. This made the sons of the king very jealous, and in their jealousy, as in all other things, Jokul surpassed all; and it was easy to see that Thorstein yielded to Jokul in all things, nor was this any reproach to him. Thorstein far surpassed all his brothers and all other men known. Jarl Viking had warned his sons not to vie with the sons of the king in any games, but rather to spare their strength and eagerness. One day the king's sons and the sons of Viking were playing ball, and the game was played very eagerly by the sons of Njorfe. Thorstein, as usual, checked his zeal. He was placed against Jokul, and Thorer was placed against Olaf, and the others were placed in the same manner, according to their age. Thus the day was spent. It happened that Thorer threw the ball on the ground so hard that it bounded over Olaf and fell down again far off.

At this Olaf turned angry, thinking that Thorer was mocking him. He fetched the ball; but when he came back the game was being broken up, and the people were going home. Olaf then with the ball-club struck after Thorer, who, seeing it, dodged the blow in such a manner that the club touched his head and wounded it.

But Thorstein, together with many other people, hurried betwixt them and parted them. Said Jokul: I suppose you think it a thing of no great weight that Thorer got a bump on his head. Thorer blushed at Jokul's words, and thus they parted. Said Thorer then: I have left my gloves behind, and if I do not fetch them Jokul will lay it to my fear. Answered Thorstein: I do not think it advisable that you and Olaf meet. Nevertheless I will go, said Thorer, for they have gone home. So saying, he turned back at a swinging pace, and when he came to the play-ground everybody had left it. Then Thorer turned his steps toward the hall of the king. At the same moment the sons of the king also came home to the hall, and stood near the wall of the hall. Then Thorer turned toward Olaf and stabbed his waist, so that the spear passed through his body; whereupon he withdrew and escaped out of their hands. They, on the other hand, had a great ado over Olaf's corpse; but Thorer went until he found his brother. Now asked him Thorstein: Why is there blood on your spear, brother? Answered Thorer: Because I do not know whether Olaf has not perhaps been wounded by the point of it. Said Thorstein: You perhaps tell of his death. Quoth Thorer: It may be that Jokul will not be able to heal the wound of his brother Olaf, though he be a very skillful man in almost all things. Answered Thorstein: This is a sorry thing that now has happened; for I know that my father will dislike it.

And when they came home jarl Viking was out-doors, and looked very stern. Said he: What I looked for from you, Thorer, has now come to pass, that you would be the most luck-forsaken of all my sons. This you have shown, as I think, by killing the son of the king himself. Answered Thorstein: Now is the time, father, to help your son, although he has fallen into ill-luck; and that you know means for this purpose I think you have shown by your being aware of Olaf's death while nobody had told you of it.

Answered Viking: I am unwilling to sacrifice so much as to break my oaths for the life of Thorer; for both of us, king Njorfe and I, have sworn to be faithful and trusty to each other, both in private and public matters. These oaths he has kept in all matters. Now I will not, therefore, show myself worse than he has been; but this I would do if I should fight against him, for there was a time when king Njorfe was as dear to me as my own sons, and it needs not be hinted at that I should give Thorer any help; he must leave, and never more come before my eyes.

Answered Thorstein: Why should not all of us brothers then leave home? for we will not part with Thorer, but stand by one another for weal or for woe. Answered the jarl: That is a matter that rests with you, my son; but great I must call the ill-luck of Thorer, if he is to be the cause of my losing all my sons and my friendship with the king too, who is the doughtiest man in all things, and besides these, my life, which is, however, worth but little. But there is one thing that makes me glad, and that is that it will not fall to the lot of any one to put you to death, although your escape will be narrow enough, and this will all be caused by Thorer's ill-luck; nevertheless, the loss of him will be felt on account of his valor.

Now, my son Thorstein, here is a sword, which I will give to you; Angervadil is its name, and it has always had victory with it; my father took it from Bjorn Blue-tooth at his death. I have no other distinguished weapons except an old kesia, which I took from Harek Ironhead; but I know that nobody is able to wield it as a weapon. Now if you are going to leave home, my son Thorstein, then it is my advice that you go up to a lake named Vener; there you will find a boat belonging to me, standing in a boat-house; go in it to a holm which lies in the lake; there you will find in a shed food and clothes enough to last you twelve months; take good care of the boat, for there are no more ships in the neighborhood. Hereupon the brothers parted with their father. The brothers all had good clothes and armor, which had been given them by their father before this happened. Thorstein and his brothers went until they found the boat. Then they rowed to the holm, and found the shed; here was enough of all things which they needed, and they took up their abode there.

XI

NOW IT is to be told that Jokul and his brothers told of the death of Olaf to their father.

Said Jokul: This is the only thing to be done, that we bring together an array and march to the house of Viking and burn him and all his sons alive in their house, and even this would scarcely be vengeance enough for Olaf's death.

Said Njorfe: I wholly forbid that any harm be done to Viking, for I know that my son has not been slain by his advice, and no one is guilty of this but Thorer. But Viking and I have sworn to each other an oath of brotherhood, and this oath he has kept better than anyone else, and hence I shall not wage any war against him, for I do not think Olaf will be atoned for in the least by slaying Thorer, and thus giving more grief to Viking. And so Jokul did not get any help in this matter from his father. Olaf was buried with the usual ceremonies of olden times, and from this time Jokul began to keep a suite of men.

King Njorfe was already growing very old, so that Jokul for the most part had to ward the land. One day it happened that two men went before Njorfe, both dressed in blue frocks. They greeted the king. He asked them for their names. One of them said he hight Oautan, the other said he hight Ogautan, and they bade the king give them winter quarter. Answered the king: To me you look ugly, and I will not receive you. Said Jokul: Have you any accomplishments? Answered Ogautan: As to that, we have not much to boast of; still we know many more things than people have spoken to us about. Said Jokul: It seems best to me then that you enter my suite and stay with me. So they did. Jokul did well by them. It had been heard at the king's hall that Viking had banished his sons. Jokul was unwilling to believe it, and went to Viking with a large suite. Viking asked what his errand was, and Jokul asked him what he knew about the miscreant Thorer. Viking told him that he had banished his sons, so that they did not live there. Jokul asked to be allowed to search the rooms of the house. Viking granted this, but said the king would not have thought that he would deceive him. They then searched the rooms, but, as might be expected, found nothing; and having done this they returned home.

Jokul did not like that he heard nothing of the brothers, and so he said to Ogautan and his comrade: Would not you by your cunning be able to find out where the brothers have their dwelling-place?

I guess not, answered Ogautan; you are nevertheless to let me and my brother have a house to sleep in, and nobody must come there before you, nor must you visit the house until after three days. Jokul saw that this was done, and a small separate house was assigned for them to sleep in.

Jokul positively forbade all people mentioning them, and he threatened the transgressor of his orders with certain death. Early on the day agreed upon Jokul came to the house of the brothers.

Said then Ogautan: You are too hasty, Jokul, for I have just awaked; still I can tell you about the sons of Viking. You know, I suppose, where there is a lake called Vener. In it is a holm, and on the holm a shed, and there are the sons of Viking.

Answered Jokul: If what you say is so, then I have no hope of their being overtaken.

Said Ogautan: In all things you seem to me to act like a motherless child, and I do not think you will be able to do much alone. Now I will tell you, continued Ogautan, that I have a belg (skin-bag) called the weather-belg. If I shake it, storm and wind will blow out of it, together with such biting frost and cold that within three nights the lake shall be covered with so strong an ice that you may cross it on horseback if you wish.

Said Jokul: Really you are a man of great cunning; and this is the only way of reaching the holm, for there are no ships before you get to the sea, and nobody can carry them so far. Hereupon Ogautan took his belg and shook it, and out of it there came so fearful a snowstorm and such biting frost that nobody could be out of doors. This was a thing of great wonder to all; and after three nights every water and fjord was frozen. Then Jokul gathered together men to the number of thirty. King Njorfe did not like this journey, and said his mind told him it would cause him more and not less sorrow; for in this journey, he said, I will lose the most of my sons and a great many other men. It would have been better if we, according to my will in the beginning, had come to terms with Thorer, and thus kept the friendship of jarl Viking and his sons.

XII

NOW JOKUL got himself ready for the journey together with his thirty men, and besides them Gautan and Ogautan.

The same morning Thorstein awoke in his shed and said: Are you awake, Thorer?

Answered he: I am, but I have been sleeping until now.

Said Thorstein: It is my will that we get ourselves ready for leaving the shed, for I know that Jokul will come here today together with many men.

Answered Thorer: I do not think so, and I am unwilling to go at all; or have you any sign of this?

I dreamt, said Thorstein, that twenty-two wolves were running hither, and besides them there were seven bears, and the eighth one, a red-cheeked bear, large and grim-looking. And besides these there were two she-foxes leading the party; the latter were very ugly-looking, and seemed to me the most disgusting of all. All the wolves attacked us, and at last they seemed to tear to pieces all my brothers excepting you alone, and yet you fell. Many of the bears we slew, and all the wolves I killed, and the smaller one of the foxes, but then I fell.

Asked Thorer: What do you think this dream means?

Made answer Thorstein: I think that the large red-cheeked bear must be the fylgia (follower, guardian-spirit) of Jokul, and the other bears the fylgias of his brothers; but the wolves undoubtedly were, to my mind, as many as the men who came with them; for, certainly they are wolfishly-minded toward us. But besides them there were two she-foxes, and I do not know any men to whom such fylgias belong; I therefore suppose that some persons hated by almost everybody have lately come to Jokul, and thus these fylgias may belong to them. Now, I have told you this my thought about the matter, and we will have to act in the manner pointed out to me in my sleep, and I would that we might avoid all trouble.

Says Thorer: I think your dream has been nothing but a scare-crow and idle forebodings, still it would not be uninteresting to try our mutual strength. Quoth Thorstein: I do not think so; it seems to me that an unequal meeting is intended, and I should like that we might get ready to go away from here. Thorer said he would not go away, and it had to be as he would have it. Thorstein arose and took his weapons, and all his brothers did likewise, but Thorer was very slow about it. At the very time when they had gotten themselves ready, Jokul came up with his men. The shed had two doors, one of which Thorstein guarded together with three of his brothers, the other was guarded by Thorer together with four men. A sharp attack then began; the brothers warded themselves bravely, but Jokul attacked the door warded by Thorer so strongly that three of his brothers fell, but one of them was driven out of the door to the spot where Thorstein stood.

Thorer still guarded the door for a while, being by no means willing to yield. Then he tarned out of the door and found his way among the enemies down upon the ice. They surrounded him, but he defended himself very bravely. Thorstein seeing this, ran out of the shed together with those of his brothers who were yet alive, went down onto the ice where Thorer was standing, and now a fierce combat took place. Thorstein and Thorer dealt many heavy blows, and at last all the brothers had fallen excepting Thorstein and Thorer; and all the sons of Njorfe had also fallen save Jokul and Grim. Then Thorstein became very weary, so that he was hardly able to stand. He saw that he would fall; and of the opposite party all had fallen but Gautan and Ogautan. Now Thorer was both weary and wounded, and the night was already growing very dark. Just then Thorstein turned against Gautan and stabbed him through his body with Angervadil, so that he fell to the ground among the other dead bodies. Then three men, Jokul, Grim, and Ogautan, arose and searched for Thorstein among the slain, and they thought they had found him, but the person they found was Jokul's brother, Finn, for they were so much like each other that it was impossible to know them apart. Grim said Thorstein was dead. Said Ogautan: That shall be put beyond a doubt, and he cut his head off, but of course it did not bleed, for he was already dead. After this they went home. King Njorfe asked them how the meeting had turned out, and learning this, he did not approve it at all, saying that he now had lost much more than his son Olaf, his seven sons and many other men having died. Now Jokul kept quiet.

XIII

IN THE next place it is to be told that Thorstein lay among the slain so tired out that he was wholly unable to help himself, but he was but little wounded. And toward the end of the night he heard a wagon coming along the ice. Then he saw a man following the wagon, and he saw that the man was his father. And when the man came to the field of battle, he cleared his way, throwing the dead out of his path, but he threw none with more force than the sons of the king. He saw that all were dead except Thorstein and Thorer. He then asked them whether they could speak at all, and Thorer said that he could. Still Viking saw that he was covered with gaping wounds. Thorstein said that he was not wounded, but very tired.

Viking took Thorer in his lap, and then it seemed to Thorstein that his father, in spite of his age, showed great strength. Thorstein went to the wagon himself and laid himself in it with his weapons. Then Viking drove on with the wagon. The weather began to grow dark and cloudy, and it changed so fast that, in a very little while, the whole ice seemed to Viking to give way. Just at the time when they had landed, all the ice had melted out of the lake. Then Viking went home to his bed-chamber. Close by his bed was the entrance to an underground dwelling, and down into it he took his sons; in it was enough of food and drink, and clothing, and all things that might be needed. Viking healed the wounds of his son Thorer, for he was a good leech. One end of the house stood in a forest; and here Viking very strongly warned his sons never to leave the underground dwelling, for he said it was sure that Ogautan would straightway find out that they were alive; and then, added he, we may soon look for a war. As to this they made good promises.

Time passed on until Thorer became altogether whole again. It was now talked abroad throughout the country that all the sons of Viking were dead; but nevertheless, it was talked somewhat after Ogautan that it was not sure whether Thorer was dead or not. Then Jokul bade him seek and try to find out with certainty where Thorer had his dwelling-place. Now Ogautan fell into deep thinking, but still he did not become any surer about Thorer.

One day it happened that Thorer said to Thorstein; I am getting very tired of staying in this underground dwelling, now the weather is fine, and my will is that we take a walk into the forest to amuse ourselves.

Answered Thorstein: I will not, for we would then break the bidding of our father.

Nevertheless, I shall go, said Thorer.

Thorstein had no mind to stay behind, and so they went to the forest and spent the day there amusing themselves. But in the evening, when they were about to go home again, they saw a little she-fox scenting round about her in all directions, and sniffing under every tree.

Said Thorer: What Satanic being goes there, brother?

Answered Thorstein: I really do not know; it seems to me that I have once seen something like it, namely, the night before Jokul's visit to the shed, and I think that we here have the cursed Ogautan. He then took a spear, which he shot at the fox, but she crept down into the ground. After this they went home to their underground dwelling, and did not let on that anything had happened. Shortly afterward, jarl Viking came there and said: Now you have done a bad thing, having broken what I bade you, by leaving the cave, and thus Ogautan has found out that you are here. I therefore expect the brothers soon will come with war upon us.

XIV

SHORTLY AFTER this, Ogautan had a talk with Jokul and said: It is indeed true that I am your right and not your left hand.

What is there now about that? asked Jokul.

Answered Ogautan: It is that the brothers, Thorer and Thorstein, are still alive at Viking's, and are hid by him.

Answered Jokul: Then I will gather together men, and not give up till we have their lives.

Jokul got together eighty men, among whom there were thirty of the king's courtiers, all well busked as to clothes. In the evening they were busked for setting out, being about to leave the next morning. Two young loafers, of whom the one hight Vott and the other Thumal, had just come there, and when they had just gone to bed in the evening, Vott spoke to Thumal: Do you not think it is wise, brother, that we arise and go to Viking, and tell him of Jokul's plans, for I know it will be the bane of Viking if they come upon him unawares, and it is our duty to go and help him.

Made answer Thumal: You are very foolish; do you not think that the watchmen will become aware of us if we travel by night, and then we shall be killed without giving any help to Viking.

Said Vott: You always show that you are a coward; but although you dare not move a step, I will nevertheless go and tell Viking what is about being done, for I would gladly lose my life if I could hinder the death of Viking and his sons, for he has often been kind to me. Then Vott arose and dressed himself, and likewise did also Thumal, for the latter had now no mind of staying in the bed alone.

Now they went their way, and came to Viking's at midnight, and aroused him from his sleep. Vott told him that Jokul was to be looked for there with a large number of men. Said Viking: Well have you done, dear Vott, and your deed surely deserves a reward. Then Viking called together some men from the neighborhood, so that he had thirty men. Then he went down to his sons in the cave, and told them the state of things.

Said Thorer: They shall be withstood if they come, for we will come up out of the cave and fight together with you.

Answered Viking: You shall not! Let us first see how our fight may turn out, and if it should look hopeless to me, then I will go to that place below which is your cave and make a great noise, and then you must come and help me. Thorstein said he would do so, and so Viking went away.

After daybreak Viking and all his men took their weapons. He took the kesia called Harek's loom in his hand; but everybody thought he would not be able to wield it on account of its weight, he being so old. A wonderful change then seemed to take place; for as soon as Viking had put on the armor he seemed to be young a second time.

A large yard was enclosed by a high wall, in front of Viking's byre; it formed a very good vantage ground, and here he and his men busked themselves for the battle, and weapons were given to Vott and Thumal.

XV

NOW IT is to be told that Jokul busked himself and all his army for starting early the next morning, and he did not halt in his march before he came to the dwellings of Viking. Viking was standing outside upon the wall of the yard, and bade Jokul and all his men come in.

Answered Jokul: Quite otherwise have you deserved than that we should accept your invitation; our errand here is that you give up those mishap-bringing men, Thorstein and Thorer.

I will not do it, answered Viking; nevertheless I will not deny that both of them have been here, but I would sooner give up myself than them. Now you may attack us if you like, but I and my men will ward ourselves. They now made a hard attack, but Viking and his men warded themselves bravely. Thus some time passed. Then Jokul tried to scale the wall. Viking and his men slew many men; but now all his own men began to fall. Then Viking went to the place over the underground dwelling, struck his shield hard, and made a fearful noise. This Thorer heard, and said to Thorstein: We ought to make haste, and for all that we may be too late, for I think our father has fallen already. Thorstein said he was quite ready, and when they came out only Vott and Thumal and three other men were standing with Viking. Nevertheless Viking was not wounded yet; he was only very tired. As soon as the brothers came out, Thorstein turned to the spot where Jokul was standing, but Thorer went where Ogautan and his men stood. Twelve of king Njorfe's men attacked Viking and his men. Viking warded himself, and was not wounded by the men who were against him. Their leader hight Bjorn.

In a short time Thorer slew all the followers of Ogautan, and stabbed at him with his sword, but Ogautan thrust himself down into the ground, so that only the soles of his feet could be seen. Thorstein attacked Jokul.

Said Vott: It is well that you are trying each other's bravery, for Jokul never could bear to hear that Thorstein was a match for him in anything.

Now there was a very hard battle between Thorstein and Jokul, and it so turned out that Jokul, scarred with many wounds, bounded back, and fell down outside of the wall. But when Jokul had gone away, Viking gave quarter to the men of the king's court that still were alive, and sent them away with suitable gifts, begging them to bring his friendly greetings to king Njorfe.

And when Jokul came home, Ogautan was there already, Jokul blamed him bitterly for having fled before anybody else. To this made answer Ogautan: It was not possible to stay in the fight any longer, and truly it may be said that we there had to do with trolls rather than with men. But Jokul found that his words rather overdid the matter. Somewhat later king Njorfe's men, to whom quarter had been given by Viking and his men, came home, bringing Viking's greetings to king Njorfe, and telling him of all the kind treatment they had gotten from Viking.

Said the king: Truly is Viking unlike most other men, on account of his high-mindedness and all his bravery, and now, my son Jokul, I speak the truth when I solemnly forbid any war to be waged against Viking from this time forward.

Answered Jokul: I cannot bear to have the slayers of my brothers in the garth next to me, and in a word. I declare that Viking and his sons shall never live in peace so far as I am concerned, and I shall never cease persecuting them before they are all sent to Hel (the goddess of death).

Answered the king: Then I shall try and see who of us two is the more blest with friends, for with all those who are willing to follow me I will go and help Viking; it seems to me to be of great weight that you do not become the bane of Viking, for if that should follow, I would be forced to do one of two things, either to have you killed, and that would be the cause of evil talk, or to break my oaths which I have sworn, namely, that I would avenge Viking if I should outlive him. And thus he ended his speech.

Viking had a talk with his sons, and said to them: Owing to Jokul's power I dare not keep you here; but there is another matter of still more weight, and that is, that I do not want any discord to arise between me and king Njorfe. Said Thorstein: What will you then advise us to do? Answered Viking: There is a man, by name Halfdan, who rules over Vags; Vags is on the other side of yonder mountain. Halfdan is my old friend and foster-brother. To him I will send you, and commend you to his good will; but there are many dangerous hindrances in the way, especially two hut-dwellers (robbers), one of whom is worse to deal with than the other; the name of one of them is Sam, and the other is hight Fullafle; the latter has a dog called Gram, with which it is almost as dangerous to deal as with the robber himself. Now I am not sure that you will reach Vags, though you may escape both of these robbers, for there is a chasm along the mountain so deep and broad that I do not know any one who has passed it but my foster-brothers and myself; but I should indeed think it more likely that Thorstein might pass it, whereas I feel less hopeful about Thorer.

Shortly afterward the brothers busked themselves for setting out, having all their weapons with them. Then Viking gave the kesia to Thorer; he handed a gold ring to his son Thorstein, begging him to give it to Halfdan as a token of their old friendship.

Now be patient my son Thorer, says Viking; although Halfdan may be peevish toward you, or does not look much to you or your errand. Then the sons took leave of their father, who was so deeply moved that the tears trickled down his cheeks. Viking looked after them as they were going away, and said: I shall never in my life see you again, and nevertheless you, my son Thorstein, will reach an old age, and become a very distinguished man; and now farewell, and all hail to you both. Then the old man returned home, but his sons climbed the mountain until they reached a hut in the evening. The door was half shut. Thorer stepped over to it, and by using all his strength, he pushed it open; and when they had entered the hut, they saw there a great deal of wares and supplies of all kinds. There was a large bed.

And at nightfall the hut-dweller, a man of somewhat frowning look, came home. He said: Are you here, you mishap-bringing men, you sons of Viking, Thorstein and Thorer, who have slain seven of the sons of Njorfe? And now all their ill-luck shall come to an end, for it will be an easy matter for me to strike you to the ground.

Who is that, says Thorer, who so boastingly insults us?

Answered the robber: My name is Sam: I am the son of Svart; my brother's name is Fullafle; he is boss in the other hut.

Said Thorstein; I see that feyness calls on us two brothers, if you alone kill both of us, and therefore I do not hesitate to test our valor, but Thorer shall stand by without taking any part in our combat.

At the same time Sam ran suddenly under Thorstein with so great speed, that the latter lost the hold he had gotten, but still did not fall.

Then Thorer ran to Sam, stabbing him with his kesia in one side so that it came out at the other side, and thus Sam fell down dead.

So they stopped there during the night and had a good rest, for there was plenty of food. They made the hut warm, but did not carry away any fee with them. In the morning they left the hut, but in the evening of the same day they came to another but, much larger than the former one. There also the door was half shut. Thorer stepped over to the door, intending to push it open, but he could not. He used all his strength, but still the door would not open. Then Thorstein stepped over to the door, and pushed it until it gave way, and so they went into the hut. On the one side there was a stack of wares and on the other one of logs; a bed was placed in the inner part of the hut, crosswise, and it was so large that they were surprised at its size. At one end of the bed was something like a large, round bedstead, and they judged that it must be the couch of the dog Gram. They then seated themselves and built a fire before them, and long after nightfall they heard heavy footsteps outside; presently the door was opened, and a giant of stupendous stature entered, carrying bound on his back a large bear, and a string of fowl on his breast. He laid his burden down on the floor, saying: Fie! here I have the miscreants, the sons of Viking, who, on account of their ill-fated deeds, are held in the worst repute throughout the whole land. But how did you escape the hands of my brother Sam?

We escaped in such a manner, said Thorstein, that he lay dead on the spot. You have taken advantage of him in his sleep, said Fullafle. By no means, said Thorstein, for we fought with him, and my brother Thorer slew him. I shall not act as a nithing toward you tonight, says Fullafle; you shall stay till to-morrow morning, and have what food you want.

Then the hut-dweller cut his game to pieces, took a table and put victuals on it, whereupon they all took to eating, and after their supper they went to bed. The two brothers slept together in some marketable cloaks. The dog growled as they passed by him. Neither party tried to deceive the other. In the morning both parties arose early. Said Fullafle: Now, Thorstein, let us try each other's strength, but let Thorer fight with my dog in another place. Answered Thorstein: That shall be according to your wish.

Now they went out of the hut and over on the lawn which fronted it, and suddenly the dog, with his jaws wide open, leaped upon Thorer. Both Thorer and the dog fought fiercely, for the dog warded off every blow with his tail, and when Thorer tried to pierce him with his kesia, he escaped by biting the weapon at every stab. Thus they fought for three hours, and Thorer had not yet succeeded in wounding him. Once Gram suddenly darted upon Thorer and bit a slice out of his calf. At the same time Thorer stabbed the dog with his kesia, pinning him down to the ground, and soon after Gram expired. But of Fullafle it is to be told that he had a large meker (Anglo-Saxon mece, a kind of sword) in his hand, and Thorstein had his sword also. They had a long and severe struggle; for Fullafle was wont to deal heavy blows, but as Angervadil bit armor no less than flesh, he fell dead, and Thorstein was wholly without a wound.

XVI

NOW THE brothers busked themselves for leaving, and continued their walk until they reached a great chasm, which it seemed to Thorstein it would be very dangerous to pass. Nevertheless, he made himself ready to leap over the abyss, and did it. He was immediately followed by Thorer, but when Thorstein had reached the other side of the chasm and looked round, Thorer had just reached the same side and was falling down into the chasm. Thorstein succeeded, however, in seizing him and pulling him up again.

Said Thorstein then: Brother, you always show that you are a dauntless fellow; so you did now, too, for you might know that it would be certain death to you if you should fall into the chasm. It did not happen this time, answered Thorer, for you saved me, as you have so often done before. Then they proceeded on their journey until they came to a large river, which was both deep and rapid. Thorstein said they must look for the ford, but without delay. Thorer waded into the river, and not far from the bank the water was so deep that the bottom could not be reached, and therefore he had to sustain himself by swimming. Thorstein, not being minded to be standing on the bank, threw himself into the river and swam after him. Thus they reached the other bank, where they wrung their wet clothes. But while they were doing this the weather grew so bitterly cold that their clothes froze hard as a stone, and so they could not put them on. At the same time a fearful snow storm arose, and it was thought that Ogautan was the cause of it.

Thorstein asked Thorer what was the best thing for them to do. Answered Thorer: I think we can do nothing better than to dip our clothes in the river, for in cold water things soon thaw out. So they did, and thereby were able to put on their clothes again. Then they went on until they came to the byre of Vags. It being night when they came there, the door of the house was locked, so they could not enter. They kept knocking at the door a long time, but nobody came to it. In the yard lay a beam twenty fathoms long. This they brought upon the roofs of the houses, and they rode upon it in such a manner that every timber began to creak, and all the inmates of the house became so frightened that they ran each into his corner. Then Halfdan went to the door and out to the front yard, and the brothers now went over to him and greeted him.

Halfdan gave them a cold and reserved answer, asking them, however, for their names. They gave him their names, adding that they were the sons of jarl Viking, and that they brought greetings from the latter to him. Said Halfdan: I cannot talk about foster-brothership between us; to me it seems that many a man keeps his word of foster-brothership but middlingly well, and no more; and as for you, who have slain the most of king Njorfe's sons, it also seems to me that you have not regarded the sanctity of foster-brothership in respect to many of Njorfe's descendants. Still, you may enter my house, and lodge here to-night, if you like. Then Halfdan went in at a swinging pace, followed by the brothers. They entered the stofa (sitting-room), where there were but few persons. Nobody took the clothes off the brothers, and thus they sat during the evening, till people began to go to bed; then a dish, containing porridge, and a spoon in each end of it was placed on the table before them. Thorer began to eat the porridge.

Said Thorstein then: You are very inconsistent in regard to your pride; and, so saying, he took the dish and threw it on the floor in the further part of the room, so that it broke to pieces. Hereupon the people went to bed. The brothers had no bed, and got but very little sleep during the night. Early in the morning they got up and busked themselves for leaving. But when they had got outside the door the old man came to them and asked them: What did you say last night, or whose sons did you say you were? Made answer Thorer: What more do you know now than when we told you we were the sons of jarl Viking? Said Thorstein: Here is a golden finger-ring, which he begged me to give you.

Said Thorer: I think he will be the worse off who shows him anything of it. Made answer Thorstein: Be not so peevish, brother! Here is the gold ring, as a token that you should receive us in such a manner that we might be comforted and protected at your house. Halfdan took the ring, became glad, and said: Why should I not receive you, and do all the good in my power for you? To do so is my duty, on account of my relations to my friend Viking. You seem to be men blest with good luck. Said Thorer: The adage is indeed a true one, that it is good to have two mouths for the two kinds of speech. Last night, soon after we had come to you, you treated us quite otherwise. I therefore am inclined to think you a coward, and you everywhere show your slyness. Said Thorstein: Let us be patient, Halfdan, with my brother, although he is cross in his words to you, for he is a reckless man in his words and doings.

Answered Halfdan: I have heard that you are the most doughty of men, and that Thorer is hot-tempered and reckless; still, I think that you are in every respect a man of more spirit. Hereupon they went into the house, their clothes were taken off them, and every attention was shown them. They stayed there during the winter, and enjoyed the most hearty treatment. But in the beginning of spring Thorstein said to Halfdan: We shall now leave this place. Answered Halfdan: What is your best advice? Made answer Thorstein: I wish you would give me a ship, manned with a crew, for I intend to set out and wage war and gain booty. To this Halfdan gave his consent.

After busking themselves properly, they sailed to the south, along the coast of the country, until they met with two vessels, which had been sent out by their father, and were filled with men and good weapons. Now Thorstein sent back the ship which had been given to him by Halfdan, and sent the crew with it; but the brothers became skippers, one on each of the two ships. They waged wars in many places during the summer, and gained much fee and fame. In the fall they landed on an island which was ruled by the bonde, whose name was Grim. He bade them stay with him through the winter, and they accepted his offer. Grim was married and had an only daughter, by name Thora, a tall and fine-looking girl. Thorer fell in love with her, and told his brother Thorstein that he wanted to marry her. Thorstein talked about the matter to Grim, the bonde, but the latter flatly refused to give his consent. Answered Thorstein: Then I challenge you to fight with me in a holm-gang, and he who wins shall be master of your daughter. Grim said he was ready for the holm-gang.

The next day they took a blanket, which they threw under their feet, and then they fought the whole day very bravely, but in the evening they parted, neither of them having received any wound. The second and the third days they fought, but the results were the same as the first day. One day Thorer asked the daughter of the bonde how it came to pass that Grim could not be vanquished. She said there was in the fore part of his helmet a stone, which made him quite invincible as long as it was not taken away from him. This Thorer told to Thorstein; and on the fourth day of their fight Thorstein threw his sword, grasping the helmet of his antagonist with both his hands with so great force that the cords of the helmet were severed. Shortly after he attacked Grim, and now Thorstein's greater strength was shown. He brought Grim down, but gave him quarter. Then Grim asked who had advised him to take the helmet. Thorstein said that Thora had told it to Thorer. Then she wants to be married, answered Grim, and it shall so be. Thus it was resolved that Thorer should marry Thora. In the beginning of spring Thorstein set out to carry on wars, leaving Thorer at home. The newly married couple took to loving each other very much, and they got a son, whom they named Harald. This was their only child. He afterward took his father's kesia, after which he was nick-named and was called Harald Kesia.

XVII

A KING was named Skate, a son of Erik, who again was a son of Myndil Meitalfsson. Skate was king in Sogn, and with his queen he had two children, a son named Bele, who was a very excellent man, and a daughter who hight Ingeborg. At this time she was not in the kingdom, having been spellbound (and thus removed from the country). Skate had been a berserk and a very great viking, and he had forced his way onto the throne of Sogn. There was a man who hight Thorgrim, and who had to defend the realm against the invasion of foes. He was a great champion and a warlike man, but not over faithful. Between Thorgrim and the king's son, Bele, there was a warm friendship. Bele had great celebrity throughout all lands. It had happened, after king Skate had grown very old, both his children still being young, that two vikings, one named Gautan and the other Ogautan, had landed in his country. They had taken the king by surprise, and offered him two conditions, either to fight a battle with them, or give up his land and become a jarl under them. King Skate, though he had no troops to meet them with, would rather die with honor than live with shame; he would rather fall in his kingdom than serve his foes. He therefore went to battle, having no other troops than his courtiers. Thorgrim escaped with the king's son, Bele, but Ingeborg remained at home in her bower. In the combat with Ogautan, king Skate fell with honor, but those of his men who escaped death in the battle fled to the woods.

Now Ogautan took the kingdom into his charge, and had the title of king given to himself. He asked Ingeborg to become his wife, but she flatly refused, saying she would rather kill herself than marry the bane of her father, and such a villain, too, as Ogautan; for you, she said, are more like the devil himself than like a man.

At this Ogautan grew angry, and said: I shall reward you for your foul language, and I hereby enchant you, so that you shall get the same stature and looks as my sister Skellinefja, and the same nature also as she, as far as you may be capable of assuming it; and, spell-bound, yon shall inhabit that care which is on the Deep River, and you shall never escape out of this enchanted state until some man of noble birth is willing to have you, and pledges himself to marry you; still you can never escape until I am dead. But my sister shall wear your looks. Said Ingeborg: I cause you to be so enchanted that you shall keep this kingdom only for a short time, and never have any good of your reign. The spells pronounced by Ogautan proved true, and Ingeborg disappeared. Soon afterward, the king's son, Bele, came thither again, together with Thorgrim and many other men. It was night, and they set fire to the upper story of the house in which the two brothers slept, and burnt it up, together with the people who lived in it, except the brothers, who escaped through an underground passage and fled, without stopping until they came to the court of king Njorfe. Bele took possession of his country again, and Thorgrim remained in his former position as warder of the king's land.

XVIII

A KING, named Vilhjalm (William), ruled over Valland. He was a wise man, and was blest with many friends. He had a daughter, who hight Olof, and was a woman of great culture. Now it is to be told that Jokul, Njorfe's son, after the departure of the sons of Viking, made Thorstein and Thorer outlaws in every place within the boundaries of his kingdom.

King Njorfe did not consent to it, for he and Viking kept their friendship during their whole life. Once Ogautan had a talk with Jokul, and asked him if he would not like to get married. Jokul asked him where he saw a match for him. Answered Ogautan: Vilhjalm of Valland has a daughter named Olof, and I think a marriage with her would add to your honor. Said Jokul: Why not then make up our minds as to this subject? So they busked themselves for the voyage, and together with sixty men they sailed for Valland. Here they paid a visit to king Vilhjalm, who received Jokul very heartily, for his father, Njorfe, was well known throughout all lands. Now Jokul asked for Olof in marriage, and Ogautan pleaded with the king in his behalf, but the latter appealed to his daughter. And straightway after this conversation thirty very brave-looking men entered the hall. The one who went before them was the tallest and fairest, and he went up to the king and greeted him. As soon as Ogautan saw these men his voice fell, his beard sunk, and he begged Jokul and his other men not to mention his name so long as they stayed in that land. The king asked the stately men what they hight, and the chief called himself Bele, and said he was the son of Skate, the king, who was ruler of Sogn.

My errand hither, he added, is to woo your daughter. Made answer the king: Jokul, the son of Njorfe, came here before you on the same errand; now I will settle the matter in this way, that she choose herself which one of the two wooers she will have. Then the king placed Bele on one side of himself, and there was a great banquet. After three nights they took a walk to the bower of the princess, asking her which one of the two wooers, Jokul or Bele, she would marry, and it soon appeared that she would rather marry Bele; but at that moment Ogautan threw a round piece of wood into her lap, whereby her nature was suddenly changed to such an extent that she refused Bele and married Jokul. Then Bele returned to his ships. Jokul and Bele had formerly been on good terms, so that some people say that Bele had got a reward for killing Thorstein and Thorer. Bele did not blame Jokul though the daughter of the king declined to marry him (Bele), for the matter depended upon her decision. Thereupon Bele went home to his kingdom, and after the wedding Jokul also repaired homeward accompanied by Ogautan.

XIX

NOW OUR saga must turn to Thorstein at the time when he was returning home from his warfare, bound for Grim the bonde, for his brother Thorer resided in that island. Jokul got news of Thorstein's voyages. He spoke to Ogautan, asking him to try his tricks and by witchcraft bring about a storm against Thorstein, in order that he might be drowned, together with all his men. Ogautan said he would try, no matter what the result might be.

Then, with his incantations, he caused so tremendous a storm against Thorstein that his ships were wrecked amid the tumultuous waves, and all his crew perished. Thorstein held out well a long time, but at last he became tired of swimming, and then he had reached the surf and was beginning to sink down. At this moment he saw an old woman, of very great stature, wading from the shore out toward him. She wore a shriveled skin-cloak, which fell to her feet in front, but was very short behind, and her face was very large and like that of a monster.

She stepped over to him and, seizing him up from the sea, said: Will you accept life from me, Thorstein?

Answered he: Why should I not, or what is your name?

Said she: My name is uncommon; it is Skellinefja; but you will have to make some sacrifice in return for your life.

Said he: What is it?

Made answer she: That you grant me the favor that I ask of you.

Said Thorstein: You will ask nothing from me that will not bring me good luck; but when shall the favor be granted? Answered she: Not yet. Then she bore him ashore, and now he had come to that island which was governed by Grim. She then wrestled with him till he grew warm, whereupon they parted, each wishing the other success. Then she walked on, for she said she had other places to call at. But Thorstein went home to the byre, and his meeting there with his brother was the cause of great joy to both of them; and so Thorstein remained there during the winter, and very much was made of him.

Now we must turn to Jokul and Ogautan as they were sailing homeward. One very fine day it happened that their ship was suddenly shrouded in darkness, accompanied by such a biting frost and cold that nobody on board dared to turn his face against the wind. They all covered their faces with their clothes; but when the weather had cleared off again they saw Ogautan hanging in the bole of the mast-head, and he was dead. Jokul looked upon his death as a great loss, and returning to his kingdom he remained quiet. Early the next spring Thorstein and Thorer busked themselves for a voyage, intending to visit their father, Viking; and when they came as far as to Deep River, before they knew of it, Jokul came there to them with thirty men. A combat between them straightway began. Jokul was very eager in the fight, and so was his brother Grim. Thorer and Thorstein defended themselves bravely, and a long time passed before these brothers received any wounds from Jokul and his men, for not only did Thorstein deal heavy blows, but Angervadil also bit iron as well as cloth. Thorer defended himself excellently, although he did not have his kesia, which he had left at home. He and Grim met, and they fought very bravely: still the end of the fight was that Grim fell to the ground, dead. By this time Thorstein had slain eighteen men, but, as might be expected, he was both tired and wounded, and so was Thorer. Then the brothers turned their backs together and still defended themselves well. Now Jokul with his eleven men, pursued them and made so valiant an attack that Thorer fell. Then Thorstein defended himself manfully until there remained no more than Jokul and three of his men. But then Jokul stabbed Thorstein with his sword, wounding him in the upper part of the thigh; and Jokul being a strong man, and bearing on the sword with all his might while he stabbed him, Thorstein, who was very tired, and was standing on the very edge of the river-bank, fell down from the crag, while it was all that Jokul could do to stop himself so that he did not fall also.

After this Jokul went home, thinking he had slain Thorstein and Thorer; and having come home he remained quiet. But now it is to be told of Thorstein, that he, having fallen from the crag, alighted upon a grassy spot among the rocks; but, being tired and wounded, he was unable to move, and yet he was in his full senses after he had fallen. Angervadil fell out of his hand and down into the river.

Thorstein was lying there betwixt life and death, and expecting soon to breathe his last. But before he had lain thus very long he saw Skellinefja coming; she was clad in her skin-gown, and looked no fairer than before. She approached the place where Thorstein was lying, and said: It seems to me, Thorstein, that your misfortunes will never come to an end, and now you seem already to be breathing your last, or will you now grant me the favor upon which we formerly agreed? Said Thorstein: I do not now find myself able to render much of any service to you. Made answer she: My request is that you promise to marry me, and then I will try to heal your wounds. Said Thorstein: I do not know as I had better make that promise, for to me you look like a monster.

Said she: Still you have your choice between these two things. You must either marry me or lose your life; and, in the latter case, you break, in the bargain, the oath which you swore to me when you pledged yourself to grant my favor after I had saved you at Grim's Island. Said Thorstein: There is much truth in your words, and it is better to keep one's promise; hence I vow that I will marry you, and you will prove to be my best helper in time of need: still I should like to stipulate with you that you get me my sword back, so that I may wear it in case my life is prolonged.

Says she: So be it. And having taken him up in her skin-gown, she leaped, as if quite unencumbered, up over the crags and proceeded until a large cave was before them. Having entered the cave, she bandaged Thorstein's wounds and laid him on a soft bed, and within seven nights he was almost healed.

One day Skellinefja had left the cave, and in the evening she came back with the sword, which was then dripping wet, and she gave it to Thorstein. Said she: Now I have saved your life twice and given you your sword back, of which you are fonder than of aught else; and a fourth thing, which is of great importance to both of us, is that I hanged Ogautan. And yet you have completely rewarded me, for you have delivered me from the spell-bound condition into which Ogautan enchanted me. My name is Ingeborg; I am the daughter of king Skate and the sister of Bele, but my only means of delivery from bondage was that some man of noble birth should promise to marry me. Now you have done this, and I am freed from bondage. Now you must busk yourself for leaving the cave and follow my advices, and you will find my brother Bele and four men with him. Among the latter will be his land-warden, Thorgrim Kobbe. From Jokul they have received some money, offered as a price for your head, and they will begin a battle with you. I do not care if you do kill Thorgrim and his companions, but spare the life of my brother Bele, for I should like to have you become his foster-brother; and if you have a mind to marry me, then go with him home to Sogn and woo me. I shall be there before you, and it may be that I will look otherwise to you then than now. Then they parted, and he had not gone far before he met Bele, accompanied by four men, and, at their meeting, Thorgrim said: It is good, Thorstein, that we have found each other. Now we shall try to win the price put upon your head by Jokul. Said Thorstein: It seems possible to me that you may lose the fee and forfeit your life too.

XX

Now we must tell about Thorstein that he was attacked by Bele and his men, but he defended himself well and bravely, and the result was that Thorgrim and three of his companions fell. Then Thorstein and Bele entered a new contest. Thorstein defended himself, but would not wound Bele. Bele kept on attacking Thorstein, until the latter seized him and set him down at his side, saying: You are wholly in my power, but I will not only give you your life, but also offer you an opportunity to become my foster-brother. You shall be king and I shall be herser, and in addition to this I will woo your sister Ingeborg, and get her estates in Sogn as a dowry. Said Bele: This is no very easy matter, for my sister has disappeared, so that nobody knows what has become of her. Answered Thorstein: She may have come back. Said Bele: I do not see how she could get a doughtier fellow than you are, and I give my full consent to the proposition. Having settled this with their words of honor, they went home to Sogn. Bele soon became aware that his sister had come back, and that she had not lost any of that blooming beauty which she had had before in her youthful days.

Thorstein began his suit, and asked that Ingeborg might become his wife. This was resolved upon. As a dowry she got from her home all the possessions lying on the other side of the fjord. The byre where Thorstein resided was called Framness, but the byre governed by Bele was called Syrstrond. The next spring Thorstein and Bele set out to wage wars, having five ships, and during the summer they harried far and wide, and got enough of booty, but in the fall they returned home again having seven ships. The next summer they went out a harrying again, but got very little booty, for all vikings shunned them; and having reached the small rocky islands called Elfarsker, they anchored in a harbor in the evening. Thorstein and Bele went ashore, and crossed that ness toward which their ships were lying. But having crossed the ness, they saw twelve ships covered with black tilts. On shore they saw tents, from which smoke arose, and they seemed to be sure that these tents must be occupied by cooks. Having taken on a disguise, they went thither, and having come to the door of a tent, they both placed themselves in it in such a manner that the smoke did not find any out-way. The cooks made use of abusive words, and asked what sort of beggars they were, as they were guileful enough to want them burnt alive or smothered. Bele and Thorstein made an ugly disturbance, and answered with hoarse voices that they came to get food; or, said they, who is the excellent man who commands the fleet lying here at the shore?

Said they: You must be stupid old men if you have not heard of Ufe, who is called Ufe the Unlucky, and is the son of Herbrand the Bigheaded. This life is the brother of Otunfaxe, and we know there are no men under the sun more celebrated than these two brothers. Said Thorstein: You tell good tidings. Shortly after, Thorstein and Bele returned to their own men, and early the next morning, having busked themselves, they rowed around the ness and immediately shouted the cry of battle. The others then quickly busked themselves, took their weapons, and a vehement battle began. Ufe had more men, and was himself a most valiant warrior. They fought for a long time in such a manner that it could not be seen which side would gain the victory. But on the third day Thorstein began to board the dragon commanded by Ufe the Unlucky, and he was followed without delay by Bele, and a great havoc they made, killing all who were between the prow and the mast of the ship. Then Ufe came from the poop and attacked Bele, and they fought for some time, until Bele began to get wounds from Ufe, who handled his weapon dexterously and dealt heavy blows. Meanwhile Thorstein came with his Angervadil, and gave Ufe a blow with it. The sword hit the helmet, split the whole body and the byrnie-clad man from head to foot, and Angervadil struck against the mast-beam so forcibly that both its edges sunk out of sight. Said Bele: This blow of yours, foster-brother, will live in the memory of men as long as the North is peopled. Hereupon they offered to the vikings two terms, either to give up and save their lives, or to have a combat. But they preferred to accept a quarter from Thorstein and Bele. The latter gave pardon to all, and they eagerly accepted it. Here much booty was taken, and having stayed three nights, during which time the wounded were healed, they repaired home in the autumn.

XXI

AT SPRINGTIME the foster-brothers busked themselves for leaving home, and had fifteen ships. Bele commanded the dragon which had been owned by Ufe the Unlucky. It was a choice ship, its beak and stern being whittled and carved and extensively overlaid with gold. King Bele got the dragon, for it was the choicest part of the booty which they took when they had slain Ufe, it always being their custom to give to Bele the most costly parts of the booty. No ship was thought better than this dragon excepting Ellide, which was owned by Ufe's brother, Otunfaxe. Ufe and Otunfaxe had inherited these ships from their father, Herbrand, and Ellide was the better one of the two in these respects, that it had fair wind wherever it sailed, and it almost understood human speech. But the reason why Otunfaxe and not Ufe had gotten Ellide was, that Ufe had fallen into so bad luck that he had killed both his father and his mother, and it seemed to Otunfaxe that if justice should be done, Ufe had forfeited his right of inheritance. Otunfaxe was the superior of the two brothers on account of his strength, stature and witchcraft. Now the foster-brothers went out a harrying, and waged wars far and wide in the waters of the Baltic, but they found but very few vikings, for everybody, upon hearing of them, fled out of their reach.

At this time none were more celebrated for their harrying exploits than Thorstein and Bele.

One day the foster-brothers were standing on a promontory, on the other side of which they saw twelve ships lying at anchor, and all of them were very large. They rowed rapidly toward the ships and asked who was the commander of the warriors. A man who stood leaning against the mast made answer: Angantyr is my name; I am a son of jarl Hermund of Gautland. Said Thorstein: You are a hopeful fellow; but how old are you? Made answer he: I am now nineteen years old. Asked Bele: Which do you prefer, to give up your ships and fee or to fight a battle with us? Said Angantyr: The more unequal your terms are, the more promptly I make my choice. I prefer to defend my fee, and fall, sword in hand, if such be my fate. Said Bele: Busk yourself then; but we will make the attack.

Then both of them busked themselves for the battle and took their weapons.

Said Thorstein to Bele: There is very little of noble courage in attacking them with fifteen ships, as they have but twelve. Said Bele: Why shall we not lay three of our ships aside? And so they did. A hard battle was now fought. Angantyr's warriors dealt so heavy blows, that Bele and Thorstein declared that they had never been in greater peril. They fought the whole day until evening, but in such a manner that it could not be seen which party would gain the victory. The next day they busked themselves again for the fight.

Then said Angantyr: To me it seems, king Bele, that it would be wiser not to sacrifice any more of our men, but let us two fight a duel, and he who conquers the other in the holm-gang shall be the victorious party. Bele accepted this challenge; so they went ashore, and having thrown a blanket under their feet, they fought bravely until Bele became tired out and began to receive wounds. Thorstein thought it evident that Bele would not gain the victory over Angantyr, and it came to pass that Bele was not only exhausted but also nigh his last breath.

Said Thorstein then: It seems best to me, Angantyr, that you cease your fighting, for I see that Bele is so exhausted that he is almost gone. On the other hand, I will not be mean enough to play the dastard toward you and assist him; but if you become the bane of Bele, then I will challenge you to fight a duel with me; and as to personal valor and strength, I think there is no less difference between me and you than there is between you and Bele. I will slay you in a holm-gang duel, and it would be a great loss if you both die. Now I offer you this condition, that if you spare Bele's life, we will enter into a foster-brotherhood upon mutual oaths.

Said Angantyr: To me it seems a fair offer that Bele and I enter into foster-brotherhood; but it seems to me a great favor that I may become your foster-brother. Then this was resolved upon and secured by firm pledges on both sides. They opened a vein in the hollow of their hands, crept beneath the sod, and there they solemnly swore that each of them should avenge the other if any one of them should be slain by weapons. Then they reviewed their warriors, and two ships of each party had lost all their men. They healed those who were wounded, and thereupon they left the place with twenty-three ships, returning home in the fall. They spent the winter at home quietly, and enjoyed great honor. Now none were thought more famous on account of their weapons than these foster-brothers.

XXII

WHEN SPRING opened, the foster-brothers busked themselves for departing from home, and had thirty ships. They sailed to the east and harried in Sweden and in all parts of the Baltic. As usual, they carried on their warfare in a seeming manner, flaying vikings and pirates wherever they could find them, but leaving bondes and chapmen in peace. On the other hand, it is to be told that Otunfaxe. when he heard of the death of his brother Iife, thought it a great loss. And of him it is to be related, that for three summers together he searched for the foster-brothers.

Now it is furthermore to be related, that Bele and his men one day laid their ships near some small rocky islands, called Brenner's Isles. They cast anchor and busked themselves well. Hereupon all the three foster-brothers went ashore, and proceeded until they came to a small byre. There stood a man outside the door splitting wood; he was clad in a green cloak, and was a man of astonishing corpulency. He greeted Thorstein by name. Said Thorstein: We differ widely as to our faculty for recognition; you greet me by name, but I do not remember that I have ever seen you before; what is your name? Says he: My name is an uncommon one. I hight Brenner. I am a son of Vifil, and a brother of your father, Viking. I was born at the time when my father was engaged in warfare, and had his home with Haloge. I was raised on this island, and have lived here since. But have you, my nephew Thorstein, heard anything about the viking Otunfaxe?

Answered Thorstein: No; or what can you tell about him?

Made answer Brenner: This I can tell, that he has been searching for you during the last three years, and now he lies here on the other side of those islands with all his fleet; he wants to avenge his brother Ufe the Unlucky. He has forty ships, all of which are very large, and he himself is as big as a troll, and no weapons can bite him. Said Thorstein: What is to be done now? Made answer Brenner: I can give you no advice unless you have a chance to meet the dwarf Sindre; and moreover he will least of all be embarrassed in finding out what ought to be done.

Asked Thorstein: Where can I expect to find him? Made answer Brenner: His home is in the island which lies near the shore, and is called the Smaller Brenner's Isle. He lives in a stone. I scarcely hope that you will be able to find him, but you are welcome here to-night. Said Thorstein: Something else must be done than to keep quiet. Then they went to their ships, and Thorstein launched a boat and rowed to the island. He went ashore alone, and when he came to a little stream, he saw two children, a boy and a girl, playing on its banks. Thorstein asked their names. The boy called himself Herraud, and the girl Herrid. Said she: I have lost my gold ring, and I know this will make my father, Sindre, cross, and I think I may look for punishment. Said Thorstein: Here is a gold ring, which I will give you. She accepted the gold ring and was pleased with it. Said she: I will give this to my father; but is there nothing that I might do that might be of service to you? Made answer Thorstein: Nothing; but bring your father here, that I may have a talk with him, and manage the matter in such a manner that he may advise me concerning those things which are of importance to me.

Answered Herrid: I can do this only provided my brother Herraud acts according to my will, for Sindre never refuses him anything. Said Herraud: You know I take your part in everything. Thorstein unbuckled a silver belt which he wore, and gave it him; to it was attached a beautifully ornamented knife. Said the boy: This is a nice present; I shall take all possible pains to promote your wish; wait here until I and my sister come back, Thorstein did so, and after a long while the dwarf Sindre came, accompanied by the boy and his sister. Sindre greeted Thorstein heartily, and said: What do you want of me, Thorstein? Made answer Thorstein: I want you to give me advice as to how I may conquer the viking Otunfaxe. Answered Sindre: It seems to me wholly impossible for any human being to vanquish Faxe, for he is worse to deal with than anybody else, and I will advise you not to fight any battle with him, for you wilt only lose your men, and hence the best thing for you to do is to turn your prows away from the island to-night. Made answer Thorstein: That shall never be; though I knew it before that I should lose my life, I would rather choose that than flee from danger before it has been tried. Said Sindre: I see that you are a very great champion, and I suggest to you that you unload all your ships this night, bring all valuable things on shore, and that you load the ships again with wood and stone. Then busk yourself early to-morrow morning and come to them before they wake; thus you may be able to surprise them in their own tents. You need to do all this if there shall be any show for you of gaining a victory over Faxe; for I will tell you this, that so far is common iron from biting him, that he cannot even be scathed by the sword Angervadil. Here is a belt-dirk, which my daughter Herrid will give you, and thus reward you for the gold ring, and I am of the opinion that it will bite Otunfaxe if you use it skillfully.

My son, Herraud, proposes this as a reward for the belt, that you shall name my name if you seem to be hard pressed. Now we must part for a while; fare you well, and good luck to you. By my power of enchanting I promise that my dises shall always follow and assist you. Hereupon Thorstein went to his boat and rowed to his men. Straightway afterward in the night he busked himself and brought the fee out of the ships, but put stones in them instead; and when this was done the old man Brenner came down from his byre, holding in his hand a large club which was all covered with iron and large iron spikes, and so heavy that a man with common strength could scarcely lift it from the ground. Said Brenner: This hand-weapon I will give you, my nephew Thorstein. You alone can manage it, on account of its weight; but yet, it will be rather light for a fight with Otunfaxe. Now it seems to me that it would be a wise measure if Angantyr would take the sword Angervadil, and you fight with this club, for, although it is no handy weapon, still it will prove fatal to many a man. Now, my nephew, I would like to be able to help you more, but I have not the opportunity. Then Brenner went back from the shore.

XXIII

WHEN THEY had made ready they rowed quickly around the ness, and then they saw the place where Otunfaxe and all his naval force was lying. Without delay they sent forth a shower of stones so hard and vehemently that they slew more than a hundred men in their sleep, having taken them by surprise; but from the moment when the warriors awoke they made a powerful resistance. Then a bloody battle was fought. A large number of the men of the foster-brothers fell, for it could almost be said that Otunfaxe shot from every finger. So it went on until night set in; then ten of the foster-brothers' ships were cleared. On the second day the battle began anew, and the slaughter was no less than on the day before. They tried several times to board Faxe's ship, and every time they made great slaughter; but they never succeeded in boarding Ellide, both because Faxe defended her and because her sides were so high. But in the evening all the ships of the foster-brothers were cleared, excepting the dragon called Ufe's naut (gift). On both days they saw that two men came from the island, and that they took their positions one on one crag and the other on another, both shooting with all their might at Faxe's ship. Here they saw the dwarf Sindre, every one of whose arrows brought down a man, and in this manner a great many of Faxe's men lost their lives. The one on the other crag was Brenner, who was shooting more like a bowman out against the ships. It did happen occasionally that stones came flying over the ships, and every stone thrown by Brenner was inclined to go to the bottom, and, as a consequence of this, many of Faxe's ships sunk.

Thus it happened that all his ships, too, had been cleared, excepting Ellide. This battle took place at that time of the year when the nights are bright, and therefore they fought the whole night. Thorstein, together with Angantyr and Bele, tried to board the dragon, but there were many men left on Ellide. Faxe ran forward, against the foster-brothers, Angantyr and Bele, and a good many blows were given and received; but no iron weapons would bite Faxe, and before they had fought very long Angantyr and Bele began to receive wounds. At this moment Thorstein approached, and with his club he smote the cheek of Faxe in the way that it came handiest for him, but Faxe did not even lout the least at the blow.

Thorstein smote again, just as hard as before; and now Faxe did not like the blows, but plunged himself overboard into the sea, so that only the soles of his feet could be seen. To both Bele and Angantyr it seemed disgusting to follow him; but Thorstein ran overboard, and swam after the fleeing Faxe, who looked like a whale. Thus a long time passed until Faxe landed; but the foster-brothers fought with those men who still were left, and did not cease until they had slain alt on board the dragon. Then they took a boat, and rowed ashore toward Faxe and Thorstein. But Faxe, having landed, seized a stone and threw it at Thorstein just as the latter was swimming toward the shore. He warded off the blow by diving, and swam out of the reach of the stone, which made a great splash as it fell. Faxe took up another stone, and a third one, both of which went the same way as the first one. But meanwhile the foster-brothers, Angantyr and Bele, approached. When Thorstein sprang overboard, he threw his club backwards, but Bele had taken it up, and, having now reached the spot where Otunfaxe was standing, he smote him in the back part of the head with the club. This he did uninterrupted again, while Angantyr at the same time was pelting him with large stones. Now Faxe's skull began to ache considerably, and, not liking to receive their blows, he plunged himself from the crag down into the sea, and swam from the shore, pursued by Thorstein, Faxe, observing this, turned against Thorstein, and a wrestle between the two swimming antagonists now took place, in which there were great, fearful tussles. They were alternately drawn into the deep by each other, and yet Thorstein found out that Faxe's strength was greater than his own; and it came to pass that Faxe brought Thorstein to the bottom, and thus he lost his power of swimming. Now Thorstein, being almost sure that Faxe intended to bite his throat to pieces, said: How could I ever want you more than now, dwarf Sindre? And suddenly he observed that Faxe's shoulder was seized by a grip so powerful that he soon sank to the bottom, with Thorstein upon him. Thorstein, who by this time had become very tired from the struggle, seized the belt-knife which had been given to him by Sindre, and stabbed Faxe in the breast, sinking the knife into his body up to the handle, and then slashing his belly down to the lower abdomen; but still he found that Faxe was not dead yet, for now said the latter: A great deed you have done, Thorstein, in putting me to death, for I have fought ninety battles, and been victorious in all, excepting this. In duels I have been the victor eighty times, so that I certainly may say I have had a holm-gang; but now I am ninety years old.

Thorstein thought it useless to let him go on prattling any longer if he could do anything to prevent it, and so he tore away from him everything that was loose within him. Now the saga goes on to tell about Angantyr and Bele, that they took a boat and rowed in it out on the sea, searching for Faxe and Thorstein, but for a long time they did not find them anywhere. At last they came to a place where the sea was mixed with blood, and quite red. They thought it must be that Faxe was at the bottom of the water, and that he had slain Thorstein, and after a while they saw some nasty thing floating upon the surface of the sea. They went nearer, and saw some large, horrible looking bowels floating there. Shortly afterward Thorstein emerged from the water, but so exhausted and outdone that he could not keep himself afloat. Then they rowed over to him, and dragged him on board. At this time there was but little hope of his life, and still he was not much wounded, but the flesh of his body was almost torn from his bones into knots. They went away and procured some relief for him, after which he soon came to his senses. They went back to the islands, and made a search of the battle-field for the slain; but only thirty men were found fit to be healed. Then they went to the old man Brenner, thanking him for his assistance. Thorstein went to the lesser Brenner's Isle to call on the dwarf Sindre, to whom he made splendid presents, and thus they parted in great friendship. Thorstein got the dragon Ellide as his lot of the booty, while Bele got Ufe's naut, and Angantyr as much gold and silver as he wished. Thorstein gave his uncle Brenner all those ships which they could not bring away with them. With three ships they left and went back to Sogn, where they spent the winter.

XXIV

IN THE spring they set out for warfare again. Angantyr asked whither they should turn their prows, saying that he thought the Baltic had already been cleared of vikings. Says king Bele: Let us then take our course into the western waters, for we have never been there a harrying before. So they did, and having reached the Orkneys, they went ashore, and waged war, destroying the inhabited parts of these islands by fire and plundering the fee; and so fearfully did they carry on their depredations that all living things fled for fear of them. Herraud hight the jarl who ruled the islands. When he heard of their depredations he gathered an army to meet them, and marched by night until he found them at an island called Pap Isle. Here it came to a battle between them, and their troops were equal. For two days they fought in such a manner that it could not be seen which party would be victorious. At last the slaughter began to lean to the disadvantage of Herraud, whose ships were cleared, so that the brothers succeeded in boarding them, and finally jarl Herraud fell, together with the most of his men. Hereupon they made expeditions through all the islands, which they subjugated, and then busked themselves for the home journey. King Bele offered to make Thorstein jarl of all the islands, but the latter declined, saying: I would rather be a herser, and not part with you, than have the name of jarl, and live far away from you.

Then he offered Angantyr the jarlship of those islands, which offer was accepted. The latter became jarl, and was to pay an annual tribute. Afterward they returned home to Sogn, where they stayed the next winter, keeping their men well, both as to weapons and clothes. And now none were thought to be superior to the foster-brothers. Children were granted to them; the sons of Bele hight Helge and Halfdan, and his daughter hight Ingeborg; she was the youngest of the children. Thorstein had a son, who hight Fridthjof. Harald grew up in the island with Grim, but when he had reached the age of maturity be set out a harrying and became a most noted man, although he is not much spoken of in this saga. He kept his nickname, being called Harald Kesia, and a large family is descended from him. Thorstein, Bels, Grim and Harald remained friends as long as they lived.

XXV

Now we must return to Jokul, Njorfe's son, who ruled the uplands after the death of Njorfe and Viking. They had preserved their friendship well until their death. Jokul won ships and fee, and was a daring viking, treating his soldiers fairly well, but no better. A few years passed in such a manner that he was the most noted viking, harrying the most of the time in the waters of the Baltic. Thorstein and Bele had not been at home long before they busked themselves for harrying expeditions, and sailing first down along the coast of the country, then through the Sound, they harried in Saxland during the summer, and got a great booty, consisting of gold and silver, and many other costly things. Afterward they intended to sail home, which they did, and having reached the mouth of Lim Fjord, they were overtaken by a violent storm, which carried them out into the sea, and in a short time the ships were separated.

Then the sea began to break over the ships from both sides, and all the men were engaged in baling out the water. And it came to pass that this storm drove the dragon Ellide, tossed by the waves, ashore alone at Borgund's Holm, At the same time Jokul also landed there with ten ships, all thoroughly equipped both as to weapons and crews. And now, as might be imagined, Jokul attacked Thorstein and his men. Thorstein was poorly prepared, for he and his crew were very much exhausted from hard work, and from being tossed about on the sea. A severe and bloody battle was fought, and Jokul, being very vehement, kept cheering his men on, telling them that they would never have a better chance to conquer Thorstein; and, said he, it will be an everlasting shame upon us if he escapes now. Then they attacked Thorstein and his men, not letting up until all his men had fallen, so that nobody but Thorstein alone remained standing on the dragon; but still he defended himself bravely, so that for a long time they could not give him a single wound. At last, however, it came to pass that they came so near to him that they could stab him with their spears; but the most of them he cut out of his reach, for the sword Angervadil bit as keenly as ever. Then Jokul made a desperate attack, and stabbed Thorstein with his spear through the thigh. At the same moment Thorstein dealt Jokul a blow, hitting his arm below the elbow, and cutting the hand off.

Meanwhile they succeeded in surrounding Thorstein with shields and capturing him. But it was near night, so that they thought it was too late to put him to death, and so fetters were put on his feet, his hands were tied with a bow-string, and twelve men were set to watch him during the night. When all had been brought ashore excepting these twelve men, together with Thorstein, he said: Which do you prefer, that you amuse me or that I amuse you? They said that he could not care much for amusement now as he was to die immediately on the morrow.

Now Thorstein, finding himself in close quarters, conceived a plan of escaping, and in a low, whispering voice he said: At what other time could I need you more than just now, my dear fellow Sindre, had not all our friendship already been broken off? Then darkness came upon the watchmen, and they all fell asleep. Thorstein saw Sindre going along the ship, approaching him and saying: You are in close quarters, my dear fellow Thorstein, and it certainly is high time to help you. He blew open the lock, then he cut the bow-string off from his hands; and Thorstein, who thus had become free, now seized his sword, for he knew where he had left it, and, turning against the watchmen, he killed them all.

Hereupon, Sindre disappeared, but Thorstein took a boat and rowed ashore, and went home to Sogn. This meeting with Bele was a very happy one, and to the latter it seemed as if he had recovered Thorstein from the domains of Hel (death). Early the next morning (after the battle) Jokul awoke, happy in the thought that he was about to take the prisoner and kill him; but when they came to the place where they had left him, the prisoner was gone, and the watchmen dead. This was to them a very great loss.

Jokul turned his prows homeward, greatly dissatisfied with his voyage, having lost Thorstein, and received scars that could never be healed. Henceforth he was called Jokul the One-handed. The foster-brothers, king Bele and Thorstein, gathered an army and went to the uplands, sending a message to Jokul, and preparing a battle-field for him. Jokul gathered men; although, on account of their friendship with Thorstein, many of his subjects sat at home, and thus, getting only a few, he durst not engage in battle, but fled out of his land, and went to Valland to his brother-in-law, Vilhjalm. The latter gave him a third part of his kingdom to rule. King Bele and Thorstein conquered the uplands, whereupon they returned home and kept quiet. Some time later there came men from Valland to meet Thorstein. They had been sent out by Jokul. Their errand was to offer Thorstein, in the name of Jokul, terms of peace. They were to have a meeting in Lim Fjord, to which both should come with three ships each, and there they should settle their dispute. Thorstein was very much pleased with this offer, confessing that it was contrary to his wish that he had had troubles with Jokul, saying that he had entered into them unwillingly on Njorfe's account, and on account of the latter's friendship with Viking. Now this was agreed upon. The ambassadors returned home, but in the summer time Thorstein busked himself for going abroad, taking with him Ellide and two other ships. To Bele this voyage did not seem a hopeful one, for he looked upon Jokul as a treacherous and faithless man. He advised Thorstein to send spies ahead, and find out whether everything was done faithfully on Jokul's part, and having found this out, they should return and meet him in the Sound.

They did so, and came back, reporting that Jokul and his party were lying at anchor in Lim Fjord, and keeping perfectly quiet. So they proceeded on their voyage till they reached the fjord. Here they held a meeting in the place agreed upon, and came to mutually satisfactory terms, on the conditions that the loss of men, the wounds and the blows, should be considered even on both sides, but Jokul should get his kingdom back, and not be tributary to anybody. Thorstein's kingdom in the uplands should fall to Jokul's lot, in compensation for the loss of his hand. On these conditions they were to be fully reconciled. Then Jokul went home to his kingdom, and kept quiet. Thorstein and Bele went home to Sogn, settled in their kingdoms, and made an end to all warfares. Ingeborg, Thorstein's wife, had already died, and Ingeborg, Bele's daughter, had her name. Fridthjof grew up with his father. Thorstein had a daughter who hight Vefreyja, who at this point of our saga had reached the age of maturity, for she was begotten in the cave of Skellinefja, and there she was born too. In wisdom she was like her mother. She got Angervadil after the death of her father, Thorstein, and many excellent men are descended from him. By all Thorstein was considered the most distinguished and most excellent man of his time. With these contents, we now finish the saga of Thorstein, Viking's son, and it is a most amusing one.

THE SAGA OF FRIDTHJOF THE BOLD

I

THE BEGINNING of this saga is, that king Bele ruled over the Sogn fylke. He had three children: a son, who hight Helge, another by name Halfdan, and a daughter called Ingeborg, a fair looking woman, of great wisdom, and the foremost of the king's children. On the coast bordering the fjord on the west side there was a large byre, called Baldershage (Balder's Meads). There was a Place of Peace and a great temple enclosed with high wooden pales. Many gods were there, yet none of them was such a favorite as Balder; and so jealous were the heathen people of this place, that no harm should be done therein, either to beasts or to men; and no dealings must there take place between men and women. The place where the king dwelt hight Syrstrand, but on the other side of the fjord was a byre called Framness. There dwelt a man who hight Thorstein, the son of Viking. His byre was over against the dwelling of the king. With his wife, Thorstein had a son, by name Fridthjof, a man taller and stronger than anybody else, and even from his youth furnished with very unusual prowess. He was called Fridthjof the Bold, and so much was he beloved that all men prayed for his welfare.

The children of the king were still young when their mother died. Hilding was the name of a good bonde in Sogn. He offered to foster the king's daughter, and so she was brought up in his house well and carefully. She was called Ingeborg the Fair. Fridthjof was also fostered by the bonde Hilding, and thus Ingeborg was his foster-sister, and both of them were peerless among children. King Bele growing old, his personal property began to ebb away from his hands. Thorstein ruled over the third part of his kingdom, and from that man Bele got more aid than from any other source. Every third year Thorstein invited the king to a very costly banquet, while the king, on the other hand, gave a feast to Thorstein the other two years. At an early age Helge, Bele's son, turned to offering to the gods, and yet neither he nor his brother was much beloved. Thorstein had a ship called Ellide, rowed on each side by fifteen oars, furnished with bow-shaped stem and stern, and strong-built like an ocean-going vessel, and its sides were clamped with iron. So strong was Fridthjof, that he, at the bow of the ship, rowed with two oars thirteen ells long, while everywhere else there were two men at each oar. Fridthjof was considered peerless among young men of that time, and the sons of the king were jealous, because he was praised more than themselves.

Now king Bele was taken ill, and when he was rapidly approaching death he sent for his sons and said to them: This illness will be my bane, but this I will bid you, that you keep friendship with the friends that I have had, for it seems to me that you are inferior to Thorstein and his son Fridthjof in all things, both in good counsel and bravery. You shall raise a mound over me. Hereupon Bele died. Soon afterward Thorstein also was taken sick, and then he said to Fridthjof: This will I bid you, my son, that you govern your temper and yield to the sons of the king, for this is fitting on account of their dignity, and besides it seems to me that your future promises much good. I wish to be buried in a how opposite the how of king Bele, on this side of the fjord, close by the sea, so that it may be an easy thing to shout to one another about things that are about to happen. Bjorn and Asmund hight the foster-brothers of Fridthjof; both of them were large and strong men. Shortly after this Thorstein died. He was buried in a how according to his request, but Fridthjof took his land and all his personal property after him.

II

FRIDTHJOF BECAME the most famous man, and the bravest in all dangers. His foster-brother, Bjorn, he valued most, but Asmund served both of them. The best thing he got of his father's heritage was the ship Ellide, and another costly thing was a gold ring, and a dearer one was not to be found in all Norway. So bounteous a man was Fridthjof that he was commonly said to be no less honorable than the sons of the king, excepting their royal dignity. On account of this they showed great coldness and enmity toward Fridthjof, and they could not easily bear to hear him spoken of as superior to themselves; and, furthermore, they seemed to have seen that, their sister, Ingeborg, and Fridthjof had fallen into mutual love.

Now the time came when the kings had to attend a banquet at Fridthjof's, at Framness, and, as usual, he entertained everybody more splendidly than they were wont to be entertained. Ingeborg was also present at this feast, and Fridthjof frequently talked with her. Said the king's daughter to him: You have a good gold ring. Said Fridthjof: That is true. Hereupon, the brothers went home, and their envy of Fridthjof grew. Shortly afterward Fridthjof became very sad. Bjorn, his foster-brother, asked him what the matter was. Fridthjof answered that he had in mind to woo Ingeborg; for, said he, though my title is less than that of her brothers, still I am not inferior to them in personal worth. Says Bjorn: Let us do so. Then Fridthjof, in company with a few men, went to see the brothers. The kings were sitting on their father's how, when Fridthjof greeted them courteously. Thereupon he presented his request, saying that he prayed for their sister, Ingeborg, Bele's daughter.

Said the kings: You do not show great wisdom in making this request, thinking that we will give her in marriage to a man who is without dignity. We therefore most positively refuse to give our consent. Said Fridthjof: Then my errand is quickly done; but this shall be given in return, that hereafter I shall never give you my help, though you may be in want of it. They said they did not care about it at all. Then Fridthjof returned home, and got back his cheerful mind.

III

THERE WAS a king, by name Ring, who ruled over Ring-ric, which also is a part of Norway. He was a mighty fylke-king, of great ability, but at this time somewhat advanced in age. Spoke he to his men: I have heard that the sons of Bele have broken off their friendship with Fridthjof, a man of quite uncommon excellence. Now I will send some men to the kings, and offer them this choice,— either they must become subject and tributary to me, or I will equip an army against them; and I think it will be easy to capture their kingdom, for they are not my peers either in forces or in wisdom, and yet it would be a great honor to me in my old age to put them to death.

Hereupon king Ring's messengers left, and, meeting the brothers, Helge and Halfdan, in Sogn, they spoke to them as follows: This message does king Ring send you, that you must either pay a tribute to him, or he will come and harry your kingdom. They made answer that they were unwilling to learn In their youth that which they had no mind to know in their old age, namely, to serve him with shame; and now, said they, we shall gather all the army that we may be able to get together. And so they did; but, as it seemed to them that their army would be small, they sent Hilding's foster-father to Fridthjof, asking him to come and help the kings.

Fridthjof was sitting at the knave-play when Hilding came. Said Hilding: Our kings send you their greetings, and request your help for the battle with king Ring, who is going to invade their kingdom with arrogance and wrong. Fridthjof answered nothing, but said to Bjorn, with whom he was playing: There is an open place there, foster-brother, and you will not be able to mend it; but I will attack the red piece, and see whether it can be saved. Said Hilding then again: King Helge bade me say this to you, Fridthjof, that you should go into this warfare together with them, or you might look for a severe treatment from them when they come back. Said Bjorn then: There is a choice between two, foster-brother, and there are two moves by which you may escape.

Says Fridthjof: Then I think it advisable to attack the knave first, and yet the double game is sure to be doubtful. No other answer to his errand did Hilding get, and so, without delay, he went back and told the kings what Fridthjof had said. They asked Hilding what meaning he could make out of those words. Answered he: When he spoke of the open place, he thought, in my opinion, of leaving his place in your expedition open; but when he pretended to attack the red piece, I think he by this meant your sister, Ingeborg; watch her, therefore, as well as you can. But when I threatened him with severe treatment from you, Bjorn considered it a choice between two, but Fridthjof said the knave must be attacked first, and by this he meant king Ring. Then the kings busked themselves for departure, but before they went they brought Ingeborg to Baldershage, and eight maidens with her. Said they that Fridthjof would not be so daring that he would go thither to meet her, for nobody is so rash as to injure anybody there. But the brothers went south to Jadar, and met king Ring in Sokn-Sound. What most of all made king Ring angry was that the brothers had said that they thought it a shame to fight with a man so old that he was unable to mount his horse without help.

IV

WHEN THE kings had gone away Fridthjof took his robes of state, and put his good gold ring on his hand; then the foster-brothers went down to the sea and launched Ellide. Said Bjorn: Whither shall we now turn the prow, foster-brother? Answered Fridthjof: To Baldershage, and amuse ourselves with Ingeborg.

Said Bjorn: It is not a proper thing to do, to provoke the gods. Said Fridthjof: Yet that risk shall now be run; besides, I rate the favor of Ingeborg of more account than that of Balder. Hereupon they rowed over the fjord, walked up to Baldershage and entered Ingeborg's bower, where she sat, together with eight maidens, and they, too, were eight. But when they came there all the place was covered with cloth of pall and other fine woven stuff. Then Ingeborg arose and said: Why are you so overbold, Fridthjof, that you have come here without the consent of my brothers, and thus provoke the wrath of the gods? Made answer Fridthjof: However this may be, I consider your love of more account than the wrath of the gods. Answered Ingeborg: You shall be welcome here, and all your men. Then she made room for him to sit at her side, and drank his toast of the best wine, and they sat and were merry together. Then Ingeborg, seeing the gold ring on his hand, asked whether he was the owner of that precious thing. Fridthjof said it was his. She praised the ring very much. Said Fridthjof: I will give you the ring if you promise not to part with it, and will send it to me when you no longer care to keep it, and with it we pledge our troth and love to each other. With this pledging of troth they exchanged rings. Fridthjof spent many nights at Baldlershage, and every day he went over there now and then to be merry with Ingeborg.

V

NOW IT is to be told of the brothers, that they met king Ring, who had more forces than they; then some people went between them, trying to bring about an agreement, so that there should be no battle. King Ring said he was willing to settle with them, on the condition that the brothers submit to him and give him their sister, Ingeborg the Fair, in marriage, together with the third part of all their possessions. The kings consented to this, for they saw that they had to do with a force far superior to their own.

This peace was firmly established by oaths, and the wedding was to be in Sogn, when king Ring came to meet his betrothed. The brothers fared home again with their troops, right ill content with the result. When Fridthjof thought the time had come when the brothers might be expected home, he said to the daughter of the king: Well and handsomely you have treated us, nor has the bonde Balder been angry with us. But as soon as you know that your kings have come home, then spread your bed-sheets on the hall of the goddesses, for that is the highest of all the houses in this place, and we can easily see it from our byre. Said the king's daughter: You have not followed the example of other men in this matter, but we certainly must welcome our friends when you come to us. Then Fridthjof went home, and early the next morning he went out-doors, and when he came in again he sang:

> Tell I must,
> Our good people,
> That our pleasure trips
> Wholly are ended;
> Men shall no more
> Go aboard the ships.
> For now are the sheets
> Spread out to bleach.

So they went out, and saw that all the hall of the goddesses was thatched with bleached linen. Said Bjorn then: Now the wings must have come home, and for us I think there will be but a short peace; to me it seems advisable that we gather folks together. This was done, and many men flocked together there. Soon the brothers heard of the ways of Fridthjof, and of his men and forces. Said king Helge then: It seems a wonder to me that Balder must endure every disgrace from Fridthjof. Now

I will send messengers to him, and know what kind of atonement he is willing to offer us, or else he is to be driven from the land, for I do not see that we have men enough at our command now to fight with him. Fridthjof's friends and his foster-father, Hilding, brought the message to him. Said they: The kings ask as an atonement from you, Fridthjof, that you go and collect the tribute from the Orkneys, which has never been paid since the death of Bele, for they are in want of the money just now, as they are about to give their sister Ingeborg in marriage, and a large amount of wealth with her. Makes answer Fridthjof; The only thing urging peace between us is regard for our deceased relatives, but the brothers will show us no trustiness. But this I will reserve, that all our possessions shall be left in peace during our absence.

This was promised and bound with an oath. Now Fridthjof made preparations for his voyage, choosing his men in reference to their bravery and ability to render service. The company consisted of eighteen men. Fridthjof's men asked him if he would not before setting out go to king Helge and make peace with him, and pray Balder to take his wrath away from him. Says Fridthjof: I make a solemn vow that I shall never ask for peace from king Helge. Hereupon he went aboard Ellide, and so they sailed out of the Sogn-Fjord. But when Fridthjof had departed from home, said king Halfdan to his brother Helge as follows: Our rule would be better and greater if Fridthjof was paid for his misdoings. Let us burn up his byre, and bring such a storm upon him and his men that they may perish. Helge said this was a thing to be done. Thereupon they burnt up the whole byre at Framness, and robbed it of all its fee. Then they sent for two witch-wives, Heid and Hamglom and gave them fee to send upon Fridthjof and his men so mighty a tempest that they should all be wrecked. So the witches sang their songs of witchcraft, and ascended the witch-scaffold with sorcery and incantations.

VI

BUT WHEN Fridthjof and his men had gotten out of Sogn-Fjord there fell upon them a violent storm and a great tempest, and the sea rolled heavily. The ship sped on swiftly, for it glided smoothly over the waters, and had an excellent form for breasting the sea. Sang Fridthjof then:

> My tarred horse of the sea
> I let swim out of Sogn,
> While the maids were drinking mead
> In the midst of Baldershage.
> The tempest now increases,
> Farewell, my brides, I bid you,

Who have a mind to love us.
Though Ellide should be filled.

Said Bjorn: It would be well if you could find something else to do than to sing about the maids of Baldershage. Made answer Fridthjof: My songs will not give out so soon, though. Then they were driven northward to the sounds near the islands called the Solunds. And now the storm had reached its highest pitch. Sang then Fridthjof:

High now the sea is swelling;
The waves and clouds unite,
Old spells are the causes
That call forth the breakers;
With anger shall I not
Contend in the tempest.
Let the ice-clad Solunds
Shelter our people!

Then they stood toward the islands that are called the Solunds, and intended to stop there; and now the storm suddenly abated. Then they took another course, and turned their prow away from the islands, having fair prospects for the voyage, for they had favorable wind for awhile; but the fair wind soon freshened into a gale. Sang Fridthjof then:

In former days
At Framness
I rowed to meet
My Ingeborg.
Now I shall sail
In the tempest cold,
Making the horse of the wave

Smoothly speed on. And when they bad sped before the wind far into the sea the waters began to be violently agitated again, and a gale blew up, accompanied by so great a snow-storm that the stem could not be seen from the stern, but the seas rushed over the ship so that the water had to be bailed out constantly. Sang Fridthjof then:

The waves are hid from sight,
For witch-wrought is the weather.
Heroes we of a well-famed band
Far out on the sea have come.
Stand we now all —

Disappeared have the Solunds—
Eighteen men a-baling

And Ellide sustaining. Said Bjorn: Varied will be his fortunes who fares far. That is certainly so, says Fridthjof, and sings:

Helge it is who causes
The rime-maned waves to swell.
This is not like kissing
The bride so fair in Baldershage;
Otherwise quite does love me
Ingeborg than the king.
I know no greater happiness
Than her wishes to fulfill.

Said Bjorn: Maybe she is looking to something higher for you than your present position, and this is not unpleasant to know. Says Fridthjof: Now is the time to trust good companions, though it would be more agreeable to be in Baldershage. They busked themselves bravely, for valiant men had gathered there, and the ship was the best that ever had been in the Northlands. Sang Fridthjof then this stave:

The waves are hid from sight,
Far west in the sea we are come.
Seems the ocean to me
Like embers all blazing.
High dash the breakers;
Hows are tossed up
By the swan-feathered billows.
On the rising ridges

Now Ellide rides. Now huge seas were shipped, so that all had to be baling out water. Sang Fridthjof:

Much must there now be drunk
To me by the maid's fair lips
East, where the sheets lay bleaching.
If it shall make me sink
'Neath the swan-feathered waves.

Said Bjorn: Do you think the maids of Sogn will shed many tears for you when you are dead? Made answer Fridthjof: That certainly comes into my mind. Then a huge sea broke over the bow of the ship, so that streams of water rushed in; but this saved them, that the ship was so excellent and the crew so hardy. Sang Bjorn then a stave:

> It seems not that a widow
> To you does drink,
> Nor that the ring-keeper fair
> Bids you draw near to her.
> Salt are our eyes.
> Soaked In the brine;
> Our strong arms are failing.
> Our eyelids are sore.

Answered Asmund: It does not matter though you do try your arms somewhat, for you did not pity us when we rubbed our eyes every morning when you rose so early to go to Baldershage. Said Fridthjof: Well, why do you not make a stave, Asmund? That shall not be, said Asmund, but still he sang this stave:

> Tight was the tug round the mast.
> When the seas broke over the ship;
> I alone 'gainst eight men
> Within board had to work.
> Better was it to bring
> Breakfast to the maiden's bower
> Than to be baling out Ellide
> Mid the roaring waves.

Said Fridthjof, laughing: You do not speak of your help in lower terms than it deserves, nevertheless you now showed something of the thrall-blood in yon, when you were willing to be a table-waiter. The storm still kept increasing, so that the breakers that roared round the ship seemed to the men who were on board more like huge peaks and mountains than like waves. Sang Fridthjof then:

> On cushioned seat I sat
> In Baldershage,
> Singing the songs I knew
> For the king's fair daughter.
> Now am I really
> To Ran's bed going.
> And another shall own
> My Ingeborg.

Said Bjorn: Great fear is now before as, foster-brother, and your words betoken anxiety, and that is too bad for such a brave fellow as you are. Says Fridthjof: There is neither fear nor anxiety, though ditties are made of our pleasure voyages, but it may be that they are spoken of oftener than need be, but most men would think themselves nearer to death than life if they were in our place; and still I will answer you with a stave:

That did I get to my gain;
With the maidens eight
Of Ingeborg did I, not you.
Succeed in negotiations.
At Baldershage we laid
Bright rings together;
Nor far away was then
The warder of Halfdan's land.

Said Bjorn: Such things as are already done, foster-brother, we must be content with. Now the seas dashed over the ship so violently that the bulwarks and both the sheets were broken, and four men were washed overboard and all were lost. Sang Fridthjof then:

Broken are both the sheets
Mid the ocean's great waves;
Four swains did sink
In the sea so deep.

Said Fridthjof: Reasonable it now seems to me that some of our men will go to Ran; but in my opinion we will not be considered fit to be sent thither unless we may come there busked like men, and it therefore seems good to me that every one of us have some gold on him. Then he cut the ring, Ingeborg's gift, asunder, distributed the pieces among his men, and sang this stave:

Before we are lost by Aeger.
Asunder shall be hewed the ring,
By the wealthy father of Halfdan owned.
Red as it is,
Gold shall glitter on the guests.
If of guesting we have need,
That will be fitting
For men of might
In the midst of Kan's halls.

Said Bjorn then: Now it is not to be looked for with any certainty that we come there, although it is not unlikely.

At this moment Fridthjof and his men observed that the ship was gliding over the waves very rapidly, but before them was a wholly unknown sea, and it was growing dark on all sides, so that no one could see the stem or stern from the middle of the ship, and the darkness was accompanied by sea-spray, storm, frost, snow and piercing cold. Then Fridthjof climbed the mast, and when he came down again said he to his companions: A wondrous sight I have seen: a large whale was swimming round the ship, and I have no doubt we must have come near to some land, and that this whale intends to keep us from reaching it. King Helge, I think, does not deal kindly with us, and he has undoubtedly sent us anything but a friendly messenger. I saw two women on the back of the whale, and they, methinks, cause this fearful tempest by witchcraft and sorcery of the worst sort. Now let us try whether our good luck or their witchcraft is more powerful, and you shall steer ashore as straightly as possible, but I shall smite these monsters with beams. Sang he then this stave:

Witches two
On the wave I see,
Has them hither
Helge sent.
Their backs shall Ellide
Cut in twain
E'er she her voyage
Completed has.

It is said that the ship Ellide had by enchantment gotten the power of understanding human speech. Said Bjorn then: Now men can see the disposition of the brothers toward us. Then Bjorn took the command of the ship; but Fridthjof seized a forked beam, ran to the prow and sang this stave:

Hail, Ellide!
Leap on the wave!
Break of the witches
The teeth and brow!
The cheeks and jaw-bones
Of the cursed woman.
One foot or both
Of this horrible witch!

Then he shot a fork at one of the ham-leapers (skin-changers), but the beak of Ellide struck the back of the other, and the backs of both were broken; but the whale dove down and swam away, and they saw him no more. Now the weather grew calmer, but the ship was waterlogged, and then Fridthjof called to his men requesting them to bale the ship dry. Bjorn said that this work was not needed. Whereto made answer Fridthjof: Have a care, foster-brother, and do not fall into despair; it has, you know, heretofore been the custom of brave men to give aid as long as possible, no matter what the result may be. Fridthjof sang this stave:

> My brave men! you need not
> Have fear of death.
> Exult with joy,
> My thanes!
> For this my dreams
> Full well do know,
> That I shall own
> My Ingeborg.

Having then baled the ship dry, and being near land, a rainy wind still blew against them. Then Fridthjof took two oars, seated himself in the foremost part of the prow and rowed rather vigorously. Thereupon the weather cleared off, and now they saw that they had gotten out of the sound of Effia, and there they landed. The crew were very much exhausted, but so stout was Fridthjof that he bore eight men over the fore-shore; Bjorn bore two, but Asmund one. Sang Fridthjof then:

> Up to the hearth
> Myself did bear
> My brave men, exhausted
> By the raging snow-storm.
> Now on the sand
> The sail I have brought;
> With the might of the sea
> It's not easy to deal.

VII

ANGANTYR was in Effia when Fridthjof landed there with his men. It was his custom when he drank that some man should sit at the watch-window of his drinking-hall, and took toward the wind and keep watch there. This man was to drink from a horn, and whenever one horn was emptied by him another was filled. He who was keeping watch at the time when Fridthjof landed hight Hallvard. Hallvard saw the coming of Fridthjof and his men, and sang this stave:

> In the violent storm
> I see on board Ellide
> Six men a-baling
> And seven a-rowing.
> The man in the prow,
> Bending over the oars,
> Is like Fridthjof the Bold,
> The valiant in battle.

And when he had drank from the horn he threw it in through the window, and said to the woman who gave him drink:

> Thou fair-walking woman!
> Take from the floor
> The horn turned over,
> Which I have emptied!
> Men I see on the sea,
> Exhausted by storm and rain.
> Who our help may need
> Ere the harbor they reach.

The jarl heard what Hallvard said, and asked for tidings.

Says Hallvard: Some men have landed here; they are quite exhausted, but I think they are good fellows, and one of them is so doughty that he is carrying the other men ashore. Said the jarl then: Go to meet them, and receive them in a seemly manner, if it should happen to be Fridthjof, son of my friend, the herser Thorstein; he is a most excellent man in respect to every accomplishment. Then took up the word the man who hight Atle, a great viking, and said he: Know it shall be found out whether Fridthjof, as it is said, has made a solemn vow never to be the first in praying for peace from anybody.

Together with Atle there were ten bad and ambitious men, who often went into berserks-gang. When they met Fridthjof they took their weapons. Said Atle then; Now it seems good, Fridthjof, that you turn this way, for as eagles fight face to face with their claws, so must we also. Fridthjof; and moreover, now is the time for you to keep your word, and not be the first to ask for peace. Fridthjof turned to meet them, and sang this stave:

> Succeed shall you never
> In cowing us down,

> You fainting cowards,
> Dwellers of these isles
> Either would I go
> Alone to fight
> With you men ten
> Than sue for peace.

Then Hallvard came to them and said: The jarl desires me to bid you all welcome, and no one shall insult you. Fridthjof said that he heartily accepted this greeting of welcome, and yet he was prepared to take either peace or war. Thereupon they went to call on the jarl, who received Fridthjof and all his men kindly. They spent the winter with the jarl, and were held in great honor by him; the latter frequently made questions about their voyages. This stave sang Bjorn:

> During ten whole days,
> And eight days more,
> We, fellows so merry,
> Continued a-baling,
> While billows dashed o'er us

From both sides. Made answer the jarl: Greatly has king Helge vexed you, and evil are such kings as do nothing but put people to death by witchcraft; but I know, Fridthjof, says Angantyr, what your errand hither is; you are sent hither to gather tribute, and thereto I can speedily give the answer, that king Helge shall have no tribute from me, but you may have as much fee from me as you please, and you may call it tribute or anything else you have a mind to. Fridthjof said he would accept the fee.

VIII

NOW IT shall be told what came to pass in Norway after Fridthjof had gone abroad. The brothers burn up all the byre at Framness. But while the weird sisters were performing their spells they fell down from the witch-scaffold on which they were seated, and both of them broke their backs. This autumn king Ring came north to Sogn to have his wedding, and a great feast was prepared for his nuptials with Ingeborg.

Says king Ring to Ingeborg: Whence has come that excellent ring that you wear on your hand? She said her father had been its owner. Answered he: It is a gift of Fridthjof; take it off your hand straightway, for you shall not be in want of gold when you come to Alfheim. Then she handed the ring to Helge's wife, and bade her give it to Fridthjof when he came back. King Ring then went home with his wife, and his love of her was exceedingly great.

IX

THE NEXT spring Fridthjof departed from the Orkneys, and parted with Angantyr on the most friendly terms. Hallvard went with Fridthjof. But when they came to Norway they learned that his byre had been burnt up, and when Fridthjof came to Framness he said:

Stout fellows, we
Formerly did drink
At Framness
With my father.
Now burnt I see
That same byre;
Repay must I
The king's ill deeds.

Then he consulted his men as to what was now to be done, but they bade him look to that himself; whereunto he made answer that he would first hand over the tribute. Afterward they rowed the boat over and came to Syrstrand. There they learn that the kings were at Baldershage, sacrificing to the dises.

Bjorn and Fridthjof then went up thither; and the latter bade Hallvard, Asmund and the other men break in pieces all the ships, large and small, that were to be found thereabout. So they did. Fridthjof and his men then went to the door of Baldershage. Fridthjof wanted to enter. Bjorn bade him go warily, as he wanted to go in alone. Fridthjof bade Bjorn remain outside and keep watch while he entered. Sang he then this stave:

Alone will I go
And enter the byre;
Little help do I need
The kings to find.
You shall throw fire
On the byre of the kings.
If I do not come
Back to-night.

Says Bjorn: That stave was well sung. Then Fridthjof went in and saw that there were but a few people in the hall of the dises; the kings were there at the time sacrificing, and sat drinking. Fire was burning on the floor, and the wives of the kings sat at the fires and warmed the gods, whereas other women were anointing the gods and wiping them with napkins. Fridthjof went before king Helge and said: Here you have the tribute. Herewith he swung the purse wherein was the silver, and threw it at his nose so violently that two teeth were broken out of his mouth, and he fell into a swoon in his high seat; but Halfdan caught him so that he did not fall into the fire. Sang Fridthjof then this stave:

> Take here your tribute,
> King of men!
> Take it with your fore-teeth
> Lest more you demand.
> At the bottom of this belg
> You find silver abounding.
> O'er which have ruled together
> Bjorn and I.

There were but few men in the room, for in another place there was drinking going on. But as Fridthjof walked over the floor toward the door, he saw that goodly ring on the hand of Helge's wife while she was warming Balder at the fire. Fridthjof took after the ring, but it stuck fast to her hand, and so he dragged her along the floor toward the door, and then Balder fell into the fire. But when Halfdan's wife caught after her quickly the god that she had been warming also fell into the fire. The flame now blazed up around both the gods, as they had previously been anointed and thence it ran up into the roof, so that the whole house was wrapped in flames. Fridthjof got hold of the ring before he went out Asked Bjorn then what had taken place during his visit in the house. But Fridthjof held the ring up and sang this stave:

> A blow received Helge:
> Smote the purse the villain's nose;
> Down fell the brother of Halfdan
> In the midst of the high seat.
> Balder had to burn,
> But first got I the ring.
> Then from the fire-place I
> Fearlessly wended my way.

People say that Fridthjof flung a flaming fire-brand at the roof, so that all the house was wrapped in flames, and that he then sang this stave:

> Wend we our way to the strand!

Then let our aims be high!
For the blue flame is bickering
In the midst of Baldershage.

Hereupon they went down to the sea.

X

WHEN KING Helge had come to his senses he gave orders to follow quickly after Fridthjof and kill him and all of his companions. That man, said he, has forfeited his life, as he has spared no Place of Peace. Now the trumpet was blown, and all the king's men came together; and when they came out to the hall, they saw that it stood in flames. King Halfdan and some of his men went to the fire, but king Helge followed after Fridthjof and his men. The latter had already got on board their ships and were lying on their oars. Helge and his men found that all their ships had been damaged, so they were forced to row ashore again, and lost some men. Then king Helge grew so angry that he became stark mad. Thereupon, with an arrow on the string, he stretched his bow and intended to shoot at Fridthjof. but he bent his bow with so much force that both' ends of it suddenly snapped off. When Fridthjof saw this, he seized two of Ellide's oars and plied them so mightily that both of them broke. Sang he then this stave:

Kissed I the young Ingeborg.
Bele's daughter.
In Baldershage.
Thus shall the oars
Of Ellide
Both be broken
Like Helge's bows.

After this the wind began to blow out of the inner part of the fjord so they hoisted the sails and sailed on. Fridthjof said to his men that they might busk themselves not to stay there very long. Afterward they sailed out of Sogn. Sang Fridthjof then this stave:

Sailed we out of Sogn,
Here sailed we a short time ago;
When flames consumed the byre
My father left to me.
But now in the midst of Baldershage
The flames have begun to blaze.

I now am an outlaw, for sooth I know that it has been sworn.

Said Bjorn to Fridthjof: What shall we do now? Foster-brother, said Fridthjof, I shall not remain here in Norway; I will try the life of warriors, and go on viking expeditions. Then they explored islands and skerries during the summer, and thus gained for themselves fee and fame; but in the fall they repaired to the Orkneys, where they were heartily welcomed by Angantyr, and they spent the winter there. But when Fridthjof had left Norway the kings held a thing, and declared Fridthjof an outlaw in all their realms, and made all his possessions their own. King Halfdan settled at Framness, and rebuilt the byre which had been burnt down; and likewise they restored the whole Baldershage, but it took a long time before the fire was put out. That which most touched the heart of Helge was that the gods had been burnt up, and it cost much to build Baldershage up again as it had been before. Sat king Helge now at Syrstrand.

XI

FRIDTHJOF WAS successful in gaining fee and fame wheresoever he came; villains and savage vikings he slew; the bondes and chapmen he left in peace; and he was now a second time called Fridthjof the Bold. He had gotten by this time a large and well-arrayed army, and had become exceedingly rich in chattels. But when Fridthjof had spent three winters in viking expeditions, he sailed west and steered up the Vik.

Fridthjof said he had a mind to go ashore; but you, said he, will have to go a harrying this winter; for I am growing tired of warfare, and I am going to the uplands to find king Ring, and have a talk with him; but you shall come back next summer and get me, and I will be here on the first day of summer.

Says Bjorn: This is no wise plan; however, your will must prevail; my wish it would be to go north to Sogn, and kill both the kings Halfdan and Helge. Makes answer Fridthjof: That is of no use; I prefer to go and find king Ring and Ingeborg. Says Bjorn: I am unwilling to run the risk of sending you alone into his hands, for although he is somewhat advanced in age, Ring is a wise man and of noble birth. Fridthjof said he must have his own way; and you, Bjorn, said he, will have to be the commander of our company in the meantime. They did as he would have it. So Fridthjof went to the uplands in the fall, for he was curious to see the love betwixt king Ring and Ingeborg.

Before he came thither he put on a large cowled cloak over the other clothes, all shagg. He had two staves in his hands, a mask over his face, and made himself look as old as possible. Afterward he met some herd-swains, and going heavily he asked them: Whence are you? Made answer they: We have our homes in Streitaland (Straggle-land), at the king's dwelling. Asks the old man: Is Ring a mighty king? Made answer they: To us you seem to be so old a man that you ought to know what manner of man king Ring is in all respects. The old man said he had been thinking more about salt-boiling than about the manner of kings. After this he went up to the king's hall. Toward the close of the day he went in, assumed a very feeble look, and stopping near the door he pulled the cowl over his head and hid his face. Said then king Ring to Ingeborg: There went a man into the hall much larger than other men. Answered the queen: Such are insignificant tidings here. The king then spoke to the man-servant who stood before the table: Go ask the cowl-man who he is, whence he comes, and where his kinsmen dwell. The swain then ran over the floor to the stranger and said: What is your name, my man? or where were you last night? or where are your kinsmen? Says the cowl-man: You ask your questions rapidly, my fellow: but will you be able to understand if I tell you about these things? Certainly I can, said the swain. Says the cowl-man; Thjof (thief) is my name, at Ulf's (wolf's) I spent last night, and in Anger (grief) I am brought up. The swain hastened before the king, and told him the answers of the stranger.

Says the king: You understood admirably, swain. I know the land called Anger, besides, it may be that this man's mind is not at ease. I think he is a wise man, and a man of great worth. Says the queen: This is a remarkable manner of yours to be so eager to talk with every carle that comes here, whosoever he may be; but so far as this man is concerned, I should like to know of what account he is. Says the king: You do not know any better than I do. I see he is a man that thinks more than he talks, and makes good use of his eyes. Thereupon the king sent a man for him, and the cowled man went to the inner part of the hall before the king; he bent forward somewhat, and greeted the king in a low voice. Said the king? What hight you, my large man? Made answer the cowled man by singing this stave:

> FRIDTHJJOF (peace-thief) I hight
> When I fared with the vikings;
> HEKTHJOF (war-thief) when
> The widows I grieved;
> GEIRTHJOF (spear-thief) when I
> The barbed shafts threw;
> GUNNTHJOF (battle-thief) when I
> 'Gainst the kings went;
> EYTHJOF (isle-thief) when I
> The skerries did plunder;

HELTHJOP (death-thief) when I
The babies did toss up;
VALTHJOF (slain-thief) when I
Higher than men was;
But now since then
With salt-boilers about
Have I been wandering;
With needy salt-earles,
Until hither I came.

Said then the king: From many things you have taken the thief's (Thjof's) name; but where were you last night? and where is your home? Made answer the cowled man: In Anger (grief) I am born, my mind urged me hitherward, but my home is nowhere. Says the king: It may be that you have been brought up in sorrow for awhile, but it may also be that you were born in peace. You must, I think, have spent last night in the forest, for there is no bonde near this place who hight Ulf (wolf); but when you say you have no home, yon undoubtedly mean that you think your home of little consequence, since your heart drove you hitherward. Said Ingeborg now: Go thief (Thjof)! get yourself other night-quarters, or betake yourself to the guest-chamber! Said the king: I am now old enough to arrange seats for my guests; come, stranger, put off your cloak and take a seat at my other hand. Said the queen: Yea, in your dotage you are, when you ask beggars to sit down by your side.

Said Thjof: It is not becoming, sir; better is that which the queen says; I am more accustomed to be among salt-boilers than to sit by the side of rulers. Said the king: Do as I will it; for I think my will must prevail this time. Thjof doffed his cloak, under which he was clad in a dark blue kirtle, and had a goodly ring on his hand; a large silver belt was about his waist; down from the belt hung a large purse full of bright silver coins, and a sword was girt to his side; but on his head he wore a large skin cap; his eyes looked dim and his face was all shaggy. Says the king: Now I dare say that things look as we would wish to have them; give him, my queen, a good mantle, and such a one as may be becoming to him.

Answered the queen: Your will shall prevail, my lord, but I do not like this Thjof (thief) much. Then a good mantle was given to him, which he donned and sat down in the high seat beside the king. The queen's face blushed red as blood when she saw the goodly ring, but still she was unwilling to converse with him, while the king was exceedingly cheerful, and said: A goodly ring you have on your hand, and you must have been boiling salt a long time before you earned it. Made answer Thjof: This is my whole paternal heritage. Says the king: May be you have more than that, but few salt-boilers are your equal; so I think, lest it should be that old he is fast creeping into my eyes. So Thjof spent the winter here, heartily treated and highly esteemed by all. He was liberal with his fee and cheerful to everybody. The queen seldom talked to him, but the king and he were always happy when they were together.

XII

THE SAGA tells that king Ring and his queen and a large company once were to go to a feast. Said king Ring then to Thjof: Will you go along, or will you stay at home? He said he would rather go along. Said the king: That suits me better. So they started, and had to cross a frozen lake. Said Thjof to the king: Untrustworthy seems to me the ice, and we seem to be going unwarily. Said the king: It is often to be observed that you have much forethought concerning us. A little while afterward all the ice broke down; then Thjof leaped to the place that was broken, and pulled up the sled and all that were in it. Both the king and the queen were sitting in the sled. All these, together with the horses hitched to the sled, Thjof suddenly put up onto the ice, and then said the king: That was a right good lift, Thjof; and Fridthjof the Bold, had he been here, would not have been able to do it with stronger hands; the doughtiest companions are such men as you. Now they came to the feast, from which we have no tidings, and the king fared home loaded with seemly gifts. Midwinter had passed, and when spring began the weather grew milder, the forests took to blooming, the grass to growing, and the ships were able to glide betwixt the lands.

XIII

IT WAS one day that the king said to his courtiers: I want you to go with me to the woods to-day, that we may amuse ourselves and see how fair is the country; and so they did, a large number of men rambled out into the woods with the king. It happened that the king and Fridthjof were both together in the woods, far from the other men. Said the king that he was heavy, and would fain sleep. Answers Thjof: Go home, my lord, for that is more becoming to a man of noble estate than to lie out-of-doors. Said the king: I cannot do that. Then he laid himself down, fell asleep and snored loudly. Thjof sat near him, drew his sword from the sheath and threw it far away from him. A little while afterward the king sat up and said: Is it not true, Fridthjof, that many things entered your mind? But you dealt wisely with those thoughts, and henceforth you shall be held in great honor with us. But I knew you immediately the first evening when you came into our hall, and you shall not speedily leave as; and I think a great future lies before you. Said Fridthjof: My lord, you have treated me well and friendly, but now

I mast soon be off, for my troops are soon coming to meet me, according to a previous arrangement that I have with them. Therewith they rode home from the woods, and now the king's folk crowded around them. All went home to the hall and drank freely. At the drinking it was made known to all that Fridthjof the Bold had spent the winter there.

XIV

ONE MORNING early there was a knock at that door of the hall where the king, the queen and many others were sleeping. Asked the king who was calling at the door. Said he who was outside: Fridthjof is here. I am now busk and bowne for my departure. Then the door was opened. In stepped Fridthjof and sang this stave:

> Now must I thank you.
> Bountifully you have feasted
> The feeder of the eagle.
> Bowne am I for departure.
> Ingeborg can I ne'er forget
> While to both of us life is granted.
> Fare she well I and take she
> This costly gift for many kisses.

Therewith he threw the goodly ring to Ingeborg and bade her accept it. The king smiled at this stave and said: So, after all, it came to pass that she got more thanks for your winter quarters than I, and yet she has not been more kind to you than I. The king then sent his servants for drink and food, saying that they should eat and drink before Fridthjof went away. Sit up, queen, he added, and be of good cheer. She said she had no mind to eat so early. Says king Ring: Let us now all eat together, and so they did. But when they had been drinking awhile said king Ring: I wish you might stay here, Fridthjof, for my sons are as yet nothing but children, but I am old and unfit to ward my land, if anybody should seek it for the purpose of harrying. Soon must I be off, my lord; and he sang this stave;

> Live, king Ring,
> Hale and long!
> The highest of kings
> 'Neath the northern skies!
> Guard well, my king,
> Your queen and land.
> Nevermore shall meet again
> Ingeborg and I.

Sang king Ring then:

Fare not thus from hence,
My Fridthjof! dearest
Son of kings,
So sad in mind!
Your costly gifts
I shall reward
Better far
Than, you are aware.

Sang he this too:

Give I the famous
Fridthjof my wife,
And therewith all
That belongs to me.

Interrupted him straightway Fridthjof, and sang:

I will not accept
Those gifts from yon,
Lest fatal illness
Threatens my king.

Says the king: I should not have given these things to you had I not thought that this was the case; for I am sick, and I wish you to enjoy this in preference to all others, for you are above all men in Norway. I give you a king's name, too; for her brothers, I think, will be less willing than I am to grant honor to you and give you the wife. Said Fridthjof: Accept many thanks from me, my lord, for your kindness, which is more than I could ask or even think; but as to my rank, I will take nothing more than a jarl's name. Herewith king Ring, taking Fridthjof's hand, gave him the government of the kingdom, which he had ruled over, and jarl's name therewith. Fridthjof was to rule until the sons of king Ring were old enough to rule their own kingdom. King Ring kept his sick-bed but a short time, and when he died there was great sorrow in his kingdom. A how was raised over him, and, according to his wish, much fee was buried with him. Then Fridthjof made a great feast, which his folk came to. At this feast king Ring's funeral and Ingeborg's and Fridthjof's wedding were celebrated together. Hereafter Fridthjof began to rule this kingdom, and was thought a most excellent man. He and Ingeborg had many children.

XV

THE KINGS in Sogn, the brothers of Ingeborg, heard these tidings, that Fridthjof had become the ruler of Ring-ric, and that he had married Ingeborg, their sister. Said Helge to Halfdan, his brother, that it was a great shame and an overbold act, that the son of a herser should marry her. So they gathered together much folk and went with them to Ring-ric with a view to slaying Fridthjof and conquering all the kingdom for themselves.

When Fridthjof became aware of this he also gathered together folk and said to the queen: A new war has come upon our realm, but, whatever the end of it may be, we do not like to see you in low spirits. Said she: It has now come to this, that we must look to you above all others. Bjorn had then come from the east to aid Fridthjof. They proceeded to battle, and, as he formerly had been wont, Fridthjof was foremost where the danger was the greatest. He and Helge came to a hand-to-hand struggle, and Fridthjof slew king Helge. Then Fridthjof held up the shield of peace, and thus the battle ceased. Said Fridthjof then to king Halfdan: Two important choices are now in your hands, the one that you surrender everything to me, the other that you get your bane like your brother. It is clear that I am stronger than both of you. Then Halfdan chose to surrender himself and his kingdom to Fridthjof. Now Fridthjof took the rule of the Sogn-fylke, but Halfdan should be herser in Sogn, and pay tribute to Fridthjof as long as he ruled over Ring-ric. The title of king of Sogn was given to Fridthjof from the time when he gave up Ring-ric to the sons of king Ring, and thereupon he added Hordaland by conquest. Fridthjof and Ingeborg had two sons, Gunnthjof and Hunthjof. Both of these became men of might.

And now here ends the saga of Fridthjof the Bold.

KING HARALD'S SAGA

By

Jennie Hall

I - The Baby

King Halfdan lived in Norway long ago. One morning his queen said to him:

"I had a strange dream last night. I thought that I stood in the grass before my bower. I pulled a thorn from my dress. As I held it in my fingers, it grew into a tall tree. The trunk was thick and red as blood, but the lower limbs were fair and green, and the highest ones were white. I thought that the branches of this great tree spread so far that they covered all Norway and even more."

"A strange dream," said King Halfdan. "Dreams are the messengers of the gods. I wonder what they would tell us," and he stroked his beard in thought.

Some time after that a serving-woman came into the feast hall where King Halfdan was. She carried a little white bundle in her arms.

"My lord," she said, "a little son is just born to you."

"Ha!" cried the king, and he jumped up from the high seat and hastened forward until he stood before the woman.

"Show him to me!" he shouted, and there was joy in his voice.

The serving-woman put down her bundle on the ground and turned back the cloth. There was a little naked baby. The king looked at it carefully.

"It is a goodly youngster," he said, and smiled. "Bring Ivar and Thorstein."

They were captains of the king's soldiers. Soon they came.

"Stand as witnesses," Halfdan said.

Then he lifted the baby in his arms, while the old serving-woman brought a silver bowl of water. The king dipped his hand into it and sprinkled the baby, saying:

"I own this baby for my son. He shall be called Harald. My naming gift to him is ten pounds of gold."

Then the woman carried the baby back to the queen's room.

"My lord owns him for his son," she said. "And no wonder! He is perfect in every limb."

The queen looked at him and smiled and remembered her dream and thought:

"That great tree! Can it be this little baby of mine?"

II - The Tooth Thrall

When Harald was seven months old he cut his first tooth. Then his father said:

"All the young of my herds, lambs and calves and colts, that have been born since this baby was born I this day give to him. I also give to him this thrall, Olaf. These are my tooth-gifts to my son."

The boy grew fast, for as soon as he could walk about he was out of doors most of the time. He ran in the woods and climbed the hills and waded in the creek. He was much with his tooth thrall, for the king had said to Olaf:

"Be ever at his call."

Now this Olaf was full of stories, and Harald liked to hear them.

"Come out to Aegir's Rock, Olaf, and tell me stories," he said almost every day.

So they started off across the hills. The man wore a long, loose coat of white wool, belted at the waist with a strap. He had on coarse shoes and leather leggings. Around his neck was an iron collar welded together so that it could not come off. On it were strange marks, called runes, that said:

"Olaf, thrall of Halfdan."

But Harald's clothes were gay. A cape of gray velvet hung from his shoulders. It was fastened over his breast with great gold buckles. When it waved in the wind, a scarlet lining flashed out, and the bottom of a little scarlet jacket showed. His feet and legs were covered with gray woolen tights. Gold lacings wound around his legs from his shoes to his knees. A band of gold held down his long, yellow hair.

It was a wild country that these two were walking over. They were climbing steep, rough hills. Some of them seemed made all of rock, with a little earth lying in spots. Great rocks hung out from them, with trees growing in their cracks. Some big pieces had broken off and rolled down the hill.

"Thor broke them," Olaf said. "He rides through the sky and hurls his hammer at clouds and at mountains. That makes the thunder and the lightning and cracks the hills. His hammer never misses its aim, and it always comes back to his hand and is eager to go again."

When they reached the top of the hill they looked back. Far below was a soft, green valley. In front of it the sea came up into the land and made a fiord. On each side of the fiord high walls of rock stood up and made the water black with shadow. All around the valley were high hills with dark pines on them. Far off were the mountains. In the valley were Halfdan's houses around their square yard.

"How little our houses look down there!" Harald said. "But I can almost—yes, I can see the red dragon on the roof of the feast hall. Do you remember when I climbed up and sat on his head, Olaf?"

He laughed and kicked his heels and ran on.

At last they came to Aegir's Rock and walked up on its flat top. Harald went to the edge and looked over. A ragged wall of rock reached down, and two hundred feet below was the black water of the fiord. Olaf watched him for a while, then he said:

"No whitening of your cheek, Harald? Good! A boy that can face the fall of Aegir's Rock will not be afraid to face the war flash when he is a man."

"Ho, I am not afraid of the war flash now," cried Harald.

He threw back his cape and drew a little dagger from his belt.

"See!" he cried; "does this not flash like a sword? And I am not afraid. But after all, this is a baby thing! When I am eight years old I will have a sword, a sharp tooth of war."

He swung his dagger as though it were a long sword. Then he ran and sat on a rock by Olaf.

"Why is this Aegir's Rock?" he asked.

"You know that Asgard is up in the sky," Olaf said. "It is a wonderful city where the golden houses of the gods are in the golden grove. A high wall runs all around it. In the house of Odin, the All-father, there is a great feast hall larger than the whole earth. Its name is Valhalla. It has five hundred doors. The rafters are spears. The roof is thatched with shields. Armor lies on the benches. In the high seat sits Odin, a golden helmet on his head, a spear in his hand. Two wolves lie at his feet. At his right hand and his left sit all the gods and goddesses, and around the hall sit thousands and thousands of men, all the brave ones that have ever died.

"Now it is good to be in Valhalla; for there is mead there better than men can brew, and it never runs out. And there are skalds that sing wonderful songs that men never heard. And before the doors of Valhalla is a great meadow where the warriors fight every day and get glorious and sweet wounds and give many. And all night they feast, and their wounds heal. But none may go to Valhalla except warriors that have died bravely in battle. Men who die from sickness go with women and children and cowards to Niflheim. There Hela, who is queen, always sneers at them, and a terrible cold takes hold of their bones, and they sit down and freeze.

"Years ago Aegir was a great warrior. Aegir the Big-handed, they called him. In many a battle his sword had sung, and he had sent many warriors to Valhalla. Many swords had bit into his flesh and left marks there, but never a one had struck him to death. So his hair grew white and his arms thin. There was peace in that country then, and Aegir sorrowed, saying:

"'I am old. Battles are still. Must I die in bed like a woman? Shall I not see Valhalla?'

"Now thus did Odin say long ago:

"'If a man is old and is come near death and cannot die in fight, let him find death in some brave way and he shall feast with me in Valhalla.'

"So one day Aegir came to this rock.

"'A deed to win Valhalla!' he cried.

"Then he drew his sword and flashed it over his head and held his shield high above him, and leaped out into the air and died in the water of the fiord."

"Ho!" cried Harald, jumping to his feet. "I think that Odin stood up before his high seat and welcomed that man gladly when he walked through the door of Valhalla."

"So the songs say," replied Olaf, "for skalds still sing of that deed all over Norway."

III - Olaf's Farm

At another time Harald asked:
"What is your country, Olaf? Have you always been a thrall?"
The thrall's eyes flashed.
"When you are a man," he said, "and go a-viking to Denmark, ask men whether they ever heard of Olaf the Crafty. There, far off, is my country, across the water. My father was Gudbrand the Big. Two hundred warriors feasted in his hall and followed him to battle. Ten sons sat at meat with him, and I was the youngest. One day he said:

"'You are all grown to be men. There is not elbow-room here for so many chiefs. The eldest of you shall have my farm when I die. The rest of you, off a-viking!'

"He had three ships. These he gave to three of my brothers. But I stayed that spring and built me a boat. I made her for only twenty oars because I thought few men would follow me; for I was young, fifteen years old. I made her in the likeness of a dragon. At the prow I carved the head with open mouth and forked tongue thrust out. I painted the eyes red for anger.

"'There, stand so!' I said, 'and glare and hiss at my foes.'

"In the stern I curved the tail up almost as high as the head. There I put the pilot's seat and a strong tiller for the rudder. On the breast and sides I carved the dragon's scales. Then I painted it all black and on the tip of every scale I put gold. I called her 'Waverunner.' There she sat on the rollers, as fair a ship as I ever saw.

"The night that it was finished I went to my father's feast. After the meats were eaten and the mead-horns came round, I stood up from my bench and raised my drinking-horn high and spoke with a great voice:

"'This is my vow: I will sail to Norway and I will harry the coast and fill my boat with riches. Then I will get me a farm and will winter in that land. Now who will follow me?'

"'He is but a boy,' the men said. 'He has opened his mouth wider than he can do.'

"But others jumped to their feet with their mead-horns in their hands. Thirty men, one after another, raised their horns and said:

"'I will follow this lad, and I will not turn back so long as he and I live!'

"On the next morning we got into my dragon and started. I sat high in the pilot's seat. As our boat flashed down the rollers into the water I made this song and sang it:

"'The dragon runs.
Where will she steer?
Where swords will sing,
Where spears will bite,
Where I shall laugh.'

"So we harried the coast of Norway. We ate at many men's tables uninvited. Many men we found overburdened with gold. Then I said:

"'My dragon's belly is never full,' and on board went the gold.

"Oh! it is better to live on the sea and let other men raise your crops and cook your meals. A house smells of smoke, a ship smells of frolic. From a house you see a sooty roof, from a ship you see Valhalla.

"Up and down the water we went to get much wealth and much frolic. After a while my men said:

"'What of the farm, Olaf?'

"'Not yet,' I answered. 'Viking is better for summer. When the ice comes, and our dragon cannot play, then we will get our farm and sit down.'

"At last the winter came, and I said to my men:

"'Now for the farm. I have my eye on one up the coast a way in King Halfdan's country.'

"So we set off for it. We landed late at night and pulled our boat up on shore and walked quietly to the house. It was rather a wealthy farm, for there were stables and a storehouse and a smithy at the sides of the house. There was but one door to the house. We went to it, and I struck it with my spear.

"'Hello! Ho! Hello!' I shouted, and my men made a great din.

"At last some one from inside said:

"'Who calls?'

"'I call,' I answered. 'Open! or you will think it Thor who calls,' and I struck my shield against the door so that it made a great clanging.

"The door opened only a little, but I pushed it wide and leaped into the room. It was so dark that I could see nothing but a few sparks on the hearth. I stood with my back to the wall; for I wanted no sword reaching out of the dark for me.

"'Now start up the fire,' I said.

"'Come, come!' I called, when no one obeyed. 'A fire! This is cold welcome for your guests.'

"My men laughed.

"'Yes, a stingy host! He acts as though he had not expected us.'

"But now the farmer was blowing on the coals and putting on fresh wood. Soon it blazed up, and we could see about us. We were in a little feast hall, with its fire down the middle of it. There were benches for twenty men along each side. The farmer crouched by the fire, afraid to move. On a bench in a far corner were a dozen people huddled together.

"'Ho, thralls!' I called to them. 'Bring in the table. We are hungry.'

"Off they ran through a door at the back of the hall. My men came in and lay down by the fire and warmed themselves, but I set two of them as guards at the door.

"'Well, friend farmer,' laughed one, 'why such a long face? Do you not think we shall be merry company?'

"'We came only to cheer you,' said another. 'What man wants to spend the winter with no guests?'

"'Ah!' another then cried out, sitting up. 'Here comes something that will be a welcome guest to my stomach.'

"The thralls were bringing in a great pot of meat. They set up a crane over the fire and hung the pot upon it, and we sat and watched it boil while we joked. At last the supper began. The farmer sat gloomily on the bench and would not eat, and you cannot wonder; for he saw us putting potfuls of his good beef and basket-loads of bread into our big mouths. When the tables were taken out and the mead-horns came round, I stood up and raised my horn and said to the farmer:

"'You would not eat with us. You cannot say no to half of my ale. I drink this to your health.'

"Then I drank half of the hornful and sent the rest across the fire to the farmer. He took it and smiled, saying:

"'Since it is to my health, I will drink it. I thought that all this night's work would be my death.'

"'Oh, do not fear that!' I laughed, 'for a dead man sets no tables.'

"So we drank and all grew merrier. At last I stood up and said:

"'I like this little taste of your hospitality, friend farmer. I have decided to accept more of it.'

"My men roared with laughter.

"'Come,' they cried, 'thank him for that, farmer. Did you ever have such a lordly guest before?'

"I went on:

"'Now there is no fun in having guests unless they keep you company and make you merry. So I will give out this law: that my men shall never leave you alone. Hakon there shall be your constant companion, friend farmer. He shall not leave you day or night, whether you are working or playing or sleeping. Leif and Grim shall be the same kind of friends to your two sons.'

"I named nine others and said:

"'And these shall follow your thralls in the same way. Now, am I not careful to make your time go merrily?'

"So I set guards over every one in that house. Not once all that winter did they stir out of sight of some of us. So no tales got out to the neighbors. Besides, it was a lonely place, and by good luck no one came that way. Oh! that was fat and easy living.

"Well, after we had been there for a long time, Hakon came in to the feast one night and said:

"'I heard a cuckoo to-day!'

"'It is the call to go a-viking,' I said.

"All my men put their hands to their mouths and shouted. Their eyes danced. Big Thorleif stood up and stretched himself.

"'I am stiff with long sitting,' he said. 'I itch for a fight.'

"I turned to the farmer.

"'This is our last feast with you,' I said.

"'Well,' he laughed, 'this has been the busiest winter I ever spent, and the merriest. May good luck go with you!'

"'By the beard of Odin!' I cried; 'you have taken our joke like a man.'

"My men pounded the table with their fists.

"'By the hammer of Thor!' shouted Grim. 'Here is no stingy coward. He is a man fit to carry my drinking-horn, the horn of a sea-rover and a sword-swinger. Here, friend, take it,' and he thrust it into the farmer's hand. 'May you drink heart's-ease from it for many years. And with it I leave you a name, Sif the Friendly. I shall hope to drink with you sometime in Valhalla.'

"Then all my men poured around that farmer and clapped him on the shoulder and piled things upon him, saying:

"'Here is a ring for Sif the Friendly.'

"'And here is a bracelet.'

"'A sword would not be ashamed to hang at your side.'

"I took five great bracelets of gold from our treasure chest and gave them to him.

"The old man's eyes opened wide at all these things, and at the same time he laughed.

"'May Odin send me such guests every winter!' he said.

"Early next morning we shook hands with our host and boarded the 'Waverunner' and sailed off.

"'Where shall we go?' my men asked.

"'Let the gods decide,' I said, and tossed up my spear.

"When it fell on the deck it pointed up-shore, so I steered in that direction. That is the best way to decide, for the spear will always point somewhere, and one thing is as good as another. That time it pointed us into your father's ships. They closed in battle with us and killed my men and sunk my ship and dragged me off a prisoner. They were three against one, or they might have tasted something more bitter at our hands. They took me before King Halfdan.

"'Here,' they said, 'is a rascal who has been harrying our coasts. We sunk his ship and men, but him we brought to you.'

"'A robber viking?' said the king, and scowled at me.

"I threw back my head and laughed.

"'Yes. And with all your fingers it took you a year to catch me.'

"The king frowned more angrily.

"'Saucy, too?' he said. 'Well, thieves must die. Take him out, Thorkel, and let him taste your sword.'

"Your mother, the queen, was standing by. Now she put her hand on his arm and smiled and said:

"'He is only a lad. Let him live. And would he not be a good gift for our baby?'

"Your father thought a moment, then looked at your mother and smiled.

"'Soft heart!' he said gently to her; then to Thorkel, 'Well, let him go, Thorkel!'

"Then he turned to me again, frowning.

"'But, young sharp-tongue, now that we have caught you we will put you into a trap that you cannot get out of. Weld an iron collar on his neck.'

"So I lived and now am your tooth thrall. Well, it is the luck of war. But by the chair of Odin, I kept my vow!"

"Yes!" cried Harald, jumping to his feet. "And had a joke into the bargain. Ah! sometime I will make a brave vow like that."

IV - Olaf's Fight With Havard

At another time Harald said:

"Tell me of a fight, Olaf. I want to hear about the music of swords."

Olaf's eyes blazed.

"I will tell you of our fight with King Havard," he said.

"One dark night we had landed at a farm. We left our 'Waverunner' in the water with three men to guard her. The rest of us went into the house. The farmer met us at the door, but he died by Thorkel's sword. The others we shut into their beds. The door at each end of the hall we had barred on the inside so that nobody could surprise us. We were busy going through the cupboards and shouting at our good luck. But suddenly we heard a shout outside:

"'Thor and Havard!'

"Then there was a great beating at the doors.

"'He has two hundred fighters with him,' said Grim; 'for we saw his ships last night. Thirty against two hundred! We shall all drink in Valhalla to-night.'

"'Well,' I cried, 'Odin shall have no unwilling guest in me.'

"'Nor in me,' cried Hakon.

"'Nor in me,' shouted Thorkel.

"And that shout went all around, and we drew out our swords and caught up our shields.

"'Hot work is ahead of us,' said Hakon. 'Besides, we must leave none of this mead for Havard. Lend a hand, some one.'

"Then he and another pulled out a great tub that sat on the floor of the cupboard.

"'I drink to Valhalla to-night,' cried Thorkel the Thirsty, and he plunged his horn deep into the tub.

"When he brought it up, his sleeve was dripping and the sweet mead was running over from the horn.

"'Sloven!' cried Hakon, and he struck Thorkel with his fist and knocked him over into the cupboard.

"He fell against the wooden wall at the back, and a carved panel swung open behind him. He dropped down head first. In a minute he put his head out of the hole again. We all stood staring.

"'I think it is a secret passage,' he said.

"'We will try it,' I answered in a whisper. 'Throw dirt on the fire. It must be dark.'

"So we dug up dirt from the earth floor and smothered the fire. All this time there was a terrible shouting and hammering at the doors, but they were of heavy logs and stood.

"'I with four more will guard this door,' I said, pointing to the east end.

"Immediately four men stepped to my side.

"'And I will guard the other,' Hakon said, and four went with him.

"'The rest of you, down the hole!' I said. 'Close the door after you. If luck is with us we will meet at the ships. Now Thor and our good swords help us! Quick! The doors are giving way.'

"So we ten men stood at the doors and held back the king's soldiers. It was dark in the room, and the people out of doors could not tell how many were inside. Few were eager to be the first in.

"'Thirty swords are waiting in there to eat up the first man,' we heard some one say.

"We chuckled at that.

"But the king stood in the very doorway and fought. Our five swords held him back for a long time, but at last he pushed in, and his men poured after him. We ran back and hid behind some tubs in a dark corner. The king's men went groping about and calling, but they did not find us. The room was full of shouting and running and sword-clashing; for in the dark and the noise the men could not tell their own soldiers. More than one fell by his friend's sword. When it was less crowded about the doorway, I whispered:

"'Follow me in double line. We will make for the ships. Keep close together.'

"So that double line of men, with swords swinging from both sides, ran out through the dark. Swords struck out at us, and we struck back. Men ran after us shouting, but our legs were as good as theirs. But I and Hakon and one other were all that reached the ship. There we saw our 'Waverunner' with sail up and bow pointing to open sea. We swam out to her and climbed aboard. Then the men swung the sail to the wind, and we moved off. Even as we went, a spear whizzed through the air, and Hakon fell dead; for the king and all his men were running to the shore.

"'After them!' they were shouting.

"Then we heard the king call to the men in his boats lying out in the water:

"'Row to shore and take us in.'

"Thorkel was standing by my side. At that he laughed and said:

"'They do not answer. He left but a handful to guard his ships. They tasted our swords. And we went aboard and broke the oars and threw the sails into the water. It will be slow going for Havard to-night.'

"Then he turned to the shore and sang out loudly:

"'King Havard's ships are dead:
Olaf's dragon flies.
King Havard stamps the shore:
Olaf skims the waves.
King Havard shakes his fist.

Olaf turns and laughs.'

"That was the end of our meeting with King Havard."

V - Foes' fear

Every day the boy Harald heard some such story of war or of the gods, until he could see Thor riding among the storm-clouds and throwing his hammer, until he knew that a brave man has many wounds, but never a one on his back. Many nights he dreamed that he himself walked into Valhalla, and that all the heroes stood up and shouted:

"Welcome! Harald Halfdanson!"

"Ah! the bite of the sword is sweeter than the kiss of your mother," he said to Olaf one day. "When shall I stand in the prow of a dragon and feast on the fight? I am hungry to see the world. Ivar the Far-goer tells me of the strange countries he has seen. Ah! we vikings are great folk. There is no water that has not licked our boats' sides. This cape of mine came in a viking boat from France. These cloak-pins came from a far country called Greece. In my father's house are golden cups from Rome, away on the southern sea. Every land pours rich things into our treasure-chest. Ivar has been to a strange country where it is all sand and is very hot. The people call their country Arabia. They have never heard of Thor or Odin. Ivar brought beautiful striped cloth from there, and wonderful, sweet-smelling waters. Oh! when shall the white horses of the sea lead me out to strange lands and glorious battles?"

But Harald did something besides listen to stories. Every morning he was up at sunrise and went with a thrall to feed the hunting dogs. Thorstein taught him to swim in the rough waters of the fiord. Often he went with the men a-hunting in the woods and learned to ride a horse and pull a bow and throw a lance. Ivar taught him to play the harp and to make up songs. He went much to the smithy, where the warriors mended their helmets and made their spears and swords of iron and bronze. At first he only watched the men or worked the bellows, but soon he could handle the tongs and hold the red-hot iron, and after a long time he learned to use the hammer and to shape metal. One day he made himself a spear-head. It was two feet long and sharp on both edges. While the iron was hot he beat into it some runes. When the men in the smithy saw the runes they opened their eyes wide and looked at the boy, for few Norsemen could read.

"What does it say?" they asked.

"It is the name of my spear-point, and it says, 'Foes'-fear,'" Harald said. "But now for a handle."

It was winter and the snow was very deep. So Harald put on his skees and started for a wood that was back from shore. Down the mountains he went, twenty, thirty feet at a slide, leaping over chasms a hundred feet across. In his scarlet cloak he looked like a flash of fire. The wind shot past him howling. His eyes danced at the fun.

"It is like flying," he thought and laughed. "I am an eagle. Now I soar," as he leaped over a frozen river.

He saw a slender ash growing on top of a high rock.

"That is the handle for 'Foes'-fear,'" he said.

The rock stood up like a ragged tower, but he did not stop because of the steep climb. He threw off his skees and thrust his hands and feet into holes of the rock and drew himself up. He tore his jacket and cut his leather leggings and scratched his face and bruised his hands, but at last he was on the top. Soon he had chopped down the tree and had cut a straight pole ten feet long and as big around as his arm. He went down, sliding and jumping and tearing himself on the sharp stones. With a last leap he landed near his skees. As he did so a lean wolf jumped and snapped at him, snarling. Harald shouted and swung his pole. The wolf dodged, but quickly jumped again and caught the boy's arm between his sharp teeth. Harald thought of the spear-point in his belt. In a wink he had it out and was striking with it. He drove it into the wolf's neck and threw him back on the snow, dead.

"You are the first to feel the tooth of 'Foes'-fear,'" he said, "but I think you will not be the last."

Then without thinking of his torn arm he put on his skees and went leaping home. He went straight to the smithy and smoothed his pole and drove it into the haft of the spear-point. He hammered out a gold band and put it around the joining place. He made nails with beautiful heads and drove them into the pole in different places.

"If it is heavy it will strike hard," he said.

Then he weighed the spear in his hand and found the balancing point and put another gold band there to mark it.

Thorstein came in while he was working.

"A good spear," he said.

Then he saw the torn sleeve and the red wound beneath.

"Hello!" he cried. "Your first wound?"

"Oh, it is only a wolf-scratch," Harald answered.

"By Thor!" cried Thorstein, "I see that you are ready for better wounds. You bear this like a warrior."

"I think it will not be my last," Harald said.

VI - Harald is King

Now when Harald was ten years old his father, King Halfdan, died. An old book that tells about Harald says that then "he was the biggest of all men, the strongest, and the fairest to look upon." That about a boy ten years old! But boys grew fast in those days for they were out of doors all the time, running, swimming, leaping on skees, and hunting in the forest. All that makes big, manly boys.

So now King Halfdan was dead and buried, and Harald was to be king. But first he must drink his father's funeral ale.

"Take down the gay tapestries that hang in the feast hall," he said to the thralls. "Put up black and gray ones. Strew the floor with pine branches. Brew twenty tubs of fresh ale and mead. Scour every dish until it shines."

Then Harald sent messengers all over that country to his kinsmen and friends.

"Bid them come in three months' time to drink my father's funeral ale," he said. "Tell them that no one shall go away empty-handed."

So in three months men came riding up at every hour. Some came in boats. But many had ridden far through mountains, swimming rivers; for there were few roads or bridges in Norway. On account of that hard ride no women came to the feast.

At nine o'clock in the night the feast began. The men came walking in at the west end of the hall. The great bonfires down the middle of the room were flashing light on everything. The clean smell of this wood-smoke and of the pine branches on the floor was pleasant to the guests. Down each side of the hall stretched long, backless benches, with room for three hundred men. In the middle of each side rose the high seat, a great carved chair on a platform. All along behind the benches were the black and gray draperies. Here hung the shields of the guests; for every man, when he was given his place, turned and hung his shield behind him and set his tall spear by it. So on each wall there was a long row of gay shields, red and green and yellow, and all shining with gold or bronze trimmings. And higher up there was another row of gleaming spear-points. Above the hall the rafters were carved and gaily painted, so that dragons seemed to be crawling across, or eagles seemed to be swooping down.

The guests walked in laughing and talking with their big voices so that the rafters rang. They made the hall look all the brighter with their clothes of scarlet and blue and green, with their flashing golden bracelets and head-bands and sword-scabbards, with their flying hair of red or yellow.

Across the east end of the hall was a bench. When the men were all in, the queen, Harald's mother, and the women who lived with her, walked in through the east door and sat upon this bench.

Then thralls came running in and set up the long tables before the benches. Other thralls ran in with large steaming kettles of meat. They put big pieces of this meat into platters of wood and set it before the men. They had a few dishes of silver. These they put before the guests at the middle of the tables; for the great people sat here near the high seats.

When the meat came, the talking stopped; for Norsemen ate only twice a day, and these men had had long rides and were hungry. Three or four persons ate from one platter and drank from the same big bowl of milk. They had no forks, so they ate from their fingers and threw the bones under the table among the pine branches. Sometimes they took knives from their belts to cut the meat.

When the guests sat back satisfied, Harald called to the thralls:
"Carry out the tables."

So they did and brought in two great tubs of mead and set one at each end of the hall. Then the queen stood up and called some of her women. They went to the mead tubs. They took the horns, when the thralls had filled them, and carried them to the men with some merry word. Perhaps one woman said as she handed a man his horn:

"This horn has no feet to be set down upon. You must drink it at one draught."

Perhaps another said:
"Mead loves a merry face."

The women were beautiful, moving about the hall. The queen wore a trailing dress of blue velvet with long flowing sleeves. She had a short apron of striped Arabian silk with gold fringe along the bottom. From her shoulders hung a long train of scarlet wool embroidered in gold. White linen covered her head. Her long yellow hair was pulled around at the sides and over her breast and was fastened under the belt of her apron. As she walked, her train made a pleasant rustle among the pine branches. She was tall and straight and strong. Some of her younger women wore no linen on their heads and had their white arms bare, with bracelets shining on them. They, too, were tall and strong.

All the time men were calling across the fire to one another asking news or telling jokes and laughing.

An old man, Harald's uncle, sat in the high seat on the north side. That was the place of honor. But the high seat on the south side was empty; for that was the king's seat. Harald sat on the steps before it.

The feast went merrily until long after midnight. Then the thralls took some of the guests to the guest house to sleep, and some to the beds around the sides of the feast hall. But some men lay down on the benches and drew their cloaks over themselves.

On the next night there was another feast. Still Harald sat on the step before the high seat. But when the tables were gone and the horns were going around, he stood up and raised high a horn of ale and said loudly:

"This horn of memory I drink in honor of my father, Halfdan, son of Gudrod, who sits now in Valhalla. And I vow that I will grind my father's foes under my heel."

Then he drank the ale and sat down in the king's high seat, while all the men stood up and raised their horns and shouted:

"King Harald!"

And some cried:

"That was a brave vow."

And Harald's uncle called out:

"A health to King Harald!"

And they all drank it.

Then a man stood up and said:

"Hear my song of King Halfdan!" for this man was a skald.

"Yes, the song!" shouted the men, and Harald nodded his head.

So the skald took down his great harp from the wall behind him and went and stood before Harald. The bottom of the harp rested on the floor, but the top reached as high as the skald's shoulders. The brass frame shone in the light. The strings were some of gold and some of silver. The man struck them with his hand and sang of King Halfdan, of his battles, of his strong arm and good sword, of his death, and of how men loved him.

When he had finished, King Harald took a bracelet from his arm and gave it to him, saying:

"Take this as thanks for your good song."

The guests stayed the next day and at night there was another feast. When the mead horns were going around, King Harald stood up and spoke:

"I said that no man should go away empty-handed from drinking my father's funeral ale."

He beckoned the thralls, and they brought in a great treasure-chest and set it down by the high seat. King Harald opened it and took out rich gifts—capes and sword-belts and beautiful cloth and bracelets and gold cloak-pins. These he sent about the hall and gave something to every man. The guests wondered at the richness of his gifts.

"This young king has an open hand," they said, "and deep treasure-chests."

After breakfast the next morning the guests went out and stood by their horses ready to go, but before they mounted, thralls brought a horn of mead to each man. That was called the stirrup-horn, because after they drank it the men put their feet to the stirrups and sprang upon their horses and started. King Harald and his people rode a little way with them.

All men said that that was the richest funeral feast that ever was held.

VII - Harald's Battle

Now King Halfdan had many foes. When he was alive they were afraid to make war upon him, for he was a mighty warrior. But when Harald became king, they said:

"He is but a lad. We will fight with him and take his land."

So they began to make ready. King Harald heard of this and he laughed and said:

"Good! 'Foes'-fear' is thirsty, and my legs are stiff with much sitting."

He called three men to him. To one he gave an arrow, saying:

"Run and carry this arrow north. Give it into the hands of the master of the next farm, and say that all men are to meet here within two weeks from this day. They must come ready for war and mounted on horses. Say also that if a man does not obey this call, or if he receives this arrow and does not carry it on to his next neighbor, he shall be outlawed from this country, and his land shall be taken from him."

He gave arrows to the other two men and told them to run south and east with the same message.

So all through King Harald's country men were soon busy mending helmets and polishing swords and making shields. There was blazing of forges and clanging of anvils all through the land.

On the day set, the fields about King Harald's house were full of men and horses. After breakfast a horn blew. Every man snatched his weapons and jumped upon his horse. Men of the same neighborhood stood together, and their chief led them. They waited for the starting horn. This did not look like our army. There were no uniforms. Some men wore helmets, some did not. Some wore coats of mail, but others wore only their jackets and tights of bright-colored wool. But at each man's left side hung a great shield. Over his right shoulder went his sword-belt and held his long sword under his left hand. Above most men's heads shone the points of their tall spears. Some men carried axes in their belts. Some carried bows and arrows. Many had ram's horns hanging from their necks.

King Harald rode at the front of his army with his standard-bearer beside him. Chain-armor covered the king's body. A red cloak was thrown over his shoulders. On his head was a gold helmet with a dragon standing up from it. He carried a round shield on his left arm. The king had made that shield himself. It was of brass. The rivets were of silver, with strangely shaped heads. On the back of Harald's horse was a red cloth trimmed with the fur of ermine.

King Harald looked up at his standard and laughed aloud.

"Oh, War-lover," he cried, "you and I ride out on a gay journey."

A horn blew again and the army started. The men shouted as they went, and blew their ram's horns.

"Now we shall taste something better than even King Harald's ale," shouted one.

Another rose in his stirrups and sniffed the air.

"Ah! I smell a battle," he cried. "It is sweeter than those strange waters of Arabia."

So the army went merrily through the land. They carried no tents, they had no provision wagons.

"The sky is a good enough tent for a soldier," said the Norsemen. "Why carry provisions when they lie in the farms beside you?"

After two days King Harald saw another army on the hills.

"Thorstein," he shouted, "up with the white shield and go tell King Haki to choose his battle-field. We will wait but an hour. I am eager for the frolic."

So Thorstein raised a white shield on his spear as a sign that he came on an errand of peace. He rode near King Haki, but he could not wait until he came close before he shouted out his message and then turned and rode back.

"Tell your boy king that we will not hang back," Haki called after Thorstein.

King Harald's men waited on the hillside and watched the other army across the valley. They saw King Haki point and saw twenty men ride off as he pointed. They stopped in a patch of hazel and hewed with their axes.

"They are getting the hazels," said Thorstein.

"Audun," said King Harald to a man near him, "stay close to my standard all day. You must see the best of the fight. I want to hear a song about it after it is over."

This Audun was the skald who sang at the drinking of King Halfdan's funeral ale.

King Haki's men rode down into the valley. They drove down stakes all about a great field. They tied the hazel twigs to the stakes in a string. But they left an open space toward King Harald's army and one toward King Haki's. Then a man raised a white shield and galloped toward King Harald.

"We are ready!" he shouted.

At the same time King Haki raised a red shield. King Harald's men put their shields before their mouths and shouted into them. It made a great roaring war-cry.

"Up with the war shield!" shouted King Harald. "Horns blow!"

There was a blowing of horns on both sides. The two armies galloped down into the field and ran together. The fight had begun.

All that day long swords were flashing, spears flying, men shouting, men falling from their horses, swords clashing against shields.

"Victory flashes from that dragon," Harald's men said, pointing to the king's helmet. "No one stands before it."

And, surely, before night came, King Haki fell dead under "Foes'-fear." When he fell, a great shout went up from his warriors, and they turned and fled. King Harald's men chased them far, but during the night came back to camp. Many brought swords and helmets and bracelets or silver-trimmed saddles and bridles with them.

"Here is what we got from the foe," they said.

The next morning King Harald spoke to his men:

"Let us go about and find our dead."

So they went over all the battle-field. They put every man on his shield and carried him and laid him on a hill-top. They hung his sword over his shoulder and laid his spear by his side. So they laid all the dead together there on the hill-top. Then King Harald said, looking about:

"This is a good place to lie. It looks far over the country. The sound of the sea reaches it. The wind sweeps here. It is a good grave for Norsemen and Vikings. But it is a long road and a rough road to Valhalla that these men must travel. Let the nearest kinsman of each man come and tie on his hell-shoes. Tie them fast, for they will need them much on that hard road."

So friends tied shoes on the dead men's feet. Then King Harald said:

"Now let us make the mound."

Every man set to work with what tools he had and heaped earth over the dead until a great mound stood up. They piled stones on the top. On one of these stones King Harald made runes telling how these men had died.

After that was done King Harald said:

"Now set up the pole, Thorstein. Let every man bring to that pole all that he took from the foe."

So they did, and there was a great hill of things around it. Harald divided it into piles.

"This pile we will give to Thor in thanks for the victory," he said. "This pile is mine because I am king. Here are the piles for the chiefs, and these things go to the other men of the army."

So every man went away from that battle richer than he was before, and Thor looked down from Valhalla upon his full temple and was pleased.

The next morning King Harald led his army back. But on the way he met other foes and had many battles and did not lose one. The kings either died in battle or ran away, and Harald had their lands.

"He has kept his vow," men said, "and ground his father's foes under his heel."

So King Harald sat in peace for a while.

VIII - Gyda's Saucy Message

Now Harald heard men talk of Gyda, the daughter of King Eric.

"She is very beautiful," they said, "but she is very proud, too. She can both read and make runes. No other woman in the world knows so much about herbs as she does. She can cure any sickness. And she is proud of all this!"

Now when King Harald heard that, he thought to himself:

"Fair and proud. I like them both. I will have her for my wife."

So he called his uncle, Guthorm, and said:

"Take rich gifts and go to Gyda's foster-father and tell him that I will marry Gyda."

So Guthorm and his men came to that house and they told the king's message to the foster-father. Gyda was standing near, weaving a rich cloak. She heard the speech. She came up and said, holding her head high and curling her lip:

"I will not waste myself on a king of so few people. Norway is a strange country. There is a little king here and a little king there—hundreds of them scattered about. Now in Denmark there is but one great king over the whole land. And it is so in Sweden. Is no one brave enough to make all of Norway his own?"

She laughed a scornful laugh and walked away. The men stood with open mouths and stared after her. Could it be that she had sent that saucy message to King Harald? They looked at her foster-father. He was chuckling in his beard and said nothing to them. They started out of the house in anger. When they were at the door, Gyda came up to them again and said:

"Give this message to your King Harald for me: I will not be his wife unless he puts all of Norway under him for my sake."

So Guthorm and his men rode homeward across the country. They did not talk. They were all thinking. At last one said:

"How shall we give this message to the king?"

"I have been thinking of that," Guthorm said; "his anger is no little thing."

It was late when they rode into the king's yard; for they had ridden slowly, trying to make some plan for softening the message, but they had thought of none.

"I see light through the wind's-eyes of the feast hall," one said.

"Yes, the king keeps feast," Guthorm said. "We must give our message before all his guests."

So they went in with very heavy hearts. There sat King Harald in the high seat. The benches on both sides were full of men. The tables had been taken out, and the mead-horns were going round.

"Oh, ho!" cried King Harald. "Our messengers! What news?"

Then Guthorm said:

"This Gyda is a bold and saucy girl, King Harald. My tongue refuses to give her message."

The king stamped his foot.

"Out with it!" he cried. "What does she say?"

"She says that she will not marry so little a king," Guthorm answered.

Harald jumped to his feet. His face flushed red. Guthorm stretched out his hand.

"They are not my words, O King; they are the words of a silly girl."

"Is there any more?" the king shouted. "Go on!"

"She said: 'There is one king in Denmark and one king in Sweden. Is there no man brave enough to make himself king of all Norway? Tell King Harald that I will not marry him unless he puts all of Norway under him for my sake.'"

The guests sat speechless, staring at Guthorm. All at once the king broke into a roar of laughter.

"By the hammer of Thor!" he cried, "that is a good message. I thank you, Gyda. Did you hear it, friends? King of all Norway! Why, we are all stupids. Why did we not think of that?"

Then he raised his horn high.

"Now hear my vow. I say that I will not cut my hair or comb it until I am king of all Norway. That I will be or I will die."

Then he drank off the horn of mead, and while he drank it, all the men in the hall stood up and waved their swords and shouted and shouted. That old hall in all its two hundred years of feasts had not heard such a noise before.

"Ah, Harald!" Guthorm cried, "surely Thor in Valhalla smiled when he heard that vow."

The men sat all night talking of that wonderful vow.

On the very next day King Harald sent out his war-arrows. Soon a great army was gathered. They marched through the country north and south and east and west, burning houses and fighting battles as they went. People fled before them, some to their own kings, some inland to the deep woods and hid there. But some went to King Harald and said:

"We will be your men."

"Then take the oath, and I will be friends with you," he said.

The men took off their swords and laid them down and came one by one and knelt before the king. They put their heads between his knees and said:

"From this day, Harald Halfdanson, I am your man. I will serve you in war. For my land I will pay you taxes. I will be faithful to you as my king."

Then Harald said:

"I am your king, and I will be faithful to you."

Many kings took that oath and thousands of common men. Of all the battles that Harald fought, he did not lose one.

Now for a long time the king's hair and beard had not been combed or cut. They stood out around his head in a great bushy mat of yellow. At a feast one day when the jokes were going round, Harald's uncle said:

"Harald, I will give you a new name. After this you shall be called Harald Shockhead. As my naming gift I give you this drinking-horn."

"It is a good name," laughed all the men.

After that all people called him Harald Shockhead.

During these wars, whenever King Harald got a country for his own, this is what he did. He said:

"All the marshland and the woodland where no people live is mine. For his farm every man shall pay me taxes."

Over every country he put some brave, wise man and called him Earl. He said to the earls:

"You shall collect the taxes and pay them to me. But some you shall keep for yourselves. You shall punish any man who steals or murders or does any wicked thing. When your people are in trouble they shall come to you, and you shall set the thing right. You must keep peace in the land. I will not have my people troubled with robber vikings."

The earls did all these things as best they could; for they were good strong men. The farmers were happy. They said:

"We can work on our farms with peace now. Before King Harald came, something was always wrong. The vikings would come and steal our gold and our grain and burn our houses, or the king would call us to war. Those little kings are always fighting. It is better under King Harald."

But the chiefs, who liked to fight and go a-viking, hated King Harald and his new ways. One of these chiefs was Solfi. He was a king's son. Harald had killed his father in battle. Solfi had been in that battle. At the end of it he fled away with two hundred men and got into ships.

"We will make that Shockhead smart," he said.

So they harried the coast of King Harald's country. They filled their ships with gold. They ate other men's meals. They burned farmhouses behind them. The people cried out to the earls for help. So the earls had out their ships all the time trying to catch Solfi, but he was too clever for them.

In the spring he went to a certain king, Audbiorn, and said to him:

"Now, there are two things that we can do. We can become this Shockhead Harald's thralls, we can kneel before him and put our heads between his knees. Or else we can fight. My father thought it better to die in battle than to be any man's thrall. How is it? Will you join with my cousin Arnvid and me against this young Shockhead?"

"Yes, I will do it," said the king.

IX - The Sea Fight

Many men felt as Solfi did. So when King Audbiorn and King Arnvid sent out their war arrows, a great host gathered. All men came by sea. Two hundred ships lay at anchor in the fiord, looking like strange swimming animals because of their high carved prows and bright paint. There were red and gold dragons with long necks and curved tails. Sea-horses reared out of the water. Green and gold snakes coiled up. Sea-hawks sat with spread wings ready to fly. And among all these curved necks stood up the tall, straight masts with the long yardarms swinging across them holding the looped-up sails.

When the starting horn blew, and their sails were let down, it was like the spreading of hundreds of curious flags. Some were striped black and yellow or blue and gold. Some were white with a black raven or a brown bear embroidered on them, or blue with a white sea-hawk, or black with a gold sun. Some were edged with fur. As the wind filled the gaudy sails, and the ships moved off, the men waved their hands to the women on shore and sang:

"To the sea! To the sea!
The wind in our sail,
The sea in our face,
And the smell of the fight.
After ship meets ship,
In the quarrel of swords
King Harald shall lie
In the caves under sea
And Norsemen shall laugh."

In the prow stood men leaning forward and sniffing the salt air with joy. Some were talking of King Harald.

"Yesterday he had a hard fight," they said. "To-day he will be lying still, dressing his wounds and mending his ships. We shall take him by surprise."

They sailed near the coast. Solfi in his "Sea-hawk" was ahead leading the way. Suddenly men saw his sail veer and his oars flash out. He had quickly turned his boat and was rowing back. He came close to King Arnvid and called:

"He is there, ahead. His boats are ready in line of battle. The fox has not been asleep."

King Arnvid blew his horn. Slowly his boats came into line with his "Sea-stag" in the middle. Again he blew his horn. Cables were thrown across from one prow to the next, and all the ships were tied together so that their sides touched. Then the men set their sails again and they went past a tongue of land into a broad fiord. There lay the long line of King Harald's ships with their fierce heads grinning and mocking at the newcomers. Back of those prows was what looked like a long wall with spots of green and red and blue and yellow and shining gold. It was the locked shields of the men in the bows, and over every shield looked fierce blue eyes. Higher up and farther back was another wall of shields; for on the half deck in the stern of every ship stood the captain with his shield-guard of a dozen men.

Arnvid's people had furled their sails and were taking down the masts, but the ships were still drifting on with the wind. The horn blew, and quickly every man sprang to his place in bow and stern. All were leaning forward with clenched teeth and widespread nostrils. They were clutching their naked swords in their hands. Their flashing eyes looked over their shields.

Soon King Arnvid's ships crashed into Harald's line, and immediately the men in the bows began to swing their swords at one another. The soldiers of the shield-guard on the high decks began to throw darts and stones and to shoot arrows into the ships opposite them.

So in every ship showers of stones and arrows were falling, and many men died under them or got broken arms or legs. Spears were hurled from deck to deck and many of them bit deep into men's bodies. In every bow men slashed with their swords at the foes in the opposite ship. Some jumped upon the gunwale to get nearer or hung from the prow-head. Some even leaped into the enemy's boat.

King Harald's ship lay prow to prow with King Arnvid's. The battle had been going on for an hour. King Harald was still in the stern on the deck. There was a dent in his helmet where a great stone had struck. There was a gash in his shoulder where a spear had cut. But he was still fighting and laughed as he worked.

"Wolf meets wolf to-day," he said. "But things are going badly in the prow," he cried. "Ivar fallen, Thorstein wounded, a dozen men lying in the bottom of the boat!"

He leaped down from the deck and ran along the gunwale, shouting as he went:

"Harald and victory!"

So he came to the bow and stood swinging his sword as fast as he breathed. Every time it hit a man of Arnvid's men. Harald's own warriors cheered, seeing him.

"Harald and victory!" they shouted, and went to work again with good heart.

Slowly King Arnvid's men fell back before Harald's biting sword. Then Harald's men threw a great hook into that boat and pulled it alongside and still pushed King Arnvid's people back.

"Come on! Follow me!" cried Harald.

Then he leaped into King Arnvid's boat, and his warriors followed him.

"He comes like a mad wolf," King Arnvid's men said, and they turned and ran back below the deck.

Then Arnvid himself leaped down and stood with his sword raised.

"Can this young Shockhead make cowards of you all?" he cried.

But Harald's sword struck him, and he fell dead. Then a big, bloody viking of King Arnvid leaped upon the edge of the ship and stood there. He held his drinking-horn and his sword high in his hands.

"Ran and not you, Shockhead, shall have them and me!" he cried, and leaped laughing into the water and was drowned.

Many other warriors chose the same death on that terrible day.

All along the line of boats men fought for hours. In some places the cables had been cut, and the boats had drifted apart. Ships lay scattered about two by two, fighting. May boats sank, many men died, some fled away in their ships, and at the end King Harald had won the battle. So he had King Arnvid's country and King Audbiorn's country. Many men took the oath and became his friends. All people were talking of his wonderful battles.

X - King Harald's Wedding

It had taken King Harald ten years to fight so many battles. And all that time he had not cut his hair or combed it. Now he was feasting one day at an earl's house. Many people were there.

"How is it, friends?" Harald said. "Have I kept my vow?"

His friends answered:

"You have kept your vow. There is no king but you in all Norway."

"Then I think I will cut my hair," the king laughed.

So he went and bathed and put on fresh clothes. Then the earl cut his hair and beard and combed them and put a gold band about his head. Then he looked at him and said:

"It is beautiful, smooth, and yellow."

And all people wondered at the beauty of the king's hair.

"I will give you a new name," the earl said. "You shall no longer be called Shockhead. You shall be called Harald Hairfair."

"It is a good name," everybody cried.

Then Harald said:

"But I have another thing to do now. Guthorm, you shall take the same message to Gyda that you gave ten years ago."

So Guthorm went and brought back this answer from Gyda:

"I will marry the king of all Norway."

So when the wedding time came, Harald rode across the country to the home of Gyda's father, Eric. Many men followed him. They were all richly dressed in velvet and gold.

For three nights they feasted at Eric's house. On the next night Gyda sat on the cross-bench with her women. A long veil of white linen covered her face and head and hung down to the ground. After the mead-horns had been brought in, Eric stood up from his high seat and went down and stood before King Harald.

"Will you marry Gyda now?" he asked.

Harald jumped to his feet and laughed.

"Yes," he said. "I have waited long enough."

Then he stepped down from his high seat and stood by Eric. They walked about the hall. Before them walked thralls carrying candles. Behind them walked many of King Harald's great earls. Three times they walked around the hall. The third time they stopped before the cross-bench. King Harald and Eric stepped upon the platform, where the cross-bench was.

Eric gave a holy hammer to Harald, and it was like the hammer of Thor. Harald put it upon Gyda's lap, saying:

"With this holy hammer of Thor's, I, Harald, King of Norway, take you, Gyda, for my wife."

Then he took a bunch of keys and tied it to Gyda's girdle, saying:

"This is the sign that you are mistress of my house."

After that, Eric called out loudly:

"Now, are Harald, King of Norway, and Gyda, daughter of Eric, man and wife."

Then thralls brought meat and drink in golden dishes. They were about to serve it to Gyda for the bride's feast, but Harald took the dish from them and said:

"No, I will serve my bride."

So he knelt and held the platter. When he did that his men shouted. Then they talked among themselves, saying:

"Surely Harald never knelt before. It is always other people who kneel to him."

When the bride had tasted the food and touched the mead-horn to her lips she stood up and walked from the hall. All her women followed her, but the men stayed and feasted long.

On the next morning at breakfast Gyda sat by Harald's side. Soon the king rose and said:

"Father-in-law, our horses stand ready in the yard. Work is waiting for me at home and on the sea. Lead out the bride."

So Eric took Gyda by the hand and led her out of the hall. Harald followed close. When they passed through the door Eric said:

"With this hand I lead my daughter out of my house and give her to you, Harald, son of Halfdan, to be your wife. May all the gods make you happy!"

Harald led his bride to the horse and lifted her up and set her behind his saddle and said:

"Now this Gyda is my wife."

Then they drank the stirrup-horn and rode off.

"Everything comes to King Harald," his men said; "wife and land and crown and victory in battle. He is a lucky man."

XI - King Harald Goes West-Over-Seas

Now many men hated King Harald. Many a man said:
"Why should he put himself up for king of all of us? He is no better than I am. Am I not a king's son as well as he? And are not many of us kings' sons? I will not kneel before him and promise to be his man. I will not pay him taxes. I will not have his earl sitting over me. The good old days have gone. This Norway has become a prison. I will go away and find some other place."

So hundreds of men sailed away. Some went to France and got land and lived there. Big Rolf-go-afoot and all his men sailed up the great French River and won a battle against the French king himself. There was no way to stop the flashing of his battle-axes but to give him what he wanted. So the king made Rolf a duke, gave him broad lands and gave him the king's own daughter for wife. Rolf called his country Normandy, for old Norway. He ruled it well and was a great lord, and his sons' sons after him were kings of England.

Other Norsemen went to Ireland and England and Scotland. They drew up their boats on the river banks. The people ran away before them and gathered into great armies that marched back to meet the vikings in battle. Sometimes the Norsemen lost, but oftener they won, so that they got land and lived in those countries. Their houses sat in these strange lands like warriors' camps, and the Norsemen went among their new neighbors with hanging swords and spears in hand, ever ready for fight.

There are many islands north of Scotland. They are called the Orkneys and the Shetlands. They have many good harbors for ships. They are little and rocky and bare of trees. Wild sea-birds scream around them. On some of them a man can stand in the middle and see the ocean all about him. Now the vikings sailed to these islands and were pleased.

"It is like being always in a boat," they said. "This shall be our home."

So it went until all the lands round about were covered with vikings. Norse carved and painted houses brightened the hillsides. Viking ships sailed all the seas and made harbor in every river. Norsemen's thralls plowed the soil and planted crops and herded cattle, and gold flowed into their masters' treasure-chests. Norse warriors walked up and down the land, and no man dared to say them nay.

These men did not forget Norway. In the summers they sailed back there and harried the coast. They took gold and grain and beautiful cloth back to their homes. In Norway they left burning houses and weeping women.

Every summer King Harald had out his ships and men and hunted these vikings. There are many little islands about Norway. They have crags and caves and deep woods. Here the vikings hid when they saw King Harald's ships coming. But Harald ran his boat into every creek and fiord and hunted in every cave and through all the woods and among the crags. He caught many men, but most of them got away and went home laughing at Harald. Then they came back the next summer and did the same deeds over again. At last King Harald said:

"There is but one thing to do. I must sail to these western islands and whip these robbers in their own homes."

So he went with a great number of ships. He found as brave men as he had brought from Norway. These vikings had brought their old courage to their new homes. King Harald's fine ships were scarred by viking stones and scorched by viking fire. The shields of Harald's warriors had dents from viking blows. Many of those men carried viking scars all their lives. And many of King Harald's warriors walked the long, hard road to Valhalla, and feasted there with some of these very vikings that had died in King Harald's battles. But after many hard fights on land and sea, after many men had died and many had fled away to other lands, King Harald won, and he made the men that were yet in the islands take the oath, and he left his earls to rule over them. Then he went back to Norway.

"He has done more than he vowed to do," people said. "He has not only whipped the vikings, but he has got a new kingdom west-over-seas."

Then they talked of that dream that his mother had.

"King Harald was that great tree," they said. "The trunk was red with the blood of his many battles, but higher up the limbs were fair and green like this good time of peace. The topmost branches were white because Harald will live to be an old man. Just as that tree spread out until all of Norway was in its shade, and even more lands, so Harald is king of all this country and of the western islands. The many branches of that tree are the many sons of Harald, who shall be earls and kings in Norway, and their sons after them, for hundreds of years."

INGOLF'S SAGA

By

Jennie Hall

Men had been feasting in Ingolf's house. But there was no laughing and no shouting of jokes. Ingolf sat in his high seat frowning and gloomy. His head hung on his breast. He was staring into the fire. Now he raised his head and looked about the hall.

"Comrades," he said, "what shall we do? Herstein and Holmstein died by our swords. Their kinsmen hunger to kill us. Besides, when Harald hears of our deed, there will not be a safe place in Norway for us. He will never let a man fight out an honest quarrel. Where shall we go?"

A man stood up from the bench.

"We have friends in the Shetlands," he said. "Let us find homes there."

Then Leif, in the high seat opposite Ingolf, stood up.

"No, not the Shetlands, my foster-brother. They are crowded already. Besides, Harald will not long keep his hands off them. Then they will be no better than Norway. England and Ireland and Scotland are old. My eyes ache for something new. What of that far island that Floki found? It is empty. We could choose our land from the whole country. There is good fishing. There are green valleys. And Butter Thorolf says that butter drops from every weed. There are mountains and deserts where we may find adventure. I say, let us steer for Iceland!"

When he stopped, many of the men shouted:

"Yes! Iceland!"

But an old man stood up.

"We have all laughed at that tale of Butter Thorolf's," he said. "But Floki himself said that the sea about the island is full of ice that pushes upon the land, that no ship can live in that water in the winter, that great mountains of ice cover the island. Did not all his cattle die there of hunger and cold, and did he not come back to Norway cursing Iceland?"

"Oh, Sighvat, you are old and fearful," called out Leif, and he laughed. Then he stretched himself up and threw back his head.

"Are we afraid of ice? Have we not seen angry water before? I have been hungry, but I have never died of it. Surely if there are fish in the sea and grass in the valleys, we can live there. I should like to stand on a hill and look around on a wide land and think, 'This is all ours,' and out upon a rough sea and think, 'Far off there are our foes and they dare not come over to us.' Besides, we shall have no Shockhead Harald to lord it over us. We can come and go and feast and fight as we please. We shall be our own kings. And our ships will be always waiting to take us away, when we are weary of it. And we shall see things that other men have never seen. I am tired of the old things. Perhaps in after days men will make songs about 'those foster-brothers, Ingolf and Leif, who made a new country in a wonderful land, and whose sons and grandsons are mighty men in Iceland!'"

Ingolf leaped up from his chair.

"By the strong arm of Thor!" he cried, "I like the sound of it. Now I make my vow."

He raised his drinking-horn.

"I vow that I will find this Iceland and pass the winter there, and that if man can live upon it I will go back there and set up my home."

"And I vow that I will follow my foster-brother," cried Leif.

And many men vowed to go.

So on the next day they began to make ready a boat. They looked her over carefully and recalked every seam and freshly painted her and put into her their strongest oars and made her a new sail.

"This will be the longest voyage that she ever made," Ingolf said.

When the work was done, they put into her great stores, axes, hammers, fish-nets, cooking-kettles, kegs of ale, chests of hard bread, chests of smoked meat, brass kettles full of flour, skin bottles of water. They stowed these things away in the ends of the ship. When they were ready they put in four head of cattle.

"We shall need the milk and perhaps the meat," Ingolf said.

Many men wished to go, but Ingolf had said:

"There is little room to spare and little food and drink. I have planned for half a year. But perhaps we must be sailing longer than that. Our food may run short. We must not have extra mouths to feed. There are thirty oars in our boat. I will take only one man for every oar, and Leif and I will steer."

So they started off. Leif stood in the prow leaning forward and looking far ahead, and he sang:

"What does the swimming dragon smell?
A stormy sea, an empty land,
Hunger, darkness, giants, fire.

Leif and his sword do laugh at that."

They sailed for days and saw no land. Sometimes they passed ships and always made sure to sail close enough to hail them.

"Where are you going?" Ingolf would call.

"To Norway," would come back the answer.

"For trade or fight?" Leif would shout.

Then would ring out a great laugh from that boat and this answer:

"A shut mouth is a good friend."

So the two ships sailed on, and the men were glad to have heard a greeting and to have called one.

But at last there were the Shetlands.

"We will go in here and rest," Ingolf said.

When they rowed to shore a certain Shetland man stood there. He watched them land and looked them all over. Then he walked up to Ingolf and said:

"You look like brave men. Welcome to Shetland. You shall come to my house and rest your legs from ship-going and fill your stomachs. I hunger for news of Norway."

So they went to his house and stayed there for three days. And good it seemed to be near a fire and in a quiet bed and before a steaming platter. When they went to the shore to start off again, the Shetland man had his thralls carry a keg of ale and a great kettle of cooked meat and put them into the ship.

"Think of me when you eat this," he said.

Then the Norsemen put to sea again and sailed for a long time.

One day a terrible storm came up; the sky was black; the wind howled through the ship. Great waves leaped in the sea.

"Down with the sail and out with the oars!" Ingolf shouted.

So the men furled the sail and took down the mast and laid it along the bottom of the boat. As they worked, one man was washed overboard and drowned. The men sat down to row, but the tumbling waves tossed the boat about and poured over her and broke three of the oars. But still the men held on. They were wet to the skin and were cold, and their arms and legs ached with the hard work, and they were hungry from the long waiting, but not one face was white with fear.

"Ran, in her caves under sea, wants us for company to-night," Ingolf laughed.

So they tossed about all night, but in the morning the wind died down. Great waves still rolled, and for days the sea was rough, but they could put up the sail. Then one day Leif, as he sat in the pilot's seat, jumped to his feet and sang:

"To eyes grown tired with looking far,
All at once appeared an island,
A stretching-place for sea-legs,
A quiet bed for backs grown stiff
On rowing-bench on rolling sea.
A place to build a red fire
And thaw the blood that sea-winds froze."

But when they came near they saw no place to land. The island was like a mountain of rock standing out of the water. The sides were steep and smooth. They sailed around it, but found no place to climb up.

"There are many other islands here," said Leif. "We will try another."

So he steered to another. It, too, was a steep rock, but one side sloped down to the water and was green with grass.

"Oh, I have not seen anything so good as that green grass since I looked into my mother's face," one man said.

There was a little harbor there. The men rowed in and quickly jumped out and put the rollers under the ship and pulled her upon shore. Then they threw themselves down on the grass and rolled and stretched their arms and shouted for joy. After that they built a fire and warmed themselves and cooked a meal and ate like wolves. They slept there that night.

In the morning before Ingolf's men started away they were standing high up on the hillside, looking about. They saw no houses on any of the islands, but they saw smoke rise from one hillside.

"Some other men, like us, weary of the sea and stopping to rest," said Ingolf.

They saw the island that they had sailed around the night before.

"There can surely be nothing but birds' nests on top of that," Sighvat said.

"Look!" cried another, pointing.

Men were standing on the flat top of that island. They were letting a boat down the steep side with ropes. When it struck the water, they made a rope fast to the rock and slid down it into the ship and sailed off.

"Some robber vikings from Scotland or Ireland," laughed Leif. "It is a good hiding place for treasure."

Soon Ingolf and his men got into their ship and were off. Old Sighvat grumbled.

"Is this land not new enough and empty enough and far enough? I am tired of sea, sea, sea, and nothing else."

"We started for Iceland," said Ingolf, "and I will not stop before I come there. I have a vow. Did you make none, Sighvat?"

Then they were on the water again for weeks with no sight of land.

"Oh! I would give my right hand to see a dragon pawing the water off there and to fling a word to its men," Sighvat said.

"No hope of that," replied Ingolf. "Only three dragons before ours have ever swept this water, and men are not sailing this way for pleasure or riches."

So only the desolate sea stretched around them. Sometimes it was smooth and shining under the sun. Often it was torn by winds, and a gray sky hung over it, and the men were drenched with rain. Once they ran into a fog. For three days and nights they could not see sun or stars to steer by. They forgot which way was north. When after three days the fog lifted, they found that they had been going in the wrong direction, and they had to turn around and sail all that weary way over again. But at last one afternoon they saw a white cloud resting on the water far off. As they sailed toward it, it grew into long stretches of black, hilly shore with a blue ice mountain rising from it. The sun was going down behind that mountain, and long lines of pink and of shining green, and great purple shadows streaked the blue.

"It is Iceland!" shouted the men.

"It is like Asgard the Shining," Ingolf said.

But it was still far off. Men can see a long way there because the air is so clear. So Ingolf and his people sailed on for hours and at last came into a harbor. A little green valley sloped up from it. On one side was the bright ice mountain. Back of it were bare black and red hills. In that valley Ingolf and his men drew up their boat and camped. At supper that night one of the men said:

"I almost think I never felt a fire before or had warm food in my mouth."

The men laughed.

"It is four months since we left Norway," Ingolf said. "Few men have ever been on the sea so long."

That night they put up the awning in the boat and slept under it.

After that some men went fishing every day in the rowboat that they had. And Ingolf took others, and they sailed along the shore, seeing what kind of a land this was. But winter began to come on. Then Ingolf said:

"Remember what Floki said of the ice and the rough sea in winter. Soon we cannot sail any longer. Let us choose a place to stay and build a hut there and cut hay for our cattle."

So they did. Their hut was a little mean thing of stones and turf. They kept the cattle and the hay in it. Sometimes they slept there, when it was very cold. But most of the time they ate and slept by a great bonfire out of doors where it was clean. Leif said:

"I like the cold air of the sea better than the bad-smelling air of a house, even though it is warm."

Now every day Ingolf and Leif and some of the men walked about the island. At night they all sat around the campfire and talked of what they had seen during the day.

"This is surely a wonderful land," Ingolf said once. "It is at the same time like Niflheim and like Asgard. Here is a spot green and soft, a sweet cradle for men. Next it is a mountain of ice where men would freeze to death. And next to that is a hill of rock that seems to have come out of some great fire. Yesterday I saw a cave on the seashore. The door of it was big enough for a giant. The waves broke at the doorstep. A terrible roaring came from the cave. I think it is the home of a giant. I think that giants of fire and giants of frost made this island. I have seen great basins in the rocks filled with warm water. They looked like giants' bath-tubs. I have seen boiling water shoot up out of the ground. I have walked, and have felt and heard a great rumbling under me as though some giant were sleeping there and turning over in his sleep. One day I stood on a mountain and looked inland. There was a wide desert of sand and black and red rock with nothing growing on it. The fierce wind blew dirt into my eyes, and the cold of it froze the marrow in my bones. When I have seen these things I have cursed the country, and have said: 'The gods hate Iceland. I will not stay here.' But then I have walked through beautiful warm valleys where the winds did not come. I saw in my mind the flowers that we found last summer. I saw our cattle feeding on the sweet grass. I thought of the sea full of good fish. I saw my house built among green fields, and my wife sitting in her home, and my children playing among the flowers and making up tales about the bright ice mountains. I saw the wide, rough seas between me and Harald and our foes. Then I thought to myself, 'It is the sweetest home on earth.' As for me, I am coming here to live. What do you say, comrades?"

"Have I not vowed to follow you, foster-brother?" said Leif. "And indeed I never saw a land that I liked better. I don't believe in your giants. My sword is my god, and my ship is my temple, and I like this land to set them up in."

They sat about the fire long that night making plans.

"You shall go home and get our women and our things, Ingolf," said Leif. "I will off to Ireland and have a frolic. There will be little play of swords in this empty land, and I want to have one last game before I hang up my battle-knife. Besides, I will come to you with a ship full of gold and clothes and house-hangings such as we cannot get here, and they will cost me nothing but the swing of a sword."

As they talked, Ingolf looked up at the sky. The northern lights were quivering there. They were like great flames of yellow and green and red.

"See," he said, and pointed. "We are not so far that the gods will forget us. There is the flash of the armor of the Valkyrias. A battle is on somewhere, and Odin has sent his maidens to choose the heroes for Valhalla."

Leif only laughed and lay down to sleep.

So in the spring they all went back to Norway. Leif got ready the boat again and merrily sailed for Ireland.

"Here I go to get riches for our new land," he said.

Ingolf set his men to cutting down pines in the forest and some to building a new ship. He had his thralls plant large crops of grain and grind flour and make new kegs and chests of wood. He himself worked much at the forge, making all kinds of tools—spades, axes, hammers, hunting-knives, cooking kettles. The women were busy weaving and sewing new clothes. Ingolf sold his house and land and everything that he could not take with him.

After about two years Leif came back. He had ten thralls that he had got in Ireland. He took Ingolf aboard his ship and raised the covers of great chests. Gold helmets, silver-trimmed drinking-horns, embroidered robes, and swords flashed out.

"Did I not say that I would come back with a full ship?" he laughed.

At last all things were ready for starting.

"To-day I will sacrifice to Thor and Odin," Ingolf said. "If the omens are good we will start to-morrow."

"Well, go, foster-brother," laughed Leif. "But I have better things to do. I will be putting the cattle into the ship and will have all ready."

So Ingolf and his men went into the forests a little way. There in a cleared space stood a large building. In front of this temple the men killed two horses for Odin. Ingolf caught some of the blood in a brass bowl. He raised it and looked up at the sky and said:

"All-wise and all-father Odin, and Thor who loves the thunder, I give these horses to you. Tell me whether it is your will that we go to Iceland."

As he said that, a raven flew over his head. Ingolf watched it.

"It is Odin's will that we go," he said. "He sent his raven to tell us. It is flying straight toward Iceland."

The men shouted with joy at that.

Now they hung some of the meat of the horses on a tree near the temple.

"For the ravens of Odin," they said.

Ingolf carried the bowl of blood into the temple. He went through the feast hall in front to a little room at the back. Here stood wooden statues of the gods in a semicircle. Before them was a stone altar. Ingolf took a little brush of twigs that lay on it and dipped it into the blood and sprinkled the statues.

"You shall taste of our sacrifice," he said. "Look kindly on us from your happy seats in Asgard."

Then they went into the feast hall. There thralls were boiling the horseflesh in pots over the fire. The tables were standing ready before the benches. Ingolf walked to the high seat. All the others took their places at the benches. When the horns came round, Ingolf made this vow:

"I vow that I will build my house wherever these pillars lead me."

He put his hand upon a tall post that stood beside the high seat. There was one at each side. They were the front posts of the chair. But they stood up high, almost to the roof. They were wonderfully carved and painted with men and dragons. On the top of each one was a little statue of Thor with his hammer.

At the end of the feast Ingolf had his thralls dig these pillars up. He had a little bronze chest filled with the earth that was under the altar.

"I will take the pillars of my high seat to Iceland," he said, "and I will set up my altar there upon the soil of Norway, the soil that all my ancestors have trod, the soil that Thor loves."

So they carried the pillars and the chest of earth and the statues of the gods, and put them into Ingolf's boat.

"It is a well-packed ship," the men said. "There is no spot to spare."

Tools, and chests of food, and tubs of drink, and chests of clothes, and fishing nets were stowed in the bows of both boats. In the bottom were laid some long, heavy, hewn logs.

"The trees in Iceland are little," Ingolf said. "We must take the great beams for our homes with us."

Standing on these logs were a few cattle and sheep and horses and pigs. The rowers' benches were along the sides. In the stern of each boat was a little cabin. Here the women and children were to sleep. But the men would sleep on the timbers in the middle of the boat and perhaps they would put up the awning sometimes.

At last everyone was aboard. Men loosed the rope that held the boats. The ships flashed down the rollers into the water, and Ingolf and Leif were off for Iceland. As they sailed away everyone looked back at the shore of old Norway. There were tears in the women's eyes. Helga, Leif's wife, sang:

"There was I born. There was I wed.
There are my father's bones.
There are the hills and fields,
The streams and rocks that I love.
There are houses and temples,
Women and warriors and feasts,
Ships and songs and fights—
A crowded, joyous land.
I go to an empty land."

There was the same long voyage with storm and fog. But at last the people saw again the white cloud and saw it growing into land and mountains. Then Ingolf took the pillars of his high seat and threw them overboard.

"Guide them to a good place, O Thor!" he cried.

The waves caught them up and rolled them about. Ingolf followed them with his ship. But soon a storm came up. The men had to take down the sails and masts, and they could do nothing with their oars. The two ships tossed about in the sea wherever the waves sent them. The pillars drifted away, and Ingolf could not see them.

"Remember your pillars, O Thor!" he cried.

Then he saw that Leif's ship was being driven far off.

"Ah, my foster-brother," he thought, "shall I not have you to cheer me in this empty land? O Thor, let him not go down to the caves of Ran! He is too good a man for that."

On the next day the storm was not so hard, and Ingolf put in at a good harbor. A high rocky point stuck out into the sea. A broad bay with islands in the mouth was at the side. Behind the rocky point was a level green place with ice-mountains shining far back.

After a day or two Ingolf said:

"I will go look for my pillars."

So he and a few men got into the rowboat and went along the shore and into all the fiords, but they could not find the pillars. After a week they came back, and Ingolf said:

"I will build a house here to live in while I look for the posts. This way is uncomfortable for the women."

So he did. Then he set out again to look for the pillars, but he had no better luck and came back.

"I must stay at home and see to the making of hay and the drying of fish," he said. "Winter is coming on, and we must not be caught with nothing to eat."

So he stayed and worked and sent two of his thralls to look for the holy posts. They came back every week or two and always had to say that they had not found them. Midwinter was coming on.

"Ah!" said Ingolf's wife one day, "do you remember the gay feast that we had at Yule-time? All our friends were there. The house rang with song and laughter. Our tables bent with good things to eat. Walls were hung with gay draperies. The floor was clean with sweet-smelling pine-branches. Now look at this mean house; its dirt floor, its bare stone walls, its littleness, its darkness! Look at our long faces. No one here could make a song if he tried. Oh! I am sick for dear old Norway."

"It is Thor's fault," Ingolf cried. "He will not let me find his posts."

He strode out of the house and stood scowling at the gray sea.

"Ah, foster-brother!" he said. "It was never so gloomy when you were by my side. Where are you now? Shall I never hear your merry laugh again?

That spot in my palm burns, and my heart aches to see you. That arch of sod keeps rising before my eyes. Our vows keep ringing in my ears."

At last the long, gloomy winter passed and spring came.

"Cheer up, good wife," Ingolf said. "Better days are coming now."

But that same day the thralls came back from looking for the posts.

"We have bad news," they said. "As we walked along the shore looking for the pillars we saw a man lying on the shore. We went up to him. He was dead. It was Leif. Two well-built houses stood near. We went to them. We knew from the carving on the door-posts that they were Leif's. We went in. The rooms were empty. Along the shore and in the wood back of the house we found all of his men, dead. There was no living thing about."

Ingolf said no word, but his face was white, and his mouth was set. He went into the house and got his spears and his shield and said to his men:

"Follow me."

They put provisions into the boat and pushed off and sailed until they saw Leif's houses on the shore of the harbor. There they saw Leif and the men who were his friends, dead. Their swords and spears were gone. Ingolf walked through the houses calling on Helga and on the thralls, but no one answered. The storehouse was empty. The rich hangings were gone from the walls of the houses. There was nothing in the stables. The boat was gone.

Ingolf went out and stood on a high point of land that jutted out into the water. Far along the coast he saw some little islands. He turned to his men and said:

"The thralls have done it. I think we shall find them on those islands."

Then he went back to Leif and stood looking at him.

"What a shame for so brave a man to fall by the hands of thralls! But I have found that such things always happen to men who do not sacrifice to the gods. Ah, Leif! I did not think when we made those vows of foster-brotherhood that this would ever happen. But do not fear. I remember my promise. I had thought that a man's blood is precious in this empty land, but my vow is more precious."

Now they laid all those men together and tied on their hell-shoes.

"I need my sword for your sake, foster-brother. I cannot give you that. But you shall have my spears and my drinking-horn," said Ingolf. "For surely Odin has chosen you for Valhalla, even though you did not sacrifice. You are too good a man to go to Niflheim. You would make times merry in Valhalla."

So Ingolf put his spears and his drinking-horn by Leif. Then the men raised a great mound over all the dead. After that they went aboard their boat and sailed for the islands that Ingolf had seen. It was evening when they reached them.

"I see smoke rising from that one," Ingolf said, pointing.

He steered for it. It was a steep rock like that one in the Faroes, but they found a harbor and landed and climbed the steep hill and came out on top. They saw the ten thralls sitting about a bonfire eating. Helga and the other women from Leif's house sat near, huddled together, white and frightened. One of the thralls gave a great laugh and shouted:

"This is better than pulling Leif's plow. To-morrow we will sail for Ireland with all his wealth."

"To-morrow you will be freezing in Niflheim," cried Ingolf, and he leaped among them swinging his sword, and all his men followed him, and they killed those thralls.

Then Ingolf turned to Helga. She threw herself into his arms and wept. But after a while she told him this story:

"When springtime came, Leif thought that he would sow wheat. He had but one ox. The others had died during the winter. So he set the thralls to help pull the plow. I saw their sour looks and was afraid, but Leif only laughed:

"'What else can thralls expect?' he said. 'Never fear them, good wife.'

"Now one day soon after that the thralls came running to the house calling out:

"'The ox is dead! The ox is dead!'

"Leif asked them about it. They said that a bear had come out of the woods and killed it, and that they had scared the beast away. They pointed out where it had gone. Then Leif called his men and said:

"'A hunt! I had not hoped for such great sport here. Ah, we will have a feast off that bear!'

"So they took their spears and went out into the woods. As soon as they were gone, the thralls came running into the house and took down all the swords and shields from the wall and ran out. In some way they met my lord and his men in the woods and killed them. Then they came back and took everything in the house and dragged us to the boat and sailed here."

"O my brother!" said Ingolf, "where is that song about 'those two foster-brothers, Ingolf and Leif, who made a new country in a wonderful land, and whose sons and grandsons are mighty men in Iceland'? But come home with me, Helga."

So they took the women and Leif's things and Leif's boat and sailed home. The next day after they came to Ingolf's house, Helga said:

"We have made your family larger, brother Ingolf. Will you not take Leif's two houses and live in them? He does not need them now. He would like you to have them."

"It would be pleasant to live there," Ingolf said. "I thank you."

So the next day they loaded everything aboard the two ships and sailed for Leif's house. There they stayed for a year. Ingolf still sent his thralls out to look for the pillars. He was careful always to have hay, so his cattle prospered. That spring he planted wheat, but it did not grow well.

"This is sickly stuff," Ingolf said. "It takes too much time and work. It is better to save the land for hay. Perhaps we can sometime go back to Norway for flour."

At last one day the thralls came home and said:

"We have found the pillars."

Ingolf jumped to his feet. He cried out:

"You have kept me waiting three years, Thor. But as soon as my house and temple are built, I will sacrifice to you three horses as a thank-offering."

"It is a long way off, master," the thralls said, "and we have found much better places in our walks about the island."

"Thor knows best," Ingolf answered. "I will settle where he leads me."

So that summer they loaded everything into the ships again and sailed west along the coast until they came to the place where the pillars were. The land there was low and green. On both sides were low hills. A little lake glistened back from shore. In the valley were hot springs, with steam rising from them.

"It looks like smoke," the men said. "It is very strange to see hot water and smoke come out of the ground."

In front of this green land was a good harbor with islands in it. Far over the sea toward the north shone a great ice-mountain.

"I like the place," Ingolf said. "I will make this land mine."

So he built fires at the mouth of the river near there, and stood by them and called out loudly:

"I have put my fire at the mouth of these rivers. All the land that they drain is mine, and no man shall claim it but me. I will call this place Reykjavik."

Then Ingolf built his feast hall. He himself carved the beams and the door-posts. Gaily painted dragons leaned out from the doors and stood up from the gables. Men and animals fought on the door-posts. For the doors he made at the forge great iron hinges. Their ends curved and spread all over the door. Near his feast hall he built a storehouse and a kitchen and a smithy and a stable and a bower for the women.

"We do not need a sleeping-house for guests," he said. "Who would be our guests?"

He roofed all his buildings with turf. It made them look like green mounds with gay carved and painted walls under them. He built also a temple, and on that was beautiful carving. In this he set up those statues that had been in his old temple. He put up, too, those pillars of his high seat that had been drifting about so long. Under them he laid the soil of Norway that he had brought in the little bronze chest.

"I have kept my vow, O Thor!" he cried.

Then he sacrificed three horses that he had promised to Thor. After that was over, he said:

"Here is a good field for sport. Let us have some of the old games that we used to play at home. Who will wrestle with me?"

So they wrestled there and ran races and swam in the water. The women sat and looked on.

"Oh, this is good to see!" Helga cried. "We are as gay as we used to be in old Norway."

But it was not many weeks before Ingolf said:

"I wish that I might sometime see sails in that harbor. I wish that I might think, 'Around this point of land is another farm, and across the bay is another. I can go there when I am very lonely.' I wish that I might sometime be invited to a feast. I wish that I might sometimes hear the good, clanging music of weapons at play. It is a good land, but we have lived alone for four years. I am hungry for new faces and for tidings of Norway."

One night as he and his men sat about the long fire in the feast hall, a servant threw a great piece of wood upon the fire. It was streaked with faded paint and it showed bits of carving.

"See," said Ingolf, pointing to it, "see what is left of a good ship's prow! What lands have you seen, O dragon's head? What battles have you fought? What was your master's name? Where did the storm meet you? Perhaps he was coming to Iceland, comrades. Would it not have been pleasant to see his sail and to shake his hand and to welcome him to Iceland? But instead he is in Ran's caves, and only his broken prow has drifted here."

Now it was not many months after that when one of the men came running into the feast hall, shouting:

"A sail! a sail in the harbor!"

All those men gave a shout with no word in it, as though their hearts had leaped into their throats. They jumped up and ran to the shore and stood there with hungry eyes. When the men landed, those Icelanders clapped them on the shoulders, and tears ran down their faces. For a long time they could say nothing but "Welcome! Welcome!"

But after a while Ingolf led them to the feast hall and had a feast spread at once. While the thralls were at work, the men stood together and talked. Such a noise had never been in that hall before.

"We have already built our fires and claimed our land up the shore a way," the leader said. "Men in Norway talk much of Ingolf and Leif, and wonder what has happened to them."

Then Ingolf told them of all that had come to pass in Iceland; and then he asked of Norway.

"Ah! things are going from bad to worse," the newcomers said. "Harald grows mightier every day. A man dare not swing a sword now except for the king. We came here to get away from him. Many men are talking of Iceland. Soon the sea-road between here and Norway will be swarming with dragons."

And so it was. Ships also came from Ireland and from the Shetlands and the Orkneys.

"Harald has come west-over-seas," the men of these ships said, "and has laid his heavy hand upon the islands and put his earls over them. They are no place now for free men."

So by the time Ingolf was an old man, Iceland was no longer an empty land. Every valley was spotted with bright feast halls and temples. Horses and cattle pastured on the hillsides. Smoke curled up from kitchens and smithies. Gay ships sailed the waters, taking Iceland cloth and wool and Iceland fish and oil and the soft feathers of Iceland birds to Norway to sell, and bringing back wood and flour and grain.

When Ingolf died, his men drew up on the shore the boat in which he had come to Iceland. They painted it freshly and put new gold on it, so that it stood there a glittering dragon with head raised high, looking over the water. Old Sighvat lifted a huge stone and carried it to the ship's side. With all his strength he threw it into the bottom. The timbers cracked.

"If this ship moves from here," he said, "then I do not know how to moor a ship. It is Ingolf's grave."

Then men laid Ingolf upon his shield and carried him and placed him on the high deck in the stern near the pilot's seat where he had sat to steer to Iceland. They hung his sword over his shoulder. They laid his spear by his side. In his hand they put his mead-horn. Into the ship they set a great treasure-chest filled with beautiful clothes and bracelets and head-bands. Beside the treasure-chest they piled up many swords and spears and shields. They put gold-trimmed saddles and bridles upon three horses. Then they killed the horses and dragged them into the ship. They killed hunting-dogs and put them by the horses; for they said:

"All these things Ingolf will need in Valhalla. When he walks through the door of that feast hall, Odin must know that a rich and brave man comes. When he fights with those heroes during the day, he must have weapons worthy of him. He must have dogs for the hunt. When he feasts with those heroes at night he must wear rich clothes, so that those feasters shall know that he was a wealthy man and generous, and that his friends loved him."

Ingolf's son tied on his hell-shoes for the long journey.

"If these shoes come untied," he said, "I do not know how to fasten hell-shoes."

Then he went out of the ship and stood on the ground with his family. All the men of Iceland were there.

"This is a glorious sight," they said. "Surely no ship ever carried a richer load. Inside and out the boat blazes with gold and bronze, and, high over his riches, lies the great Ingolf, ready to take the tiller and guide to Valhalla, where all the heroes will rise up and shout him welcome."

Then the thralls heaped a mound of earth over the ship. This hill stood up against the sky and seemed to say: "Here lies a great man." Sighvat put a stone on the top, with runes on it telling whose grave it was. All this time a skald stood by and played on his harp and sang a song about that time when Ingolf came to Iceland. He called him the father of Iceland. People of that country still read an old story that the men of that long ago time wrote about Ingolf, and they love him because he was a brave man and "the first of men to come to Iceland."

A SAGA GLOSSARY

Atgeir – A kind of javelin.
Belg - Animal skin. Can refer to an animal skin worn or one used as a bag.
Berserk or berserker – Warrior who fights with frenzied rage in battle.
Bonde – Farmer.
Busk – Make ready; prepare.
Byre – Cottage, dwelling or house.
Chapman – Merchant.
Dises (female guardian spirits).
Dragon – Powerful warship made of wood and iron.
Feyness – The Approach of foreboding of death.
Fylgia – Guardian spirit.
Garth – A farm or farmyard.
Ham-leaper – A shapeshifter. One who is able to change his shape.
Hel – Goddess of Death.
Jarl – A Scandinavian chieftain; earl.
Hight – Called or named.
Holm – A flat tract of land by a river.
Hyre – Farm, farmhouse.
Kirtle – Man's tunic.
Meker - Anglo-Saxon sword.
Naut - Gift.
Ness - Peninsula.
Stofa - Sitting-room.

Made in the USA
Middletown, DE
27 October 2023

41454126R00215